RIVERSONG

TESS THOMPSON

For the "Valley Kids" and the teachers who helped form us.

PROLOGUE

1988

LEE TUCKER SAT on the front steps of the covered porch at her family's farmhouse, a sketch pad and wire-bound notebook in her lap. She wrote the date on the top of a notebook sheet and then, pushing her glasses farther onto the bridge of her nose, searched her mind for possible calamities to write on her worry list. Each morning she captured potential misfortunes in writing, having come up with the idea as a way to manage her anxiety when she was eight years old, after the night her inebriated mother fell down the stairs and broke her arm in three places. It happened in the middle of an ink black night: a scream, the sound of glass breaking on a hardwood floor, a succession of thuds, and then a loud thump. Lee ran from her room, eyes heavy from sleep. She saw her mother crumpled, unmoving, like a discarded rag doll at the bottom of the stairs. Eleanor, dazed, said to her daughter, "Call an ambulance." The ambulance took them both to the hospital. Lee sat in the lobby while they fixed her mother's arm, and she made her first list on the back of a magazine order form.

Back then she'd had a childlike belief that writing a list would keep the bad things from happening; that which was named could be kept at bay, she'd thought. But she was eighteen now and knew better. Writing the words on a clean sheet of paper was merely a way to curtail the fear. She knew by now her mother would do what she would do. Lee didn't factor into the equation.

June 1, 1988

(59 days until I leave for college)

List of Worries

Mom will find my bus fare and spend it all on booze before I can leave.

I will have no way to get to college.

I will wither away day after day here in this hot house while Mom collects more and more papers and books and other stuff until the walls collapse in on me, causing me to suffocate.

She tapped the pencil eraser on the paper. She always wrote in pencil so she could modify later in the day, as thoughts occurred to her. A ladybug landed on the toe of her sneaker. The sun was warm on the top of her head. She looked beyond the overgrown yard to the mountains jutting from the earth in magnificent peaks against a brilliant blue sky. Summer had come overnight to southwestern Oregon, bringing a dry heat that by July would bake the rich soil and turn the grasses every hue of yellow.

Lee heard the hum of a vehicle and looked up to see Mrs. White's old yellow Ford truck racing down the dirt road. Ellen White was a spare, sinewy woman. Her bony hands gripped the large steering wheel as the truck bounced through the many potholes on the Tuckers' part of the road so that it appeared as if she were attached to the steering wheel itself. Her long braid, the color of a speckled hen, jerked with every bump, like a live snake down her straight spine.

Ellen White was the Tuckers' only neighbor for miles. The houses shared a swimming hole with a sandy shore, deep water, and a rope swing no one used—property divided equally by Lee's grandparents and Ellen and Ralph White years ago when they first settled in this valley. Not that it made any difference to Lee. She wasn't allowed to swim. Her mother was afraid of water.

Lee lifted a hand to wave. Instead of driving past like she did most mornings Mrs. White stopped, turning off the engine and hopping out of the truck in what seemed like one fluid movement. "Mornin'," Mrs. White said. She was dressed in a long skirt, a blouse buttoned up to her neck, square practical shoes: English teacher clothes.

"Mornin'," Lee said.

"Senior skip day, isn't it? Why you sittin' here?" She had an unequivocal way of speaking and an economical way of moving.

"Not going," Lee said.

"Why's that?"

"No way to get there."

"Your mother's old Dodge broken down?"

"I can't drive." She felt herself go hot, ashamed.

Mrs. White put her hands on her hips and shook her head, pursing her lips like she did during English class when someone hadn't read the assignment. "Your mother didn't teach you to drive? How you supposed to go off to that fancy college if you can't drive?"

Lee shrugged, watching an ant make its way across the weathered board of the porch step. "She's afraid of cars."

Mrs. White nodded, her eyes darting upward and then returning to Lee's face different than the moment before. Flat dry eyes, the color of faded denim, Lee thought. Seemed everyone in town knew her grandparents had died in a car accident before Lee was born and that Eleanor had raised her alone. No husband, no family. "Regardless, a person needs a way to get around," Mrs. White said, crossing her arms over her spare chest.

"I'll take the bus. The bus system in Seattle's real good."

"Really good. Though I 'spect you could come up with a better description than 'good.'" She pulled up her sleeve and looked at her watch. "All my morning classes are cancelled due to senior skip day, so there's no need for me to hurry in this mornin'." As if her word decided everything, she said with finality, "I'll drive you up there."

"You know about the party?"

"I've been teaching high school since before you were born. There isn't a thing I don't know about you kids."

Lee shrugged, as if she didn't care. "No one expects me."

Mrs. White peered at her. "What does that mean?"

"I don't really want to go."

"Why?"

"For one, I don't have a bathing suit."

Something flickered in Mrs. White's light blue eyes. Anger maybe. Lee couldn't be sure. "That's ridiculous. How could you not have a suit?"

Lee didn't say anything, thinking Mrs. White asked a lot of questions. Mrs. White's gaze flickered to the window of Lee's mother's bedroom and then back to Lee. "You have shorts and a t-shirt?"

"Yeah."

"Those'll work fine. What's the other thing?"

"Huh?"

"You said 'for one thing.' What's the other?"

Lee put her finger on her sneaker and the ladybug crawled onto it. "I won't know what to do there."

"Preposterous. You'll eat chips, put your toes in the water, listen to that god-awful Michael Jackson you kids like on one of those, what are they?"

Lee smiled. "Boom boxes." The ladybug took flight from Lee's finger, heading for an empty flower box.

"Right."

"But, I—"

Mrs. White put up her hand and shushed Lee with a quick click of her tongue. "Go get your shorts on. You're going to the party if I have to drag you up there by your red hair."

They drove up the winding mountain road toward the river spot Lee heard the other kids call "Six Mile." The cab of the truck smelled like rubber and gasoline and she felt slightly queasy. They drove higher and higher. The hay fields in the valley below soon appeared as rectangular patches of green, the farm houses like dollhouses. Her heart beat loud in her chest. She told herself not to be scared of everything like her mother was. People drive this road every day, she thought. But the road was carved into the mountain and if they were unfortunate enough to take a corner too fast they might fall over the cliff and be killed instantly. She shivered, imagining the car tumbling over the side of the mountain and crashing into the canyon below. Had she known about this turn of events she would have included it on her worry list.

As the road became steeper, Mrs. White slowed the car, keeping her eyes on the road. "Your mother sleeping in this morning?"

Lee examined her profile, wondering what Mrs. White knew about them. "Yeah," she answered, turning her gaze to the passenger side window. There was wire tacked to the side of the mountain to keep boulders and rocks from falling onto the road. There were dangers everywhere, she thought, vowing never to come up here again.

The road curved sharply and Mrs. White shifted gears. The truck made a lower pitched hum. "Eleanor ever tell you her mother was my best friend?"

"Nope." Then, afraid she'd sounded rude, added, "We don't talk much."

"Your mother and I had a little falling out, years ago." She glanced at Lee. "When you were a baby."

Lee was curious about what she meant by a "falling out" but was too shy to ask. She figured it was something nasty her mother had said or done. That's the way it was with drunks: anger, belligerence, paranoia. Lee knew that by now.

Silence for a few minutes and then she saw a dirt parking lot, packed with cars and trucks. "This is it," Mrs. White said. "You want me to pick you up later?"

"I hadn't thought about it."

"I best come get you. Most of these yahoos will be drinking. Be a miracle from God if no one gets killed. Pick you up at four?"

Lee looked at her watch. It was only 9:30. "That seems like a long time." A long time to not know what to say or do, she thought. An eternity to sit around feeling ridiculous in her faded shorts and her skinny white legs and her flat boobs.

"Three then." Mrs. White flicked her hand toward Lee's door. "Go on now. Don't want any kids to see me up here."

After Mrs. White drove away, Lee looked around, wondering if it was too late to chase after the truck and tell Mrs. White, forget it, I don't need this much humiliation. I get enough at home, she might add. Then she saw some kids heading toward a sandy trail between some birch trees and decided to follow them, feeling the pain of self-consciousness in every step, clutching her canvas bag that held her sketch pad and notebook to her chest. The path led to a sandy beach and a deep green swimming hole as perfectly shaped as if it were a man-made pool. The beach was scattered with kids in bathing suits and shorts. There were coolers stuffed full of beer. Chips and cookies peeked out of grocery bags. Someone had a boom box blaring Madonna's "Papa Don't Preach." She smelled marijuana smoke and saw some kids behind a tree passing a joint.

On the other side of the swimming hole were boulders jutting ten or so feet above the water where kids sat, dangling their legs over the sides or tanning themselves against the rocks. Suddenly a boy did a Tarzan yell and dove from the tallest point into the jade-colored water. Lee gasped, realizing she was clutching the sides of her own arms with fright until the boy's head bobbed out of the water, hair covering his face. He whipped his head to one side and his hair fell back in place. Then he swam the crawl back toward the rocks, head poking out of the water and moving from side to side in a way that reminded Lee of an overgrown puppy. Christina Brown, big hair, black-lined eyes, from sixth period health class, stood beside her. She gave Lee a look like, who are you and why are you here? Then she adjusted her bikini bottoms and waved to the boy in the water.

Lee walked to the water's edge. She took off her sneakers and put her feet into the water. The sand was soft, the water as cold as iced tea. Her feet looked whiter than usual under the water. Minnows came to nibble at her toes. Someone was distributing bottles of beer. She surprised herself when she held up her hand for one and used her shirt to twist off the cap. She sipped it tentatively. It tasted bitter and the bubbles tickled going down her throat but she took two long swallows. Then she sat back against a rock and tossed stones into the river, wishing she hadn't let that bossy Mrs. White talk her into coming. She didn't belong here, amidst all the laughter, abandonment, the war cries of freedom. These other kids were alive and vibrant. She was chained and invisible. She understood she wasn't offensive to the other kids like Ronnie Myer who didn't shower and smelled badly or Sally Wagner who had a nervous tic and one eye that crossed and a strange habit of talking to herself in the lunchroom. Lee was just benign, someone no one thought of, like she didn't really exist. Maybe she wasn't really here or there or anywhere. Her thoughts were turning jumbled. Could it be the two sips of beer, she wondered?

She forced herself to take another long sip. It still tasted terrible. She poured some of it onto the wet sand. The beer turned into white foam and then made air holes in the surface.

She wandered along the edge of the river. Climbing onto a boulder, she saw a patch of sand nestled between large rocks, almost like a cave. No one was there. Holding her beer in one hand and her bag in the other, she clambered over the smooth round granite to perch on an indentation that was like a seat. She took out her sketch pad and began drawing a cluster of poppies. The green buds hadn't opened yet, merely hinting at the vibrant orange that would soon be revealed.

She lobbed a pebble into the water and, hearing footsteps, turned her head to see Zac Huller approaching, walking lopsided, holding a beer. He was class vice president, an athlete. Some girl had written "babe" in lipstick on his locker last week. Lee knew his parents owned the town sawmill. "Born with a silver spoon in their mouth," her mother said once, sneering. Zac stopped, looking disappointed. "Oh, I thought you were someone else." He plopped down on the sand, inches from her bare legs. "What're you doing?"

She tossed another pebble. "I don't know."

"Everybody's getting loaded." He tipped the beer into his mouth, his Adam's apple moving up and down with each swallow.

Lee chucked a small flat rock and it skipped over the water in three leaps.

Zac threw his empty bottle and it shattered into jagged pieces. "Man, I can't wait to get out of this shit-hole." Brown glass lay in shards on the sand and he kicked one with his foot, pulling another beer from his shorts.

"Me too."

"I heard you got a big scholarship. What for?"

"Art."

"I saw your paintings hanging in the cafeteria. Freaked me out but I don't know crap about art. I'm going to the community college up by Eugene. My dad's got a boner over college, so here I go." He kicked the sand and sipped his beer. "My dad just wants to get rid of me now that my mother left him. She went to Florida with some rich guy she met when she went to visit my aunt. She hated it here. Always talking about how much she missed the city and what a hick my old man is. I guess she hated me too because she's gone, gone, gone." He tore the label off the beer bottle and crumpled it between his fingers. "Wanna hear something messed up?" He looked at her, eyes half closed. "Do you?"

"I guess."

"I saw my mother porking that guy in Florida. I walked in on them one day after school. It was disgusting. I hate him. My dad's a jerk, always on my ass about everything, but this guy, this guy's a complete waste."

Lee remembered then that he was gone the first part of the school year. "Did you come back after that?"

"Yeah, I came back to live with my dad. He thinks I'm a complete screw-up, so that's a lot of fun." He flipped his hair out of his eyes and stared at her, slapping her ankle. "You know, you're not so ugly underneath those glasses." Lee looked at him, thinking he was interesting in a science project kind of way, and lobbed another pebble.

He lurched to a standing position and dropped with a thud on the rock next to her, waving his hand between them. "What do you think about this?"

Lee's eyes darted away from his face to the sun glistening on the water. "About what?"

"Y'know, me talking you up?" His fingers grasped her knee and then went up her leg to the soft flesh of her inner thigh. "You ever think this would happen?"

Lee put her legs together. "Exactly what are we talking about?"

"I'm Zac and you're a, what are you? A non-person. I've watched you in that bullshit health class and I wonder if you're a girl or a robot." His words slurred and there was spittle in the corners of his mouth. "Maybe I could loosen you up. Make you scream a little, break the robot out of her shell." He pulled on the collar of her t-shirt with his index finger. "This could be a good spot to y'know." He raised his eyebrows and patted the sand with his foot. "Nice and soft."

"It's not really soft, as a matter of fact."

The vein on his forehead bulged as his face turned a shade of purple. "See, like that, the way you're so stiff and shit. It's weird." He yanked her glasses from her face and tossed them onto her canvas bag. He pulled her to the sand. He was on top of her. Sharp pebbles dug into the backs of her legs. His wet tongue wiggled around inside her mouth like a slug and his breath smelled of beer and Doritos. He panted, his hands clutching at her breasts like he was trying to pluck them from her body.

She wheezed against his weight, attempting to push him off. He was heavier than he looked. "Don't you have a girlfriend?" He grunted. "Screw Lindsey. She's been blowing me off." He yanked at her shorts.

She reached behind her, hoping for a rock but found instead a sharp-edged piece of the broken beer bottle and slammed it hard into the back of his right thigh. He shrieked, jumping to his feet and twisting his upper body to see the wound, looking like a rabid dog chasing his tail. "You stabbed me?" He held up his fingers. There was a small amount of blood on them. "I'm bleeding. You bitch." He lunged for her but tripped and fell onto the sand. She grabbed her glasses and bag and scrambled over the rocks, slipping in her tennis shoes and scraping her knee. She kept running until she reached the crowd.

Lee waited the rest of the afternoon in the hot parking area for Mrs. White. Finally, shortly after three she pulled up in the yellow truck. Without getting out of the vehicle, Mrs. White leaned across the seat to the passenger side and opened the door. "Hop in," she called out to Lee.

Mrs. White had changed into Bermuda shorts and a t-shirt, her white legs surprisingly muscular for an old lady, Lee thought. "You're red as a lobster," Mrs. White said. "Don't you know about suntan lotion?"

Lee looked at her arms. They were bright pink and starting to sting. Her skin was hot to the touch. Great, she thought, a sunburn to top off what had been a horrific day. This just proved it, bad things always happened to her whether she wrote her list or not. As a matter of fact, it was the things she didn't think of that happened.

As Mrs. White backed the truck onto the road she said, "You have any fun?"

"Not really."

"A lot of drinking?"

"Yeah, I guess."

Mrs. White looked at her sharply but didn't ask any other questions. Lee's eyes were heavy. She put her head against the side of the truck and fell asleep. When she woke they were pulling up to her mother's house.

She sat up, rubbing her eyes. "Sorry, didn't mean to fall asleep."

But Mrs. White wasn't listening. She was looking at the house with a worried expression. "What's wrong?" Lee asked her.

Mrs. White swore under her breath and leaped from the truck, sprinting toward the porch. Lee followed, her heart beating hard inside her chest. They entered through the front door, Lee on the older woman's heels. The screen door slammed behind them. It smelled different but she couldn't think of what. Then it came to her. Smoke.

"Those damn cigarettes," Mrs. White yelled, running toward the kitchen.

The coffee table, covered with magazines and newspapers, was on fire. Her mother lay on the couch, inches from the flames, not moving.

Lee screamed. Without thinking, she ran past the fire to the couch and dragged her into the foyer. Once on the floor, Eleanor's eyes fluttered and then she coughed the rattled smoker's cough, her chest rising and falling.

"Mommy, are you alright?" Lee took her mother's hand that felt like crepe paper, sobbing.

Without opening her eyes Eleanor murmured, her face slack, "My chest hurts."

Lee heard the clang of a pan and then water running from the kitchen. Mrs. White ran past them with a pan of water. Lee watched her douse the fire. It went out instantly, as if it knew there

11

was no denying Ellen White what she wanted; the remains of its rebellion were soggy, charred magazines and blackened remnants of the town newspaper.

They put Eleanor to bed and cleaned the mess left by the fire. Afterwards they sat on the steps of the front porch. "How did you know?" Lee said. "About the fire."

"Oh, I've got a nose can smell most anything. It's a curse most of the time. Always figured my family must've been the types smelled the Queen's dishes for poison."

Lee made a pattern in the dirt with her foot. "Glad we got here when we did." She shivered.

Mrs. White looked at her, eyes sharp. "Is it always this bad?"

Lee shrugged, looking at the ground. "I guess."

"You ever tell anyone about it, like a teacher at school or anything?"

"Nah, what could they do?"

Mrs. White looked like she might say something but then thought better of it, examining her fingernails instead.

"Mrs. White, I'm leaving in the morning." And as she said it, she knew suddenly that it was true. She was finished with high school. She'd miss the graduation ceremony but who cared? She was done living in this crazy house. "College starts in late August but I'll go now, get a job for the summer. I can live in the dorms during the summer as long as I have the rent."

Mrs. White nodded. "You'll need some money."

"I've got a little saved." Not much, she thought. Enough for a bus ticket and one month's rent. But it could get her through until she found a job.

"I'll float you some. You can pay me back when you're a rich and famous artist."

She wanted to protest but knew she couldn't. "Okay. Thanks."

"I'll take you to the bus station in the morning."

"The bus to Seattle leaves at 11:30." She'd memorized the schedule years ago, planning her escape.

"I'll be here to get you."

She slept fitfully that night and woke late the next morning, hot under her bed covers. The air reeked of smoke. Her sunburned skin stung. She threw back the covers, longing for the feel of water on her scorched arms and legs. She dressed in a ratty pair of shorts and t-shirt. On her way down the hall she paused in front of her mother's room, leaning for a moment on the closed door. A bird's summer song drifted in through the open hall window. Her mother snored softly inside the room. She put her hand on the doorknob to go in like she did every morning but then hesitated. The familiar sadness crept in but she forced the feelings inside, scratching her sunburned arms with her fingernails, drawing blood. The river beckoned to her, as if it called her name. She withdrew her hand from the door and walked away, down the hall and the creaky stairs, all the while hearing a call to the river, knowing that she would not look back again.

In the yard the sky felt long and hazy, different than the day before. She knew it would be a scorcher, unusual for June. She walked the path towards the swimming hole. At the swing, she paused, holding the rough rope between her fingers, wondering what it felt like to fly over the river and then plunge into the mystery of its waters without fear or hesitation. She took the worn path to the water, slipping several times but going on anyway, determined to be brave. At the river's edge, she inched in, her overheated skin shocked at the cold. When the water reached her shoulders she moved her arms in a circular motion, pretending to swim, keeping her feet anchored to the sandy floor. Then she bent her knees, closing her eyes and submerging her head under the water. She stayed like that with her eyes scrunched closed until the coolness seeped in through her skin and reached the place inside her where hope and despair lived side by side. She imagined the pain of her childhood diminishing to flecks of ice. Her feet came off the ground and she opened her eyes. She was floating. Her hair streamed out in front of her as her t-shirt ballooned around her body like a safety device, bubbles escaping from her shorts. The gray floor of the river hosted several red crawfish and a school of minnows swam around her. Infinitesimal specks of fluorescent algae drifted through the water, illuminated by the pelting sunlight. She felt triumphant. She was refreshed, cool at last.

Later that morning Mrs. White came in her truck, beeping her horn to let Lee know she'd arrived. Eleanor was on the porch already. Lee took her suitcase in hand, looking around the shabby house one last time. She wanted desperately to go but felt that nudge of guilt, knowing she was all her mother had in the world.

Eleanor leaned against a porch post, smoking a cigarette, dressed in a faded blue, tattered housecoat. Mrs. White's acute eyes watched from the truck. Lee reached to hug her mother, smelling the familiar scent of vodka and cigarettes, but the suit-cases made it an awkward bump of shoulders. "I'll visit soon," said Lee, lying.

"You'll be back soon enough. It's not as easy out there as you think. You'll see."

"Alright, well, I love you." The words felt strangled, unfamiliar.

Her mother took a drag of her cigarette and swept her hand in the air as if she were ridding herself of junk. "Go on now, Ellen's waiting for you." Lee turned and walked down the steps of the porch and into the waiting truck, raging suddenly against her mother for making what should be a victorious sweep to art school one last bitter moment in Lee's mouth.

They drove the thirty minutes to the bus depot in silence. Lee's stomach was nervous, her mind racing. She started to cry when she saw the bus depot sign. Mrs. White handed her a tissue. Lee took it, blowing her nose angrily. Lee was relieved that Mrs. White didn't say something trite, meant to be comforting like adults sometimes did. She just parked silently and hauled the suitcase out of the back of the truck with one hand.

Lee walked to the booth and bought a one-way ticket to Seattle. She checked her suitcase but kept her canvas bag with her wallet, a book, and sketch pad for the trip. Mrs. White handed her a paper bag that smelled of cinnamon. "I baked you a few things. It's a long ways. You best call me when you get there. Collect."

"Alright. You'll tell my mother?"

"Sure thing."

Then they stood on the hot cement that smelled of urine and spilled oil, waiting for the sign to board. Lee sniffed and wiped her eyes with the tissue.

After a time Mrs. White cleared her throat and without looking at Lee said, "My husband was a drunk too, mean as the day is long after a half a bottle of Jim Beam. It's a heartbreaking way to live and I'm sure if your mother could help it, she would live a different way. But that isn't your concern any longer. You've done your time. I'll look after your mother, so don't worry about her. Just go live your life."

"What if I don't know how?" The tears started again, in furious little streams down her cheeks.

Mrs. White crossed her arm and pursed her lips, looking over at her with flashing eyes. "Nonsense. You'll figure it out. Don't let anyone tell you differently." She nodded towards the bus. "It's time." She gave Lee a slight push. Before Lee put her foot on that first step, she turned back to Mrs. White and called out, "Thank you."

"Go get 'em," she called back, smiling.

Inside the bus it was air conditioned and smelled of stale cigarette smoke. It was nearly empty so she chose the front seat, close to the driver, for safety's sake. She looked out the window. Mrs. White was still there. Lee waved. Mrs. White waved back.

CHAPTER ONE

LEE SHUTTERED under the awning of her condominium building on Seattle's Second and Blanchard, searching vainly in the dark for the man who called himself Von. It was midnight and the wind off the Puget Sound was fierce, bringing the scent of seaweed and fish along with a chill that seemed to penetrate through her clothing and into her bones so that her teeth chattered like a child's at an early morning swimming lesson. Across the street was a black sedan, parked in the same spot for a week, a man watching her every move. For the fifth time in five minutes she felt the inside pocket of her mint green pea coat for the cashier's check and, reassured it was there, withdrew her hands into the sleeves. The rain pooled on the roof of the glass awning and dripped onto the cement in a steady, mind numbing rhythm. A sudden distant shout from late night drinkers feeling a different kind of buzz made her jump.

Then she saw a shadow across the street, a figure dragging one foot slightly behind the other in a limp. He nodded at her and walked across the street to where she waited, feeling small and more frightened than she'd ever been in her life.

"You able to get it?" He stood in front of her, shaking the rain from his Mariners' cap, a splash landing on her face. With the palm of his hand he smoothed the few wisps of brown hair on his otherwise bare head.

"Yes."

He stepped closer and she smelled rank cigarette smoke on his coat. "Good."

She handed him the envelope and wrapped her arms around herself to stop shaking.

He licked his index finger and lifted the check from the envelope. His eyes darted to the amount and then to her face. His eyes glittered but his voice was low, without emotion. "This is only half."

Her voice wavered and cracked. "I couldn't get it all."

He put the check in his jacket and Lee caught sight of the shiny handle of a handgun. He put a cigarette in his mouth. "I said all of it."

"I sold everything we had."

He lit his cigarette and took a deep drag, exhaling slowly. "You gotta get me that money."

Lee's eyes stung from the smoke that drifted around her face. She bit her bottom lip to stop it from trembling. "This is to show you I'm good for it, that I don't plan to cheat you. I can get it eventually but I need some time."

"You're out of time."

"I just don't have it." She tasted blood and realized it was from inside her own lip.

"We'll give you another week. I'll meet you right here a week from now."

"What if I can't get it? What then?"

He threw his cigarette on the ground and stomped it with his heel. "Do I have to spell it out for you?"

She shook her head no and put her hand to her mouth. "I want you to know, this is not who I am. I'm a respected businesswoman in this town. I'm an honest person. This was all a terrible mistake."

He took another cigarette from his pack and held it in the air almost as if he expected her to light it for him. "Lady, it don't matter to me what kind of person you are. I'm hired to get the money owed to my boss. Nothing more nothing less." The corners of his mouth turned up in a smirk. "A fact's a fact. You owe my boss this money and he don't care one whit if you've been deluding yourself about who you really are or who your husband was. This money you owe, that's who you are to him."

She chastised herself silently, telling herself to stop talking and just get out. He was correct, she had been delusional but her eyes had been recently pulled open like a person on a torture device, one sickening revelation after another. She said, "Fine, I'll see you next week."

"Don't stand me up, Lee Johnson. It wouldn't be pretty."

"I won't," she lied. There was a woman headed towards the glass door and Lee scurried behind her into the lit lobby.

A few moments later Lee sat on the master bedroom toilet, wearing a bra, her panties around her ankles. She held a new pregnancy test in her hands. It was shaped like a pen and had two display windows. She pulled off the plastic cover and stuck it between her legs, aiming her urine stream at the spongy end of the stick like the directions said. Some of it splashed her thighs. Holding the test in one hand like a sword, she cleaned up with toilet paper. Sweat dribbled between her breasts. She waited, never taking her eyes from the test. The line in the first window turned pink. According to the package it would take at least a minute for the line in the other window to appear. If it did she was pregnant. "Please be negative," she whispered to herself. "Please."

This was torture, she thought. Couldn't they make a faster test? Her eyes landed on the soaking tub, wondering bitterly if the new owners would love it as much as she had.

She breathed in through her nose and out her mouth like in Pilates class. She counted to twenty. At twenty-one, she peered at the test. Two dark pink lines showed in the second window.

She was pregnant. She'd known it. But here it was in pink and white. She said inside her head, "No, no, no. This can't be." She crossed her arms over her tender breasts, fighting the urge to cry. She ordered herself to hold it together as she pulled up her panties and threw the test in her bag, on top of a pair of jeans and a t-shirt. Then she pulled on a traditional Islamic dress and fastened a full Burka over her head. She looked in the mirror. She didn't recognize herself. Maybe no one else would either.

She went to the window and moved the drawn shade a crack to see that it was still drizzling. A layer of fog hovered just above the center of the skyscraper across from where she stood. She looked to the street below. The black sedan was still there.

She grabbed her bag and went out to the living room. Her friend Linus paced by the front door. He stopped, staring at her. "Well, it's a good disguise, I'll give it that." A muscle twitched in his cheek. "But keep your head down anyway." His voice was grave and shaky. He plucked nervously at the purple knit scarf around his neck.

"I know. We've been over and over the plan."

"What took you so long?"

She paused, and for the first time in their fifteen-year friendship she held something from him. She wouldn't tell him she was pregnant. It was too much for him to absorb, after all they'd gone through these last several weeks.

The moment had come to say goodbye. She wanted to express her love and gratitude to him but she felt awkward, clumsy. She tried anyway, clearing her throat. "Linus, I don't say it enough, don't know if I've ever said it, but I love you." Her voice broke. "I want you to know that, in case anything happens. Maybe if I'd said it more to Dan, he'd still be here."

He put up his hand to quiet her. "Please, Lee, you've got to stop punishing yourself. What he's done is not your fault." His voice was angry now, his cheeks flushed.

"It occurred to me this morning that when I disappear it's not only from these awful people but from you too. It didn't sink in until today. Isn't that stupid?" She started to cry.

"I know. Me too." He wrapped his arms around her.

"We've spoken almost every day for fifteen years."

"I know."

"I even called you on my honeymoon. Remember?"

He smoothed her hair and rested his chin on the top of her head. "This isn't forever. Just get your mother's house sold so you can pay off this bastard. Then I'll come pick you up. You can stay with me when you come home. Start a new life. I'll give you a job at Figs when you get back."

She smiled, hiccupping. "I don't know anything about food."

He chuckled. "And you don't drink. You can't work in a restaurant without drinking. It's against the restaurant code."

She tried not to cry but tears fell from her eyes one after the other. "Don't forget about me. I don't want to come back and find you've replaced me with some other woman."

He moved his hands to her shoulders and looked into her eyes. "Unless George Clooney whisks me off to his villa in Lake Como, I'll be here." His eyes were full of tears now too. "I've got to go before I lose it. Please be careful." He kissed her on the cheek and left through the door he'd come and gone through so many times before.

She looked around the bare condo for the last time, at the vaulted ceilings, granite counters, marble fireplace, designer paints on the walls. Everything had been decorated just so. "We'll be so happy here," her husband had said the night they moved in. And now he was dead. Out of habit she touched her ring finger to play with her wedding ring. But it was no longer there, sold for cash like everything else. There was nothing but the slight indentation in her skin to prove their five-year marriage ever existed.

She peered down the length of the eighth-floor hallway for human shadows. There was no one, no sounds or movement. She punched the elevator button and held her breath until the doors opened and closed. All the way down she fidgeted until the elevator came to a stop. She walked into the lit lobby and out the door. The rain was coming down harder than before. A car passed but the street was mostly empty. Across the street the man still sat in the black car, reading a newspaper. He might have glanced at her but she couldn't be sure. She forced herself to walk at a casual pace, watching out of the corner of her eye, holding her breath. At the corner there was a homeless man, his bearded bleary face half hidden behind a cardboard box. She saw the man in the sedan turn the page of the newspaper, uninterested in her. He hadn't recognized her, she thought. She put her head down and walked up the hill to Fifth Avenue.

Parked in the alley behind a bar was a friend of Linus's in a blue Prius. Lee got in the passenger seat without speaking. He nodded and gave her a half smile, white knuckles clenched on either side of the steering wheel. Then they sped down the alley, up Denny Avenue, and onto I-5 South, on their way to a gray Dodge Minivan and new cell phone that waited in Olympia, registered under a false name.

CHAPTER TWO

IN THE MINIVAN, Lee headed up Olympia's main street to the I-5 South entrance. At each stop light she looked in her rearview mirror to see if she was followed, but saw nothing suspicious. Rain pounded against the windshield as she merged onto the freeway, holding her breath each time a car passed. For several miles there were no lights behind her. She relaxed somewhat and began to feel cold from the sweat that had soaked through the Islamic dress. She adjusted the heat and thought longingly of the heated seats in her BMW. The seats in this van were cold. It smelled of cheap plastic and a vanilla- scent air freshener shaped like a tree that someone had hung around the mirror.

She'd been chilled for three weeks now. It was an iciness that had seeped into her bones and made her teeth chatter with the emptiness that comes with a sudden grief.

Three weeks ago—to be exact, 21 days, 5 hours and 8 minutes ago—Lee's assistant Paula had stepped inside her office conference room in the middle of her company presentation to representatives from the press and distributors about their new product. Paula's face was ashen and Lee knew something was wrong with Dan. She'd known it when he hadn't shown up for a day he'd been working towards for months. But she'd pushed it aside in order to do the presentation and appear as if everything was normal.

Paula stammered, gripping the handle of the conference room door. "I, I'm sorry but there's something—we need Lee to come out to the lobby. It's urgent."

She began to shake and her legs were like liquid under her as she made her way to the front desk. There were two policemen standing at the reception area.

"Are you Dan Johnson's wife?"

She nodded, unable to feel her arms. "Yes, I'm Lee Johnson." There was a high-pitched scream inside her head.

The heavyset, ruddy policeman looked at her without blinking. The wiry bushy one stared at the beige carpet. "We're sorry to inform you that your husband has been found dead. We found his body with what we believe was a self-inflicted gunshot wound to his head in his car at the waterfront park downtown."

She heard herself say, "No," like it came from someone else. "Dan doesn't even have a gun." She wasn't sure if she said the words or if they were inside her own head.

The older one rested his hand on her arm. "We're very sorry for your loss, Mrs. Johnson."

The room tilted and her knees buckled. The fuzzy policeman reached to steady her, his thick eyebrows knitted together in concern, his mouth moving, but the whirr between her ears drowned the words. She staggered to the potted plant by the glass doors and heaved three, four, five times, until her stomach cramped and she gulped air, unable to stand upright. Her eyes focused on the policeman's black shiny shoes. His hand was on her back. His speech sounded like gibberish down a deep tunnel. The younger officer guided her to a chair. She looked past him to Paula, who stood slumped against the reception desk, hands clasped and her face white and stricken. Lee had whispered, "Call Linus."

Two days later, Linus held her hand as they walked towards the lobby of her condominium complex. They had come from the funeral home, where Linus made the arrangements while Lee stared helplessly at her hands that seemed to have lost all their blood.

Afterwards she slumped against Linus's sturdy frame as they rode the elevator up to her condominium unit. There was a man lurking near her front door, dressed in tan pants, a white button-down shirt, and tennis shoes. He leaned against the wall, ankles crossed, holding a newspaper in his right hand. His index and middle fingers were stained with what Lee recognized as nicotine and tobacco smoke. Her mother's fingers had been the same.

"Can we help you?" Linus asked, tucking Lee's arm under his own.

The man approached them, favoring his right leg with a slight limp. "I work for Gaspare DeAngelo. You owe my boss some money." She got a whiff of musk aftershave mixed with cigarette smoke and garlic.

He scowled at Lee's blank look. "Don't play dumb with me, lady. Y'know, Mr. DeAngelo, the guy who gave you a million bucks last year to keep your little business going while Danny boy worked out these, whad'ya call 'em, bugs, yeah, bugs in the software." He coughed and his lips parted, showing teeth stained the same brown of chewing tobacco she remembered from the men who stood on the sidewalk outside of her mother's grocery store job when she was a child.

"I know we have an investor but I don't know the terms of the deal. Dan handled it," said Lee.

"I'm sure you know the terms better than I do, lady. But maybe you're a little stressed, so I'll review the highlights for you. Listen close. Mr. DeAngelo gives you and Danny a million bucks at twenty-five percent a year, payable by February 21st. Otherwise Mr. D. takes the company, if he wants it. February 21st was yesterday, but Mr. D. starts thinking, Danny's brain is the company and now it's splattered all over his fancy car, so now Mr. D.'s thinking he just wants his money."

Lee heard what he said, but her mind seemed incapable of understanding.

Linus took a step forward. "Let me understand this. Are you threatening her?"

The man kept his eyes on Lee. "Very good. At least your, uh, friend is starting to catch on."

She stared at him. "Even if what you say is true, I don't have a million and a quarter to give you."

"My boss said to give you a few weeks." He gave her a business card with his name, Von Marshal, and a phone number printed in black and white. "You call me to make the arrangements. My boss isn't someone who likes to be played. People who don't understand that have a way of, uh, not showing up at work one day, y'know what I mean?"

Thirty minutes later, Lee sat shaking in front of her gas fireplace. Linus brought her a heavy wool sweater and they stared at one another for a long moment, too shocked to think of anything to say. After a few minutes, Linus got up and went into the kitchen. Lee heard him rummaging through cupboards and then a pop of a wine cork. The doorbell rang and she turned to see Linus rush in from the kitchen, holding his hand up to indicate she should stay on the couch. He put his eye to the peephole. "It's just Paula," he said, relief in his voice.

Paula had dark circles under her eyes and her nose was red and raw. "Lee, when I was cleaning out the offices I found this on top of Dan's computer." Paula handed her an envelope with "Lee" scrawled in Dan's block type print. She took it, splitting the envelope open with her finger while walking towards the bedroom. Alone, she shut the door, sinking heavily onto the edge of the bed. Dan's red woolen slippers were placed neatly by the end table. She slipped her feet into them, unfolding the papers.

But it wasn't a note. There were no explanations, no words of love or sorrow. It was the terms of the agreement with DeAngelo, listed just as Von had described.

She began to rock back and forth on the bed. And then, like a movie she didn't want to watch, she imagined his last moments. He sealed the document in the envelope, scrawling her name in a guilty rush and taking a long swig of the whiskey he kept in his desk drawer for the courage to do what he had to do. Then he was in his car, parked in a busy lot at the waterfront park with its view of the Olympic Mountains. Here the reel became blurry. He might have watched the joggers, mothers with baby strollers, truant teenagers sneaking drags from a pot pipe, maybe thinking how much he would miss the world with its simple beauty and pleasures. Or perhaps he merely stared at the dashboard, overwhelmed with despair and panic, and nothing registered in his mind but "get it over with," so the pain and hopelessness could end. Possibly it was like a tunnel that sucked and twirled him into blackness and he thought of nothing but the doing of it, the mechanics of his own death. The pulling of the trigger.

She wept into his pillow, yearning to smell his aftershave but it smelled clean, like soap and fabric softener. He'd been sleeping at the office for weeks, working towards the product release date.

She thought then, where did he get the gun and why did he do it in the car and how did he become that hopeless? What was the last thing he thought as he pulled the trigger? Was it of her or just his failures?

CHAPTER THREE

ABOUT FIFTY MILES NORTH of the Oregon-Washington border the radio went to static. Lee moved the radio dial until she found the only station, country and western. That would be it from now until Portland, she thought. She drove another fifteen miles before stopping at a rest stop to use the facilities. It was dark now. She scanned the parking lot and then sprinted to the women's restroom. The smell of human excrement and damp cement made her nauseous. She stood for a moment over the toilet, thinking she might vomit and wondering if this was the beginning of 'morning sickness.'

Outside, she spotted a vending machine and remembered a friend saying she ate crackers during her pregnancies to help with the nausea. She put two quarters in the slot, choosing animal crackers. As she headed for the minivan, she heard a rustle in the bushes. Terrified, she ran the rest of the way to the van, jumping behind the wheel and locking the door. She turned on her head-lights and saw a possum creep out of the bushes, scuttling along the sidewalk. Somewhere between a rodent and reptile, his skin, long tail, and pointy nose made him appear like a creature from another planet.

The gruesome image lingered with her as she drove the I-5 corridor through southwest Washington, crossing the bridge over the Columbia River from Vancouver, Washington to Portland, Oregon, along the flat green fields of the Willamette Valley, and as she wound up and around the mountains near Roseburg. She stopped at one of the small towns along I-5 to refuel and find something to eat.

She stood at the Dairy Queen counter, attempting to ignore the smells of fried meat and old grease. She ordered a Heath Bar Blizzard, thinking this small desolate town was similar to where she was headed. They all had Dairy Queens.

Since Dan's death and the subsequent nightmare days and nights that followed, her skin seemed to ache all the time. She fought the urge to put her head on the counter and weep. Instead she stuffed several napkins and a straw into her purse. She watched an older couple in the corner booth. The woman, missing several teeth and with gray hairs hanging from the sagging skin underneath her chin, shoved a breakfast sandwich in her mouth, all the while berating her male companion and rubbing the silver cross that hung below her ample breasts. "It's your problem," she said. "She's nothing but a druggie. I'm not taking her brats into our house."

The man's skinny legs rested in the aisle because his beach ball sized stomach couldn't fit in the booth. Like a pregnant woman, he rested one arm on the top of his stomach and turned the pages of a newspaper as if he couldn't hear her. He took four fries in his hand and scratched his head, leaving a layer of grease on the pink shiny scalp.

Woozy, Lee turned to see if her order was ready. The teenager was at the drive-through window, talking into the speaker. Behind her she heard a child's yell and looked over to see toddler twins chasing each other around and between the plastic tables. The mother, bones showing under sallow skin, with greasy limp hair and yellow in the whites of her eyes, stared at the wall. Her baby, trapped in the cheap wooden high chair, blubbered and held up his arms. "Mama, up. Mama, up." Without looking at him, she threw fries onto the table in front of him. "Eat."

Across the restaurant the older woman huffed, her voice a harsh rasp. "Why some people don't control their monsters, I'll never know." The mother flipped the old woman the finger.

Lee paid for her order and left. She sat in the vehicle. Her breath fogged the windows. She thumped her head against the steering wheel several times before dialing Ellen White's phone number from the cell phone. There was no answer, just a click from an outdated message machine with a recording of Mrs. White's voice, sounding startled. "It's Ellen. Leave a message at the beep."

"Hi Mrs. White. This is Lee. Just wanted to let you know I'd be there in about three or four hours. Uh, well, thanks. See you soon."

Ellen White had kept her promise to Lee all those years ago and looked after Eleanor. She checked on her every day, made meals, did her shopping, and paid her bills with money Lee sent every month. At the first of every month Mrs. White sent a note on plain white paper with an update on Eleanor's health and a detailed account of expenses. She often included a personal note in a P.S., written in a brief, almost telegram-type style, as if the personal side of things should be kept brief. All those postscripts over the years had never failed to make Lee smile.

Ten years ago Mrs. White had written, "P.S. Retired last month. I assume they were glad to get rid of an old bat like me but gave me a grand sendoff with cake and champagne. I'll miss teaching Hemingway and such but glad to have more time to garden."

Lee, in turn, wrote brief notes in the same style included with the monthly checks. On her admittance to the MBA program at Wharton she'd said, "Off to graduate school to study business. The art world is fine if you don't mind starvation. Hoping to add more dollars to these checks in a couple years."

Mrs. White wrote back to her new address in Chicago. "P.S. I'm proud of you. Don't forget to take out those paints once in a while just so you can remember who you are. My beans are taking over the garden—will take me a month of Sundays to can all of them."

From Wharton Lee wrote, "Graduate in one month. I've met a man in the program named Dan Johnson. He's full of fire and ambition. Not sure of the future."

About Dan Mrs. White wrote, "P.S. Hope this fellow deserves you. Don't marry him unless you're absolutely sure. It's the most important decision you'll ever make. I won first prize for my pie at the county fair. Stupidest contest in the world but what can I say, I'm a vain woman."

After her wedding Lee wrote a quick note from her new desk in Redmond, Washington, along with a check for twice the amount she had been sending. "Was married last month to Dan Johnson. Had a small wedding in between interviews at Microsoft. Writing this from my new desk in the marketing department."

Mrs. White sent a beautiful pine easel for a wedding present and a note, written on a card with a painting of tulips, without a P.S.

"Congratulations. Once you get married it seems you have to share everything—the bad and the good. So here's a little something just for you. Even if you just paint on the weekends it will feed your soul.

"I imagine you as a grown married woman, capable, sophisticated, beautiful, and wish I could see you in person sometime. Maybe you'll come for a visit one of these years? You could bring your young man. Of course, you could stay with me, seeing as your mother's filled her house almost completely with junk. Be well. Be happy. Warmly, Ellen White."

But a year ago Mrs. White called on the telephone instead of sending news via a card. Eleanor was dead. She'd asked to be cremated. Would Lee like to come for a memorial service or to spread the ashes? Lee declined. Mrs. White said, "Don't blame you. But I'll keep the ashes in case you change your mind."

Lee had told herself there was no reason to pretend that a memorial service was something her mother would have wanted, since she hadn't cared if Lee visited when she was alive. Not to mention, Lee thought, of her angry alcoholic disdain for most people in the small town where she lived. Anyway, Lee couldn't face all the memories that waited there in that town, in that house, all of which she tried to pretend never happened. She hadn't wanted to think about the girl she once was, or her complicated, excruciating relationship with her mother. Starting the month after Eleanor's death, she sent the budgeted money to AIDS Alliance and worked late so she didn't have to think about her mother's cremated ashes poured into a little ceramic container.

Lee sent Mrs. White a card thanking her for her kindness and asking if there was something she could do to repay her.

Mrs. White sent a note back that said, "No need to thank me for the care of your mother. She was a pain in the ass, but it made me glad to think of you free and, hopefully, happy. I'll keep an eye on the house until you can make it down here. Stay in touch. Warm regards, Ellen White."

Lee took a last sip of her milkshake and pulled back onto the freeway, resigned that her destination was the only option left.

CHAPTER FOUR

IT WAS THE MIDDLE OF THE MORNING when she turned onto the dirt road to her mother's house. Large puddles jostled the car and splashed the windows as she drove the last corner and turned into the driveway. The white farmhouse, built in the mid-century, was perched on a slight hill, with a large front porch and two cherry trees on each side. Lee parked the car next to the house and stared out the window for a few minutes at her last possession, her inheritance from her mother. It surprised her to see the yard looked well-kept even though no one had lived there in over a year. The wild grass outside the small fenced front garden and the patchy grass inside the dilapidated fence were cut short. Against the covered front porch the cherry trees were in full bloom, their pink flowers fluttering against the chill of the early March breeze. Ellen White's doing, she supposed.

She took a deep breath and tried to move, but her limbs were lead. This place made her numb. She stared unseeing out the window, remembering the day she and Linus had come up with the plan that had brought her to this moment.

The day after Dan's funeral she found Linus on a stepstool in her kitchen, putting away wine glasses.

He looked into her face and gave her a quick hug. "You slept."

"Those little pink pills are powerful." From the window over the breakfast nook she could see snow scattered on the jutting peaks of the Olympic mountain range. She sat on the white wood bench of the nook and gazed out the window. "There's a guy watching my window in a car across the street."

"I saw him too." Linus's face was red as he pushed his coffee cup to the middle of the table. "How could Dan do this to you?"

She hadn't seen before that Linus was angry. She put her hand on his arm and watched a drop of rain drip down the outside of the window.

Linus's hands shook on the tabletop. "What do you want to do?"

"I've got to figure out how to get the money."

"I'll give you everything I have in savings and stocks. It's about 150k."

"I can't take your money, plus it's not enough to make a dent into this." She took his hands, and they were silent for a moment. "I'm late."

He flinched and his neck flushed red. "Late, late?"

"Yeah, that kind of late."

"How late?"

"Two weeks."

"It's probably just the stress. That can cause missed periods, right?"

She put her head in her hands. "I'm sure that's it." It was the forgotten birth control pills the month before that worried her but she kept that to herself, afraid to even say it out loud.

After a moment she pulled her hands from his and tapped her fingers on the surface of the table. "I have an idea of what to do, how to get the money. I did some calculations and I think if we could auction all my stuff and this condo I could come up with at least half the debt."

Linus raised his eyebrows, his eyes full of fear. "What about the rest?"

"Did I ever tell you I inherited my mother's house in Oregon?"

He looked surprised, raising his hands in the air with a flutter. "Uh, no, I don't think you mentioned that."

"It's in the middle of nowhere."

"Like the country?"

"Right, the country. I could fix up the house and sell it for the rest of the money."

"You think you could sell it for a half a million?"

"I don't know. I'm sure it's a mess. My mother never threw anything away and never left the house."

"I saw somebody like that on Oprah. There's a name for it, but I can't think what it is."

She said without thinking, "Agoraphobic." She went on, wringing her hands. "My grandfather built the house in the forties. It has an old-fashioned front porch on twenty acres and a river runs through the property. The land alone must be pretty valuable."

She put her hair behind her ears and took a big breath, reaching into her pocket and pulling out Von's card. "I'm going to call this guy and see if I can buy some time."

She punched in the number and Von picked up on the second ring. "It's Lee Johnson. I have a few questions."

"Yeah?"

"I can get you half of the money in a week but I need more time for the other half."

"How much time?"

"Couple of months."

"Listen, lady, my boss wants the money now. He's waited long enough. Meet me on Tuesday, ten p.m. in front of your building. Bring the full amount." He clicked off and Lee put the phone in the charger and sat back at the table, shaking and staring into space.

"He wants all of it next Tuesday. What am I going to do?"

Linus got up and paced in front of the refrigerator. "This house, where is it exactly?"

"Southern Oregon. It's a one stoplight town and my mother's house is about ten miles out."

"Has anyone ever heard of this place?"

"Not really."

"So, you could hide out there while you're fixing up the house?"

She looked at him. "How would I get there without them following me? These guys have me staked out."

He sat across from her at the table. "We've got to figure that part out."

She went to the sink and filled a glass with water. She felt tears start again and let them flow, hanging her head. Linus stood behind her, patting her shoulder. "This is going to be alright. We're going to get you out of this. I'm going to call all my gay friends and have them help us organize an auction. They love this kind of thing."

She nodded, wiping her face and turning to look at him. "Linus?"

"What is it?"

"What did he look like? When you identified the body, I mean?"

He backed up from her, putting up his hands. "No, don't go there."

"I need to know how he did it."

"Why? It's better not to know."

"I thought that, but it isn't true. Please, tell me how he did it."

"I'm not talking about this."

She grabbed his arms and shook him. "Yes, I deserve to know. I want to know how he did it." She shook him again and then pushed into his chest with her open palms. "Tell me how he did it."

"He put it in his mouth."

Lee dropped to the floor, hugging her knees and wailing. "Why? Why did he do this?"

Linus was on the floor next to her and he pulled her to him. "I don't know. I don't know." He held her, rocking her in his lap like a child.

There was a thump on the window and Lee jumped, startled out of her memory. It was Ellen White, older, grayer, but the same. She wore a cotton dress with work boots and held plastic kitchen gloves between strong fingers. Lee opened the car door and slid her feet to the ground. Mrs. White grabbed her and for a moment Lee thought she might hug her, but instead she shook Lee's hand in a brisk, firm handshake. "Good to see you. I was in the kitchen cleaning and saw you drive up." She smelled of Palmer's cocoa-butter lotion and cookies.

She went on, pushing back a bit of stray gray hair from her forehead. "You can't believe the amount of crap in that house." Her face was etched with wrinkles, but her body was still lithe and muscular, radiating youthful energy. She squinted, looking at Lee from head to foot. "You look about the same as the day I drove you to the bus station."

Lee grimaced. She took Mrs. White's hands, forcing herself to smile. "I've changed a little, haven't I? I have contacts now."

Mrs. White looked at her again, cocking her head as if examining a rare specimen. "You're just as pretty as a picture. I knew you would be."

"It's good to see you," said Lee, fighting back tears.

"Sure was pleased to get your letter last week." Mrs. White still had the long braid, gray now, and coiled on top of her head. "Was shocked as could be to hear you were coming for a visit." She peered around Lee into the van. "You bring much?" She still had the efficient way of speaking and moving that made Lee feel like a child ready for a nap, inept and incompetent.

"It's in the back." Lee opened the back of the van and grabbed the large suitcase. Mrs. White took the other, smaller bag.

"That it? Thought you were staying for a while?"

"Traveling light these days." Lee gestured to the yard. "You've cut the grass?"

"Sure did. Bought myself one of those rider mowers when I turned seventy."

CHAPTER FIVE

THEY HESITATED at the top of the stairs. Lee looked down the hallway at the doors of the two small bedrooms, the bathroom, and master. The house smelled of mildew, dust, and the bottom of an ashtray after the butts have been emptied. Mrs. White pointed to the doorway of the master. "Better sleep in there."

"You mean the shrine?"

Mrs. White chuckled and moved down the hall to the master bedroom. "The other rooms are full of junk." As if it was decided, Mrs. White flung open the master bedroom door. The room was empty but for a mid-century, four-poster bed, a bureau with a round mirror, and faded yellow cotton curtains. "Your mother got really bad about the stuff at the end, but she never touched this room." Mrs. White pulled back the curtains and pushed open the windows. The outdated faded wallpaper peeled at the corners and the pine floorboards were dull and nicked. "The stench isn't as bad in here. I've had the windows open the last several days."

The room possessed the feel of frozen time and expectancy, like its mistress and master might still return. As if she read Lee's thoughts, Mrs. White nodded her head. "Yep, feels like the room's waiting for something. I never understood why she didn't move in here after your grandparents were killed. Shoot, that was the year you were born and what are you, thirty-four?"

"Thirty-five."

"Holding on to the past never works, you know, people gotta move on. Not that I was a good example, mind you."

Lee wondered what she meant but was too tired to invite conversation by asking. She moved to the bureau and looked at the framed photo of her grandfather in his World War II uniform. Mrs. White dusted it with the front of her cotton dress. "Your grandfather built this house with his bare hands. They don't make houses like this anymore. He'd turn over in his grave if he saw how your mother let it go to pot." She picked up the other framed picture, of Lee's grandmother, and held it near Lee's face. "You sure look like her. Rose was a redhead too. Both of us were redheads, y'know? We used to laugh about that. All that fiery temper in one room." She gestured towards the bed. "There was some money hidden in the cookie jar downstairs, left over from what you used to send every month, so I got you a new mattress and sheets. Hope you don't mind but I knew you couldn't sleep on the old one."

Lee raised her eyebrows and stuttered. "Gr…Great. Thanks."

"I used to take two-thirds of the check you sent every month to pay her bills and buy groceries and leave the rest in the cookie jar. I plumb forgot it was in there. Eleanor got so she didn't trust the bank and of course you know she didn't leave the house, so that money just sat in there, except for what she used to buy the booze."

"Let me guess, someone, out of the kindness of their heart, delivered that to her door?"

"The derelict who owns the Rusty Nail. Used to drop a box the first of every month. Bastard knew your checks came like clockwork." She walked to the bed and smoothed the top of the patchwork quilt, the squares each a pattern of a geometric red flower. "Washed your grandmother's homemade quilt and it's good as new."

Lee fingered the thread along one of the squares, imagining her grandmother's fingers pushing the needle through the fabric. "Do you know what happened to my grandparents' clothes and stuff?"

"I came and packed them up the year after they died." Mrs. White lowered her voice, as if someone were listening. "Matter of fact, I used to come up here and clean when I brought groceries and such to your mother. She used to space out in front of the idiot box in the afternoon."

"I snuck in here one time when I was a kid. Looking for clues about them." She sat on the side of the bed and shivered. "But all I found was the back of my mother's hand."

Mrs. White plumped a pillow, eyebrows knitted. "I could tell you anything you want to know."

"I'd like that sometime." Lee shivered and jumped from the bed to shut one of the windows. "It's raining."

"March. Nice one minute, cold the next." Mrs. White pulled on the front of her dress and crossed her arms over her chest. "You hungry?"

Lee shrugged and walked towards the door. "A little."

They moved in silence down to the kitchen. The counters and floor looked scoured, as did the appliances. Mrs. White gestured towards a chair. "Sit, I'll fix you something before I go." On the table was a fresh pie, berry juice seeping through the top of a browned crust. Mrs. White hustled about the kitchen and Lee, feeling like a guest, sat in one of the metal chairs and watched. Mrs. White pulled a carton of eggs from the 1950's refrigerator, yanked an old frying skillet out of the cupboard, poured oil in the pan, turned on the burner, and, hands on her bony hips, watched the pan heat. "Shoulda got you some bacon. I didn't think you'd be so skinny." When the room filled with the smell of hot grease, she cracked two eggs into the pan. They sizzled and snapped and she flipped them in the air without using a spatula. She slipped the eggs onto a plate, set it in front of Lee, and then poured a glass of milk. "You need your calcium if you want to be moving around when you're seventy."

Lee poked an egg with her fork and the yolk squirted onto the flowered surface of the old plate. Her stomach turned and she felt the crackers make their way to her throat. She ran to the back door, yanked it open, and vomited into the wet dank earth of the flowerbed next to the back steps. She wiped her mouth with her hand and limped up the steps into the kitchen. The smell of fried egg lingered in the air. She went to the sink, turned on the water, and slurped from her cupped hand. A branch of a cherry tree, dripping with pink flowers, wavered outside the kitchen sink window, rain beading on the soft pink petals. She splashed the frigid water over her face and then collapsed onto the chair.

Mrs. White stood at the stove and watched her. "Please don't tell me you're a drunk?"

"What? No, of course not. I don't drink."

"Thank God. Y'know, they're saying now it's hereditary."

"Don't touch it. Always figured it was best not to start, given Mom."

"I'm awfully glad to hear you say it. I worried about you up there in that mean old city all these years. The temptations are many, I imagine." She put her hand on Lee's forehead. "You don't feel hot. You think you're sick?"

"I've been feeling kind of sick all afternoon but I'm probably just tired. It's been a hard couple of weeks."

Mrs. White scrutinized Lee for a moment and then sat in the other chair. "What happened to bring you here?"

"Dan died. Unexpectedly." Lee watched the sprinkles of rain turn to drops outside the kitchen window, staying silent until she was sure the tears weren't about to start. She made her tone matter of fact. "Shot himself."

"I see." Ellen crossed her arms over her chest and matched Lee's understated tone. "What was wrong with him?"

"It's complicated."

"It always is."

"He took a loan from someone he shouldn't have but couldn't get our product to work in order to pay it, the consequence of which was the loss of our company. I guess the idea of that kind of failure was too much for him."

She shook her head as if she'd heard the same story many times before. "Son of a bitch. Gosh durn selfish bastard."

"Dan was so driven, Mrs. White. Crazy half the time over this idea of making it. He just took me along for the ride. I didn't know about the construct of the loan or any of the details of it. The sad thing is, his product was good. It was a game for serious gamer types. Do you know what that is?"

"Sure, it's those pasty, stoop-shouldered idiots that play ridiculous games instead of living their lives."

She smiled. "That's right."

Mrs. White grinned, patting her bun. "I stay informed for an old lady."

Lee looked towards the ceiling, trying to control the wobble in her voice. "I've lost everything."

The way Mrs. White looked at her, Lee saw she had it figured, how desperate she was, how broke, how alone. "Except for this beat-up old house," said Mrs. White. She swept her hand against the tabletop in a half circle. "Well, it's something to start with." She traced the rim of her coffee cup with her pinkie finger until she reached the crack above the painted rose. "My husband was killed in a logging accident in the woods when my son was ten years old. I had enough money to last exactly two months. Your grandmother helped get me through it. We ate dinner at this very table every night for I don't know how long." She paused and patted the top of her coiled bun. "You'll be alright."

Lee's eyes filled with tears and she wiped them with the back of her hand. "How? I don't see how."

Mrs. White looked out the window, tapping her finger on the surface of the table. "Y'know, I had to, that was one thing. My boy needed me. But, the thing I did then was go back to work. I'd been trained as a teacher and I started subbing at first and then they hired me on to teach full-time. Then I'd come home and take care of my place and my son. I guess work got me through, now I think of it."

Lee stared at the tabletop, wiping the end of her nose with the back of her sleeve. "Thought I'd fix up the house to sell."

"I hate to see it go out of your family, but I'll do what I can to help."

"You've done enough, dealing with my mother all those years."

"I've known your family for what feels like all my life. Your grandmother Rose and I were twenty years old when our husbands built these houses. We were twenty-one when we had our babies. Your grandmother was the best friend I ever had." Mrs. White's eyes reddened. She put her cup in the sink and it clinked against a fork. "I held your mother the day she was born."

"Did she have vodka in her baby bottle?" Lee looked out the screen door. The sun poked through the gray rain clouds, illuminating the multiple shades of greens in the yard and forest.

Mrs. White's eyes were sad. "She was the prettiest, smartest baby you ever saw. Her life just went in the wrong direction. It was too much, being alone with a baby and so young."

"You did it."

Mrs. White blinked and nodded her head. "So I did, but I'm a different sort than most. Shoot but your mother caused me fits half the time but now she's gone, I miss having someone to look after. My son died when he was eighteen, but once a mother, always a mother."

Lee put her hand over Mrs. White's and shivers went up her spine. "Mrs. White, I never knew that. I'm so sorry."

She looked at her, and Lee read surprise in her stoic face. "He died in the car accident with your grandparents."

Lee stared at her. "I had no idea. My mother would never talk about them, so I don't even know how they died exactly."

"They went to pick up Chris from the county fair. He was showing his FFA pig," said Mrs. White. "It was a way to make college money, raising an animal for market at the fair. The kids used to stay the whole week, get their animals judged and then auctioned off. Matter of fact, your mother had the flu that night or she would have been with them too. Your granddaddy offered to get him for me so I wouldn't have to drive the thirty minutes by myself. A car drifted into their lane on the mountain pass." She ran her hand across the table again, like there might be a stray crumb. "None of them suffered. I was always grateful for that." Mrs. White touched the top of her bun and then held up a hand. "Shoot, I don't know why I'm talking about all this morbid history. I've got to go and let you get some rest." She headed towards the door. "I sure would like it if you'd call me Ellen. I spent too many years as Mrs. White teaching school."

Lee agreed and walked her to the door. She touched the woman's wiry arm as she stepped from the kitchen to the top step of the small back patio. "Thanks for the pie. And for everything all these years with my mom, and the mattress. I can't repay your kindness."

"Why, you're welcome. I don't have much else to do these days, especially now. I'll be glad to see a light from your window on a dark night, for however long you stay. Now you call me tomorrow and I'll help you come up with a plan to get this old place fixed up."

CHAPTER SIX

LEE WATCHED the woman's purposeful stride as she disappeared out the creaky gate and down the dirt road. So much loss in one lifetime, Lee thought. Was life only a series of griefs? The fortitude it must have taken Ellen White to keep moving, to continue fighting was humbling. Was it the measure of character?

Hungry now, she remembered the pie on the counter. She'd allow herself one piece before she went upstairs and rested. Not bothering to cut into it, she scooped some onto a fork, juice dripping onto the tabletop. The blackberry filling was fragrant and fresh, with a hint of tartness. Perhaps some lemon juice had been added, she thought. It was the perfect combination, not overly sweet like pies from the grocery store. The crust was flaky and light, tasting of butter on her tongue. She ate two more bites, enjoying them. And then she thought of Dan. His mother made a pie every year for his birthday. He'd loved pie. The reality of the last several weeks came to her in a rush, the anxious hollow feeling returning to the pit of her stomach. She pushed away the pie and stared out the window, fighting the sobs that came anyway. She'd not known grief would come in waves, brought on by the smallest of things. Nor had she realized that ordinary acts of living would continue even after the loss of a love and that it would remain possible to get caught up in the moment of a simple pleasure before remembering.

And it washed down upon her in an inescapable truth, this bath of grief. Her husband was never coming back. He was gone and nothing she did would bring him back.

A thousand "what ifs" came to her, as they had for days and weeks now, all useless to the outcome but unavoidable. The biggest of which was, what if she'd been in the marriage with open eyes instead of simply getting through the day, the week, the month. If only she'd been awake to really see him, perhaps she could have saved him.

Her thoughts jumped to this new knowledge that she was pregnant. It settled into her mind for the first time. She'd put it aside for the miles between Seattle and now. Hard as the pregnancy was to fathom, it was time to think it through, to figure out what must be done.

They hadn't touched in months. They'd been to a party that night and he'd been almost like his old self, joking and laughing with friends in the kitchen. He'd had several drinks so she'd driven them home. He'd been quiet in the car but strangely attentive, twisted in the seat, watching her with soft eyes like he'd done when they were first together. At home he ran his fingers up the sides of her arms. He spoke softly, earnestly, "No matter what happens, remember I've loved you since the moment I met you." She choked up and put her arms around his neck, holding him close.

It was the last time. And now there was a pregnancy.

She rummaged in her bag for the test, needing proof suddenly that she hadn't imagined the pink lines. The test was there at the bottom of her bag, evidence of a new life that she could see and hold in her hand, while the evidence of her husband's death seemed somehow without substantiation. She understood the ritual of the funeral was supposed to give her this symbol of closure but she remembered so little of it that it seemed almost like someone else's dim nightmare.

They'd had the memorial service at an old Seattle church, all dark wood and ornate carvings on the beams and benches. It smelled of incense and burning candles and the powdery florist shop smell of the roses in oversized vases in front of the pastor's pulpit. His mother looked shrunken, slumped against his father. His sister's tears soaked through the paper program in her hands, the husband next to her.

She remembered that the pastor prattled from his script the facts of Dan's life from the obituary. "Dan Johnson was born in 1974, raised by Ralph and Betty Johnson in Seattle, Washington. He graduated in 1996 from Stanford University with a degree in computer science and went on to get his MBA in Finance from Wharton in 2000. He co-founded, with his wife, Lee, Existence Games, Inc." He said something about the arms of Jesus and she looked left to the stained glass depiction of Mary holding her baby. And Jesus couldn't have felt farther away than in that moment.

It was then that Linus walked to the pulpit to speak. The crowd was silent. The microphone squeaked as he adjusted it up to his height. He explained that he was in the restaurant business and that he'd thrown their wedding reception. He cleared his throat and wiped the corner of his eye with a lime green handkerchief before continuing. "When I met Dan I remember thinking he was the ultimate golden boy, what with his crown of blond curls, his movie star smile, his pedigree of Stanford and Wharton, his athletic prowess. And yet I was skeptical of this man that wanted to marry my Lee, wondered if he was good enough for her, wanting to be sure this man deserved her. What happened next I will never forget. Dan could not dance. Not a move without stepping all over his partner's toes. Two months before the wedding he asked me if I'd teach him to waltz. He wanted to surprise Lee at their wedding reception." He made a frame with his hands. "Picture straighter than straight, masculine Dan, and little ol' me waltzing around his living room." He choked up, breathing heavily into the microphone. "Dan learned how to dance to please Lee, and as many of you may have observed, he was beautiful that night, dancing with his bride. No matter what, we all have that memory of him and I have to believe he was happy in that moment. I hope that might give us all some peace in the days and months to come."

Now, sitting in her mother's kitchen, she closed her eyes, recalling the night of their reception. "Dance with me," he asked. Surprised, she'd looked at Linus and he'd nodded, yes. She put her hand in Dan's and he walked her to the middle of the dance floor. He nodded to the band and they began to play a waltz. He guided her in perfect time, his silk tuxedo against her bare arms. Dan looked into her eyes and she whispered tearfully, "Thank you." And she thought to herself, this is the beginning of my real life, the one I was meant to have. Everything was right.

Now, at her mother's old kitchen table, she wiped her eyes, wondering if anything would ever feel right again.

CHAPTER SEVEN

LEE SLEPT THE REST OF THAT FIRST DAY and through the night, awakening to birds chirping outside her window. She reached over to Dan's side of the bed with her foot but there was nothing but a cold fold of bed sheet. In that instant between sweet insensible sleep and consciousness, it was as if the previous month hadn't happened. Once fully awake the sick ache roared through her. She got out of bed and looked out the window, still nervous that somehow Von followed her. But there was nothing in the driveway but her minivan. She shivered, yawned, and, rubbing her eyes, shuffled to the bathroom. She glanced in the mirror and gasped, shocked by the greasy hair and dark circles under her eyes. She tugged at the rusty faucets in the shower until they trickled russet-colored water into the yellow-stained tub. She sat with her arms around her ankles, head resting on her knees, and rocked until the water cleared.

She went to the hall closet for a towel. It smelled of old neglected wood. There were two ratty towels, the material so thin she could see through it, folded in squares on the second shelf that Ellen must have washed and put away for her. Steam drifted into the hallway from the bathroom.

She stood under the warm spray with her eyes closed. Compared to the shower at home, the water was a trickle on the back of her neck. But it was hot and comforting to her skin that felt beat up from the strain of the last weeks. She moved her hand over her stomach, taut and bloated. It was hard to comprehend there was anything inside her except longing and despair instead of a multiplying mass of cells that would turn into a human baby.

She scrubbed her body with soap and as the suds washed her clean she began to sort through and organize her thoughts, as she had with all new ventures, devising a plan that she would execute step by step. She saw it unfold in five phases: fix up the house, sell it, pay DeAngelo, move to a new city, and get her career back on track.

She washed her hair, holding her breath because the smell of the shampoo brought nausea in waves, and tried to focus on breaking down the first step of the plan. This morning she would conduct a full assessment of what it would take to get the house ready to sell. If the house foundation and construction were as strong as Ellen White indicated, she might be able to sell it for more than she owed DeAngelo. After the assessment, she would gather any items she could sell to get started on the repairs.

She stared at her image in the mirror on the bureau. Her tender breasts strained against her blouse, enlarged from their usual modest size to the size of large apples, and made her feel like a porn star. She popped a cracker in her mouth, slipped on a long cardigan sweater, and surveyed the master bedroom. There were two bedside tables, the bureau, and the bed, all brought with her grandmother from the east when she married in 1943. They might be considered antiques. She swept her hand on the smooth wood of the headboard, calculating its worth. She jotted that amount in a small notebook under a "To Sell" category, next to "Grandmother's furniture" with a circle bullet, in her precise angular printing.

She wandered down the hallway. The wallpaper, once a light

brown with small blue flowers, was now faded to tan. The hallway's hardwood floor showed burns from dropped cigarettes, most notably between her mother's bedroom and the bathroom. She wrote in her notebook under "Repairs" the estimated cost for the floor to be refinished and what it would cost to have the wallpaper replaced.

At the end of the hallway, Lee opened the door to her childhood bedroom six or so inches before it pushed against something. She poked her head in the crack and saw piles of newspapers, Ladies Home Journals, Reader's Digests, and romance and mystery paperbacks, stacked on the bed and floor. She felt a tightness in her chest and her right eyelid twitched. She closed the door with a slam. Her mother's bedroom was also stacked with worthless junk. She wrote under "To Do" in her notebook, "Burn contents of bedrooms," along with estimated costs for repairs.

She walked to the ground floor, the hardwood stairs creaking with her footsteps and the stair railing swaying in her hand. From the foyer at the bottom of the stairs, Lee moved into the curved archway of the living room, felt for the light switch along the left wall, and flipped it, but the bulb was burned out. In the dim light she saw stacks and stacks of papers with a path to a stained and sunken couch. She walked through the path to the window and pulled back the worn burgundy velvet draperies. There was a small rickety end table next to the couch, damaged with rings from her mother's drink glasses; a small television on an apple box; and piles of magazines, newspapers, and paperbacks. In the rare places where the wall showed, paper hung in strips. The smell of cigarette smoke permeated everything. She jotted in her notebook, "Burn or dump all contents of living room."

She trudged up the stairs, sat on the bed, and added the estimates for kitchen upgrades and repairs to the list. Altogether the costs of cleaning and repairs were shy of fifteen thousand dollars. She had five hundred dollars cash in her wallet that Linus insisted she take, several thousand in the bank, no idea how to do any repairs, and no money to pay anyone. The only answer was to find a job in town, scrimp, and use every spare dollar for the restoration.

She heaved herself off the bed to unpack the few belongings she had left. She'd kept the bare essentials, only what would fit in one suitcase. Her intent was to hang her clothes in the closet by type, with color-coded hangers she brought from her closet in Seattle. But each item she unpacked evoked thoughts of Dan and her former life. The light blue cashmere sweater Dan chose for her at the Nordstrom sale last autumn, the white cotton panties he called her 'granny underwear,' the cocktail dress she wore to their last business event. She stopped unpacking and stared at the pine floorboards.

Later that morning she sat on the steps off the kitchen. The yard was a grassy area and outside the fence was untouched forest, heavy with Douglas firs, pines, madronas, and low-growing ferns. It was chilly and the air smelled of damp earth and the unique freshness of early spring. The crab apple and cherry trees hinted of their summer bounty with white and pink flowers, while the lilac and hydrangea bushes sprouted green buds. Only the daffodils and tulips opened to their full glory. There was the sound of a truck changing gears on the highway and birds chirping. She looked up into the tall trees outside the fence and beyond to the vast blue sky. As a child, in the summer months, the backyard was a place of solace. After her mother slept, she crept out to the yard, lay in the grass, and listened to the deep croaks of the bullfrogs with the high-pitched song of the crickets. She would gaze at the stars until the night's vast sky enveloped her and she became a star herself and was at peace in that moment of connection to the largeness of the universe. But today it did not comfort her. Today, it amplified her feelings of isolation from the world, even from herself, as if mocking her with its beauty.

CHAPTER EIGHT

LEE WAS THIRSTY. She rummaged through the cupboards for a glass. They were bare except for a few cracked plates; a cereal bowl; four faded salad plates, chipped on the edges; and one lone teacup, cracked but still intact. This was all that was left of the original set. Lee had given it to her mother for a Christmas gift when she was young.

This old kitchen was cold and full of memories, she thought.

The year she was seven Lee's mother lost her job at one of the grocery stores in town. Neither of them knew then it would be her last job. Lee shopped for the groceries each Saturday morning at the other store, the one on the other side of town. Eleanor sat in the car, a floating head amidst the smoke from her cigarettes, a hand flicking the ashes out of a small slit in the window. Lee filled their basket with the same items every week: coffee, milk, peanut butter, cheese, bread, and ground meat. She paid with the Food Stamps her mother picked up every Monday afternoon. The autumn Lee was eleven, the store put up a display of dishes you could purchase with Green Stamps. The first time she saw them, Lee stopped to look at the display, wanting more than anything to give them to her mother for Christmas. She touched the light brown ceramic plates and ran her fingers over the white flower pattern etched on the edges. She held one of the dainty teacups and pretended to drink from it, until she heard her mother beep the horn and motion for her to pay for the groceries and come to the car.

The entire dish set, which included four place settings, cost one-thousand Green Stamps. Each week the ladies at the check stand gave her fifty stamps, more than she should have earned for the amount of food she bought, not to mention that technically you weren't eligible unless you paid with real money. But, at age eleven, Lee didn't know and accepted the stamps, bliss in her heart each time. She couldn't help but notice that the checkers glanced out at the smoke-filled car with a disapproving look when they put the stamps in her hand.

One week before Christmas she counted out one-thousand stamps to the lady with the blond beehive named Bridget. Bridget called the rest of the ladies over. "Lee's got enough, girls. She's got enough for the whole set." They all cheered for her, and the lady named Sue with the long brown hair who looked like Jaclyn Smith on the show Charlie's Angels offered to bring it to her house the next day. "Can you bring it at night?" Lee asked her, glancing at the car. "My mother goes to bed early." The ladies exchanged looks and Sue said, "No problem. I get off at eight." That's perfect, Lee thought, because Mom will be asleep on the couch by then.

Her steps were light that day and her tummy did little flops. That night after writing in her worry journal, she imagined sitting on the floor next to an enormous tree, decorated with small ornate glass ornaments and twinkling lights. Under the tree were many presents in store-bought wrapping with giant bows, all for Lee. She and her mother were in new Christmas pajamas and slippers, sipping cocoa. Her mother, eyes twinkling like Pa's from Little House on the Prairie, patted her hand. "I wish we had some new cups to drink this cocoa from." And Lee said, kind of casually so as not to give away the surprise, "Maybe you should open my gift now." Her mother's face lit with excitement as she opened the box and saw the cups. "How were you ever so clever to think of it?" Lee shrugged modestly. Her mother took them out of the box one at a time, examining them in ecstatic excitement. "They're so beautiful. Maybe we should have a dinner party!"

But of course it wasn't that way.

When her mother tore open the newspaper Lee used in place of wrapping paper, she looked at them, a mixture of disdain and displeasure on her face. "What do we need all these for?"

"It's how they come, Mom. They don't come in packages of two."

She reached farther into the box and pulled out a salad plate. "What are we gonna use these for?"

Lee's face turned pink. "They're for salad. Or dessert."

"May as well just put everything on the same plate. Less to wash." Her mother picked up the packaging and stuffed it back in the box. "You can put them away later, once you figure out what to do with the perfectly good dishes we already have." Lee excused herself, ran to the bathroom, and sat on the floor crying until she heard her mother call from downstairs that she needed more ice from the freezer in the shed.

After that she didn't allow herself any fantasies that involved her mother.

Now, Lee drank several teacups of water and then washed the cup and put it into the cupboard. She leaned next to the sink and looked at the ancient stove and remembered a cold night, two frozen dinners heating in the oven. Her mother leaned on the counter, flicking her cigarette in the glass ashtray and sipping vodka on ice. Lee sat at the table, drawing a picture of an exotic bird from a photo in a magazine. The house seemed cozy, like they were a family from one of Lee's fantasies. She imagined her father would arrive home from work any minute, dressed in a suit and holding a briefcase. He might kiss her on the head and call her "honey." Her mother lifted her glass in a gesture towards the drawing. "What is that now, a bird?" "A parrot, Mommy, but it's not right because I need color markers to make the feathers." Her mother snatched the paper from the table and ripped it in two. "You think I have money growing from trees to buy you anything you want?" She slammed her glass on the counter and an ice cube fell on the floor. "Do you?" Eleanor poured more vodka in her glass and yanked the hot tin dinner from the oven. "You want to keep eating?" "Yes, Mommy." She threw the tin on the table, and drops of Salisbury steak gravy splattered onto Lee's homework folder. "Then shut up about pens."

Lee felt hot from the memory and washed her face at the sink. She wished she could call Linus but knew she could not risk alerting Von to her new location. It seemed like a month since she left him when really it was just fourteen hours since she'd said goodbye.

It felt like the last eighteen years were a dream, and maybe she'd never really left. She felt the old sensation of being invisible, unsure if she even existed.

She stared into the empty sink, thinking about the old adage that you learned how to be a mother from your own mother. If that was true, there was no way she could have a baby. The fact that her life mirrored her mother's, even with all her efforts to break the cycle, made her feel almost hopeless. She had never known the feeling of wanting to give up before and it disoriented her. Even during all the difficult years in this house she always had a plan, a vision, for what her life could be. She used to think if she could just make it to her eighteenth birthday intact, she would have a chance to steer her own destiny.

She looked around the faded kitchen and thought there was no way she could bring a child into her messed up life.

Not letting herself think, she called information from the leased cell phone, asking for the nearest Planned Parenthood office. She asked for an appointment for an abortion. The calm voice on the other end of the line explained she must have an initial consultation before the procedure could be scheduled.

"But I've made up my mind."

"Sorry, Miss, it's policy." They scheduled an appointment for three days later.

CHAPTER NINE

THE NEXT DAY, Lee slowed her minivan to 25 mph as she crested a slight hill, glancing at the sign, "Welcome to River Valley, pop. 1432." Her stomach tightened, thinking the population was the same as when she left, eighteen years before. Like many of the small towns that peppered the West, the population of the city limits did not reflect the residences scattered throughout the area, down country roads, deep into the woods, perched on sides of mountains—around 5,000 people total, Lee guessed. Regardless, she thought, there had been no growth in this area for twenty years even as the rest of the West expanded with opportunity.

From the city limits sign, she saw from one end of town to the other. It was one main street with a series of shabby, worn-out buildings that held the essence of despair. It was the sag of the town, the way it looked like it had given up, that depressed her. It possessed all the same things every small town has, two grocery stores, two gas stations, five or six bars, eight churches, a library, schools, a bank with a sign that tells you the time and temperature, and the state-regulated liquor store. There was nothing remarkable in it, she thought, except the way the dramatic mountains surrounded the valley and the expansive sky made her want to hold out her arms and soar up into the blue. Perhaps it was the giant sky or the loom of the mountains that made the shriveled faded town lose heart. Next to their splendor, anything man-made might feel beleaguered but especially these low slung, sad structures.

As she drove, she saw several wooden signs that read, "Thank you to the Beautify River Valley committee for these improvements." Looking for the professed improvements, she guessed it must be the flower boxes and the turquoise paint color scheme adopted by many of the businesses.

She turned left off the main street and drove by the junior high school, curious to see if it was still standing. Behind the brick building were the football field and bleachers where Mark Caldwell and Doug Flanders yelled out to her one day. "You know what a blow job is?" "No, but I'll give you one if you don't shut up," she called back. For years she wondered why they fell over each other with laughter. She smiled thinking of it, though the feeling of confused embarrassment, knowing there was something risqué or sexual in their request but too naïve and unaware to understand what, lived near the surface of her, even now.

She drove farther up the street past the high school. She turned back onto the main street and parked, checking her hair in the rearview mirror and reapplying her lipstick before surveying the line of businesses. She chose Ray's Accounting, Taxes, and Bookkeeping. She walked into the small office, warm air blasting her face from the overhead heating as the door closed behind her. The office was bare except for a desk with a computer and a bookshelf of tax manuals. A man between fifty and sixty, with a helmet of brown hair that Lee suspected was a toupee, sat at the desk playing a game of solitaire on his computer. When the door closed he sprung from his desk, knocking his stapler on the floor. "You need your taxes done?" He wore a short-sleeved, wrinkled, button-down shirt, and brown polyester pants with a mustard stain on the left leg.

Lee slung her bag over her shoulder. "No, I'm new to town and wondered if you needed any help?"

He came around his desk, and Lee detected the sour smell of Bengay. "Gosh, I don't have enough business for a helper." He held out his hand, introducing himself as Ray Zander. He stroked his chin, his pace of speech slow and drawn out. "Sure wish I did." He scratched his arm, and flakes of dry skin floated through the air, propelled by the blast of hot air from the heater vent. "Only folks making any money seem to be the crystal meth makers, and they don't pay taxes."

The back of Lee's throat ached. She forced politeness in her voice. "That's a shame."

"We got a couple of new wineries outside of town. I do their books but they're not hiring right now."

Lee moved her bag to the other shoulder. "What about the banks? Think they have any openings?"

"Unlikely. Where'd you come from?"

"Seattle. But I grew up here."

Ray arched his eyebrows. "That right? What's your name?"

"Lee Tucker." This was the first time she'd said her maiden name in five years and she felt like an imposter.

"What brings you back?"

"My mother died last year and I'm fixing up her house."

"What kind of work you do?"

"I was the president of a small high tech firm."

"Dot com? You go bust? I told my investment club all those crazy ideas would flop. Everybody jumping on the whole ecommerce thing like a bunch of sheep!"

She tucked one side of her hair behind her ear, all of a sudden hot in her sweater. Sweat beaded on the tip of her nose and she resisted the urge to wipe it with her fingers. "We started our business after the dot com bust."

"That right? What kind of product?"

"A computer game, for extreme gamers."

He looked at her blankly and she turned towards the door,

noticing rain drops on the sidewalk. "Thanks for your help." She pushed the door open with her shoulder and stepped onto the sidewalk, already two steps down the street before she realized he was on her heels.

Hands in his pockets, Ray strolled beside her, continuing the same slow pace of talking. "What happened to your company?"

She stopped walking and wondered how much she should reveal? It would be all over town in a matter of minutes so she needed a sustainable story, especially if she wanted anyone to hire her. "My husband died unexpectedly and I lost the company."

Ray's eyes softened and he patted her arm. "Sorry to hear that. I lost my wife last year to cancer." He rubbed his eyes with his fingertips and his tone shifted to lower in his chest. "Just brings it back for me every time I hear of someone else losing their spouse." He studied her face and then looked up at the sky, snapping his fingers. "You know, there is one place to try. It wouldn't be the type of thing you'd want long term but it'd keep the wolf away, if that's what you need. Mike opened a little restaurant six months ago." He pointed down the street. "You remember where the old grocery store was?"

"Sure." It was run by Steve Turner, reputed to give free groceries to needy customers and hire the down and out, before one of the big chains opened in the mid-eighties and forced him out of business. Lee remembered him as a gentle soul, lids half closed, slipping her a piece of chocolate every now and then. "My mother worked there for a while in the seventies."

"You said your last name is Tucker? By golly, your mother was Eleanor Tucker. Sure, I remember her now." He shuffled his feet and glanced again at the sky. "She had some health problems?"

"You could say that."

His face softened as he connected her to the memory. "I remember you too, now you mention it. Little redhead, thick glasses, sweet thing huddled behind your mother's check stand." He half smiled and shrugged his shoulders. "Embarrassed to say I used to go in there for smokes. Kicked the habit now but I was in there every other day and if your mother was on shift in the late afternoon or evening, there you'd be, curled up with your nose in a book." He cocked his head to one side and said with admiration in his voice and a hint of surprise, "You turned out real pretty."

"I got contacts."

"It's more than just the contacts. You've done well for yourself, I can see that, in spite of your..." He cleared his throat, but Lee knew what he thought, even though he was too courteous to say, in spite of your mother. This she hated, this small town peculiarity, where everyone thinks they know everything about you, but in fact it is only a half truth, a piece of your life that is public, the rest of you obscured by the collective narrative.

He lowered his voice to just above a whisper. "Mike opened this restaurant in the old market space and his son's running it. Rumor has it, the boy's mixed up in some bad stuff. Mike, he's kind of our honorary mayor and he's always talking about how to get tourists in here and thought a nice restaurant might tempt folks to stop on their way through, but so far they just keep on driving." He glanced around as if someone might hear. "Now I shouldn't say this, but I do their books, and the restaurant's bleeding cash. Course he's rich as all get out, his family's owned the mill for three generations, but Mike doesn't like to lose money. They could use a real business woman to help them out, get it profitable." He patted her shoulder again.

She wanted to rip the toupee off his head and dash it with her high-heeled boot. She could be ten years old the way his kindness ripped her of pride and made her the meek, impoverished charity case. She dared not look in the window below the hand painted Ray's Accounting sign for fear she'd spy the reflection of the pitiful little girl and her drunken mother stumbling out of the grocery store on their way home to their cold, cigarette-infested house, to eat their television dinners in front of the black and white television with the broken sound, the clink of ice cubes in the highball glass occasionally drowning out the show.

Ray puffed out his chest, clapping his hands, his toupee

shifting higher on his forehead. "Tell you what, I'm gonna call Mike right now. Come on back to my office."

When she stepped inside the restaurant, she waited for her eyes to adjust to the muted light, holding her breath against the odors of grease and stale beer. Plastic tables, folding metal chairs, and artificial plants were scattered about the room. There were two guitar amplifiers and a microphone in the front corner. A man, his back to the door, sat at one of the red-checked-plastic covered tables, punching numbers into an adding machine and scribbling in a notebook. "We're not open." His hand jerked when the lead of his pencil snapped. "Dammit."

"Excuse me, I'm here to meet Mike." Her boots squeaked on the rough uneven slabs of wood, dull and scratched from dirt and wet shoes. She sneezed and grabbed a napkin from one of the tables. There was dust and grime along the floorboards and her boot squished on a limp greasy fry on the floor.

"This time of day he's at the mill."

He raised his head and Lee stifled a gasp. It was Zac Huller from high school, except his face seemed expanded like there was a centimeter of water under the surface of his skin.

He stopped writing and looked at her. "You look familiar." He came over to where she stood, putting his hands in his pockets and staring at her. "Lee Tucker?"

She nodded. "Zac."

"I haven't seen you since that one party on senior skip day. That was some party! What I remember of it anyway." He chuckled and rubbed his hand on his back pocket. "Some weird shit went down that day."

A trickle of sweat made its way down Lee's back. "It's been a long time."

"What've you been up to?"

"I've been in Seattle."

"That right? You visiting?"

"My mother died last year so I'm here to take care of some things."

"Bummer." He stared at her and his eyes blazed. "You married?"

Lee adjusted her sweater over her stomach. "No."

"I married Lindsey. You remember her?"

"Sure."

"We got divorced after a couple of years. She turned out to be a crazy bitch."

"That's too bad."

"I'm the manager here. Temporarily. I'm just helping my dad out for a few months and then I'm moving south, to the beach."

"Great."

He moved closer. "Well, you look different. I'm impressed."

"Oh, thanks." Lee clasped her hands together to control the shaking. "I should go."

"Stay, have a beer with me. We can talk about the old days. Man, it seems like yesterday."

Lee tried to sound polite. "The time does go quickly."

A man's voice called for Zac. He stiffened and rolled his eyes. "Great. My dad's here."

A man in his sixties strode through the front door. He was a rustic kind of handsome: cowboy hat, straight spine, biceps bulging under the rolled-up sleeves of his dress shirt. He pulled his cowboy hat from his head and the room seemed to both shrink and fill with electricity. He gripped Lee in a handshake that bobbed her arm up and down. "Welcome back, Lee Tucker. Ray says you're looking for some work?" His voice was low and centered deep in his chest.

Zac glared at the floor and mumbled. "We don't have any work for her here."

Mike pulled a chair out for Lee. "Sit. You hungry?" Mike raised his eyebrows at Zac. "Make us some lunch, bud. I could eat a horse. Not that we serve horse here, Lee. We're a bunch of hicks, but we won't feed you horse. Might taste like it, though. Can't find a decent cook to save our lives."

Zac, face dark, glowered at Mike and turned his gaze on Lee. "There's nothing wrong with our cook."

"It'd be darn hard for us to know since nobody orders any food, now wouldn't it?"

Lee fingered the collar on her blouse and tried to sound light-hearted. "I'm not hungry anyway. My neighbor brought me a pie and I've practically eaten the whole thing."

Mike nodded, slapping the table. "Nothing better than pie." He waved Zac towards the kitchen. "I don't have all day."

Zac left for the kitchen without commenting. Mike seemed to relax the second Zac was out of sight. He scooted his chair up to the table, metal clanking on the wood floor. "I was real sorry about your mother. I didn't know her too good but your grandfather bought lumber from my father way back when." Mike's eyes, the same blue as a hazy summer sky, scrutinized her like he was looking for something important in her face.

"I never knew him."

"Broke my heart when they were killed. I was already working at the mill by then, learning how to run it from my dad and I was in awe of your grandfather. I never met a man who seemed to love life more." He paused and Lee saw a flicker of sadness behind his eyes. "My buddies say I'm getting sentimental in my old age, but it gets to where half the people you used to know are dead. Awful good to see his granddaughter in the flesh though, all grown and beautiful."

"That's kind of you. Thank you." A feeling of muted discomfort and a faint embarrassment washed over her. It was strange to learn about her grandfather from a complete stranger when she knew almost nothing from her own mother.

Mike shifted in his chair. "Let's talk business. Ray said you had a muckety-muck job up there in Seattle?"

"I was the president of a game company. My husband developed a game called Random. Have you heard of it?"

"Can't say I have. I don't know much about computers. Just got one last year and am finally on the internet like the rest of the world."

"That was our first game, which we then sold to Gamester and were working on a new game when my husband died a month ago. Unexpectedly. And, I lost the company."

Mike leaned back in his chair. "That's a tough break, kid. You come here to get a fresh start?"

"And to fix up my mother's house to sell." For the first time since it happened she wished she could go on, tell him all the sordid details. "But I need a job."

He placed his hands on the table. "My family's owned a sawmill here for over sixty years. You might be too young to remember how the timber industry died in the eighties and this town died overnight. Before that there were three sawmills and between us we employed over five hundred men." He chuckled and winked at her. "And a few women too. Secretaries in those days of course, before you all got liberated." He played with the brim of his cowboy hat and shook his head. "My mill's the only one left and we only employ eighty people. Most of the young people leave as soon as they graduate high school and never come back. Families leave because there's no work. What does that leave us?"

Lee shrugged her shoulders. "I don't know."

"A bunch of old people like me." He smacked the table with his hand. "But I have some ideas to get tourists in here spending money."

"Isn't the Beautify River Valley Committee in charge of that?"

He chuckled. "Did you see the turquoise paint?" Lee nodded and they laughed together. "Someone on the committee heard about these towns that have color codes, but anyway, the minute Ray called me, I remembered all those art prizes you used to win at high school and how Zac always said you were one of the smartest girls in his class." He leaned back in his chair. "I'd like to see this place turned into a first-rate restaurant." He looked at her and raised his hands in the air. "You think you could do that?"

She thought of Linus. "Maybe. I have to be honest, I don't know the restaurant business. Matter of fact, I don't know a thing about food or wine."

"My father said if you had a task seemed too big, break it up into parts and do it bit by bit. We'll use the same concept I have out at the mill. You start on the floor before you move up. You come in and wait tables, observe the kitchen, and after four to six weeks, come to me with a business plan."

"What about Zac?"

He lowered his voice. "I thought this would be a good job for him, but he's made a mess of it. Women, booze, the whole bit." He trailed off and glanced towards the kitchen. "He's had some problems. When he was seventeen, his mother left us. She wasn't a great mother to begin with but Zac always worshipped her. Zac and me, we've had a distant relationship at best. He was with his mom for a while in high school and when he came back he was never the same. After high school he went to junior college but flunked out after a couple months. He's been kind of lost ever since." Mike put his hands on the table. "He needs a job until he can figure out what he wants to do. So, Zac stays. You have to figure something to do with him."

Just then Zac came through the swinging doors with two plates of sandwiches. He set them on the table, hard. Mike grabbed a sandwich and patted Lee's shoulder. "Zac, great news. Lee's agreed to come work for me. See if she can figure how to make some money out of this place."

Zac stared at the middle of the table and his voice was soft. "What, you find one of your miracles?" He looked at his father and made quotes in the air with his fingers.

Mike glared at him but Zac plopped in a chair, crossed his legs, and waved a sandwich in the air in rhythm to his words. "My ol' pop here had a dream God wants him to save the town and he's been on the lookout for his disciples for a year now."

Mike was red and a small muscle on the side of his face twitched. He massaged it with his index finger. "Be quiet, Zac."

Zac's eyes flickered but his voice was flat. "When does she start?"

Mike's voice matched his son's, the air vibrating with unspoken words. "Tomorrow. She's gonna learn the business and come up with a new plan by May. Get used to the idea of a real boss." Mike took the top piece of bread off his sandwich and fingered the salami, lettuce, cheese, and tomato before reassembling it and taking a bite. "This needs more mustard."

CHAPTER TEN

TWENTY-FOUR HOURS LATER, Lee held her coat over her head and pounded her fist on the locked restaurant door. She had tried for an hour to get into the building and was soaked through from the driving rain that fell in an angry torrent. Shivering, she cursed, turned for the car, and almost smacked into a tall figure in a gray rain poncho. She looked up to see a man with light brown skin and dark eyes grinning down at her. He held an enormous yellow umbrella like it was an extension of his arm, which gave the impression that he was in harmony with his surroundings instead of in dispute against the onslaught of rain and chill.

"You need an umbrella." He put the emphasis on the um of umbrella, in a slight southern drawl. He moved the umbrella over her and smiled. His teeth were white and there were deep creviced half circles around his mouth. "The restaurant doesn't open until six." His lackadaisical self-confidence, the way he appeared unbothered by the water that cascaded from the vinyl fabric to the cement, disarmed her.

"You work here?" she said.

"In a manner of speaking."

"I was supposed to meet Zac here at four to start work but he hasn't shown." The wool fabric of her coat was beginning to give off the odor of wet dog.

Thick eyebrows lifted and his mouth twitched in a half smile. "Working here?"

She nodded and glanced at her watch. "At four."

He reached into his pants pocket and pulled out a large set of keys. "I can let you in." He unlocked the door and held it for her.

The door closed behind them. It was dark. Lee was suddenly frightened to be alone with a stranger. What if he worked for DeAngelo? How could she be this stupid to walk into a dark room with someone she didn't know? Holding her breath, she heard the whoosh of the man's umbrella closing, his boots squeaking on the wooden floor, and a click of a light switch. The room filled with the white glow of fluorescent light. She blinked and stared at him, trying to make out if he carried a gun under his fleece jacket. The man stared back at her, leaning on his umbrella like a walking stick. "Zac doesn't get here until after five. I usually come at four to set up but I was late today."

The smell of astringent chemical cleaning products clung in the air, making her nose itch and eyes sting. She sneezed and opened her bag to look for a tissue.

"Bless you." The man ducked behind the counter and handed her a box of tissues. "My band plays here weekends."

Lee blew her nose. He was a musician, she thought —thank God.

He put out his hand. "I'm Tommy Gonzales."

Lee shook it. "Lee Tucker."

He put his umbrella by the door. "What's your job?"

She wiped under her eyes with the tissue and tried to sound nonchalant. "I'm a business consultant. Mike's hired me to upgrade the place."

He cocked his head and studied her. "I didn't think you were from around here."

"Good."

He chuckled and pulled his rain poncho over his head, showing a glimpse of a lean, brown stomach before adjusting his fleece jacket over the belt of his pants. "You do restaurants mostly?" His dark wavy hair stood up from the electricity of the rubber poncho and he rubbed his hands through it. He wore a chain with a cross around his neck.

Lee squeezed the piece of tissue into a ball in the palm of her hand. "Sure."

There was a knock on the front door. A teenager in a backwards baseball cap waved to them. The man motioned for him to enter. "What's up, Oliver?"

"Hey, Tommy, we can't get into the center 'cause Marlo's sick and the doors are locked. And we got enough kids for a game."

Tommy looked at Lee and winked. "Guess this is my day for unlocking doors." He pulled a key off the set and threw it to the boy. "I'll swing by and get it after I'm through here."

The boy grinned. "Thanks, dude." He left out the front door with a wave.

The kitchen doors squeaked and Zac strolled in. He nodded at Tommy and draped his arm around Lee's shoulders. "You're wet. What'd you do? Walk here?" He reeked of booze.

Lee backed away, shuddering. "I was waiting in the rain for you to open the door. I thought you said to be here at four?" She stood behind one of the tables and tossed her wet coat on the bar counter. The hairs on her arms stood upright and she rubbed her skin with her hands. Tommy followed her movements, and their eyes locked for a moment before Lee looked away.

"Dad said four." Zac walked to the counter, flipped a spout, and filled a plastic glass with foamy golden beer. "I didn't tell you anything. I'm still the manager here."

The aroma of yeast and hops and the lingering stench of astringent chemicals made the nausea rise to her throat. She put her hand over her mouth and swallowed hard, wondering why they called it morning sickness when it was clearly all day sickness.

Tommy unzipped his fleece and handed it to Lee. "Put this on."

She was about to decline when she shivered again. She took it from his outstretched arm and pulled it over her head. The fabric was soft like a baby's blanket next to her wet skin and his collar smelled of citrus-toned aftershave that calmed her nausea. "Thanks."

He glanced at Lee's water saturated shoes. "Zac, turn on the heat, man." Tommy wore a dark blue t-shirt with "Los Fuegos" in yellow letters across the chest.

Zac raised his beer glass towards Tommy. "The local hero. Rescues dogs, kids, and recent widows."

Tommy's eyes darted to Lee and she saw him see her with this new information. He spoke in clipped words to Zac with his eyes still on her, and his face was dark. "Like I said, turn on the heat." He turned and the two men stared at each other until Zac shrugged and ambled towards the kitchen.

"The heater's in the back, Lee. When you're running things, you can turn it on yourself." The doors swung closed.

Tommy scrutinized her face. "You know him before this?"

"High school."

"You scared of him?"

She averted her eyes so he didn't see she was lying. "No, he just creeps me out."

"Can't stand the guy myself, for lots of reasons I won't go into on your first day. But I've seen him do some strange stuff after some beers, so you let me know if he gives you any trouble." He smiled but his eyes were somber dark pools.

A few minutes later, Zac yanked chairs off of the tabletops and waved his hand at Lee. "You can tag along tonight. See me do my thing."

Lee chose another table and began putting the chairs on the floor. "Do you have job descriptions for the staff?"

Zac laughed. "Job descriptions?"

She counted to three in her head before she spoke. "I need to understand how things currently work before I propose any changes."

His back stiffened, his cheeks flushing. "You need to watch and do." He slammed a chair to the floor. "Doesn't matter anyway. If you're as smart as my dad thinks, you'll figure out he's a nut and there's no way to make any money in this town selling fries, even if they're on a pretty plate."

She calculated the situation. She knew nothing about running a restaurant, let alone developing a business plan to make it profitable in this one-horse town, and this man-child would thwart her at every opportunity. She pulled another chair from a table and spoke in a casual but respectful voice. "The business climate is tricky, no question. I need to assess the situation, come up with a viable business plan, and market the heck out of it. And, I need your help. I mean, you've been here, you know the business. We could make a great team."

He rolled his eyes. "Is that the kind of bullshit you talk about for a living?"

She ignored his comment and took a conspiratorial tone. "I know how frustrating it can be when things don't take off, but there could be a great business here, with a few changes."

Zac had puffy bags under his eyes. With slumped shoulders he gaped at her. "Wherever you've been the last fifteen years isn't even the same planet I live on."

"I'm just saying—"

"This town is nothing but a bag of bones. You'll be gone in a couple weeks, and I'll still be stuck here. People like you don't stay." He went behind the counter and poured himself another beer.

The way his Adam's apple moved up and down as he guzzled the beer turned her stomach, and her patience snapped. He was nothing but a pathetic drunk, just like her mother. "Look, we can either make this friendly or antagonistic. Regardless, your dad hired me to do a job and whether you think it's bullshit or not doesn't matter, because I'm here and I need this job in a way you could never understand, having had everything handed to you all your life."

Zac's face turned purple. "Don't get me wrong. I could give a shit about this place. But I don't want you here, in my business." He swept his arm across the counter and knocked a stack of plastic cups to the floor. The sound echoed in the empty restaurant.

Her mouth hung open, amazed at how like a child he was. The front door squeaked and she turned to see Tommy standing in the doorway, holding a guitar case. "Everything okay?" His eyes fixated on Zac, the muscles in his forearm twitching as he gripped the handle of his guitar case.

"Don't worry about it, amigo. Lee's just educating me in bull-shit 101." Zac downed the rest of his beer and stormed to the kitchen.

She hugged the fleece to her body and looked at the floor. She felt lightheaded and knew it was from the stress and lack of food. She put her hand on the table and took a deep breath. "That could have gone better."

"You're white as a ghost." Tommy pulled a chair out from under the table. "Here, have a seat."

She crumpled onto the chair and whispered, more to herself than him, "This is going to be even harder than I thought."

He kneeled next to her. "He's got reasons to make this hard for you."

She put her face in her hands. Zac was right about one thing, this town, this life, felt like another planet from the one she'd left. She looked up at Tommy and felt there was something he wasn't telling her about this situation. She thought to ask him what he knew but his gaze on her was intense and distracted her. She sensed he was the type that saw other people with a swift clarity, noticing every nuance, twitch, and flush. She wondered what he had catalogued about her today?

Tommy pinched his lip with his thumb and finger as he'd done earlier. "This is none of my business, but, I don't think you should take this job."

"You have another one lined up for me?"

He stroked the scar on his face with his thumb. "I'm just saying this might be more trouble than you care to get involved in. Given the family dynamics and all."

She sighed and ran her fingers through her matted hair. "I have to make it work."

He smiled and the corners of his eyes crinkled, knees cracking as he rose from the floor. "If that's the case, you're going to fit right in around here." He patted the back of her chair. "Keep the jacket 'til you're warmed up. I don't need it."

She felt the warmth of his hand as if he'd touched her skin instead of the chair, even as he walked to the doorway and picked up his guitar.

Minutes later, she sat on the toilet in the bathroom stall and sobbed a heaving silent wail. Here it was again, without warning, a stab of uncontrollable grief. Yet another part of her life that was different. Years of controlled behavior, measured emotion, were replaced with these blind waves of pain. This time it was from Tommy's kindness, the engagement from his eyes, the sense that he understood, that triggered it.

After it subsided to the usual dull ache, she scrubbed her face and hands, reapplied her make-up, fluffed her hair, and walked to the kitchen.

A young man wearing a chef's hat, with sloped shoulders and blubber like a tire around his middle, peeled carrots near the sink. Zac hovered behind him. Neither looked up when she came in. She stood next to the counter and planted a polite half smile on her face.

Zac put his hands in his pockets, leaned on the counter, and pointed at the young man. "This is Billy."

Billy glanced over his shoulder and said, "Hey," without discernable emotion. He turned on the deep fryer next to the grill and placed a wire basket into the cold oil. Using a large square knife, he chopped the heads of lettuce in half, making a loud thump on the wooden cutting surface.

"Nice to meet you, Billy. I'm Lee. Mike's hired me to see if we can make the place a little busier."

The blade stopped mid-air and his eyes darted to her and then Zac. He turned back to the lettuce and brought down the blade on another head of lettuce. He cut the lettuce halves into shreds and added them to a monster silver bowl that contained shredded carrots and purple cabbage.

"You ready for tonight? It's Friday, so we'll be packed." Zac patted Billy on the shoulder. Billy flinched, strode to the walk-in refrigerator, and pulled out another head of lettuce, along with a container of Velveeta cheese. He tossed them on the counter and opened the industrial-sized freezer, pulling out two bags of uncooked frozen French fries and two bags of onion rings.

Zac yanked a folding step stool out of the corner and used it to reach a giant plastic container of ketchup. With his back to her, he pointed at the back counter. "Go fill the ketchup bottles. Then put them out on each table."

Billy stopped chopping. "Code says you're supposed to empty and wash them before filling them up again."

"That right? Good thing the inspector only comes once a year." Zac laughed and hit Billy on the back another time. "Make me some white fett. I'm starved." He left through the swinging doors.

"Whatever you say, asshole," Billy muttered into the lettuce. He adjusted the heat of the deep fryer. The vat sizzled and the odor of hot oil filled the kitchen. She put her nose to the collar of Tommy's fleece to stifle the nausea.

After she filled the ketchup bottles, Lee wiped the plastic-covered menus with a wet cloth, swept the floor, put the salt and pepper shakers out on the tables, and changed the beer keg. Meanwhile Zac drank another glass of beer and read the paper in-between giving her instructions. Around 5:30 he went into the kitchen and came out with a steaming plate of Fettuccini Alfredo. The smell made Lee's stomach rumble with hunger.

"So, what's the policy on dinner?" She spoke as if it didn't matter either way. "Is it alright if I eat before we open?" She winced at the squeaky sound in her voice.

Zac, hunched over the bowl, wrapped the fettuccini around his fork and slurped up the noodles, half of them dangling out of his mouth before he sucked them in, smearing sauce over his chin and mouth. He swiped his mouth with a paper napkin and pulled the newspaper closer to his plate. "You pay half for whatever you eat." He took another bite. "Write it on a ticket."

"A ticket?"

"A ticket." He shook his head and rolled his eyes. "What you use for writing down an order."

"Where do I get those?"

"Ask the waitresses when they come in."

Lee walked to the kitchen where Billy stirred a huge metal pot on the stove. It looked like boiling glue with little green specks and smelled of cooked peas from school lunches.

"What is it?" said Lee, pointing at the pot.

He glanced at her and then looked back to his task. "Broccoli cheese soup." He pointed at a package on the counter. "Comes from a mix. I'm not really a cook." He tilted his head and flushed. "I used to be the dishwasher but the other cook quit, so now I'm both." She asked where the order tickets were kept. "In his office." He pointed at a closed door with his stirring spoon and turned the knob underneath the burner.

The office was small, no bigger than the closet in her former condo. Posters of Hawaii and California beaches covered the small wall space. The desk, bookshelf, and filing cabinet overflowed with papers, files, menus, invoices, and employee timecards. On the top of the largest heap was a purple children's diary, with a fairy on the cover and a lock on it. She reached to grab one of the ticket books and her arm brushed the diary. It fell on the floor and the lock popped, opening to a page with a list of names, a series of dates, dollar amounts, and one other number notation in the far right column. Some of the names were highlighted in yellow. She glanced behind her, alarmed at what those figures could mean. She closed the diary, picked the top ticket book off the stack, and went back into the kitchen.

Billy stood at the counter tossing spices into a mixing bowl. "The soup's kinda disgusting. You want my specialty?"

Lee smiled and wondered what his specialty could be, given his recent promotion from dishwasher. "Great."

He went to the walk-in refrigerator and pulled out a package of hamburger. "This is my secret stash of good meat. The stuff we feed the customers ain't fit for a dog." He dropped the hunk of meat into a bowl, reached under the counter, and pulled out a silver shaker. "I got a secret spice combo that makes it special." He sprinkled a generous amount over the meat, rolled it into a ball, flattened it between his hands, and pressed it into the hot grill. It made a sizzling sound and the scent of grilled meat filled the kitchen. Lee's stomach growled, even as the smell made her nauseous. She shouldn't have waited so long to eat but she needed the little cash she had left for gas, not groceries.

"You want cheese?" Billy asked her. "I got some decent cheddar here I bring from home." He held up a large chunk of orange cheese.

"Sure."

He turned the patty once and pressed it down with the spatula before placing the cheese over the top. He reached into bins under the counter and pulled out onions, lettuce, and pickles. He toasted a bun on the grill, squirted pink sauce on one half and mayonnaise on the other. He scooped the burger off the grill and onto the bun.

"I just made the first batch of fries." He rested his elbow on the counter, peering at her. "You want some?"

"Oh no, this is plenty." Lee took a bite of the hamburger. "This is good," she said, and ate another bite. "What's in the spice shaker?"

He grinned and his face turned pink. "Can't tell you that." He lowered his voice. "Zac won't let me make it for the customers, says the meat costs too much. No one ever orders anything but fries and nachos unless they're from out of town." He went back to the grill and scraped the tidbits left by the burger meat into the trash.

"We should put this on the menu."

"No, it's nothing, really."

The back door to the alley swung open. A tall big-boned woman with enormous bleached blond hair burst into the kitchen, chewing a piece of green gum enthusiastically. She wore tight jeans and a low top, which her breasts threatened to fall out of at any moment. The door slammed behind her as she tripped on a crack in the industrial tiling. The oversized straw bag she carried fell out of her arms and out spilled a curling iron, lip gloss, and sparkle body powder. When she leaned over to pick up the items a handgun fell out of the side pocket of the bag. It made a loud thud on the cement floor. "Hey Billy baby! Sorry I'm late but I had to stop for a cof a cuppa. Since I turned fifty my get up and go has got up and gone." She threw back her head with a loud cackle and tossed everything in her purse, except for the small handgun, which she polished with the end of her shirt before tucking it into a pocket on the side of the bag. She spotted Lee. "Holy crap!" She put her hand to her heart. "You scared me." She came closer, pulling the glasses hanging on a chain around her neck up to her eyes. "You new?"

Lee stood up and put out her hand. "Today's my first day. I'm Lee."

"I'm Cindi. That's with an 'i,' not a 'y.'" She looked Lee up and down. "You're a tiny little thing!" She looked over at Billy at the grill and chomped her gum faster. "Billy Baby, did Zac finally get rid of Deana?"

"No, Lee's a…" He looked over at Lee. "What are you again?"

"I'm a consultant. Mike's hired me to come up with some new ideas for the restaurant."

Billy turned back to the grill. "I just made her my specialty."

Cindi winked at Lee. "He must like you."

Billy turned pinker and scurried into the walk-in refrigerator.

Cindi put her bag on one of the hooks by the door. "Damn, I didn't know we was getting a consultant." She glanced at the door to the dining room and lowered her voice. "This mean Zac won't be here as much?"

Lee took her plate over to the commercial dishwasher and stacked it onto a tray. "Maybe."

Cindi sidled next to Lee and said into her ear, "He gonna focus full time on his other job?"

Before Lee could ask her what she meant, Zac came into the kitchen, dropped his empty plate on the counter, and washed his hands at the sink. "Deana called. She's not coming in."

Cindi rolled her eyes and said under her breath, "Big surprise. It's Friday night." She pointed at Zac's back and mouthed the words, "He's nailing her."

Zac, still at the sink, dried his hands. "Lee'll cover for her."

"Me?"

Zac turned from the sink. "Part of your consultant duties." He pushed open the swinging door with his foot and glanced back at Lee. "I'll make sure to put that in your job description."

Lee watched Cindi stack red plastic glasses on the shelves under the bar counter. Each time she leaned over to put another stack away, Lee got a waft of spearmint gum and cheap hairspray.

"Could you give me a synopsis of what I'm supposed to do tonight?" said Lee. "As you can probably tell, I have no clue."

Cindi smiled and looked pleased. "I'm not sure what a synopsis is exactly but I'd be more than happy to show you the ropes. You got kind of the deer in the headlight look, but I've been doing this crap since before you was born, so you just stick with me." Cindi spat her gum into a cocktail napkin, squirted diet soda from the tap into a cup, and took a dainty sip. Her teeth protruded slightly and made Lee think of a bunny from a children's story.

"Most weekends, there's two of us girls on the floor. We split the room in half unless one side's busier than the other." She pulled a ticket book out of her apron pocket. "You'll need to write stuff down real fast so you write ff for French fries, rings for onion rings, and nc for nachos. That's most of the orders anyway." She put another piece of gum in her mouth. "The most important thing to remember is Zac. He does nothing but get in our way and cause us more work, so the best thing to do is keep his beer glass full." She pointed to where he sat with a group of women. "That's his normal table. He can get scary, so don't cross him."

"Scary how?"

"Y'know, if he drinks too much he gets even meaner and starts slamming things around. Stuff like that. One time I saw him throw one of his girlfriends against the wall for bringing him the wrong beer. Broke her damn arm. You just never know what he's gonna do." Cindi took a damp cloth and ran it across the top of the bar. "We got some regulars, especially on Fridays when the band plays." She indicated two women at the table near the band equipment. "Them two come in every Friday night." She scrubbed some dried ketchup off the surface of the bar. "School teachers. They have a thing for Tommy and baskets of fries. Did I mention we give one free refill on those?" She shook her head, whispering in Lee's ear, "They should lay off the fries, if you know what I mean."

Lee was about to ask how she kept track of refills, but didn't have the chance because Cindi talked without a pause. "Now the band. The singer. Gorgeous." She said it in three elongated syllables. "He reminds me of that actor on Law and Order. Only not so serious. He opened an athletic center over behind the library for kids in trouble. The women are crazy for him. 'Course there's not much to choose from around here. Not that it bothers me none. I got my own man at home." She shook her head and lowered her voice in that way people do when they love to be the one in the know. "Between you and me, he pretty much came right out and told me he got hurt something fierce. People always tell me things, that's just the kind of person I am. Anyway, he acts like he could care less when the ladies throw themselves at him. Not that he likes boys or nothin' like that." A group of boisterous men burst into the room, pushed two tables together and waved at Cindi and Lee.

"Go on, girl. I'll just watch from here but you call me over if you need anything."

At the table, Lee handed out menus, grabbed the pencil from behind her ear, and asked for their drink orders. The oldest of the bunch, gray beard, huge belly, clad in overalls, spoke first. "You're new."

She nodded and put her hand on her hip like she'd seen Cindi do. "Sure am." She sounded stiff and fake, like the first time she'd said a curse word in junior high.

He raised his bushy eyebrows and looked around at his buddies. "We've never had a redhead before." They all laughed.

She dropped her arm to her side. "What can I get you?"

A man at the end of the table wearing a baseball cap and with an unshaven greasy face raised his hand. "You on the menu?" Again, they all laughed. Another glanced at her crotch. "You a real redhead?" he said.

Cindi appeared at Lee's elbow. "You boys behaving yourselves?" The way she stood, hands on hips, indulgent smirk, her voice a mixture of banter and authority, reminded Lee of a Madam at a whorehouse. And Lee was the sweaty, quaking, sacrificial virgin right before she went upstairs for her first night on the job.

The bearded ringleader put his hands up in the air. "Of course, Miss Cindi."

"What can we get you then?" said Cindi.

"Beers. Couple of pitchers. Burgers all around. Get Billy to sneak us extra fries."

Cindi nodded and shook her finger at him. "Not that you boys deserve it, but I'll see what I can do. You be good, or I'll be saying goodnight early."

Lee carried the pitchers in one hand and six plastic beer mugs in the other. She wasn't sure what to put down first and the beer was heavy. The young greasy one got up and came around the table. "Let me help you." He reached for the pitchers at the same time Lee moved to put them on the table. The pitchers slipped and beer spilled down Lee's front, causing her shirt to cling to her breasts.

The men stared, whooped and hollered. "Didn't know it was wet t-shirt night." The table exploded with laughter, whistles, and boot stamping. Cindi came to the table and they quieted.

"How much you boys drink before you got here? I have a right mind to cut you all off." They all moaned. The greasy one slapped the table and another got down on his knees. "Please, Miss Cindi, it wasn't our fault."

The bearded one stood. "We're sorry. We'll be good the rest of the night."

There was more laughing and back slapping and Cindi whispered in her ear, "I have an extra shirt in my locker. I'll be right there."

Lee ran to the kitchen, past Billy, and into the back area where there were several lockers. She sat on the chair. How will I make it through the rest of the night, she thought? She felt a hand on her shoulder and looked up to see Cindi. "Now, listen, sugar, don't worry about it." She opened her locker and handed Lee a shirt. "Take off your wet shirt and put this one on." She grabbed an apron from one of the hooks. "Here, I forgot to tell you to put this on."

"I don't know if I can do this." Lee pulled the dry t-shirt over her head.

"Sure you can." Cindi tied the apron on Lee and gave her a squeeze. "It's just beer and perverts."

The back alley door opened and Zac strolled through the kitchen with a half smile on his face. He strode past them to his office and slammed the door shut.

Cindi clicked her tongue and her eyes were hard. "Bastard's gonna get us all killed."

Billy's voice sang out from the grill. "Order up."

Cindi helped her take the burgers out to the table. The men were finished with the first two pitchers and asked for more, but seemed to have forgotten the wet t-shirt contest.

The two school teachers waved her over and one of them put her plump hand on Lee's forearm. "You have any low fat cookies?"

"We have oatmeal chocolate chip. They looked kind of healthy."

"We'll take three each."

Tommy was at the microphone, guitar around his neck, when she came back to the table with the cookies. The two women leaned forward in their chairs, eyes in a school girl glaze, fixated on Tommy, the corners of their mouths lifted in shy smiles. Lee set the oversized cookies on the table. The blond one grabbed the largest without taking her gaze off Tommy.

Tommy adjusted his guitar and spoke into the microphone, his voice and body fluid, relaxed. "Thanks for making it out tonight, even with the terrible weather. We're Los Fuegos. Got a couple of tunes to keep you entertained this evening. This first song I wrote myself." He smiled at the school teachers. "You regulars will recognize it."

The ladies giggled and clapped their hands together. Lee watched from the bar, fascinated but scornful of their adoration for this small town singer. She began to pour another pitcher of beer from the tap.

Then he sang.

Lee looked up from pouring the pitcher and stared. His voice was a melodic baritone, soulful and emotional, James Taylor mixed with Jackson Browne. There was something unusually frank in it, like you could hear into the place most people kept hidden. The song was a ballad, kind of folk and country mixed. He sang the chorus, eyes closed. "See you in a stranger's gait, cry each time it

85

isn't true, how I wonder where you wait, was heaven waiting there for you?"

Her scalp tingled and she felt tears sting the corners of her eyes.

"Are you in the blades of grass, are you the breeze of mountain air, do you swim with river bass, how I wish I saw you there."

She looked down and realized she'd forgotten to let go of the beer spout and it overflowed onto the plastic pad and dripped to the floor. She pushed the spout shut and wiped the excess beer with the towel from the sink. Cindi came around the counter, grabbed Lee's hand, and talked in an important, self-congratulatory way, like she was personally responsible for his talent. "Don't he sing like an angel? This song's about his dead brother. He lived in Nashville for a long time but never could make a deal. He says no one wanted to sign a Hispanic country singer. There was no American Idol back then or I bet he would've won."

Lee swallowed to rid the lump from her throat. "What's he doing here?"

Cindi shrugged her shoulders, fluffed her hair, and sniffed. "Some folks love it here, you know."

The song ended and Lee found herself clapping along with the rest of the restaurant. He acted comfortable, like he was in his own living room instead of a mob of half-drunks that she imagined could turn at any moment. Lee practiced for hours when she had to do a presentation for clients and couldn't imagine what possessed someone to perform. She remembered a college friend, a drama student, explained the quality as "owning the stage": the way he talked into the microphone like they were all old friends, like he was there to make their pain a little less potent, the way he opened his mouth and his soul poured out. The crowd couldn't take their eyes off him, even the men. "Thanks so much," he said. "This next one should liven things up a bit, get you all moving." He pointed to a young couple holding hands. "Mark and Laura just found out they're having a baby, so this one's for you. Little Chuck Berry diddy called C'est la Vie."

The first licks of the classic rock song shook the room, and several people got up to dance. The young couple danced close and slow, arms around each other. Their happiness radiated across the room and she felt a pang of jealousy and the familiar anger.

She shifted her eyes from the couple to Tommy. Lee had to admit, he was sexy, in a dark, Latin kind of way. If you liked that type. Regardless, the first thing on her list of recommendations to Mike—keep the band.

More people wandered in. They all ordered fries or onion rings and an occasional plate of nachos dripping with Velveeta. The tables filled and they clapped to the music, or chatted, heads close together to be heard over the music, or danced in the small space in front of the band. The night wore on and seemed almost festive. The crowd cheered after each song and their feet tapped to the music—Birkenstocks, tennis shoes, pointy cowboy boots, and work boots. It was an assortment of small town people enjoying themselves after what she imagined was a long week of worries. We all have that in common, she thought.

Zac emerged from his office around nine, joined several rowdy women in tight clothes, and ordered pitchers of beer on the house. He disappeared from time to time out the back door but returned within minutes, redder and more animated with each glass of beer. By midnight he stumbled and slurred his words. At a quarter after, he disappeared out the back door with one of the women, who, according to Cindi, "Took him home to help him sober up, if you know what I mean."

Cindi and Lee sat at the table near the kitchen. It was after one a.m. and the restaurant was empty of customers. A few of the band members, plus Tommy and Billy, ate leftover fries and drank beer. Cindi counted her tips, licking her thumb to separate the bills. She looked over at Lee. "How'd you do?"

Lee took the beer-soaked bills out of her apron pocket. She flattened and organized them in the same direction before she counted. It was thirty-three dollars. She rubbed her temples. "Was this a busy night?" She thought how naïve she had been just hours before as to the level of transformation needed to make this place profitable and how many nights it would take to save up the kind of money she needed.

"Yeah." Cindi took off her shoes. "Doesn't seem like much after all that work." She sighed and put her feet up on the opposite chair. "I know."

"How do you live on this?"

"I gotta little coming from one of my ex-husbands." She fluffed her hair. "It helps. Plus, my kid is grown."

"There has to be a better way than this," said Lee.

"Amen, girl."

CHAPTER ELEVEN

IT WAS A THUMP and a metallic bang that awakened her from a deep sleep two nights later. She half opened her eyes, feeling drugged, not sure if she heard the noises in her dreams. The clock read 2:30. There was another crash and this time she knew the sound came from her backyard. Heart pounding, fear the taste of metal in her mouth, she grabbed a flashlight and her cell phone and stumbled to the window. She aimed the light into the yard, expecting to see Von, but the trash cans were on their sides, and out of the end of one was something large and black. The trash can moved and Lee gasped, fingers sweating on the plastic of the cell phone. The figure had a black coat and enormous paws with long black claws.

It was a bear.

Relief flooded her at first, but then the animal lifted the trash can and slammed it against the ground. She felt the force of him ripple through the air and into the house. He backed out of the can, pawing out the remnants from one of Ellen's pies, lapping at the tin pan with his long pink tongue and then tossing it on the fence, berry juice dripping down the weather-beaten boards.

Upright, he smeared his paw on the fence, interrupting the drips into swipes of magenta. He dropped back on all fours and paced the yard, shaking his head, smelling the ground, green eyes glowing in the beam of her flashlight.

He ambled over to the garden shed, got up on his hind legs and looked in the small glass window, human-like. He turned, let out a long growl, and crept on two legs closer to the house, all rolling muscle. His fierce eyes stared at Lee. She stood mesmerized, a jolt of energy racing through her body, goose bumps on her arms, unable to look away. Even through the closed window the air was heavy between them like before a thunder storm. She imagined she could smell the gamey rank of his oily fur and some kind of telepathic connection to the bear's thoughts. A revelation, an unearthing, hung in the air between them, but just out of her grasp like one of her early childhood memories. She touched her fingertips to the window as if to say, I can't get it. Her small movement seemed to break the spell between them and the bear threw back his head and roared, the sound shaking the window. Like from a dream she awakened and filled with terror, the reality that a rickety house was the only thing between her and this beast. Her mind raced with a jumble of thoughts. Should she call 911? What would she say, there's a bear in my yard, and they'd say, good luck lady, we don't do bears, call animal control? Did they even have that here? Could he get in the house? What could she do to scare him away? And then, a coherent thought: call Ellen, she'll know what to do.

Ellen answered on the third ring, sounding groggy and thick with sleep. "Lee, you alright?"

"There's a bear in my backyard."

"Is it Clive?"

"What?"

"That's what your mother and I called him, Clive."

"Was he big and black and scary?"

"Sounds like him. I'll be right there." The line clicked off before she could say, no, don't come, he's right outside the house, there's no way to get in.

Lee stood, pressing her forehead on the window next to the front door, searching the darkness for Ellen. Clive was still in the fenced backyard. She could hear him pacing and pawing at the garbage cans. Ellen emerged from the night, lantern in hand, in a walk-run down the dirt driveway, her long gray hair in a braid and dressed in a flannel nightgown and work boots. She was carrying a long gun—a shotgun, Lee supposed. Lee opened the door a crack and yelled to her, "Hurry, he's in the backyard."

Ellen began to run towards the door. Lee opened it wider, pulled her by the arm into the house, slammed the door shut, and bolted the lock. "You must be insane, running around outside with a bear on the loose."

"I've had the pleasure of his acquaintance five years in a row now." She held the shotgun with ease, like an umbrella. "He always appears this time of year." Ellen started up the stairs to the bedrooms. "He's hungry after the long winter."

Lee followed her. "What are you going to do?"

"Get rid of him." They reached the second floor and Ellen marched to the window. "This is the best place to get a shot at him if he's in the yard."

"I don't think we should hurt him," Lee said. "Isn't that illegal or something?"

Ellen opened the window and put the barrel of her shotgun through the opening. "Don't worry, I won't kill him." She lifted the gun to her shoulder. "Too messy. We'll just scare him off."

Ellen pulled the trigger. The sound was deafening. The air filled with the smell Lee remembered from firecrackers at Fourth of July. Lee moved closer to the window and Clive gazed up at her, his head tilted like he was confused. She had the distinct, crazy feeling once again that she could almost hear his thoughts, but they were a jumble of confusion, disappointment, anger, instead of information. He snapped his jaws and lunged toward the house, disappearing from view under the awning of the kitchen's door. They heard him pushing the door, the wood creaking with his weight. Ellen fired another shot out the window. Lee collapsed to the floor, hugging her knees, afraid to look. Ellen fired again and then they heard a scrambling noise at the side of the house.

Ellen backed a few feet from the wall. "He's climbing up the side of the house."

Lee hugged her knees tighter and squeezed her eyes shut. "What?"

Ellen's voice was raised an octave, yelling like an excited child. "He's using the awning for leverage!" Lee opened one eye to see Ellen creeping towards the window and peering up. She heard claws on the side of the house, and it sounded as if he were making deep holes into the wood siding.

"What's happening now?"

"He's reached the top. Good Lord, he's on the roof." There was the sound above their heads of wood splintering and falling in the attic space between the roof and the ceiling. Outside the window several shingles floated to the ground. Lee expected to see him break through and land on the floor in front of them. She jumped up and grabbed Ellen's arm. They looked in each other's eyes and fear passed between them. "What does he want?" said Ellen.

For a moment there was silence and then more back-and-forth movements as he walked the roof-line. "Clive, what do you want?" Ellen raised the shotgun and the barrel followed the sounds, her blue eyes intense. "I'm ready if he falls through."

Lee backed towards the window, and for several minutes they heard him pace until finally his footsteps descended the slope of the roof and then there were several loud thumps. They ran to the window just as Clive reached the ground. Ellen raised her gun and aimed it at his head. "The mess be damned, I'm gonna shoot the son of a bitch."

Lee, standing behind Ellen now, saw beyond the fence a dark shadow and grabbed the flashlight from the window sill. She aimed the light towards the movement. "Oh my God," Lee said. She saw two bear cubs. "Don't shoot." She gripped Ellen's shoulder. "Clive has cubs."

Ellen lowered the gun. "Clive's a girl?" She leaned closer to the window. "Clive's a girl. Well, I'll be."

Clive scurried over the fence and growled direction to her babies. They ran to her and she nuzzled them for a moment before looking back at the house. Lee touched the window with the palm of her hand and felt something enter her, not words exactly but a feeling. It came from Clive through the air, a small zap like electricity inside her mid-section where she imagined her uterus dwelt and then the thought: I want this baby. Clive shifted her gaze away from the house to her cubs and led them towards the thick trees at the edge of the woods. Lee watched from the window until they disappeared into the night. She sat on the edge of the bed. Had Clive come to tell her to keep the child? Ellen had asked what Clive wanted. Could it be that Clive wanted her to have the baby?

Ellen sat next to her on the bed. "We're safe now." She patted Lee's leg. "I thought Clive was going to fall right through that old roof." She chortled and shook her head back and forth.

Lee giggled and her shoulders began to shake, tears sliding down her face.

Ellen began to laugh too and the more they tried to stop, the harder they laughed. Ellen hobbled to the window and rested her hand on the sill, doubled over, breathless. "Stop. My stomach hurts."

Lee sobered. She folded her hands in her lap. "I'm pregnant."

Ellen's face shifted like someone slapped her. A split second later she went still. "I see."

Lee brushed her hair from her eyes. "Did you know a fetus has fingernails at ten weeks?"

Ellen looked as if she wanted to say something but walked

back to the bed and sat next to her, the bed squeaking with her weight.

"Do you think God could talk through an animal?" said Lee.

They stared at each other and an understanding passed between them, an agreement that such a thing could exist, a mysterious act of God or nature or the universe. "Stranger things have happened." Ellen patted Lee's hand. "Oddly enough, your mother never let me shoot at Clive."

"Why?"

"She never said."

"Ellen."

"Yeah?"

"I'm afraid to turn into my mother."

"I know." She shook her head and patted Lee's leg. "But having a baby doesn't turn you into your mother."

"Dan never wanted children. Thought it was too much to leave to chance—all the things that could go wrong in terms of the massive gene pool, mutations you didn't expect, characteristics that we wouldn't know how to handle. It sounds ridiculous as I say it, but I agreed with him, because of my mother. I didn't think it was a good idea to have a child that turned out like her."

"What about one that would turn out like you?"

Lee smiled and rolled her eyes. "I'm not so great, trust me." She looked at her lap. "Dan told me once that a child was the end of your life. From the moment of their birth it would be nothing but sacrifice. The part of you that mattered, that had dreams and ambition, died because you poured it into the child. He thought that's what happened to his father, that his children ruined his life. My mother made sure I knew that her life ended with my birth. She made that perfectly clear time and time again."

"Nonsense. The drink ruined her life. Had nothing to do with you. Your grandmother would've been so proud of you. Heck, I'm proud to be your friend, watching how you're rebuilding your life." Ellen jumped from the bed and plumped a pillow. "Listen, each generation has the chance to put right the mistakes of the one came before. It's a choice, y'know. To let go of the past and move on. Nothing but a choice." Ellen stood and pulled at the covers of the bed. "C'mon, scoot in there. If you're going to have a baby you've got to take better care of yourself." She tucked the covers around Lee's small frame. "Sun's almost up. Clive won't be back. She did what she came for."

Lee searched Ellen's face. "You think I can do it?"

"Oh, for Pete's sake, of course you can. Smart girl like you can do anything you put your mind to."

"Ellen, do you remember when you took me to the bus station?"

"Sure. Why do you ask?"

"Because I always wondered how you knew I needed to hear from you that day that it was okay to let go, to leave her here so I could have my own life."

"When I was a young woman I was in love with a man my father disapproved of. My biggest regret in life was that I didn't defy his wishes and marry this man. He was my one true love and I let him go because I didn't want to disappoint my father. Instead I married the man my father wanted me to—a man that slapped me around when he drank and had trouble keeping a job. All my dreams, all my desires disappeared as fast as tissue paper in a fire. That day I picked you up I saw the same look in your eyes and I didn't want you to hold yourself back because of your mother. I didn't want you to waste your life."

Lee was crying and wiped the tears from her face with her fingers. "I never thanked you properly. I hope someday to repay the gift you gave me that day. That's what it was, the gift of freedom." Fresh tears rolled down her face. "But I squandered that freedom by choosing the wrong man, the wrong path."

"Ridiculous. You did what you thought was right at the time. You've had a blow, no question, but we're gonna get you back on top once more. Tomorrow is a new day, a chance to start over again. You hear me now?"

Lee wiped her eyes and attempted a brave smile but her lips trembled. "Alright."

Ellen smoothed Lee's hair. "Now, get some rest. I'll check on you in the morning, bring you something to eat."

Lee yawned and relaxed into her pillow. "I think the baby likes pie."

"That's more like it."

CHAPTER TWELVE

THE NEXT MORNING, Lee dreamt of Dan. He stood at his desk, dressed in swimming trunks. Drops of water dripped from his hair to his bare shoulders.

"Why?" Lee said.

"I couldn't do it."

"But I'm having a baby." She glanced down at her stomach, extended to the size of a beach ball. She looked back at Dan. He backed towards the door. "Wait," she called to him. She felt cold water seep into her shoes and looked to see the floor flooded. Dan trudged through the water. At the doorway he turned back to her. "I'm sorry, so sorry. Take care of my baby." The water rose, to her knees, her stomach, her neck. She could no longer see him. She tried to swim after him but her limbs were lead. She opened her mouth to call out, no, you can't leave me alone like this, but the water covered her mouth.

Lee jerked awake. The room was lit with sunshine. The clock read five minutes after ten. Her feet were freezing. She tucked them under the blanket, turned on her side, and stared at the peeling paint next to the light switch.

She remembered the appointment scheduled for that afternoon

at Planned Parenthood. No dogs, no kids—that was their pact, she and Dan. The power couple. She flattened her hand on her stomach and lay, gazing at the crack that ran along the ceiling.

She thought about the loneliness of her marriage as she watched the clock's minute hand move in little ticks every sixty seconds. Two memories came to her, like bookends of the beginning and end of the five-year marriage. The first was a month or so after their wedding. It was a Saturday and she'd purchased tickets for them to attend a matinee production of A Doll's House at the Intiman Theatre. He'd forgotten and instead invited five former fraternity brothers over to watch the college games. She asked him to cancel. "It's one of my favorite plays and I'd love to share it with you."

"Babe, the boys would never let me live it down if I went to a play instead of watching the games. I mean, c'mon."

"But I told you about the tickets several weeks ago."

"I'm sorry, hon, I forgot about it. You sure I knew it was a Saturday? I would never schedule something during college ball."

"I don't know. Maybe not."

"C'mon, don't be mad. Call Linus. He loves that kind of stuff."

She had called Linus and the 'boys' came and watched the games, shouting and standing, shaking fists, resting their feet on her coffee table. By noon beer bottles were scattered around the room that now smelled like a bar. They ate greasy chicken wings, onion rings, and fried mozzarella sticks, the crumbs scattering on her clean carpet. Before she left for the play, she stood in the foyer watching the scene in her living room and felt a hole in the pit of her stomach, thinking, was this marriage just a continuation of the loneliness she felt all her life?

The other bookend was a Saturday morning six months before he died. She and Dan sat at the breakfast nook in their condo, sipping coffee. She worked on a list in her pocket-sized notebook of the errands she must make that day: dry cleaner, Whole Foods, Nordstrom. Across from her, she could feel Dan's foot moving up and down in what she knew to be nervous energy. He asked, without shifting his gaze from the window, "What're you doing tonight?"

She wrote her grocery list as she answered him, "Opera with Linus. You?"

"Poker."

"Should I add creamer to the grocery list?"

"I don't know." He poked her notebook with his finger and she looked at him, noticing the dark smudges under his eyes. "You want to do something together tomorrow?" he said. "Maybe a movie?"

She smiled and shook her head. "We wouldn't be able to agree on what to see, I'm certain."

He sighed, looked out the window. "Probably not." He paused and rubbed his eyes. "My dad called this morning, ostensibly to tell me about this guy I knew in high school who just took his company public and is now worth a half a billion dollars."

She went to the refrigerator to see if they needed lettuce. "Good for him."

"Right. Good for him." He got up from the table and poured more coffee into his cup. "You think that'll ever happen to me?"

She shut the refrigerator door and turned to look at him. "Worth a half a billion? Is that what you mean?"

He shrugged, nodded, took a sip of coffee. "Yeah."

"If we keep working hard, maybe."

He spoke quietly, his voice so calm as to seem disengaged. "You really think that all it takes is hard work? That's so naïve. You know the way the world works, just when you think you have it all figured out, wham, life or some asshole causes everything to blow up."

She put down her pencil and closed her notebook. "Why do you have to be worth a half a billion dollars? Can't it be enough to just enjoy our life? I mean, when will it ever be enough?"

He pushed against the table and stood. His voice was loud and he began to pace back and forth in front of her. "Because I won't know who I am if I can't make Deep Black the next huge game. Don't you get that?"

She stared at him, bewildered. "No, I guess I don't. Is this just a mission to please your father? Because he's proud of you regardless of what happens with our game."

He shouted now and raked his hand distractedly through his blond curls like he might pull the strands from their roots. "This is more complicated than just pleasing my father. I'm doing this because he never had the chance to do it himself. He was raised in poverty and had to scrape his way to lower middle class. I refuse to let another generation of Johnson men be ashamed of their life."

"This life we have is good, better than ninety-five percent of people in America. We've had opportunities to go to the best schools and have a successful business. We have the American dream. Honey, it's just one product. If this one doesn't work, we'll come up with another. Don't you get that?"

He was hoarse from shouting and leaned his forehead on the refrigerator door, speaking into it, sounding resigned and sad. "I get that you still think like a small town girl, all wide-eyed and grateful. That's what I get." He jerked back and opened the refrigerator. He pulled out a carton of half-and-half. "This is empty."

She raised her eyebrows and was cool when she said, "I just asked you if you needed more creamer."

He looked at her, face blank. "Did you?"

The clock struck 11:00 on the bedside table, pulling her from the memory. She pulled the bed covers up to her chin. She hadn't realized in that moment with Dan, or the subsequent months after, how dark and hopeless he had become. She understood now that he must have been frantic to get the game to work, especially as they crept closer and closer to the date the loan was due. Suddenly it came to her that his mind was like a reflection of Deep Black—no matter what you did, you couldn't win. And she'd been blind to it, to his suffering. Even now, knowing the outcome, she was lost as to how she could have saved him. Perhaps there was no saving him. Whatever damage roamed through his psyche was pervasive by the time she met him. As was her damage, she thought. She'd been unable to reach him because of her own limitations, her inability to connect with him the way he obviously needed but didn't get. Living together for five years, doing their best to love each other, had not been enough to save either of them.

That thought caused her to think again of the baby. She must figure a way to emerge from this rubble and make a life that could provide the life for her baby that every child deserved. She swung her legs to the floor and reached for the phone. She dialed the Planned Parenthood number. "Hello, this is Lee Tucker. I won't need to come in after all."

That afternoon, seized with a sudden frantic energy, she decided to spend the afternoon ridding the house of junk. She carried as much as she could at one time into the front yard and threw it into a huge pile. After twenty trips, the two small bedrooms were empty except for the small pieces of furniture. She was covered in dust and dirt and the pile was almost as tall as the house. She found a rusted gas can in the shed, half full. She used a butter knife to pry the cap loose and accidentally knocked the can over, spilling gas onto the steps. She wiped the spill with a rag and tossed the rag onto the top step of the stairs.

She doused the pile, threw a lit match into the heap, and watched it burst into flames. The fire was hot on her face and hands. She backed away just as the fire sped along an invisible trail of spilled gas until it reached the porch. The dry wood of the steps, protected by the overhang and untouched by rain, caught in an instant. Before she could take a breath, the entire porch was engulfed. She dragged the water hose from the side of the house, spraying in the direction of the fire, but the stream was not enough to extinguish the gas-fueled flames. Smoke billowed around her head and she gulped for air. She ran through the smoke to the side of the house, coughing until her stomach knotted.

Ellen, breathless, ran into the yard, jeans tucked into work boots. "Lee, I saw smoke. I called 911. What happened?"

Lee put her face in her hands. "I was trying to get rid of all this junk." She stumbled to the hydrangea bushes and fell to the ground on her knees. Ellen picked up the hose. She covered the nozzle with her thumb and pointed it at the flames but the spray was no match for the hot fire. Billows of gray smoke made a swath around the yard and porch. She heard a siren, stopping and starting like it had a short. She turned to see an ancient fire truck racing down the dirt road. The threadbare tires bounced in every pothole, looking like with each jerk they might whirl from their axles. The truck lurched to a stop twenty feet from the fire, steam puffing from the engine, with two firemen sitting in the cab. The one in the passenger seat lowered himself to the ground, favoring his left leg.

The other fireman pulled the fire hose from the side of the truck. She rubbed her eyes. It was Tommy. Even with the uniform and hat she knew it was him. Her mind tumbled, confused, and she didn't have time to reason out how he was a fireman too, before he turned a large lever on the side of the truck and yelled to them, "Ladies, get out of the way, this'll knock you over."

Lee was frozen but Ellen grabbed her arm, yanked her to her feet, and dragged her away from the truck.

Water gushed out of the big hose, dousing the flames on the porch first, reducing them to smoke and scarred wood, and then soaking the bonfire.

The yard spun, black spots appeared before her eyes, and then a tunnel. Feeling as though she might faint, she lay on the ground and closed her eyes. A few moments later she opened them to see Tommy's face above her. "Let me take a look at you," he said. "I'm an EMT. Don't worry, you're gonna be fine."

"But you're a musician."

"This is my day job." He felt under her chin and his fingertips were thick and callused. "Do you have any medical conditions?"

She hesitated for a moment before saying, meekly, "I'm ten weeks pregnant."

He raised his eyebrows, catching his lower lip between his thumb and forefinger. "Did you breathe in a lot of smoke?"

There was a lump in her throat. "Yeah. I coughed for a while."

He pulled out a stethoscope from the bag next to him and listened to her breathing, his brows knitted, staring at the ground. He reached for her arm resting underneath the blanket. "You need to see our doc." His fingers moved to her wrist and took her pulse. "You seen her yet?"

"No."

"Why's that?"

"I've been busy."

"At ten weeks you should see a doc, okay?"

Irritation cleared her mind somewhat and she wondered who this guy thought he was, telling her to see a doctor. What did he know about babies? "You have children?"

He smiled and took out a small light from his bag. "Look up for a minute." He shone the light into one eye and then the other. "I do not have children, however, I'm a trained medical professional, so I know about these things. We'll take you there now, have you checked out." He put the light back into his bag and cocked his head, examining her face in a way that made her want to look away and hide. "You don't like people telling you what to do." He said it as a statement of fact and as if it amused him.

Irritated at his obvious enjoyment, she replied in her remotest tone, "It depends." She stared at the blue sky poking through the branches of the cherry tree above them. The branches had dumped their blossoms weeks before, and she picked up a soggy, fallen flower from the damp ground beneath her and crushed it between the tips of her fingers.

"We'll have to take you to the doc in our truck."

"No, I can drive myself."

"Policy. I have to take you in."

"What kind of policy is that exactly? Don't I have the right to refuse treatment?"

"Not on my watch." He chuckled and put his hand out as if to help her stand. She ignored his outstretched reach and rolled on her side, preparing to get onto her feet. "I sounded kind of like a cop on television with that." He mocked himself, making his voice deeper, "Not on my watch, little lady."

Lee smiled in spite of her best efforts to stay distant. Tommy called out to the other fireman, "Verle, we're gonna take Lee to the doc."

Verle rested on his shovel, panting. "Righto," he said. "We're pretty much done here."

Lee tried to sit but became light-headed once more and lay back on the ground. "For goodness sake, let me help you," said Tommy. "Put your arms around my neck." She did as he said and he scooped underneath her, holding her like they were newlyweds entering the honeymoon suite. Further adding to her mortification, he carried her that way over to the truck. This day kept getting worse and worse, she thought, as Tommy put her gently into the cab of the truck.

Ellen and Verle gathered around the cab. Verle bowed to Ellen. "Thank you, madam, for your help. Tommy, this lady's a pistol. We should get her to join the department."

Ellen sniffed but it lacked bluster. "I'm much too busy to help you boys, though I'm sure you could use it." She poked her head in the cab of the truck. "Lee, I'll follow you in my car."

Lee nodded and rested her head on the back of the seat, staring at the ceiling of the cab. Tommy hopped up and settled behind the wheel. Verle hooked the shovel onto the side of the truck and, after two attempts, swung into the cab. They pulled out of the driveway and onto the paved road that led to the highway. The truck bounced. She winced as her breasts bobbed and her tender nipples rubbed against the rayon material of the tight bra. She placed her arms over her chest but the smell of smoke on her clothes made her pregnancy nausea worse. She put her head in her hands and took deep breaths.

"You alright?" said Tommy. "Do I need to pull over?"

"I'm really nauseous. All the time, actually." For some reason, out of nowhere, she felt as if she might cry. An ache started at the back of her throat as she tried to get control of herself. An image of the unformed person inside her, perhaps an acorn-sized fist balled against an ambush of smoke and fumes, flashed across her mind. It was her fault, she thought. She shouldn't have been messing with fire and now she might have hurt the baby.

Tommy reached out as if to pat her hand, but pulled back at the last second. "Don't worry, our doc is really good."

Verle snorted and then snored, head back, mouth ajar.

She glanced at Tommy and to her dismay a high-pitched giggle escaped from her throat. Tommy's lips twitched and he covered his mouth with his hand. "Verle could fall asleep anywhere, I swear. Once he slept through an entire outdoor concert of mine, plus fireworks after." Out of the corner of her eye, she examined Tommy. He was tall and his energy so profuse that in spite of his slim frame he appeared to fill the entire cab. Lee felt petite and feminine sitting next to him.

His hand fidgeted with the top button of his shirt. "Would it help to chat or would you like quiet?"

"Chat."

"Where'd you move from?"

"Seattle." She looked out the front window and hoped he wouldn't ask any specific questions.

He tapped the steering wheel with his long fingers like he was playing a tune. "I'm from Enumclaw." His voice was low pitched and melodic. Lee felt her shoulders relax, her eyes heavy with strain, smoke, and lack of sleep. She shocked herself by wondering what it would feel like to rest her head on his shoulder.

Tommy ran his hand over the top of his dark wavy hair. "You know where that is?"

Her lips were numb. "Sure."

"It's only a little bigger than this town."

"They're all the same."

"Small towns, you mean?"

"Yeah."

"We used to go to Seattle sometimes when I was a kid." He glanced at her and then back at the road. "You know what our favorite thing was?"

"No."

"Going to Dick's."

"Right, Dick's."

"Best burgers in the world." He turned into the clinic's driveway. "And fries. They have great fries."

"I don't eat fries."

"Really?"

"They probably aren't as good as you remember."

"Yeah?"

"You probably wouldn't even like it now."

"I think I would." He smiled. "There's some things you don't forget." He pulled into a gravel parking spot in front of the clinic. "Here we are. Now, you wait until I can help you down."

The doctor, a handsome woman in her forties with a gray frizz of hair and unshaven legs under her hemp skirt, gave Lee a full examination, assuring her it wasn't enough smoke to hurt the baby. She pushed gently on Lee's stomach. "This your first baby?"

Lee looked out the window at the fir tree that swayed in the spring breeze, light green new growth on the end of each branch. "Yes."

"Planned or unplanned?"

"Unplanned."

"Do you have a partner?"

"My husband passed away two months ago." Lee pulled down her gown. "Unexpectedly." She didn't know why she was compelled to add the unexpected part. After all, who would have a baby if they knew their spouse was dying?

"I'm sorry. Do you have a good support system, family or anything to help you through this?"

"Sure." She scratched her arm, noticing drops of rain caught in a spider's web outside the window.

The doctor's freckled hand patted her arm. "Shall we see if we can find anything on the ultrasound?"

"What?"

"We should be able to see a baby by now." She dragged a machine on a cart into the room and asked Lee to scoot down and put her feet into the stirrups. She squirted goop on a wand that looked like something out of a science fiction movie and felt cool but not uncomfortable when she slid it into Lee to look at her uterus. There was a black and green blur on the screen and then something that looked like a small mass and a pulsating dot. "There it is!" The doctor smiled. "The beginning of a life, a heart beating strong." She punched some numbers into the machine. "I'm measuring to see if we can tell how far along you are." She pushed another couple of buttons and a small piece of paper printed out of the machine. The doctor gave it to Lee, pointing at the blur that looked like a peanut. "There's your baby, measuring about ten weeks."

The doctor pulled out the wand while Lee gawked at the printout. Could that mass be a real baby?

"We need to schedule regular monthly visits until your due date."

Lee sat up and pulled down the robe to cover her exposed midriff. "I probably won't be here that long. I'm here working on my mother's house. I'm leaving before the baby comes."

"Regardless, you need to come in once a month."

"How much will those visits cost?"

The doctor ruffled through her file. "You don't have insurance?" There was a note of disapproval in her eyes.

Lee flushed, embarrassed and angered at the same time. "No. I'm between insurance policies at the moment."

The doctor stiffened and backed away from the table. "Well, you'll need to pay before you leave today. The receptionist shouldn't have let you in without insurance." She slammed the file shut and headed towards the door. "We'll have to put you on a payment plan if you can't pay. Having a baby's expensive." She was in the doorway. "Good luck to you."

Lee dressed, marched past the receptionist, and burst onto the porch, clutching the ultrasound picture between sweaty fingers. She shook with anger and shame, knowing she wouldn't be able to pay the bill today or anytime soon. She wanted to weep, but pushed the feelings down as she stepped onto the porch. Ellen was nowhere to be seen but Tommy sat on the steps reading a collection of Eudora Welty short stories. He jumped up and crossed to her. Behind him, Verle slept in the porch swing on the clinic's rustic front deck. "Everything okay?"

"The baby's fine except I don't know how I'm going to pay for it."

He didn't comment, simply waved his hand down the road. "Ellen will be right back. She went to the grocery store. Said something about getting you some decent food." He looked at her hand. "Ultrasound picture?"

"Yeah." She glanced through the window at the reception desk, walking down the steps to his truck. "Can we get out of here?"

"Sure thing." He peered at her in that way of his that made her feel like she was under the magic goop and wand of the ultrasound machine, like he could see every part of her, in formation.

Tommy nudged Verle. "C'mon Verle. Time to wake up."

CHAPTER THIRTEEN

THE RESTAURANT WAS EMPTY, except for several regular customers chasing greasy food with sips of beer. The band didn't play during the week and without them the restaurant had the desolate feel of a beach resort town the week after Labor Day. The weather had turned hot overnight on the second day of May. Lee, warm from pregnancy hormones, wore a sleeveless blouse made of stretch material, which, she realized after she left home, clung to her. She dropped a beer at the table of a young logger and felt his eyes linger at her breasts. She flipped the serving tray to cover her front section and glared at him with what she knew to be her coldest look. This was her fourth week at the restaurant and the leering and innuendoes were as tiresome as they were her first shift.

She returned to the counter and wiped the sticky layer of cola syrup stuck in the crevice behind the soda machine. As she worked, she thought about her plan for the restaurant, the beginning of a vision nestling near the surface of her mind. Over the last several days, for reasons she wasn't clear about, she felt a twinge of her former interest and energy for life, vowing to have the business plan in Mike's hands at the beginning of her fifth week at the restaurant. She understood her own strengths, how her brain worked to dissect and reassemble all the elements of something into a new form, like a pile of toddler's blocks made into a tower. Unlike the other parts of her life—the baby, the fear of DeAngelo creeping into every moment—she was at ease with the process of creation, even as her current situation was dire.

After four weeks of shifts, she had made a total of two hundred and fifty-three dollars in tips plus minimum wage, the total of which covered her utility bills, gas for her car, the minimum of groceries, and no extras. And she didn't even have a house payment.

Deana, the other waitress on shift, sat with Zac at his regular table. She had a barrel chest, wide shoulders, tummy fat that hung over her tight pants, and legs so skinny Lee wondered how they held her stout body. There were two empty beer glasses, a newspaper, and a plate of fries on the table between them. Deana ate fries one or two at a time, dunking them in ranch dressing before reaching out with her tongue to pull them into her mouth. The way she held the fries in her hands, shifting her eyes to the left in a way that looked guilty or sly, reminded Lee of a squirrel.

Zac read the paper, frowning and drumming his fingers on the plastic surface of the table. Without raising his head, he motioned to Lee to bring another round of beer by snapping his fingers and pointing to the empty pitcher. She filled a large plastic pitcher with the amber-colored microbrew, the yeasty smell turning her stomach. As Lee neared the table, Deana got up, straddled Zac, and tented the newspaper over their heads. A raspy cigarette laugh floated from underneath the paper as Lee poured them each a glass of beer. Zac's head poked out from under the newspaper. "Lee, it's too slow for both of you to be on shift, so Deana's taking the night off."

From underneath the newspaper, Deana laughed. "I have other things to do." Zac's head disappeared once again under the paper.

"No problem." Lee gritted her teeth and set the pitcher on the table, drops of foam landing on the plastic table.

The paper came down and Deana took a big drink of beer, smacking her lips. Foam lingered above her mouth and she wiped it with the back of her arm.

Lee averted her eyes, soaking up spilled beer with a spare napkin. "You guys want food?"

Zac folded the newspaper and shoved it towards Lee. "Nachos. Extra jalapeños. Take this piece of shit paper with you."

Billy was at the stove in the kitchen taking the temperature of the hot oil in his fryer. Lee said hello and asked for a plate of nachos for Zac. She threw the newspaper into the recycle bin, reading the headline on the front page. "Local Sheriff Needs Funds for Drug War." The caption under a picture of the sheriff read, "Newly elected sheriff says budget too small to battle drug crisis."

She opened the back door and breathed in the early evening air while Billy made the nachos. A quarter moon showed in the blue sky above the mountain. "What's the deal with Deana?"

"I think she's on something."

"You think she's high here at work?"

"I guess so. All I know is she used to be kind of nice before she started working here. She's all messed up now." He placed a plate of nachos covered with slices of jalapeño peppers on the pick-up counter.

Lee put her hand on the plate and looked at Billy. "Is this what he means by extra jalapeños?"

Billy looked at her, deadpan, and shrugged his shoulders. "He always sends them back, says there aren't enough peppers, so thought I'd give him what he wants."

Lee smiled, picking up the plate. "I should talk you out of this but I'm weak."

Billy laughed and sprinkled a couple more over the top. "It's my funeral."

Back at the table, half the pitcher gone, Deana sat in a chair across from a gaunt man with a nervous twitch fiddling with a matchbook. Zac sat with his legs crossed in the style of a country gentleman. Lee placed the nachos in the middle of the table. Zac looked at the plate and sat up, glaring at Lee. "This a joke?"

Lee widened her eyes. "Something wrong?"

"Tell Billy to get his ass out here so I can fire him." His words slurred and he shoved the plate across the table. As fast as a lizard's tongue after a fly, the twitchy man flung his arm out and caught the plate mere centimeters from the edge of the table.

Deana caressed Zac's arm, her eyes bloodshot slits, her voice a low scratch with traces of phlegm. "Don't worry about it, baby. He's just a dumbass who doesn't know what extra means. Lee'll take it back and get a new one."

Zac shoved her arm aside and the drunk, unsteady force knocked her off the chair and onto the floor. She popped up, lunging towards Zac. Obscenities streamed from her mouth as she pushed him off his chair.

They wrestled on the dirty floor until one of the male customers lifted Deana off Zac, holding her next to his chest. She punched and kicked the air, hair askew and jeans unzipped. The man hauled her out the front door of the restaurant. His friend put Zac back in his chair, with a hand on his chest. "Just chill out, dude." Zac tossed his head and said, "Yeah, man. It's all good." The twitchy man laughed in a high-pitched squeal before slapping the table and walking out the front door.

Lee stood in the middle of the restaurant, tray clutched to her chest, overwhelmed with the feeling that she was in a foreign land with no direction, no map with which to find her way back to her real life.

Zac looked at her and motioned her over to his table. "Lee, come over here and keep me company."

"I have work to do."

"Oh, come on, we should be friends." He leaned back in his chair, his eyes in slits. "We should be friends, like the old days."

She stood next to the table. "We were never friends."

He slapped the table and pushed a chair out with his foot. "C'mon now, that isn't true. All the girls loved me back then."

She placed her hands on the back of the chair. "Do you want something to eat?"

"Nah, I got beer here, that's all I need. I was thinking about you though, Lee." He leaned back in his chair and looked at her, eyelids half closed. "Yeah, I was thinking about you and thinking how we should be friends. I'm leaving soon and we should be friends, y'know. Friends are good to have, don't you think?"

"I'm going to bring you some of the white fett you like, okay?"

"Yeah, Billy always makes me that, good ol' Billy. He's a good kid." He looked at Lee and grinned. "Do you remember Lindsey, from high school? I ever tell you I married her?"

"I think you mentioned that, yes. You stay here and I'm going to get Billy to make you some dinner."

He nodded and waved his hand towards the kitchen. "I'll stay right here, but you have to promise to come back so I can tell you about Lindsey, how she ran off with a girl. Yeah, she turned out to like girls, can you believe that?"

She left him at the table and went into the kitchen to order the food for Zac. After giving Billy the order, she went to the locker area, sat on the bench, and tried to stop shaking. Zac's drunkenness pushed her to the dark automatic mode of caretaking and cajoling that she used with her mother. It made her feel out of control and hopeless and scared. She put her head between her legs and breathed in and out—telling herself that he was nothing to her and that it wasn't her fault he was drunk and that it didn't matter if he was, that he couldn't hurt her—until the panic subsided. She went back to Billy and picked up the fettuccini, pretending everything was fine.

When she got back out to the table Zac was talking to the man who carried Deana out of the restaurant. Lee put the food in front of Zac and went to her post at the counter, trying to ignore his loud, drunk voice, but it was impossible. "Yeah, my wife Lindsey, she took up with some chick from Klamath Falls. Just up and left me for a fucking chick." The man nodded and helped himself to more beer from Zac's pitcher. "She was the love of my life, man, and she left. Women, they all leave, y'know, after a while. My mother left because of this place, she was a classy lady and didn't want to live in this piece of shit town. She lives in Florida now and I asked her if I could stay with her for a while when I move down there and she said no. She's such a fucking mother of the year. I went there when I was in high school and I should've stayed 'cause I loved it. The beach was so rad and anyway, I'm going back there soon. Gonna buy a place, a better place than my mother's and then I can say 'fuck you' anytime I want. She sent me back here 'cause of some guy she thought was gonna marry her and then he dumped her anyway." The man nodded his head like he was listening, but his eyes were unfocused, giving Lee the impression he'd heard the story before. She was relieved when she saw Tommy come through the front door. He waved to her and came over to where she stood at the counter. His eyes were lazy instead of the intense focus they had the day her porch burned. "You missed the Jerry Springer moment," she said.

"I heard Deana yelling about it in the parking lot. I've seen enough scuffles in here to last a lifetime."

"Did Deana go?"

"Looks like she left with her skeleton friend, vowing never to set foot in here again, along with an impolite gesture to Zac. But, they had a similar thing a couple of weeks ago, so I doubt we're so lucky to be rid of her."

"Billy says it's drugs."

Tommy sighed and wiped spilled salt from the counter. "That's what I hear." He leaned against the counter. "But, enough about her, I actually came by to see how you're feeling."

"Fine." Lee wiped the spotless counter with a wet towel and avoided his eyes.

"No more coughing?"

"Right."

"Quiet in here tonight."

She looked up at him. "It's always like this unless you guys are playing."

He grinned. "That's good for us, I guess. This mean you'll keep us around even if you change the place?"

"That why you came by? To see if you've still got a job?" She meant it to be a tease, but it came out as an accusation.

"No, I came by to see you." His smile was gone and the way his eyes glittered she knew she'd hurt his feelings. "Matter of fact, I don't know what you've concluded about me, but I don't need this gig. I do it because I like Mike."

"I didn't realize there were so many venues in which to play in this thriving metropolis."

"It might serve you better to withhold judgment about a person until you know more about them." He gazed at her for a moment. "I guess I'll see you around." He walked out, without looking back.

Lee sat cross-legged outside the back door of the restaurant, hidden behind the stairs, Billy's version of a chef salad on her lap. She watched streaks of orange and pink across the sky as the sun set behind the mountain, picking through the strips of American cheese and cubes of processed turkey to find the least limp piece of lettuce. She breathed in the sweet spring air and ran over the conversation with Tommy in her head. There was an undeniable energy between them, but he moved toward the attraction with the lightheartedness of the unscathed, and she fought it with the intensity of the walking wounded. On the surface he seemed the type of man all women wanted: sensitive, strong, someone to take care of you. But she knew there was no such thing as Prince Charming, especially for a pregnant Cinderella. She'd believed in all that once. But now she was a grown woman and could not allow herself, even under the current circumstances, to believe in a savior. Because underneath Tommy's sensitive eyes, and caring attitude, even his heart-wrenching talent, was something hidden, some kernel of weakness, or meanness or hardness, with which her life could be unraveled. If her mother, the last five years with

Dan, and the shocking revelation of the last few months had taught her anything, it was that life was like Dan's games. Not only were there random occurrences of bad or good luck, but often there were obstacles from people you loved that seemingly came from nowhere.

She knew she'd hurt Tommy's feelings tonight and probably turned him off her forever, which was good in the long run. Still, after he walked away she felt more alone than ever. She flicked her hair and chided herself. Dan died three months ago and she was thinking about a man she'd known for a month.

The sun did its final descent behind the mountain and only the orange shadow remained in the evening sky. She heard voices behind the trash bin and the flick of a cigarette lighter. The back door thudded open and then there was the sound of footsteps on the stairs. She looked over to see Zac strut across the parking lot, pulling a sandwich bag out of his pants pocket and disappearing behind the wooden structure that stored the trash bins. There were muted mumblings and then Zac's voice as he came into view. "Tell him to text me. I've got some of the stuff he likes." Two young men came out from behind the Dumpster. They had identical hollow cheeks and starved eyes and skin that stretched across jutted wrist and arm bones outside of the sleeves of their t-shirts. They were like freakish twin brothers in a circus, except one was short and one tall. They darted their heads around the parking lot before shuffling to a beat-up truck parked near the alley, jumping in and speeding onto the street.

Lee held her breath until she heard Zac run up the stairs and close the door.

The bastard was dealing drugs.

CHAPTER FOURTEEN

THE NEXT DAY BEGAN OVERCAST, but by mid-morning the spring clouds broke and sun streamed into her backyard. She knelt in the wet dirt, pulling weeds and dropping them into a plastic bucket. Too poor to get her hair cut since leaving Seattle, and the pregnancy hormones speeding the growth, her hair was long enough that she wore it in a ponytail to keep it out of her eyes. As she worked, the ponytail kept sliding to one side of her neck. It was pleasurable, the way it tickled her skin. Lord, I'm turning into nature mama, she thought, smiling. As her fingers dug the spring weeds from the dark soil, she was reminded of the life-giving properties of this land. Beautiful things sprouted from within this mineral-rich dirt. She thought of Ellen's garden, the food that grew from the tiny seeds planted each spring. She stopped her work for a moment, noting at least four shades of green in the leaves of the hydrangea plant. She looked around the yard. As a child, the simple beauty of the hydrangeas, rhododendrons, the twin dogwood trees, the crab apple trees, all planted by her grandmother before she was born, had nourished her soul with their beauty and inspired her to be a painter. She breathed the scent of the soil, the sun warm on her back, and thought how the landscape ran through her still, even after all the moments in between the last time she plucked weeds from this flower patch and now.

There were footsteps and a knock on the fence. She straightened, shaking the dirt from her hands, seeing the top of Tommy's head above the top of the gate. She opened it, saying hello. He backed away as the gate swung towards him and then stepped towards her and for a moment Lee felt he might move to hug her but then he stopped just inside, resting his shoulder on the frame. He gave a wry smile that seemed wrong on his face, so different from his usual grin that rearranged his features into a series of attractive lines and angles. "Hey, Lee."

Her stomach fluttered at the sight of him leaning on the fence, his hair moving slightly in the breeze, dressed in jeans that clung to his muscular legs and a white t-shirt that draped his slim torso. She had the urge to run her fingers inside the waist of his pants, to feel what his stomach felt like next to her skin. She swallowed and moved her eyes to his face, gesturing for him to come into the yard.

As he moved past her into the yard, she had a fleeting thought that he gave her the same feeling of the sun suddenly disappearing behind the clouds on a spring day, the way he was distant and guarded and so unlike his usual self. She followed him farther into the yard, unable to take her eyes off the curve of his backside. She breathed in a gulp of air. "Thanks for coming by."

He stopped at the steps and turned to look at her. "What's going on?" he said.

She shuffled her feet and looked at a knothole in the fence. "I'm sorry about yesterday. I didn't mean to sound the way I did." She glanced back at him and attempted a humble smile. She hated apologies. "Sometimes when I try to be funny or flippant, it comes out sounding cold." She surprised herself by how honest she was and immediately felt vulnerable. She backed up several feet to the fence. "I'm not a funny person. My friend Linus tells me that all the time."

The corner of his mouth twitched. "Don't worry about it."

"Did you know Zac's dealing drugs in the parking lot of the restaurant?"

He raised an eyebrow and clicked his tongue. "So that's why you called."

She flushed and blew a wisp of stray hair from her damp forehead. "You said if I needed anything to call you."

He grinned and his upper torso relaxed. "So I did. To answer your question, yes."

She crossed her arms across her chest. "Why didn't you tell me?"

He shrugged. "If you recall, I suggested you reconsider taking the job."

She moved to the steps and sat, wrapping her arms around her knees. "Do you think Mike knows?"

He sat next to her, legs stretched out over the grass. "Doubtful. Denial and all that."

"Why does he do it, do you think?"

"Lazy. Doesn't want to do the work of a real job."

She remembered Zac's confession that day long ago at the river and wondered about his mother. "Does Mike ever talk about his ex-wife?"

"Never." He looked at her then and she felt him take her in, all of her sensitivities and insights. He saw things that others didn't. She felt anything but invisible. And for some reason she told him the story of the river and Zac. In the telling of it, something occurred to her that she hadn't known. "I think what he did messed me up more than I knew. It was the first time anyone touched me in that way and it was pretty awful."

His eyes were soft, like a caress. "Of course. It would."

She felt her skin tingle as if he touched her. She got up from the steps and walked over to the hydrangea bush. "What do you think I should do?"

"Make the place successful so you have some leverage with Mike, and then run Zac out."

"Of town?"

"You know that kid who came by the other day for the rec key?"

"The basketball player?"

"His mother dropped him at his grandmother's and disappeared somewhere, either screwed up on meth or dead because of meth. Zac's a big part of the problem here, and if it was up to me his sorry ass would be in jail."

"Why don't you turn him in?"

"I have. The police are too few and too lame to get solid proof."

"If it wasn't him, wouldn't it be someone else?"

"Not necessarily. It takes a certain kind of talent to run that kind of business. Mike says Zac's no businessman, but I disagree."

"Why do you care so much?" she said.

"Same story you've heard a thousand times. My brother died of a drug overdose at fifteen."

Lee sat next to him again. "My mother was a drunk."

"She ever get sober?"

"No, she died from it eventually." A robin redbreast hopped in the branches of the Japanese maple.

He shifted on the steps to look at her face. "How did your husband die?"

"He committed suicide." Her voice was thick and she fanned her face with her fingers to stop the tears. "It's still hard to say it out loud."

He placed his fingertips on her forearm for the briefest of moments, his eyes kind but also shocked. "I'm very sorry. Do you know why?"

"I suppose the easy way to explain it would be that he killed himself over a bad business deal." She told him of Existence Games and Dan's arrangement with DeAngelo, and that she hadn't understood the details of it until after his death. "But, he was a complicated man, even more so than I understood until it was too late. He had this obsession with success, especially financial, and I believe he couldn't face it—losing the company and having this giant debt, but I don't know for sure because he didn't leave me a note or any explanation, other than the deed to the loan." She stopped herself before she told him the rest, that she was essentially hiding from DeAngelo's people. She didn't want him to be in danger by knowing the truth. Plus, she was ashamed to be this desperate and to have allowed this to happen to her life. She said only, "I had to sell everything to pay the debt, and obviously I lost the company. And I'm pregnant. It all happened in an instant—one day I'm on top of the world, the next day my husband's gone, the company's gone, my financial security is gone."

"It's awful to watch your dreams slip away."

"I keep wondering what I should've done differently."

He murmured something Lee couldn't hear and then reached down, plucked a blade of grass and flicked it with his index finger. "My brother and I were Irish twins, if you can be that when you're Hispanic—ten months apart." He rubbed the scar on his cheek. "The drugs just kept sucking him away until the person he really was disappeared. Even after all this time I wake in the night and wonder if there's something I should've done differently. I understand that emotion only too well, but I also know that you can't move on until you've accepted that you did the best you could."

"I don't know how to do that." She was chilled and zipped up her sweatshirt. A frog croaked from somewhere in the yard. "I'm haunted with 'what ifs.'"

He turned his face towards her, and her heart constricted. "I know. I've never gotten over the loss but I live each day with gratitude that I'm still here, that for some reason God spared me from the fate of my brother and so many of our friends who got into drugs and gangs. I make the most of this life—try to make it more beautiful with my actions and my music." He laughed and shook his head. "Do I sound like a pretentious ass?"

She wanted to reach for him but instead mumbled, "Not at all."

Her voice threatened to break and she took a deep breath. "What you said was lovely. I just don't know if I can do it."

"You're strong. You'll get through this." His gaze shifted to rest on her mouth.

Her lips parted and she felt herself lean towards him as if an outside force controlled her movements; something in the air was stronger than her own will, which was telling her to move away from him. He had a muscle that ran from his ear to the collar of his shirt and she wanted to put her mouth there to see if it was warm and salty as she imagined. "I should get back to work," she said.

"I'll go then." They stayed like that for a moment, heat between them, until he moved his eyes from her mouth and back to the blade of grass in his hand. "Would you have dinner with me sometime?"

"I can't."

"Too soon?"

"Too everything." She took the blade of grass from him, rubbing it into a ball. "I still feel married, for one thing. I'm pregnant." She poked him with the blade of grass, trying to sound light. "Anyway, normal men don't date pregnant women."

He smiled but there was something in his eyes that looked sad, and how she wanted to kiss him then, to feel his body next to her. "I'm not normal." He pulled the ponytail holder from her hair, and she felt him breathe her in and out, the scent of his breath chocolate. "Does your hair smell like strawberries because of its color?"

"Tommy."

"Yes?"

"I'm only staying here long enough to get back on my feet. I don't belong here."

He let go of her hair, and a half-smile crinkled the corners of his eyes. "Say it isn't so." He stood and moved towards the fence. "Don't hold it against me if I keep asking you out. I was born an optimist."

Lee peeled dampened wallpaper from the hallway, short pieces at a time. She was now two days into her fourteenth week of pregnancy and awakened that morning to find the nausea gone as quickly as it had come, replaced by a surge of energy and a resolve to make progress on the house. On a footstool, she reached for a strip of wallpaper near the top of the wall. Sweat trickled down her back and wet gobs of paper stuck to her forearms and back of her hands. Just as she peeled a stubborn strip with her fingernails and dropped it in the bucket, she heard a knock on the front door. Wiping her hands on the front of her sweatpants, she ran down the stairs. A young woman and a boy stood on the charred porch.

"I'm sorry to bother you," the woman said. She appeared to be in her mid-twenties and wore a long cotton dress and Birkenstocks. "We broke down. My car." She pointed toward the road. "It did this shake, shake, shake thing and then it just died. I had to leave it there."

The boy looked around the porch. "Did you have a fire?" He had big brown eyes, dark skin, and straight black hair. "Did a fire truck come?"

"It did."

"I'm in first grade and a fireman came to my school." His long brown eyelashes swept his cheeks and he clutched his stomach. "Mom, I'm starving." He peeked at Lee from underneath his brown bangs. "I wanted to eat at Dairy Queen but my mom says you shouldn't put all that junk in your body." He leaned on his mother, wrapping his arms around her legs.

The woman stroked the back of his hair, introduced them as Annie and Alder Bell, and asked to use her phone. Lee motioned them in and handed Annie her cellular phone. "I just moved in, so you'll have to use my cell."

Annie's face was blank as she looked at the phone. "I don't know who to call."

"A tow truck?"

"Does that cost a lot?" said Annie.

"I think so."

"I guess I'll have to call my boyfriend." Annie touched her fingertips to her mouth. "He won't be happy."

Lee raised her eyebrows at Alder. "How would you like some lunch while your mom uses the phone?" Alder grinned and nodded his head.

Annie put her hand up, resting the tips of her fingers next to her heart. "No. It's bad enough we barged in on you."

"Nonsense. C'mon Alder, I'll show you my kitchen." Lee took Alder's hand, which felt hot and plump in her fingers. She thought how beautiful he was and of her own child growing inside her. Would his or her fingers be so luscious, she wondered? In the kitchen, she pointed to a chair. "Sit down here." She looked at him, shrugging her shoulders. "What do you eat?"

"You got peanut butter?"

"I do. You like strawberry jam?"

"Yeah! That's my favorite."

Lee set the bread on the counter and pulled the peanut butter from the fridge. Her fingers fumbled with the plastic fastener of the package of bread, dropping it on the floor. She ignored it and put two pieces of bread on a plate, then plunged a spoon into the peanut butter and plopped a cold, stiff dollop on one of the pieces of bread. Alder's eyes were wide. "My mom only puts this much on." He held up his fingers to show half as much.

"You'll have extra today." She tried to spread the peanut butter on the bread but instead of smearing it made a hole in the soft bread.

Alder came to the counter. "You ever done this before?"

"I hate peanut butter. It was on sale."

"You're not supposed to keep it in the fridge."

"Everything goes in the fridge." She spread the jam on the other piece and put it on top of its lumpy partner. "I'm afraid of bugs." She handed him the plate.

He sat at the table, taking a big bite and talking with his mouth full. "You got any milk?"

"Sure." Lee poured him a glass of milk and sat down across from him. Annie's voice wafted in from the other room. "No. Don't be ridiculous. Just forget it."

Alder stopped eating. He looked down at his plate, poking what was left of his sandwich. Lee cleared her throat. "You want some fruit?"

"No thanks."

"Hey, I've got pie."

Alder looked up and smiled. "My mom doesn't let me eat dessert very much."

"This is homemade pie, so it can't hurt you." Lee went to the refrigerator and took out the latest pie from Ellen and cut him a big piece. "It has berries. Those are healthy."

Alder took a huge bite, eyes round. "Man, this is good stuff."

They heard Annie's voice yelling in the other room. "Leave Alder out of this!"

Alder chewed another bite of pie, gazing at the edge of his plate with a glazed look in his eyes. "My mom's boyfriend's a real asshole."

Lee looked at him, shocked. "That's not a word for a little boy."

His eyes shifted to her face and his voice was flat. "But it's true."

Lee sat down, put her chin in her hand and wiped a spot off the table with her finger. "Does he live with you?"

"No, he just comes for sleepovers."

Annie came into the kitchen, eyes red.

Lee stood up, ready to apologize. "I gave him some pie."

Annie nodded and said in a small voice like she wasn't listening. "Sure, it's fine." She sat and stared at a spot on the table.

"Would you like a piece?" Lee asked.

"No..." She looked at the pie, brushing her tight blond curls from her forehead and pinching her soft middle section. "I'm trying to lose weight." Her smooth pink skin reminded Lee of a ripe succulent peach.

"Can I give you guys a lift somewhere?" said Lee.

Alder sat up in his chair. "That'd be great 'cause I don't want to walk anymore and it sounds like asshole isn't gonna pick us up."

Annie snapped her head. "Alder! I told you not to say that word."

Alder looked down at his plate. "Sorry, Mom."

Annie swept her hair back from her forehead. "You know what? I will have a piece of pie."

No one spoke while Lee cut another piece and put it in front of Annie. She took a small bite and then picked up the crust with her fingers and examined it. "This crust is well done. You make this?"

Lee shook her head. "No, I don't cook. A neighbor up the road."

"My mom's a real good cook," said Alder.

"I went to chef school." Annie rested her arms on the table top and Lee noticed burn scars on the top of her hands and bruises on her forearms. "Not that it matters anymore."

"Where did you study?"

"My mother had an Italian boyfriend who was a chef and we moved to Tuscany to live with him when I was in high school. He taught me everything he knew. But then my mother broke up with him and we came home. After high school I went to culinary school but I couldn't afford anywhere decent. I knew more than the teachers because of Franco."

"Are you cooking at a restaurant in town here?"

"Hardly. I'm a checker at the market. But, I can't get to work with a broken truck."

"What're you going to do?"

Annie sighed, her face crumpling. "I don't know. I don't have any money to get it towed or fixed." She wiped tears from her cheeks.

Alder jumped up and put his arm on his mother's back. "I can walk. I don't mind."

Lee, eyes stinging, picked up Alder's plate and put it in the sink.

Annie wiped her face and hugged Alder. "Don't worry, I

always figure something out." She took a shaky breath and headed to the sink with the other dishes. "Alder, why don't you run outside and look at Lee's yard." She turned on the faucet and added some dish soap.

He skipped down the back steps, calling out to Lee, "I always miss the good stuff."

The women laughed. Annie blew her nose into a napkin. "I'm sorry. We're a mess."

"It's alright. I understand."

Annie wiped her forehead with the back of her arm. "I doubt it."

Lee watched Alder running back and forth across the lawn. She thought about Linus and how much she missed him. She needed a friend here, a real friend. She turned to Annie. "You might be surprised. How's this? My husband killed himself. And I'm pregnant."

Annie stopped washing. "Oh, shit. That how come you're here?"

Lee peered into the soapy water. "I probably won't stay long."

"I followed a guy here. Had one quarter of chef school to go, and chucked it all for a man. I was pregnant too." Annie washed the last glass. "I'm always so broke I can't leave." She sighed. "This is my life now."

"What's with your boyfriend? Why won't he pick you up?" said Lee.

"I don't know. He's a selfish prick." She dried a dish and put it in the cupboard. "I'm going to break up with him. I just kept thinking he'd change. Turn into a good guy all of a sudden. I don't know why I keep thinking that will happen. It's always the same."

Alder came bounding up the stairs. "Mom, I saw a bunch of slugs out there." Skin flushed, he jumped up and down. "Lee, can I put salt on them? That's the best way to get rid of them."

"We'd need a big salt shaker to get rid of all the slugs we know," said Annie.

They laughed and Alder looked back and forth between them. "I don't get it."

"Never mind." Annie motioned towards the door. "We've got to go now."

"But it's fun here."

Lee smiled at him. "You can come back soon."

Lee drove slower than normal, the curves of the country road unexpected and Alder chirping from the backseat. Everywhere she looked there were shades of green: grasses in small meadows just beyond the road, proud firs and pines jutting into the brilliant blue of the afternoon sky. A slight breeze rustled the new leaves of maples and dogwoods. After several miles, Annie said to turn left onto a dirt road. They rambled along, bumping through muddy puddles, Alder bouncing up and down with the car. After a few moments, Annie told her to stop in front of a sagging mobile home. In front of the house was a car up on blocks, a child's rusted bicycle with only one wheel, and several lawn chairs overturned and covered with mildew. Lee felt Annie shift in the seat and looked over to see the woman's face flushed with what Lee intuitively knew was shame.

"It's not much, I know," said Annie.

Lee smiled, glancing back at Alder. "Looks like you have tons of room to run. You're lucky."

Alder looked at her, solemn, but his big brown eyes portrayed the unflinching honesty of the young. "I can't invite any friends here. I don't want them to see where I live. Do you still like us?"

Lee reached into the backseat to touch Alder's face for a moment. "Where you live doesn't matter one bit to me. I've had a little trouble myself lately. When you're friends it doesn't matter where you live or what kind of things you have. You understand?"

"I guess," he said, smiling and jumping from his open door to the damp ground.

Annie looked at Lee, touching her arm. "Thank you."

"He's a great boy. You're obviously a good mother. Maybe you can give me some tips." Lee gave Annie a slip of paper with her phone number. "Give me a call if you need a lift to your truck or anything."

Annie gestured at Lee's stomach. "You let me know if you need anything."

Lee smiled. "Will do." She waved at Alder. "Bye, Alder. I'll see you again soon."

"Bye, Lee." He ran up to their front door.

As she backed out of the driveway, she saw Alder at the window waving, his hand like a flutter of a bird's wing. She waved back and rested her hand on her stomach. She wondered for the first time about this place she used to call home and if there was something more, some new way she should look at it. There was Tommy and this attraction between them. And this feeling that she wanted to unburden it all, to tell and show him every detail of her life. None of which made sense because she was haunted by Dan's death and this vacillation between anger, sadness, and guilt that followed her everywhere she went.

And now to meet Annie and learn she was a chef. Was it a turn of fate or coincidence or whatever Thomas Hardy used to call it? Was it like Clive, did it mean something? She thought about the restaurant and the town and how much potential there was. Mike was right. It was breathtakingly beautiful. The rivers and mountains offered many possibilities for rich tourists if there were any decent-caliber restaurants and inns. She wondered about Annie and what kind of talent was inside her. Something about the way Annie's face looked when she crumbled the crust between her fingers gave Lee the feeling that she was good. With a real chef, they could have a real restaurant. She turned down her dirt driveway, her mind spinning with ideas.

It was midnight and Lee tossed in her bed, thinking of Tommy on the steps, the way the light hit his face and his full mouth with his big white teeth. What was wrong with her? This attraction she felt for him must be false, just a way for her mind to twist all the fear and pain about her life onto another track—the ultimate distraction. She wondered what it might feel like to kiss him. Would it be as she imagined, all lust and passion, or would it just be a mouth with saliva and intruding tongue and gnashing teeth?

She should be thinking about the restaurant and how to make it a success, not about the muscles in Tommy's legs she had spotted under his jeans. She threw off the covers and traipsed downstairs, made a cup of peppermint tea, and sat on the back steps. She gazed at the stars sparkling against their black backdrop and remembered as a child counting them and wondering why the Milky Way had the same name as a chocolate bar. The night sky was brilliant without city lights diminishing their brightness. She'd forgotten the stars.

An owl hooted and the breeze rustled in the fir trees. She ran her hand along the wooden railing and thought about her grandfather, building this house from nothing but the trees in these woods. Something out of nothing. She sipped her tea, sighing. The air was chilly but smelled of lilacs, evergreens' new growth, and cut grass. She shivered, pulling her sweater tighter and kicking the grass with her foot.

What would she tell the child about his or her father? Her mother told her nothing of her own father and she sometimes even now wondered if he was out there in the world. Did he know about her? Did he ever think of her? The one time Lee had the courage to ask her mother about him, the response was, "Long gone." Lee surmised he was a man who passed through town for a brief time, or someone her mother met the one and only year she went to college. As a child she convinced herself he didn't know of her, because the thought of his rejection was unbearable. The fantasies about him started when she was about six and, other than details—sometimes he was a prince, sometimes a teacher—the basic story was the same. He learned of her through a series of fate-like coincidences and then moved heaven and earth to find her, rescuing her from the clutches of her angry mother and taking her away with him.

She shivered and went inside to find a blanket. She pulled the throw off her bed, wrapped it around her shoulders, and went back to the steps. Lee left her teacup on the steps and lay on the grass. The ground smelled of wet dirt and spring grass. She spotted Orion and the Bear in the constellation, which made her think of Clive and her cubs and of Annie and Alder, how they were the same, bonded through naked primal love for one another —a mother and her babies. The stars felt so close they might swallow her and she floated and breathed the night into her chest. She looked for a falling star but there were none and she remembered they showed in August, one after the other plummeting through space, exploding somewhere light years away, never to be seen again. She felt like one of those shooting stars. She'd been a vibrant light in the sky until the big fall, the descent to earth where she exploded, never to be seen again.

August, what was it about August that nagged her? The baby would come in September. The new restaurant could open in August. She watched the stars for many minutes as pieces and ideas stacked together, one by one, until she saw it in its entirety. She said a silent prayer, fastening her eyes to the constancy of Orion's belt, "Please, God, let Annie be able to cook. Give me the strength to want to shine again. Fill me with light."

The next morning rain pelted the hood of her old raincoat and boots she'd found in the hall closet as she trudged through the field looking for the path from her daily walks twenty years before. Each day, no matter the weather, she had dropped her school books in the hallway, grabbed an apple, and ran all the way to her 'studio' to lose herself for hours in her art projects. But the path was gone. The light green grasses were wet and came to her hips, pressing against her and soaking her pants as she slogged along, even as she sweated underneath the plastic raincoat. After several minutes she came upon the shed, the siding gray and decayed. The one-sided roof sagged. Lee pulled on the rustic door handle, carved and assembled long ago from her grandfather's tools. Inside, besides smelling of mildew and decaying wood, it was just as she'd left it. There was an easel by the window. Old paint tubes and colored pencils were organized neatly on the shelf. She fingered a tray of pastels, their hued dust staining her skin.

She opened one of several boxes underneath the crude table and found it stacked with papers, the corners of which were curled and covered with mildew. She flipped through landscapes of the rivers and the mountains. She paused at a self portrait, an assignment from high school art class. On the canvas was her small white face with empty holes where the eyes should have been. Around the neck was a band of red, like a scarf or a noose.

At the bottom of the box was a painting of her mother, also an assignment. The painting was an image of a twisted body, the face hidden by an arm, and a billow of gray smoke floating around the head. Lee touched her fingers over the brush strokes of oil paint on the canvas, trying to remember the girl she'd been when she painted them. She could still remember what it felt like to paint that way, the release of emotion onto the canvas. She wondered where the girl was, the one that thought art would be her life work. Maybe she disappeared under the reality of tuition loans, rent, and the fear her talent was imagined and wouldn't hold up under scrutiny. Maybe she lost the reason for doing it amongst the critiques and competition of art school and the realization that it was a business with no profit potential instead of an expression of her unique point of view.

Lee stuffed the paintings back in the box and shoved it under the table. She rummaged through a box labeled 'supplies' and found a blank sheet of mildewed watercolor paper. She tucked the paper, a bag of pastels, and a small portable easel under her arm and opened the door to the outside. The rain had stopped while she was inside. Overhead, large rain clouds drifted north, letting the sun cascade down on the wet land. She walked along until she came to a spot along the river where water splashed over large rocks as mild rapids. She sat on a boulder near the water and propped the easel in her lap. She sketched images that leapt to her mind for the restaurant with the pastels: pear green for the walls, a bar and tables in dark brown, a blue awning facing the street. The water gurgled through the rocks and she began to think of it as a song in accompaniment to her drawing. The river had its own song, she mused, like Tommy. The song of the river. The river's song. Riversong. She would call the restaurant Riversong. She wrote Riversong in the left hand corner of the paper with black letters and then closed her eyes to better hear the river's voice.

The oatmeal sat cold and crusted over on the table as Lee's fingers flew over the computer. The business plan, corresponding financial spreadsheets, and a slide presentation for Mike were nearly completed. Her back ached and she realized she hadn't gone to the bathroom in hours. Her legs were stiff as she rose to her feet, stomach growling.

There was a rustle at the back door and she saw Ellen on the stairs with a basket in her arms. Lee opened the door for her, pleased to see her. She breathed in the aroma of butter and cinnamon and it felt like medicine to her aching spirit.

Ellen's eyes took in the laptop and her eyebrows knit in surprise. "You working on something?"

"The plan for the restaurant."

Ellen opened the basket, pulling out a cinnamon roll and plopping in a chair. "Let's hear it."

She handed Ellen the financial spreadsheets and went through the presentation, computer slide show and all. She proposed an intimate romantic setting with gourmet food, fresh ingredients found locally, full bar, and an extensive wine list. The space would be renovated to accommodate a new bar area complete with a curved counter and mirrored shelving for liquors, wines, and glasses, and an upgraded formal dining area. There would be two menus, one for the dining room and one for the bar. The bar menu would begin after nine p.m. with reasonably priced appetizer offerings to get the late night crowds looking for live music and drinks. Revolving art exhibits by local artists would be displayed on the walls of the dining room. There would be monthly local wine tastings, paired with the chef's custom-tailored meals, and quarterly Sunday afternoon art openings with wine and light appetizers.

After she was done, Ellen knitted her brows. "Where will you get a cook?"

Lee sat on the edge of the table. "I met a professionally trained chef the other day. Matter of fact, she prompted the entire concept for the restaurant. I hope my instinct about her is right." Lee shuffled the papers on the table.

"Where are you going to get the customers?"

Lee laughed. "I forgot to tell you that part. I'm using my instincts here, which I hope to God are right, but I think it will be a combination of tourists, retirees with disposable income, professionals like teachers, our doctor, the dentists, and people celebrating special occasions."

Ellen nodded her head, pursing her lips. "That sounds right. Anniversaries, stuff like that?"

"Exactly."

"Yeah, and the bridge ladies."

"What's a bridge lady?"

"There's these ladies around town here, most of 'em widows, play bridge three or four times a week. They've got money and time. They're always talking about how they wish there was a decent place to eat here in town."

Lee bit into a cinnamon roll. "This is good. It's kind of flaky like a croissant. We could sell these at the restaurant."

Ellen flushed and waved her hand in the air. "I'm too old to make my baking a business. I like to bake for friends. But I'm interested in this idea you have about local produce. I could help you find some local farmers and such."

Lee clapped her hands. "Perfect. Y'know, there's a whole 'eat locally' trend across the country."

Ellen chuckled and said, "I know there are some local farms in the area that would love to grow for a restaurant like this." She nodded her head. "I think this is a hell of an idea. I'm proud of you."

"Really?"

"You bet. Now listen, I found a little something for the baby while I was out yesterday." She pulled something from a plastic shopping bag next to the basket and handed it to Lee.

It was a yellow onesie with a duck on the front and matching socks that seemed no bigger than her thumb. "Ellen, this is so sweet." She fingered the socks and then held them to her cheek. "Will the baby really be this small?"

"Only for what will seem about two days. They're grown before you know it."

Lee had the urge to hug her suddenly but instead put the gift back in the bag. "This is nice. Thank you." Feeling awkward, she backed towards the door. "I should get dressed." She looked at the clock. "It's four in the afternoon!"

Ellen thumped the side of her head. "Shoot, I almost forgot the whole reason I came over here. I hired you a handyman."

Lee stared at her. "What?"

"He's more of a carpenter I guess. Anyway, he's coming by this afternoon at five." Lee opened her mouth to say no but Ellen put up her hand. "I won't take no for an answer. You're never gonna get this place finished at the rate you're working."

"I can't pay for it."

She waved her hand in the air. "Don't worry about that. You gotta learn to accept help. Otherwise you'll turn out like me, old and lonely."

"But it's so expensive."

"Pay me back when you sell the house." Ellen walked toward the door. "I need to run. I'm picking up some plants at the nursery. It's supposed to rain this afternoon."

The handyman came at five minutes after five. He had long gray hair in a ponytail, shorts, and Birkenstocks with socks. "Hey, how's it goin'?" His voice was mellow. "I'm early. I hope that's cool."

Lee looked at her watch. "I have five after."

"Really? Weird." He elongated the words, swinging his ponytail and lifting his arms above his head. He stretched his torso into a half backbend, and the stench of his underarms mixed with the smell of patchouli made Lee feel light-headed. He popped upright and closed his eyes for a few seconds. "Wow. Stressful day. Yeah, man, I'm working for this lady in town. She's so uptight. I mean, really uptight."

Lee gestured for him to come in and showed him around the house. They discussed a plan, which included painting, refinishing the floors, repairing the stairwell, getting rid of the rest of the junk, and rebuilding the porch. "I don't know what Ellen discussed with you regarding how much this might cost?"

"She's cool. I've known her for a long time and told her I'd do the whole thing for five grand plus material. Altogether I think we can get it done for ten grand."

"Really? The floors too?"

"If you don't mind laminate instead of real wood."

"I guess." Lee wrinkled her brow. "I'm repairing this house in order to sell it, so it's important the job is professional."

"This is a cool house, man, and I'll get her humming again." He stroked the wood of the stairwell. "You have to respect the materials, you know, merge the past and the present into something beautiful." He pulled the ponytail holder from his hair, shaking his long gray tresses. "You mind if I do some yoga on your grass here before I go, clear my head for the drive home?"

"I guess."

And right there in her yard he took off his shirt and began the yoga practice of salutation to the sun.

Lee closed the door, resting her forehead on it for a moment, trying not to laugh out loud. At least she wasn't bored, she thought. She had the urge to call Tommy and tell him that for such a small town, there was an endless supply of interesting people. He'd agree. She knew that for sure.

CHAPTER FIFTEEN

MIKE MARCHED through the front door of the restaurant, threw his hat on the table, and gripped Lee's hand in a firm handshake. "Good to see you, young lady." He plopped in a seat and thrust his hands behind his head. "Been looking forward to this all week." Dust floated in the streaks of sunlight that streamed through the grimy restaurant windows. He sniffed the air and shook his head. "This place always smells of old grease. Makes me think of nothing but big-bottomed women, and I don't mean the good kind. Sure hope your plan doesn't include a deep fryer."

Lee squared her shoulders. "We keep the deep fryer and I'll tell you why."

He crossed his legs and leaned back in his seat. "I'm all ears."

Using the presentation software on her laptop, she ran through the concept of the restaurant. After the fourth slide she glanced nervously at his face, hoping to discern his reaction. His face was impassive but attentive. She swallowed her nervousness and continued. She explained the numbers on the spreadsheet next, how she came to them and why she believed they could make money. "As you know, margins on alcohol are fifty percent at least and when people drink they want bar food." Mike pulled on his ear and he leaned forward a few inches. "This will bring in another type of diner, one that won't want to spend money on a full dinner but are willing to pay for appetizers and drinks."

Next she pulled a sheet from the concept board and propped it against the table. It was complete with her sketches of the dining room and bar, fabric and paint samples, ideas for the furniture, pictures of glassware, silverware, and the linens she would choose. She concluded with the budget, the hiring plan, and projected profits for the first year.

With his ring finger, Mike moved the financial projections in little circles on the table. He stared at the board. Lee could see the machinations of his brain, calculating and surmising, but was uncertain of his conclusion. He crossed his left foot over his knee and gripped the top of his boot with his right hand. "Your work is impressive. You've got class, little lady, but it might be too fancy for the folks here."

"I've done the research and the demographic supports the idea. Think about it, rich retirees, professionals, special occasion customers, and tourists for the dining room. A young local crowd for the bar." Lee sat down across from him and pointed at one of the lines on the spreadsheet. "All we need is some good press, a product that delivers, and people will flood in here. There's nothing else like this. Give them something they didn't even know they wanted. That's business."

He tipped back in his chair. "I don't know about the artsy-fartsy stuff."

"The revolving art attracts a certain clientele. It's all part of the package. I'm right about this." She raised her eyebrows in a tease. "Just 'cause you don't go for that kind of thing."

"I'm more a golf and fishing guy myself." He smiled and tipped back in his chair. "You can't charge big city prices. Is that factored in?"

"Of course."

He picked up the spreadsheet again. "This is a hell of a lot of money you want from me." He put down the paper, crossing his arms and scrutinizing her. "I hope you know what you're doing."

"I know business. It's black and white, dollars and cents, do this, do that, this happens. It's the other stuff in life I have trouble with."

He glanced at the door of the kitchen as if Zac were there. "Yeah. Me too."

Lee took a deep breath. "I'll open the place for you and help you determine who you want to run it after I'm gone."

His eyes were still on the kitchen door. "Guess it can't be Zac."

"I would highly recommend you find someone else."

He glanced out the front window for a moment and sighed. "This consultant thing, it lacks commitment."

She waved her hand as if to ward off evil spirits. "I can't stay here. I'm fixing up the house and I'll be gone as quick as I can sell it."

"You have a place to go?"

"Not exactly."

"Tell you what, you commit to this for real. Stay in town for a while, come work for me as the manager of this place, and I'll fund the whole idea, hook, line, and sinker."

She drummed her fingers on the table, calculating numbers in her head—the house sale, plus a salary, plus a bonus if they were profitable after a year. It might be enough to pay off DeAngelo. She wrote a number on a scrap of paper and pushed it over to him. "If I were to commit, I need this salary and a lump sum bonus at the end of twelve months if we make the profits I projected in my spreadsheet."

He slapped his hand on the table and grinned. "Shoot, you're a fast thinker." He leaned back in his chair, his eyes gleaming. "But so am I. I agree to the salary but not the lump sum. I'll split the profits with you 50/50 but you have to come on as a partner."

"Why would you do that?"

"Because if you own part of something, you'll work harder. That's just human nature."

She fluffed the front of her blouse to cool her damp torso. "I'm pregnant."

He raised his eyebrows and stared at her for a moment. "Well, I had no idea. Congratulations."

"I didn't know until after my husband died." She paused and took a breath. "My husband committed suicide over a bad business deal. You still want me as a partner?" She tried to sound light-hearted but the words came out a croak.

He shrugged, smiling at her. "Call it an old man's eccentricities, but I have a feeling about you. You're a scrapper and a fighter. I want a girl like that on my team."

"I can't pay the doctor bills for this baby with what I'm making now. I want health insurance for me and everyone on the staff. Starbucks style."

"Starbucks style?"

"Benefits for part-time workers. Anyone over twenty hours, we kick in for a portion."

"Done," he said.

"You've got yourself a deal." She reached to shake his hand but he moved around the table and squeezed her in a bear hug. He pulled back and looked in her eyes. "You know, a baby's a blessing no matter when they arrive." He let go of her, glancing at his watch. "I'll talk to my attorney and get something formal put together."

Lee clasped her hands together, smiling. "What have I done?"

Mike re-tucked his dress shirt into his jeans. "Commitment. Highly underrated these days."

"Can you ask Zac to clear his stuff out of the office?" she said. "It's a bit awkward for me to talk to him about it."

"That's fair." He reached into his pants pocket and pulled out a huge set of keys, slipping two from the ring. "Here's the keys. One for the back door and one for the office." He collected his papers and put on his hat. "Only one thing. Now we're partners, you've got to find something legit for Zac to do."

After Mike left she walked back to the manager's office, using her key to open the door. It was in its usual state of disarray. She looked through the piles of papers on the desk until she found the fairy diary with Zac's notes. She dropped it in her purse and crossed the street to Ray's Accounting and Taxes. Ray was in his usual place at the computer, smiling when he saw her. She sat in the visitor's chair and told him her plans for the restaurant. "Wanted to thank you for introducing me to him."

"Oh, that was my pleasure," he said.

"We'll continue to need your help with the books and taxes once we're open for business."

He smiled, crossing his arms over his chest. "That'd be just super."

"Maybe we'll have some profit to report by the end of the year."

"I believe you will, Lee. I surely do."

She reached for her bag. "Actually, I came by to ask a favor. Could I use your copy machine?"

"Why sure."

She pulled the fairy diary out of her purse. "Just a little tidying up to do before I take over Zac's office."

"Help yourself." He pointed to the copy machine in the corner. "Then you have to let me buy you a Blizzard at Dairy Queen to celebrate. I hear they have a new flavor."

"Perfect. I'm starving." She smiled and put her hand on her stomach, thinking she'd tell Ray about the baby over their Blizzards.

Later that day, Lee and Annie sat in the empty restaurant. The business plan spilled out of Lee in a rush of words. Annie's eyes were glassy. "You want me?"

"What do you think?" said Lee. "You up for it?"

"I could merge it with the Italian tradition of three courses, only with a Northwest flavor." Annie's eyes misted. "What do I have to do to get this job?"

"I want you to cook a full meal for me at my house Monday night. If it tastes the way I think it will, it's all yours."

Alder bounced up and down in his chair. "She's the best cook in the whole world."

Lee put her hand on Alder's head. "You come too. I'll invite my friend Ellen."

Alder, grinning, gave Lee a paper. "I made the baby a picture." He pointed at the crude drawing. "See, there's me and there's the baby. She's pink 'cause she's gonna be a girl."

"We'll see you Monday." Annie hugged her. Lee resisted the urge to rest her head on her soft, maternal shoulder.

Twenty minutes later, still at the restaurant, Lee plugged her time-line into the project-planning tool on her laptop. She'd just completed it when Tommy walked through the door. He pointed towards the parking lot at the back of the restaurant. "There're some shady characters out back."

"You recognize any of them?"

"Look like local lowlifes to me." He sat on one of the empty tables, swinging his legs, a vein protruding from his bulging calf muscle. "You don't work after dark, do you?"

"Don't worry about it."

His voice was tender. "But I do." He crossed his arms and stared at her for a moment.

She avoided his eyes by looking out the window, feeling nervous to be alone with him. "I met with Mike this afternoon. We agreed on a plan for this place."

"Can I hear too?"

She smiled and looked at him. He seemed genuinely interested and it gave them something to talk about. Less chance for him to ask her personal questions, she thought. She gave him the entire presentation and he listened all the way through without comment.

"What do you say? Want to be our main band?"

He smiled and clapped his hands together, twice like it was time to belt out a song right then and there. "I'd be honored. I guess Mike was right about you." He crossed his feet and arms, his voice teasing. "This mean you're going to stick around for a while?"

Lee looked down at her computer, playing with the mouse. "Not necessarily." She hooked her ankles under the chair and told herself to breathe.

Strolling over to her, he put his elbows on the table. He looked over the top of her laptop. "Why do you hate it here so much?"

His gaze unsettled her. "I don't." Her voice quivered and she tried to stop the prickly sensation behind her eyes by pressing her fingertips into them. "I just worked so hard to have a different kind of life. Away from here. Away from my mother and all the…" She paused and took in a deep breath. "Away from all the memories. Being here makes me feel like the little girl who was sad all the time. It's hard to explain."

"Are the memories still that strong?"

"I don't know. Sometimes. I've been remembering the good things too, though. I forgot how much I loved the air here. And the stars at night."

"You could replace all those bad memories with good ones, if you gave it a chance." He shrugged and grinned. "Gave me a chance, for example." His eyes danced, like he was teasing, but she knew it was a serious question.

She could feel hot splotchy red spots on her neck, and covered them with her hand. "Why do you love it here so much?"

His eyes were soft. "I love who I feel like when I'm here. The first time I drove through, and this was fifteen years ago, I thought, someday I'll come back here and live. It felt like home."

"I'd hate to see where else you've lived if this was your first choice."

He smiled and picked up her cell phone. "You're cute when you're grouchy. May I put my number in here in case you ever need me to come pick you up?"

"In the fire truck?"

He laughed and punched some keys on her phone. "When I was in fifth grade I loved a redhead named Minnie Stewart. She was sassy and had freckles too." He crossed his arms and leaned on the edge of the table. "But then her brother called me a Spic and that ended our ill-fated love affair."

"A name calling is all it took to change your mind?"

He smirked and raised his eyebrows. "Depends on the girl."

"I'm sure."

"Actually, I beat the crap out of him and she dumped me."

"Is that how you got the scar?"

He covered the scar with his hand. "No, I got this from my brother when I tried to flush his cocaine down the toilet."

"Your brother cut you?"

"Don't get between an addict and their drug of choice." He stepped towards the door. "It's not safe for you to be here alone after dark. I'll be back in an hour to walk you to your car." Before she could protest, he was gone, the door closing behind him so quickly that she wondered if she imagined he was ever there.

There was a warm breeze an hour later when Tommy walked her to her car, holding the door while she scooted behind the wheel. She turned the key but nothing happened. The battery must be dead. She looked at Tommy before fingering the car light knob. "Crap, I left the lights on."

Tommy grinned and put his hand on the back of her seat. "See, this is why you need me around."

She glanced at him and then back at the blank dashboard. "Do you have jumper cables?"

"I have some at home, in my garage."

"Well, you might want to keep those in your car if you've taken it upon yourself to be my rescuer."

"How is it that you're so damned cute even when you're being a pain in the ass?"

She laughed in spite of herself and threw up her hands. "I don't suppose you'd give me a lift home?"

He gave her his hand, helping her out of the van. "I thought you'd never ask."

She and Tommy walked up the new steps of her porch. The handyman, in the course of a week, had torn out the charred wood and replaced it with oak slabs. The porch was not yet stained, still smelling of fresh, newly shaved and cut wood. Joshua's handiwork was impressive. From her kitchen window, she had watched him as he stood the wood upright alongside the house and then ran his fingers along the surface of each board like it was a woman's leg, seeming to look for imperfections. She asked him about it later and he said he liked the pieces to fit closely together without a lot of sanding and cutting. When it was finished the boards fit so snugly together that it looked like one slab, except for the fine lines that proved they were once separate boards.

Tommy was next to her at the door. She could smell his lime aftershave and for a second wished she could just back up a half a foot and melt into him. But instead she unlocked the door and reached inside for the light switch. "This is what I'm talking about," said Tommy. "You need a porch light out here."

"Have you always been this bossy?" She stepped into the light of the foyer.

He ran his hand through his hair, peering behind her into her house. "First off, yes. Second, it's clear that you don't understand the extent of Zac's business, nor do you take proper care to protect yourself. Leaving your car lights on, no porch light. Need I say more? These tweakers are unpredictable. I wouldn't put it past one of them to follow you home in some paranoid rampage."

"Are you trying to scare me?"

He shook his head. "No, I'm sorry. I'm compelled to look after you. I can't control myself."

"I'm fine, plus, Joshua, my handyman, is installing the light tomorrow. Have you forgotten I managed to burn down the porch?"

"How could I forget that?" Something unsaid hung there for a moment before he shrugged his shoulders and turned to go. "You call me tomorrow and I'll take you to your car, get it jumped for you."

It was late, past eight and she was hungry. Not knowing what possessed her, she put her hand on the sleeve of his jacket. "You want to come in, have something to eat?"

He looked surprised, raised his eyebrows. "You're inviting me to stay?"

"It was nice of you to pick me up. Least I could do is feed you. Unless you've eaten already?"

"I have, but I'm always hungry."

"I'm not much of a cook, but Ellen leaves me mystery dishes in the fridge."

He followed her into the house and she felt him behind her all the way to the kitchen as if they were tethered by an electrical current. She switched on the light in the small kitchen. "The kitchen is next on Joshua's list, then the floors, then painting," she said. "Have a seat. I'll see what I have in here." She opened the refrigerator and sure enough Ellen had left a plastic container labeled "Chicken Stew." Lee put the old saucepan on the largest burner. Tommy sat at the table, watching her. "You want something to drink?" she asked him. "Joshua leaves beers in the fridge if you want one. I don't know exactly why he has to have them at my house but his work is beautiful and his rates so inexpensive I figured it was a small thing to ask." She stopped, feeling like she was rambling, and sighed.

"What's wrong?" he asked her, propping his cheek in the palm of his hand.

"I don't know. You make me nervous, for some reason."

"You don't know why?"

"Do you?" she asked, fiddling with the metal hanger on the end of the pot's rubber handle.

"What do you think?"

She laughed and turned down the heat on the stew. "I'm the one asking the questions here."

He grinned and held up his hands as if to shield himself. "I've got this John Hiatt song called 'Stood Up' running through my head. Ever heard it?"

"I don't think so."

He sang, "I guess she never understood what she could do, With all her flaming red hair, But I could not stand the heat in her kitchen, So, Jack, I got out of there."

She felt herself go hot, embarrassed, and turned back to the stove.

He went to her. "I'm sorry. I've made you uncomfortable." His voice was low, near her ear.

The stew made a popping sound and Lee stirred it, the glaze over the top having softened. The room filled with the smell of rosemary, onions, and roasted chicken. He was still behind her and she could almost feel what it would be like to have his arms encircle her waist, to feel his hands on her thighs. "Looks great," he said. She felt his breath at the top of her head. She scooted away from him and opened the refrigerator door. She found a beer in the door called "Rogue" in a brown bottle with nice artwork on the label. "You like this?"

"Sure. Thanks." He kept his eyes on her as he tilted the beer into his mouth.

Lee's mouth filled with saliva and she swallowed, chastising herself for thinking about the way his lips gripped the opening of the beer bottle. She touched a finger to her temple, thinking she needed to get serious control of herself before she did something stupid.

She found two bowls and filled them with stew. They sat at the table and began to eat. The stew had rounds of tender carrots, pearl onions, red baby potatoes, and shredded chicken that tasted like it had been roasted over a wood-burning flame, accompanied by a hint of rosemary and fresh thyme. "This food Ellen brings, it reminds me of this restaurant in Seattle called the Five Spot—kind of down-home cooking with a flair. I've started to imagine Ellen's house actually is the kitchen at the Five Spot. Something about her is bigger than life. She's so full of energy and ideas, especially when you consider she's in her seventies."

"She's a great lady," he said.

"I'm going to get fat if she keeps feeding me like this."

He grunted and scooped another bite into his fork. "Doubtful."

"She's appalled I don't cook."

He smiled and ate another bite of stew. "You been to the doc again?"

"Next week."

"You feeling alright?"

"Now that the all day sickness is gone, yes."

"You taking your vitamins?"

She pointed to the bottle of prenatal vitamins on the windowsill. "A horse pill a day."

"How about food?"

She nodded, keeping her eyes focused on the stew in her bowl. "Three hundred extra calories a day. What's with the interrogation?"

He shrugged. "You're really thin and pale. Not sure you take good care of yourself."

She blinked and felt herself blush. "I've gained exactly five pounds since I've been here. I weigh myself every day. I've always done that."

He leaned back in his chair, watching her. "Is it exhausting trying to control everything in your life to such a degree?"

She surprised herself by laughing. "It is exhausting, but it's the way I am."

"I suppose it's because your mother was so unpredictable."

Her eyes widened and she opened her mouth to tell him that she made it a rule not to talk about the crazy old drunk but instead her eyes filled, and she twisted her fork over in her hand. "Something like that."

"You never knew what she'd do, what state she'd be in, every day you walked in the door from school."

She stared at him. "How did you know that?"

He looked at her, his eyes serious. "I don't know."

She spoke quietly. "How do you know so much about me?"

"I can feel you."

"But why?"

"I don't know." He put his empty bowl in the sink and then sat back at the table, rubbing the scar on his cheek.

"Do you want anything else?" She avoided his eyes but felt his gaze just the same.

He leaned forward, moving her bowl an inch sideways. She looked up into his brown eyes. "I want to kiss you. Bad."

Her stomach tightened and she felt her breath catch. "You should go."

"Do you really want that?"

"Yes." Her hands were shaking and she stared at his mouth, wanting to feel it on her own. She closed her eyes, forcing herself to think of Dan. She hated herself for being here, for wanting this man to stay and hold her in his arms.

She felt his fingers brush the side of her face. She opened her eyes, trembling, feeling a lump rise in her throat. "Please," she said. "I can't." She felt the tears start to come and pushed her fingers into her eyes.

His voice was still soft as he tugged at her hands. She let him take them between his own. "I've scared you, pushing too hard. I do that."

"It's my fault." The tears came then, sliding out of her eyes of their own free will. She pushed back her chair and put her bowl blindly into the sink. Facing away from him, she said, "I'm fine." She hated the tears in her voice.

He was behind her now, touching her shoulder with the tips of his fingers. "Lee, I'm sorry."

She wiped the tears from her cheeks, whispering. "Please, just go."

"I'm so sorry," he said again. And then he was gone, closing the door softly behind him.

Saturday morning, Lee sat with Mike at the back of the restaurant, twitching her foot under the table, waiting to begin the presentation to the staff. Billy and Cindi sat together. He sipped from a large glass of diet soda and Cindi blew on a steaming coffee cup. Deana, legs crossed, flipped the pages of a movie magazine. They all waited for Zac. The ice machine made a thump as a layer of cubes slid from their rack into the bin. At ten after the hour, Mike whispered to Lee, "He's not gonna show. Let's get started."

Mike stood up and scanned the faces. "Good to see you all here. Thanks for coming in on a Saturday morning. We're making big changes to the restaurant. Lucky for us, Lee's decided to come on as partial owner and manager."

No one moved.

Mike cleared his throat. "She's gonna take it from here, explain the new business and answer any questions."

Billy's mouth hung open. Cindi stared at her with a half smile, her eyes flicking from side to side. Deana, magazine still open, squinted and played with a section of her hair. Lee grabbed the concept board from the table and tacked it onto the wall, her knees wobbling like when she was in high school and had to speak in front of the class. "The first thing I want to say is there will be a job for anyone who still wants one."

Deana let out an extended sigh, crossing her legs and rifling through her purse.

Lee gave a condensed version of the presentation, without the financial information, and handed out a list of possible positions for which they could apply. Listed were: bartender, host/hostess, servers, head chef, assistant chef, dishwasher, and busser. "All these positions will require training, which we will provide you."

Billy raised his hand. "Lee, what if you can't be trained?"

"Anyone could learn one of these jobs. That's not a problem."

Cindi laughed, tossing her hair, her mouth a thin line. "Oh, we're not too stupid to learn how to be a busboy." She tapped her high-heeled boot on the floor, crossing her arms over her tight shirt. "Last time I checked I already knew how to wait tables. Better than some, I might add."

"No, no, I know you all know how to work in the environment as it is, but the new restaurant will require formal training in the areas of service. We'll be training under the same regimen as a five-star hotel or restaurant, with the same standards."

Cindi scooted her chair a little closer to Billy. She whispered something under her breath. Billy started to laugh, saw Lee looking at him, and clamped his mouth shut, shifting his gaze to his feet.

"Like I said, all the jobs are open." Lee glanced at the paper. "Except the Head Chef."

Deana rolled her eyes, ambled near the front door, and leaned on the wall. "Five-star service. What the hell does that mean?"

Billy wiped his forehead with the back of his sleeve. "Who would teach us all this stuff?"

"I haven't worked all the details out yet, but we'll bring in a trainer," said Lee. "An expert in fine dining," she added, voice faltering.

There was a bang from the kitchen like someone dropped a large pan. A few seconds later Zac came through the swinging doors. He stood in the doorway with his arms crossed, his eyes on Lee.

Deana leaned against the front door, smiling at Zac like they were conspirators of some private joke. She turned to Lee, arranging her overgrown bangs over one eye with a coy shift of her head. "How come you're in charge now? You never even worked in a restaurant before."

Mike spoke in a cold tone Lee had never heard him use before. "Lee's come up with a hell of a concept and we've agreed to a partnership. Take it or leave it."

Deana popped a piece of gum in her mouth. "This place is fine the way it is."

"This place hasn't made a blessed dime since it opened," said Mike. "If you all want a job to come to five days a week, we gotta turn this place on its head."

Cindi stood, clutching her purse against her chest. "So Lee's an owner now?"

"Yes," said Mike.

Billy wiped the condensation from his soda glass with his thumb. "Lee, are you our boss now?" He glanced in a guilty way at Zac and then sipped his soda, looking at the floor.

Lee looked at Mike for help, who glanced at Zac, and then nodded to Billy. "Lee's the manager. Zac will be taking on a different job."

The corners of Billy's mouth turned up in a brief smile.

"How do we know you aren't just gonna push us out?" said Cindi. She put her hand on Billy's arm.

Lee started to answer, but was interrupted by Billy. "Maybe this'll be good for us. You know, like more money and stuff."

Deana guffawed, tossing her hair. "Billy, don't you get it? The only people gonna get rich around here is Lee." She paused and pointed at Mike. "And him."

Cindi nodded and looked out the window. "This won't be a place for people like us."

Lee moved toward their table and tripped in her high heels. She steadied herself on a chair. "Look, I need this to work as much as you guys do."

Cindi put her purse over her shoulder. "Different table cloths don't mean it's any different than yesterday. We're still broke."

"Yeah, but we'll be trained." Deana pantomimed a tray above her head and curtsied. "No one's gonna come to a fancy ass place just to get a drink." She threw her purse over her shoulder. "I don't need one of your shit jobs anyway. I'm outta here." She flounced out, the door swinging back and forth several times before shutting with a soft swoosh.

No one spoke. Zac left through the kitchen door. Mike glanced at Lee and followed Zac. Billy and Cindi looked at their feet.

Lee turned from them and took the concept board off the wall, surprised at feeling hurt. She'd imagined everyone would meet the new idea with excitement and enthusiasm. She flashed to a time in fourth grade when a group of girls gathered around her in the playground and told her they all took a vote and agreed they hated her and would no longer count her as a friend. This was the same feeling of shock, betrayal, and being misplaced in the world. Betrayal, she thought, is that what Cindi thinks this is?

"We're going to be shut down for a couple of months," said Lee. "There will be plenty of work getting this place ready if anyone's interested."

She turned to see Billy amble to his feet. "Yeah, well, thanks, Lee."

Billy and Cindi headed for the door, and Lee followed them. "Wait a minute."

They turned towards her. "You two think I don't know what's going on here?" said Lee. "That you're proud and intimidated at the same time. Look, I grew up in this town. My mother was a drunk and we were on food stamps and government cheese and every other humiliating program you can think of." She choked, tears springing to her eyes. "The only reason I got out is because I got a couple of breaks along the way. Y'know, a chance, someone who saw something in me and that's what this is. A chance." Her mouth filled with the saliva of unshed tears. "I'm no different than you."

They stared at her.

Billy wiped his forehead again. "You think maybe I could work for the chef? Learn how to be a real cook?"

"I do." She swiped at the corners of her eyes. "I'll make sure of it."

Cindi cocked her head. "You'll be different now, that's what happens when people become the boss."

"Believe it or not, I was a boss before I came here and my employees liked me a lot."

"I thought you were leaving here soon anyway," said Cindi.

"Do you know why I came here?"

"Not exactly," said Cindi.

"My husband killed himself and left me penniless and pregnant."

Cindi's face softened and she stared at Lee's stomach. "You're having a baby?"

"In September. So, I've got to get this place up and running before the baby comes."

Cindi crossed her arms and shook her head. "You hear this, Billy? You ever do that to a girl I'll kick your ass."

Billy pulled on his shirt where his soft middle protruded. "I don't even have a girl."

Cindi put her arm around Billy. "I know, but you will. Lee, I raised a baby on my own after my no-good husband ran off. He was a worthless son of a bitch too." She gestured to the board. "This bar, it's gonna be real drinks?"

Lee nodded.

"I always thought about being a bartender. People always telling me personal stuff as it is."

"We have enough time for you to go to bartender school before we open. We'll pay for you to go if you're serious."

Cindi nodded and placed her hands on her hips. "Maybe. Yeah, maybe."

After they left, Lee sat at the table and shuffled through the business plan. She knew getting this restaurant ready to open and the staff trained would be difficult even for someone with actual experience, like Linus. Experience she obviously didn't possess, given the interaction with the staff just now. She stared out the window, wondering what Linus would do. She ached for her old life, especially for Linus. She picked up her cell phone just as the kitchen doors swung open. Zac walked in, hands in the pockets of his long shorts. "My dad said to come see you." He paused and then added in mock reverence, "Boss."

"Have a seat."

He sat down across from her, tipping back so that the two front legs of his chair were several inches off the ground. "Look, all that stuff I said before about this place, the truth is I hated running this joint. I was just doing it because the old man wanted me to. Go at it."

"Your dad thinks you should work here."

Zac put the chair down on the floor. "I know."

She sighed and looked at him for a moment. His hair was graying at the temples and there were fine wrinkles around his eyes. She flashed to what he looked like in high school and thought how disheartening it was to see someone from your youth beaten down by life. She wondered if he saw the same in her. The thought softened her. "Zac, do you know what I used to dream about when I was in high school?"

He squinted and shook his head, like he was ready for battle. "Haven't a clue."

"I wanted to feel safe and live in a beautiful home with someone who loved me and have work that meant something to the world."

"Yeah?" His voice was softer than usual and she knew he was listening even though he still assumed the posture of someone who didn't care, leaning back in his chair, arms crossed over his chest, the macho guy thing she remembered from high school. "You get any of those things?"

"I thought I did. But, I'm here, trying to make a new life for myself."

He flicked the sleeve of his jacket with his thumb, looking at the table. "Yeah, that's all you can do, I guess."

"What did you dream about in high school?"

He shrugged and grinned. "Getting laid, probably."

She laughed like it was funny. "What do you want now? Please tell me it's more than that?"

He gazed over her head. She saw a glimmer of regret about a life gone irretrievably in the wrong direction cross his face. "What I want you can't possibly give me."

"Try me."

He blinked and stared at her. "You really want to know?"

"I do."

"I want to leave this town and never come back. I want to learn to surf in the ocean. I want to feel good instead of this fucked-up feeling all the time. I want to give a shit if I get out of bed every morning."

She flattened her hands on the tabletop, leaning forward a few inches. "Why don't you go?"

He tossed his head. She saw the fear in his eyes, the uncertainty that he would ever go. "I've got plans to get out of here but I need a few more months."

"I understand." She opened her folder and picked up her pen. "There's a position in high-end restaurants called the Food and Beverage Manager." She almost smiled, thinking the beverage part was perfect for him. "You want me to tell your dad that's your job? I'll just call if I need you?"

He smiled and his shoulders relaxed. "But you won't call, right?"

"Exactly. It can be our secret." Her left eye twitched. She ran the tip of her pen along the fake wood pattern of the plastic table. "There's only one thing you have to do for me."

He raised his eyebrows and winked. "I thought Tommy was in line for that job?"

She managed not to cringe and shook her head. "No, not that. I've seen you with your little baggies of goodies out the back door. It makes me nervous. I'm afraid it'll keep customers away."

His demeanor changed to dark in an instant, his face purple, eyes hard. He laughed without mirth, yanking at the lobe of his ear. "Quite an imagination you've got."

157

She didn't answer. Her silence seemed to enrage him. He jerked from his seat, the chair flying behind him, towering over her, smelling of the inside of a seedy bar, inches from her face. "Don't get in my business." He put one hand on the back of her chair. "Understand?"

"Isn't there someplace better than the parking lot of this restaurant?"

He shook his head and started tapping the back of the chair with his fingers. "No, no, no. Why are you talking about this? It's none of your concern. I have it all figured out and you can't mess this up for me. I have a plan, do you understand?"

"I don't understand why you're doing this at all. Your dad would do anything to help you—"

"Shut up." He yanked her off the chair and slammed her against the wall. "Just shut up about my dad. You don't understand how he is, how nothing I do is good enough, how every single day of my life I've been a disappointment to him and finally I don't care. So, just shut up about my saintly father because you have no idea how it feels to be a fuck-up." He had one hand on her neck and the other squeezed the top of her arm, his teeth clenched. "I'm gonna finally get out, live at the beach. Get the life I was meant to have. You can't get in my way." He pushed on her neck and his eyes glistened with tears. "Or you'll be sorry. You'll be very, very sorry."

She couldn't speak with his hand on her neck but nodded like she understood.

He let go of her and rested his forehead on the wall, next to her face. He spoke like he was exhausted and she held her breath in order to hear him. "I'm sorry if I hurt you," he said. "I don't want to hurt you. I'll move to another location if you want, if you'll keep your mouth shut to my dad. He doesn't know and I don't want him to. We can't ever talk about this again. Ever again."

She made her voice soft, soothing, like she was talking to a child. "It's alright, I won't tell Mike, if you stay out of the parking lot."

He pulled his forehead back from the wall, the front of his hair flopping in front of his eyes, his skin glistening with sweat. "I don't want to be someone who hurts women."

She touched her neck, her eyes focused on the collar of his shirt. "I know."

"Lee, I would stop if I could, but I'm in too deep. Do you get it?"

"Yes, I understand."

He nodded and wiped under his nose with the back of his sleeve. "I'll see you around, then." He left through the kitchen door like a blind man without a cane.

Lee slumped into a chair and folded her hands together to stop them from shaking. She looked at the clock on her phone. It was 3:00 in the afternoon but it might be midnight for how tired she felt. The afternoon sun streamed through the front windows into the spot where the checkout counters had been when her mother worked here thirty years before.

Her mother had worked at the register while Lee sat hidden at her feet, listening to the voices of the customers and her mother's breathy voice in response to their questions. Lee was inconspicuous and so obedient that she was invisible and the world went on above her, without her. She began to draw with her mother's Bic pen, stick figures with big round heads in varying haircuts, Christmas trees and suns with lines that reached out to the very edge of the paper.

By the time she was seven there was schoolwork to do and books to read. The hours passed with the smell of ripe fruit and cardboard in her nose. She was safe. But one day her mother picked up a box of canned tomatoes and screamed from pain, clutching at a spot in the middle of her back. Eleanor couldn't work after that and told Lee about a word called disability for people who got hurt at their job. Now Eleanor's back ached all the time. She drank clear liquid with ice after breakfast and wore her bathrobe all day. "Can you get me more ice from the shed?" Eleanor asked Lee each day when she came in from school.

Now, Lee looked around the empty room. She thought of Tommy then, with his contagious smile and inquisitive eyes, the citrus smell of his skin that filled with her with longing. Without thinking, she pulled up his name on her cell phone and dialed, telling herself that she could allow kindness into her life.

Tommy answered on the first ring.

"It's Lee."

"I know," he said, his voice tentative, hopeful.

"I'm at the restaurant. Will you come get me?"

"You sure?"

"I'm sure."

"I'll be right there."

CHAPTER SIXTEEN

TOMMY'S HOUSE was a surprise. It was newly constructed and full of light, perched on beams and jutting out over the grassy bank of the river. The main level was a great room with a kitchen on one end and a slouchy comfortable lounging area on the other. Guitars stood in one corner, with a brown leather chair and an old upright piano on the eastern wall. Sun came in from the picture windows that opened to a large deck.

As her eyes took in the open rafters and extended ceiling, she said, "Makes me think of a ski lodge."

He followed her gaze, shoving his hands in the back pockets of his jeans and rocking on his heels. "Had it designed for light and comfort. Oh, and the view." He pointed to the river. Across the water was a flat sandy area with two lawn chairs.

"You own this place?" she asked him.

"Yep. Bought the property years ago when prices were low. Moved here three years ago and had the house built."

She must have looked skeptical because he went on, somewhat defensively, as if offended he had to explain it to her. "Listen, I sold a song to a female singer that hit the country top ten and the royalties paid for this house."

"I thought you came here because you couldn't make it in Nashville?"

"Who told you that?"

She shrugged her shoulders, flushing.

He laughed then and seemed to relax. "What did you think? I was just some loser musician?"

"I guess I figured the EMT thing was your steady job."

He nodded. "It is. The life of a songwriter, you never know when or if you'll sell another song, so I like to keep my bases covered. Let's just say I'm conservative with money." He paused and sank into the couch, resting his feet on the rustic-looking wooden coffee table. "Although, women in my past have referred to it as cheap." He sighed and raised one eyebrow in a gesture that made her wonder what those other women were like. And how many were there? Crossing his arms, he grinned. "This make you like me better?"

Her voice was dry. "Where you live has nothing to do with who you are."

"I agree," he said.

Lee's gaze drifted to twin paintings of red poppies that hung over the couch. "The paintings are nice."

"Thanks. One of my sisters painted them." His voice was soft but wary. She understood he was worried he might frighten her away. "I'm glad you called."

She imagined sitting on his lap, feeling his arms around her. "I'm sorry about the other day," she said.

He put up his hands. "Don't apologize. It was my fault. I've been kicking myself ever since." He glanced at his guitars and then back to her. "I can't stand to see you cry. To think I caused you any further pain, it makes me crazy."

"Not you. Never you." The tears were there again, in the back of her throat.

"I don't ever want to be the person who makes you cry."

"I know," she said, gently.

He was quiet for a moment and when he spoke his words sounded thick. "Lee, why did you call?"

"I wanted to talk. Not to just anyone. To you."

He raised his eyebrows. "Really?"

She smiled. "You've worn me down. What can I say?"

"I say I love it."

"Zac came by about a job and we had a little episode, so to speak." She pushed her hair behind her ears.

He sat up, swinging his feet to the floor. "Your neck is all red. Did he do that to you?"

She pushed her fingers into the soft skin of her neck, mildly surprised to find it tender. "Yes, but it's fine." She told him then what happened with Zac, sparing no details. He listened quietly, becoming absolutely still when she told him that Zac threatened her.

After she finished he got up and began to pace behind the couch. "You have no idea how I want to take him behind the restaurant and beat the crap out of him."

"Tommy, I'm not telling you this so you can beat him up. I'd like to share something with you but it's hard to say. Especially when you're moving around like a caged animal."

He stopped and looked at her. "Anything." He put his hands on the back of the couch as if that would keep him from moving.

She took a deep breath. "Something in Zac's eyes made me think of my husband. And my mother. You see, Dan conceived and developed a game for our first company based on a world view of randomness. In the game, metaphoric life threw you unexpected joy and tragedy and your job was to maneuver around it and if you were clever and hard-working enough you could win. But his second game, Deep Black, was based on the world view that no matter what you did, your weaknesses combined with chance would destroy you and there was nothing you could do about it."

"Sounds fun," said Tommy sarcastically.

"He thought for gamers it would be the ultimate." She went to the window. "But in the irony of ironies, he couldn't get the damn thing to work. And ultimately it destroyed him."

Tommy was staring at her now, a helpless quality on his face. She went on. "There was this darkness in Dan that I pretended not to see, this way of looking at the world that made him feel defeated even in the midst of all the fortunate things that happened to us. My mother was the same. She gave up hope of ever winning the game, succumbed to this idea that everything was stacked against her so why do anything but drink? They were afraid and I've been too, all the time, even before Dan died." She put a hand on her stomach and saw Tommy's eyes follow her movements and then fix back to her face. "I had my lists and my work and my perfectly ordered home with the coordinated hangers in my closet, all to manage my fear." She paused, trying to find the words to say what she meant.

"Go on," he said.

She gazed at the rafters of his living room, steadying her voice. "For the first time this afternoon I understand what went wrong with their lives. They gave into the fear. And I felt compassion for them, maybe even forgiveness." She threw up her hands. "And I don't know where that leaves me, except really sad." She stopped talking, as suddenly as she started, and stood with her hands poised in the air as if she might go on but instead closed her mouth and gazed at Tommy.

He moved to the couch and sat with his hands folded in his lap. His eyes were open and seeing. "What else?"

She paused for a moment, trying to find the right words. "I wonder if there's something in me that made the two most important people in my life turn dark and hopeless?"

He inched forward to the edge of the couch as if he might stand. He brushed his hands through his hair. "Lee, their demons had nothing to do with you."

"Do you have demons? What keeps you up at night?"

He smiled, running his middle finger along the top of his lip. "The thought of you keeps me awake lately. But my demons were put to rest a long time ago, with God's help. Now I find peace everywhere."

"What does that even mean?"

He smiled. "Sounds a little woo-woo, huh?"

She nodded. "Yes."

"This morning I sat on my deck and listened to the sound of the river, which I've come to think of as alive because it's ever changing, like us. This time of year the water's still pretty high and, if you listen carefully, you can hear the current moving towards the ocean, the sound almost imperceptible because it's so quiet—a low steady drone punctuated with burbles over rocks and the gush of the mild rapids just down from my swimming hole. The sun was warm on my back and I sipped an espresso I made for myself with a smidge of half-and-half, just the way I like it. I felt abundant and at peace and grateful—this surge of wholeness that I know is God."

She sighed and looked toward the river. "I used to feel that as a child, but it's been a long time since I felt that kind of peace. Or hope." The sun on the water sparkled in little bits of light. She had the sudden desire to strip off her clothes and dive in deep, to feel it ripple next to her skin and run through her hair. She turned to him and smiled with a slight tremor in her voice. "Something about this place," she said, indicating outside the window, "something about you, makes me less guarded. I find myself revealing things lately that I usually keep to myself. And I don't know why. I don't know why it's you. Or this place."

He got up from the couch and stood next to her at the window. "Whatever the reason, I'm pleased." He tilted her face and they stood for a moment, their breath intermingled, her lips slightly parted, his gently closed, until she shifted towards him, almost like a fall. And he caught her mouth with his, moving in a soft capture of her top lip and then inside to the warm flesh of her mouth. His lips were soft, not hard as she'd imagined. He tasted faintly of chocolate. Everything disappeared but the feel of the kiss, of him. Finally he pulled away, tracing her jaw with his fingertips, and she watched the pulse at his neck that seemed to beat with her own hammering heart. "I don't know what I'm doing," she said.

"You're letting me kiss you." He kissed her again, harder this time, and she let her body melt into him, feeling the muscles of his legs press into her own.

She put her face into his collarbone, breathed in his scent, felt the heat through his t-shirt. "This can't go anywhere," she said. "It's too soon, and I'm not staying in town."

"Alright."

"I still feel married."

He nodded and felt the tender spots on her neck, looking into her eyes. "I can understand that. It's too soon. I'm rushing you."

She smiled and plucked at the collar of his shirt. "That's what I just said."

"I learned that technique in therapy. It's called mirroring."

She laughed. "It's very disarming."

"Let me take you to dinner. Dinner's harmless enough."

She moved away, placing her fingertips on the glass window, suddenly cringing, thinking of Dan's eyes the last time she saw him. She changed the subject. "Why are the chairs on the other side of the river?"

"Because the sand's soft and fine over there. Keeps you from making excuses about jumping in the water if you have to swim to the chairs."

"What about a book? How do you get that to the other side?"

"I have a raft. Good for books and beer."

"What if you can't swim?"

"You can't swim?"

"No."

"Want me to teach you?"

"I'm too old to learn to swim."

"Nonsense. The feel of that sand between your toes—it'll be worth it."

They were quiet as they drove south in Tommy's truck until they crossed the Oregon border into California. Lee felt shriveled and strange in the seat next to a man, on a date when only months before she'd been married. Her vow to act with bravery diminished.

"You're sorry you agreed to come." He said it as a statement.

She was apologetic. "It's not you. Just that...I don't know. It feels like homesickness almost. That kind of strange."

"You want to turn back?"

"No." The road began to curve along the highway above the Smith River. They traveled at a slow pace along the two-lane highway carved out of the side of the mountain. There were blind curves where you couldn't be sure what awaited, as in another car, a logging truck, or even a deer. She watched Tommy to discern if he was a skilled driver.

"You can relax, I've driven this road many times in the last couple of years," he said.

"My grandparents were killed on a road like this."

He put his hand on her knee for an instant. "I'll take good care of you, don't worry."

After a few miles she decided he must be good at all things physical, including maneuvering this dangerous but beautiful span of highway. He adjusted the car's speed at the curves and accelerated just beyond their crests. At one point they fell behind a slow truck but instead of trying to pass he seemed in no hurry, so she settled into her seat and soaked up the view.

They drove south, next to the mountainside. On the other side of the highway was the Smith River. Every mile or so, she saw the green water playing and sparkling in and around the gray river stones. She waved her hand around to indicate the terrain. "Since I've been back here, I'm struck by how dramatic the beauty is. Everything's so big."

"Vivid." Tommy smiled at her, taking his eyes from the road for an instant. "For a person who doesn't want to stay here, you sound like you're falling in love again with a childhood sweetheart."

She laughed and brushed her hair behind her ear. "You don't know what you're talking about."

"We'll see about that," he laughed in return.

Along the way, Tommy answered her questions and offered information about his life, surprising her with his candor. She listened, resting her head on the back of the car's seat, eyes shifting between his moving lips and the river in the canyon below, absorbing his story, absorbing Tommy.

He was forty-two years old and it astonished him to be middle-aged because he felt the same about things as when he was young. The possibility of everything still ran through him and he began most days with excited anticipation in his stomach, like he remembered from Christmas Day as a child. His life felt good to him, like he was where he belonged. He was thankful to have the freedom to play music and write songs. He looked forward to his shifts at the firehouse and playing with the band in the evenings. He loved the feel of the air in this corner of the world because it was dry and unspoiled by smog or anything man-made. It was the arid heat of the summers that he loved the most, the way the sun dried and warmed your skin after a swim in the river water.

He believed life held endless possibility, even after two marriages and a somewhat inconsistent musical career. He attributed it to his early childhood, when they were migrant workers, recent immigrants from Mexico. His parents talked about what a blessing it was to be in this country. "Nothing but possibility in America," his father said at family dinners.

"Do you wish you were a rich and famous singer?" Lee asked him, hoping the question wouldn't offend.

"I can't remember if I ever dreamt that large." He remembered the bands that played the county fair when he was a kid and that he was overwhelmed with the beauty of live performance. He thought it was glorious, how the music floated out from the stage and touched him where he sat in the bleachers with his brother. "I guess I wanted to be like them but now I get a thrill from expressing my unique point of view in a song I've composed. I love it when the crowd—small as they may be some nights—enjoys my performance."

His mother said he sang before he talked. It started with an old guitar his father had around and he strummed on it, trying to figure out how to make it sound like the records on their old phonograph. When he was ten his mother found him a guitar instruction manual at a used bookstore and little by little he taught himself how to play and read music.

His freshman year in high school he had an English teacher named Ms. Cooper. She made them all try to write a poem. He saw they were songs without music. He stayed up until 2:00 a.m. the day their poem was due, working on it, trying to find the particular words that would articulate his thoughts. When Ms. Cooper passed back the poems days later, there was a sticky note attached to his paper. It said, "This work is impressive. Try putting it to music and you might have magic."

It was the little things that inspired him. The pudgy fingers of his baby niece or the way a tulip bent in a vase like a bowing ballerina. The words just kind of stacked together in conjunction with the notes until it became a song.

He spent over fifteen years in Nashville, trying to break into the business. One day he thought, this is no kind of life. It occurred to him that his songs caught more attention as demos to bands and singers that already had recording contracts. The songs made him unique. That year he got an agent who peddled his songs to the major talents and since then he'd sold at least one a year. It was a decent living and allowed him to live his life next to the river. "I can never walk away from the music. It's cost me some things too, along the way. But it's all about measurement—how much can you give up for something you love."

Lee nodded, thinking of the baby growing inside her.

Tommy glanced at her, taking his eyes off the road for a split second. "You look sleepy. Am I boring you?"

"No, it's your voice. It relaxes me."

"Is that a good thing?"

She yawned and nestled further into the seat. "Can't be bad. Nothing else seems to work. Keep talking so we can test the theory."

He was the second in a line of six children, the oldest now his brother was gone. His parents were married for fifty years and died within months of each other three years ago. His four siblings were all girls and he loved growing up surrounded by all those women. When the girls talked, which they did constantly, he learned a lot of useful information. Their house was bilingual and you never heard such a racket as four girls talking, bickering, and laughing, two languages intermixed into a sort of music.

He missed his mother. Before her death he talked to her twice a week over the telephone. Sometimes he still picked up the receiver to call her before remembering. The loss was fresh each time, like an empty spot in his heart. "After she died I realized no one will ever know me, understand me, or love me as much. She was interested in every small and large accomplishment, the details of what I ate for breakfast, even the process of every song I wrote."

"You were lucky."

He looked over at her and she dismissed her comment with a wave of her hand. "Never mind, we're talking about you, not me."

He went on to tell her about a time when he was five years old and was up on top of a ladder picking apples. There was a kind of seat on one of the branches, so he straddled it and watched a cloud that looked like an elephant drift by until his eyes got sleepy. The next thing he knew, he jerked awake as he fell out of the tree, hitting the ground hard but unhurt. His mother screamed from where she was across the orchard. She ran to him and felt his legs. Then she smacked him with a stick twice on his bottom hard enough that it stung. "I said to her, 'Why are you beating me?' and she said, 'Because you scared me.'" He glanced at Lee and laughed. "I made sure never to fall asleep in a tree again.

"My sisters are like my papi, cerebral, mathematical," he continued, keeping his eyes on the highway. "They're practical about life instead of thinking in emotion and metaphor like I do.

I'm like my mother, emotional and artistic. After my brother's death, we fell into the pain. The girls analyzed it to try and make sense of it. Grief catches up with you eventually and when it does it's more painful, like an earthquake that shakes with more and more ferocity. Anyway, life isn't understandable. Only God understands and we have to wait until the end, where I imagine I'll see my questions answered, spread out across the heavens in waves of clarity."

The highway forked, one way to the California Redwoods, the other to Brookings, the first coastal town in Oregon when traveling north on Highway 101. "We're heading up to Brookings," he said. "My friends own a Mexican restaurant north of town."

She was sleepy, murmured a response, and closed her eyes. She felt his hand touch the side of her face. And then she was asleep.

She awakened when Tommy braked for a red light, and she sat up in the seat, looking out the window at the gray, soggy town. "Sorry, I fell asleep."

"No problem. I have that effect on women." He grinned and braked for another light.

"I'm just so tired lately."

"My sisters say the first trimester's like that."

She wiped the side of her mouth, hoping she hadn't drooled in her sleep, and reached for her purse at her feet. She ran a comb through her hair and swiped her nose and forehead with a powder compact. She coated her lips with a smear of peachy lipstick. "Do you know a lot about women because of your sisters?"

"Not as much as I need to." He laughed.

It was cloudy and sixty-two degrees according to Tommy's temperature gauge when they pulled into the parking lot of a run-down strip mall and parked in front of a Mexican restaurant. "This is where we're eating?" she said. She looked up and saw a neon twirling sign, reading Los Gatos.

Tommy laughed as he pulled the parking brake. "Don't be such a snob. Best Mexican food in Oregon." He reached across her, brushing her leg, and pulled a bottle of wine from underneath her seat. "Terrible wine though, so I always bring my own."

"No ocean view?"

He put his arm on the back of her seat and kissed her neck, sending a shiver up her spine. "Wouldn't that be kind of predictable?" he asked, his eyes on her mouth.

"I guess," she began to answer but he covered her mouth with his in a gentle kiss that made her heart pound.

He grinned, pulling back and grazing his finger along her bottom lip. "Sorry, I had to do that before we went in or I wouldn't have been able to focus on my dinner. Stay where you are. I'll get your door."

The air smelled of salt, seaweed, and fish. As was her habit now in any public place, she scanned the parking lot for Von. It was empty except for several teenagers clothed in black, smoking cigarettes. He escorted her inside with his hand on her back. The restaurant was small, with an orange and yellow patterned linoleum floor, grease stains on the dingy walls, and cheap prints of Mexican art on the walls.

A round, gray-haired Mexican woman with a heavy accent greeted them. "Tomas, so good to see you." They embraced, lingering for a moment, her soft short frame next to his tall, lean one. Maria turned to Lee. She enfolded Lee's chilled fingers into her plump warm hands. "I'm Maria. Welcome." She tweaked underneath Lee's chin. "So beautiful. Come sit." Mexican music played overhead. Laughter and voices in Spanish came from the kitchen.

They slid into a booth with shiny green plastic, cracked in places, the stuffing exposed. Maria set two menus and two glasses of ice water in red plastic cups on the table. They were the only people in the dining area except for a middle-aged couple in a back booth. She wagged her finger at Tommy. "Nothing too spicy for the señorita." She turned to Lee. "He order everything fire hot."

"Whatever Lee wants." He handed Maria the bottle of wine, which she tucked under her arm.

Maria put a hand on the top of Tommy's head. "He so fancy after he come back from Nashville has to bring his own wine." She fluffed his hair. "I remember him so little, picking apples from a ladder." She took her hand off his head and pulled out a small pad from the front of her apron. "He sing all the time so we always knew where he was. Up in trees, singing and singing."

"Now don't tell all my secrets." He winked at Lee. "I knew I shouldn't bring you here."

Maria left with the wine, promising chips and salsa when she returned. Tommy pointed to the kitchen. "Maria and her husband were friends of my parents, before we moved to Bellingham. We all picked fruit back then."

Maria dropped off their chips, the bottle of wine, and took their dinner order. Tommy poured Lee a half glass of wine and a generous one for himself.

She pushed the glass away from her. "I don't drink."

"All the time or because of the baby?"

"All the time."

He looked like he might ask a question but thought better of it and moved the glass closer to him. "Sorry, I should've asked before I poured." He watched her. She could see the clicking of his thoughts as he figured and wondered about her.

"You drink a lot?" She tried to sound light but even to herself she sounded anxious for the answer to be no.

"Not enough to be a problem. Ed, from the band, we're always on the lookout for a good ten dollar bottle of wine. We enjoy it, but for fun, not survival." He thumped on the table with his fingers and scooped salsa on a chip. "To that end, I have a little something to celebrate tonight." He popped the whole chip in his mouth and chewed.

She looked around the place and lowered her voice, teasing him. "I'd hate to see where you'd take me if it was just a regular night."

He put his hand on his heart and laughed. "That hurts." He scooped more salsa onto a chip and waved it in the air as he talked. "Actually, I sold a song to a fairly major recording artist in Nashville. Just found out this morning."

He ate another chip, wiped a stray diced tomato off the side of his mouth, and pulled a thin paper napkin out of the dispenser next to the salt and cleaned his finger. "The weird thing is, I never thought of myself as a country songwriter, but there you go. I mean, whoever heard of a Mexican country singer?" He smiled and looked to the ceiling. "But who am I to question God?"

Her voice was teasing but even she heard the bitterness at the edges of her tone. "I'd like to ask God a few questions."

He looked amused and swirled his wine. "What would you ask him, or her?"

The question surprised her. "I was teasing. I'm not used to people talking so freely about God as if He really exists. My friends in Seattle never talk about this kind of thing—they're too busy being smart."

"I remember that from my Nashville days." He cocked his head, serious now. "Really, what would you ask God if you could?"

She spoke quietly. "Why does he hate me?"

His eyes filled with tears. "Lee." He reached for her hand but she withdrew it from the table's surface, resting it on her lap. They sat like that for a few moments, the weight of her comment between them. She stared at the salsa bowl, empty except for flecks of cilantro and spices stuck to the insides of the curved ceramic. "Lee," he repeated her name, this time so tenderly that she lifted her face to look at him. "God doesn't hate you and both He and I wish we could take away your pain."

She felt the tears start and reached for his hand. "I'm sorry. I'm a terrible date."

"No, you're perfect."

"Thank you. Thank you for taking me out." She pulled her hand away and fiddled with her hair, suddenly self-conscious. "You a recovering Catholic then or you still with the church?"

He smiled. "Recovered. The Catholic Church is not for the free spirited. Oh, I shudder when I think what my mother would think if she heard me say that. She'd yell at me in rapid Spanish. She might even try to beat me with a stick." He paused and they both chuckled, the tension gone. He twisted in the booth, one of his feet brushing against her crossed ankles. A shot of energy ran through her. "As a kid I kept looking for God in the midst of all that ritual but found him inside my own heart after my brother died."

"I'd think that would make you doubt God, not get closer to him."

"I hit so low the only thing I could find was God, way down deep inside me." He blinked and ran his hand through his hair. "Am I scaring you off with all this religious talk?" He held his lip between his thumb and his index finger, studied a chip and said under his breath, "That's part of my problem with women."

"You talk too much?"

His brown eyes were sincere. "Yeah and about all the wrong things."

Maria set steaming plates of enchiladas, tamales, and refried beans on the table. "Enjoy, mi amor." She patted Tommy's shoulder and he rested the side of his head for the briefest of moments on her hand, the familiarity between them of people who've known and loved each other for a lifetime. Lee felt a rush of envy and like an outsider. She ate a small bite of enchilada, detecting a slight smoky flavor from the sauce. "Delicious."

"Best Mexican you'll ever have," he said.

They ate in silence for a few minutes and Lee was surprised to see Tommy's meal almost gone when she looked up from her plate. She put down her fork, her appetite suddenly replaced with the familiar guilty feeling in the pit of her stomach. How could she be enjoying herself this much?

As if he read her thoughts, he said softly, "It's just dinner."

"I know," she said.

He said, "After my first divorce—"

She interrupted, "First divorce?"

"Uh, yeah. I've been married twice. I mentioned that earlier."

"Yes, I guess you did. It just didn't sink in until you said it again." She sat with this knowledge for a moment. What kind of man married twice? A good one with either bad luck or terrible taste in women or both? "Two? Really?"

He raised an eyebrow and smiled. "Right. Two. What can I say? I'm an eternal optimist."

"Two. Well, better than three, I suppose." After all, who was she to pass judgment, given everything? Strangely, it made him more appealing. Maybe she wasn't the only one with some history. She felt relieved. Two divorces was a kind of failure that he must feel deeply. He wasn't perfect after all and he might understand how another person was flawed, how they might have a trunk full of baggage. Yes, she thought, I could live with that. But then she remembered she had a cold-blooded killer looking for her. Not exactly the same, she thought, as two benign ex-wives. She wasn't free to fall in love with this man. She knew she should tell him the truth before it was too late. But she remained silent, pushing aside the thoughts.

Tommy was looking at her now, trying to read whether his past was some kind of stop sign or not. She went on, casually, trying to put him at ease. "Have you dated much since your last divorce?"

"I don't think I should answer that."

She laughed. "Oh, God, how many girlfriends has it been? A dozen? Two dozen?"

His face was somber. "This is my first serious date since my second divorce."

She felt a shot of ice go through her. "That's impossible. I see how the women look at you."

He cleared his throat. "Look, I'm not a saint. There have been a few women I've spent time with over the years, so to speak, in a casual way. But they knew the score going in—nothing serious. I learned a lot from my marriages but they were so difficult to get over I haven't wanted to risk getting my heart broken again." He paused and she could see him weighing whether or not to say it. "Until now."

She changed the subject, fast. "Tell me about your marriages. What happened?"

The first marriage was to Sherri, the piano player in his band when he was just out of college. She was this willow branch of a girl, tall, pale blond, with long fingers that whipped up and down the piano keyboard with such grace that it mesmerized him. But there was this part of her that craved attention from other men. He wanted to extinguish it by making her belong to him and talked her into getting married. It was a mistake to try and cage something that wanted to be free, but he was young, romantic, in love. She had this need to be desired by men as a validation that she was worth something, combined with a compulsive attraction towards older men. All of which made him worried all the time that she would cheat on him. He was suspicious and jealous, never able to relax into the relationship because of it. He was only happy at the end of the night when she was tucked next to him on their lumpy mattress in their cramped apartment. He knew in those moments that she was his for at least the next seven hours.

One day after his afternoon shift at a coffee house, he came home early. He opened the door as quietly as he could in case she was napping. Their band played late into the night and she was pale all the time, like she was tired and malnourished. He worried about her and wished he made enough money so that she wouldn't have to work at the diner in the mornings as a waitress. For all these reasons he tiptoed over the hallway's musty green carpet to their front door and made sure his keys didn't rattle and twisted the doorknob so it wouldn't make a clicking sound when he closed it. So he didn't actually see them, he heard them. There was a soft moan, one he knew like it was eternally etched into his heart, and the creak of the bedsprings, then the man's voice.

The voice belonged to their next door neighbor, who was fifty if he was a day. Tommy stood rooted in the doorway, unable to move or think. After a moment he turned and walked out the door, as soundlessly as he entered. He sat in his '82 blue Honda Civic, watching the window of their bedroom. After a while, the curtains moved and he saw her open the window a crack and then move away from view. After a few seconds she stepped back into the frame of the window and looked towards his car. She flinched when she saw him sitting in his car, a small movement illustrating guilt. Then he saw her understand that he knew. She stood in the window for a long moment as if considering what to do next and then she turned, disappearing from sight. A few minutes later the door to the apartment building opened and she came out with his light blue suitcase, her mouth set and determined. She walked to his car, opening the passenger door with her long beautiful fingers and then shoved the suitcase onto the floor mat over the coffee stain from her spilled coffee cup months before. She said, "You can get the rest of your stuff later. I'm sorry, but I don't want to be married. I'm too young and the way you are, well, it makes me feel like I'm suffocating."

He concluded his story by saying, "It took me eight years before I was willing to try again."

Lee pushed her plate aside and wiped her mouth with the napkin. "But you did."

"I did. Blindly, too. Without reserve." He was twenty-nine the year he met Heather, and thirty when they were married. She was the daughter of a Dallas doctor, a debutante, with an art history degree and a job in a modern art gallery in Nashville. She was spoiled but intelligent, feisty, funny, the life of every party. Her father threw them a huge wedding, the kind that is written about in the society section of the newspaper. He remembered standing in one of the upstairs bedrooms of her parents' palatial Dallas home before the ceremony, wondering if this was the right thing. He was a poor musician, still trying to make it as a singer, and she was the daughter of sophisticated, white Texans. Heather's mother watched him and he imagined her calculating how dark their children would be once he broke into their blond, blue-eyed gene pool. He knew she hated him and wondered if that hatred would spill over into their marriage. He worried that one day Heather might wake up and see his dark skin, his depleted bank account, and his crazy loud Mexican family as a liability instead of a quirky, interesting novelty. But as he stood that day looking into the garden of her parents' house, he couldn't imagine she could ever change and he married her because he loved her. He quit the band and went back to school to become an EMT. He got a job with the fire department and they decided to try for a baby. They tried and tried, and she did change, with each day that passed without a pregnancy. She got this hard quality, fed by her obsession, taking her temperature twice a day and plotting ovulation, calling him at work to tell him to come home, that it was time to make a baby. Their intimate life became more and more forced and he began to feel depressed and isolated. He spent more time away from their home, away from her, because he could see how she watched him, blaming him for their lack of children. After a year she insisted he get tested and it turned out it was him, just as she suspected. The doctor thought it might have something to do with the pesticides when he was a child, but really they couldn't know why. They had been married for four years and although she said she didn't blame him, it all fell apart after that. They lived together like hostile roommates for another year. He could feel her seething with anger and blame, hating him for who he was, an immigrant's son poisoned by a rich man's orchards. He started going to therapy. He tried to get her to go with him but she wouldn't, saying no one in her family was ever crazy and that she didn't need to be cross-examined by some shrink. He tried to explain to her that the therapist wasn't an attorney and that they help you work through issues and it wasn't about being crazy or not. But she was gone, the fun-loving open girl he married. After another year he left. They were divorced six months later. Six months after that she married the young, blond doctor at her father's practice. He heard they had four children now.

Lee shifted in her seat, played with her knife, shook her head. "I'm sorry. I mean, about the baby thing."

"It's been difficult, thinking I won't get to know what it feels like to be a father. My former shrink would probably say that's why I have this compulsion to help the kids in town. Y'know, fulfilling some kind of fatherly need."

"Doesn't matter if that's the case. You're still doing a lot of good. When I was a kid, my mother was, well you know. It was the art department at school that saved me."

He gazed at her for a moment. "May I ask you something?"

"As long as I don't have to answer if I don't want to."

"Fair enough. Were you happy with your husband?"

She avoided his eyes by studying the Mexican print of a cross between a row of cactuses. "I didn't think much about it. Happy, not happy, what does that really mean? I was committed. We had a shared vision about the kind of life we wanted."

"Vision?"

"Dan was obsessed with this mantra, 'Millionaire by Thirty,' and we made a lot of decisions around that idea."

"Is that what you wanted, too?"

Her face was damp with perspiration. "Honestly, I don't even know. I was afraid to spend my life in poverty. I craved security, stability, all the things I needed as a kid and didn't get." She picked up the salsa bottle and rubbed her fingers over the ridges on the glass. "I was lonely a lot because he worked all the time. We weren't close like I imagined we should be but we never fought. He was always nice to me, generous, respectful. There was love but there was also a large distance between us. Looking back I see how disconnected we were and how willing I was to accept things the way they were without asking for more."

"Why didn't you?" he asked her, his eyes probing but his voice gentle.

"I didn't know how, which he interpreted as remote, unemotional. But it's not the case and I always thought I'd have time to tell him, later. I didn't know there would be no later."

"I'm sorry."

She put down the salsa bottle. "There was no passion between us and I longed for that."

He ran his fingers up the inside of her arm. "I find it hard to believe a man could keep his hands off you given half the chance."

Her arm tingled with goose bumps. "In the beginning he worked hard at that part of our relationship but after a while he gave up on me."

He shook his head, grasping her arm in his hand. "Give me half a chance and I'll show you how good it can be."

"I might disappoint you."

"No way."

"All the stuff you went through, did it make you this way?"

"What way is that?"

"So comfortable with yourself."

"I know what I want. I know exactly who I am. That's what you get when you've lived and loved as deeply as I have. That's the prize." He took a gulp of wine. "I don't want you to think I'm a stalker or anything but I saw you the morning before I met you at the restaurant."

"Let me guess, was I wandering the streets looking for a job?"

"No, you were coming out of the grocery store and you had on this lime green pea coat and tall black boots. There was a little girl giving away puppies and you leaned over to pet them, so graceful, the way you moved, and I could see the profile of your face as you held one of them and I can't explain it, because it's never happened to me before, but I sensed you on another level than just what I could see with my eyes. I thought, the man that's with that beautiful creature is the luckiest man on the planet. And then there you were that afternoon at the restaurant, beautiful even soaking wet, and I couldn't believe my luck that you didn't wear a ring.

"Then we got the call about your fire and finding you sick and scared and pregnant and, I don't know, I guess I thought it might be fate."

"Fate?"

"I know. Everything logical says to give you time, but this feeling of urgency just keeps poking at me, like it has to be now or it will never be."

She stared at him. "You don't know me."

"I know you have a secret. I know it's something that scares the hell out of you because you have the look of a hunted animal. And I know you should tell me what it is so I can fix it and we can live happily ever after."

She smiled. "You're a lunatic."

He shrugged his shoulders, sighing without a hint of apology. "I know."

On the way home they were quiet, listening to an old Emmylou Harris CD Lee remembered from her childhood. When they reached River Valley she should have insisted he drop her at her home, she knew that. Instead, she kept silent when he passed the turnoff for her driveway, closing her eyes and enjoying the rhythm of the car over the bumpy road and the lyrics of the song. "I would walk all the way from Boulder to Birmingham, just to see you, to see your face."

Inside his house, she sat on the couch, listening to his movements from the kitchen, the opening and closing of a cupboard, the whistle of his tea kettle, and the clank of a cup and saucer. He came into the room carrying a tray. "Just tell me I haven't scared you off." He sighed, put the tray on the coffee table, and ran his hand through his hair, looking like a worried puppy.

Right then she wanted to tell him about DeAngelo, how it hung over her and affected everything she did and thought but instead she motioned for him to sit with her. She brought his hand to her face and breathed in his skin, salty and clean. She played with the calluses on the tips of his fingers and pictured them moving on the neck of his guitar and then imagined them running along her skin. "I can't commit to anything. I'm leaving town as soon as I get on my feet."

"Alone? With a baby?"

"I've been alone all my life."

"I see that but everyone needs help at some point."

"Last time I trusted someone, look where it got me. It's best to rely on yourself."

"Like I said, I was born an optimist and I aim to change your mind." He smiled, with an inkling of sadness around his eyes, and kissed her, long and hard, until they were breathless and pressing into one another like crazed teenagers. He looked into her eyes, frightening her with his intensity, and she moved her eyes to his mouth, wondering what and how much he saw when he gazed at her that way. "Stay with me tonight," he said. She nodded, yes.

He pulled her from the couch and led her to his bedroom. The bed was a four poster king, elevated from the floor at least four feet and she wondered how she could get in it without looking like a clumsy ox. He lit two candles on the bedside tables, turned off the lamp, and joined her in the middle of the room. "I want to be able to see you," he said. He unzipped her dress and it fell to the floor around her feet. He ran his hands along the skin of her arms, gazing at her body, and she stiffened, inert with fear, unable to step out of the discarded dress, naked and vulnerable.

"Have I scared you?"

"I was married for a long time."

"We can stop right now and have tea."

She whispered, "No."

He smiled and pulled her close. "Alright then, put your arms around my neck." He lifted her onto the bed and she collapsed onto the pillows, self-conscious of the slight swell of her stomach.

"Just remember I warned you that I'm no good at this," she said.

He propped himself next to her on the bed, casual, like they had all the time in the world. He played with the lace of her bra and she felt her nipples harden and wished for his fingers to reach under the fabric. "When you say no good, what exactly do you mean?"

"I'm sort of stuck, in a manner of speaking."

He kissed the inside of her arm. "Is that code word for orgasm?"

She smiled, blushing. "I guess."

"I guarantee you will not be stuck by the time I'm done with you." The way he spoke, his voice low in his throat, so self assured and good naturedly powerful, made her body ache for the feel of him. As if he read her mind, he slid her panties down her legs, his mouth drifting along with his fingers as he tugged. He unbuttoned his own shirt and took off his pants, picked up her dress from the floor and draped them, like they were lovers themselves, on the back of a large armchair in the corner. He joined her on the bed, hands on her thighs, mouth hot against the cool skin of her neck. He unhooked the clasp of her bra and her heart beat inside her chest. He took an intake of breath when he slipped the bra from her shoulders, revealing her bare breasts. She moved her arm in front of them, blushing. "They're not always this big."

"I'll enjoy them while I can then." He pushed her back on the pillows, kissed her mouth again, this time pulling at her bottom lip with his own, and then moved down to her breasts where his tongue flicked her nipples and something molten ran through her body and she drifted away from anything but the sensation of the electricity between them. He parted from her, breaking the spell for a moment, and opened the drawer next to his bed. "I've been tested, but I'll use a condom until we can have a proper discussion," he said. She stared at the ceiling, thinking how naive she was to not have thought about that kind of protection, and wondered how many women had been in this bed before her. She felt him crouch beside her and heard the snap of the condom but instead of jumping on her like Dan always had, he lay on his side and ran his fingers up and down her thighs and back to her breasts, commanding responses from somewhere inside her. His mouth made trails up her legs, between her legs, her breasts, until she heard herself whimper, and when she thought she couldn't stand another moment, he put his fingers between her legs and stroked her until she moaned. He moved on top of her, holding himself above her on his strong arms to avoid crushing the small roundness of her stomach and she raised her hips to meet him. Her mind blanked of coherent thought, except for the feeling that there was a seed at the core of her body, and it sprouted and grew with each of their movements until she was a throbbing, exploding blossom, pink and ripe.

The only sounds in the room were the low hum of the air conditioner and his ragged breath and her murmurs as they rocked against each other. She felt like an animal, and his movements next to her were like a wild creature too, unrestrained, ardent, and his excitement elevated her own until the climax made her cry out, back arched, legs wrapped around his, hands clutching the skin of his lower back. A split second later, he uttered a short, explosive breath, the side of his face on her neck.

He rolled to his side, his face relaxed, the corners of his mouth lifted in a half smile. He ran his hand over her thigh. "Like I said, his problem, not yours."

She trembled and tears started at the corners of her eyes. He wrinkled his brow and wiped the tears with his thumb. His voice was soft, tender. "Lee, what is it?"

She shook her head, too shy to say she felt somehow unleashed, free, and most of all, grateful. "I've never, not with someone else anyway, had that before."

"It's about time, then, isn't it?" He kissed the sides of her face. "Lee, I have to know something. Was the baby planned between you?"

She looked at the ceiling. "No. He didn't know about it before he died. A baby was never in our mission statement, so to speak." Her voice was hollow. "We hadn't slept together in six months and the year before that it was a handful of times. I don't know if it was that he'd lost the attraction towards me or if it was just symptomatic of his stress over our company. I guess I'll never know."

He swept her hair away from her face. "It wasn't you, trust me." He pulled her to him and they made love again until they fell wet and spent onto the pillows. He turned on his other side and slept, his legs curled just slightly, one side of his face nestled in a soft pillow, the comforter covering the bottom half of his body.

Wide awake, she got out of bed, quiet so as not to wake him, and put on his shirt from the chair, pausing for a moment to breathe in his aftershave from the collar. She tiptoed to the hallway and pulled from her purse a small notebook where she kept her lists and ideas for Riversong. She found a sharpened pencil in the bottom of her purse and tiptoed back to Tommy's room. She sat cross-legged in the oversized armchair and opened to a blank page. In sleep his face was soft and she imagined what he must have looked like as a child. His dark lashes lay against his high cheekbones. His mouth was slack and his breath moved his chest up and down in a steady rhythm.

She sketched the curve of his shoulder first, trying to capture the bulge and bristle of the developed muscle group. As she worked she told herself she should analyze why she was in the bedroom of a stranger after just burying her husband and carrying his child inside her. She should think about how she and Tommy were doomed to part and that she might hurt him and herself the longer she stayed. But those thoughts were so distant as to not even be real. Her mind seemed unlike her own, empty of the precise rational thought she'd built her life around. She was only a body. A body that only yesterday was drained of warm blood and soft tissue and was now rushing, pulsating with life. Her skin that had been reduced to dry crepe paper was replaced with the flush of sweet dewy cells. She was weak and thirsty for this love, for the touch of this man's hand, for this bloom. She would drink from the well as long as she could, as it would have to last her a lifetime.

She sketched until the dawn brought the first of the day's light, watching him, trying to capture every nuance of his face and torso on the page. She had four drawings by the time she heard the first morning bird's song and was suddenly tired and cold. She climbed into bed then, pulling the comforter up to her shoulders and resting her head next to his on the pillow. He stirred and reached out, pulling her to him. His fingers felt along her hip and down her leg like they were reading Braille. She sighed and closed her eyes, putting her hand on the side of his torso. His skin was cold there and she pulled the comforter over him and moved so their bodies were against each other. He whispered in her ear, "You didn't sleep, did you?"

"No. It's just five o'clock now."

"Sleep. I'll keep my hands off you until at least nine."

"How did you know I didn't sleep?"

"I don't know. I just did."

CHAPTER SEVENTEEN

ON SUNDAY, in her backyard, Lee draped a white sheet over a borrowed table from the restaurant. She arranged canning jars filled with flowers and tea lights in the middle of the table. She set four places with plates, silverware, wine glasses, and white table napkins folded like small hats. She smiled to herself, enjoying the simplistic beauty.

Annie, in Lee's kitchen, hummed along to the radio amidst the sounds of chopping and clanging pans. Alder kicked his soccer ball outside the gate in an imaginary game, his cries of triumph making their way over the fence.

She walked to the front yard as Alder dropped his ball and jumped up to a tree branch to hang like a monkey. Lee sat in the rocking chair on her repaired porch and watched a pair of hummingbirds drinking the nectar of the hibiscus Ellen had planted in the hanging planters.

Two weeks into May now, the thermometer hanging by the door said seventy-six and the air smelled like promise and fresh grass. She heard a low hum of a truck engine and tires crunching on the gravel road and looked up to see Tommy's truck bouncing down the driveway. He stopped next to the patch of grass and jumped from his truck to join her on the porch. "What time you leave this morning? I woke up and there was no trace of you."

"I had an early meeting with a supplier."

"What's that smell?"

"Dinner. First meal cooked in there since 1972."

He laughed. "That the chef?"

She nodded and pointed to Alder, who was now chasing his ball in a circle around the yard. "That's Alder. Her son."

He sat on the new steps and stretched his legs. "What're we eating?"

"This is a work thing."

His face sobered. "You sleep in my bed two nights in a row and I can't come for dinner?"

"It's not Mayberry supper club."

He picked up a pebble from the flower bed next to the step and lobbed it across the grass to the gravel road. "Dinner too much of an admission we're involved?"

"Don't make this complicated."

"That's what you do." He hoisted off the steps and stood. "Mike was at the rec center this afternoon. Why didn't you tell me you committed to a partnership with him? He's talking crazy, like you're going to help us save the town."

She shrugged but said, earnestly, "There's something about Mike. I can't say no to him."

"But you can to me?"

"What? No. It's different."

"How?"

"Because I shouldn't have a boyfriend when my husband's been dead less than four months."

"Is that what it is?" He stared at her, cheeks flushed, eyes sharp, a vein in the middle of his forehead bulging. "Or is it something else?"

"I need the money. What do you want me to say?" Her hands shook and she felt the sting of tears behind her eyelids.

He rested his head on a beam and looked towards the driveway. "I hear from Mike that you said you'd stay but you tell me you're leaving. Which is it?"

"I, I don't know."

"I should go."

"No, please stay." She moved to where he stood on the steps. She touched a strand of his hair that curled around the neck of his shirt and breathed in his skin's citrus, salty scent. "I'm still working some things out." She couldn't think what else to say and played with the collar of his shirt. "Starting to see why my husband killed himself?"

He stood stiff, silent, rubbing the scar on his cheek. "You do this joke thing when you want to avoid saying the truth. To answer your question, no, I can't see one reason why any man could bring himself to leave a life that had you in it."

"Is that a lyric from one of your songs?" she said, softly, feeling the tears form at the corners of her eyes.

He shook his head and smiled. "You're going to drive me crazy."

She put her arms around his neck and pressed into him. "I'm sorry, just stay for dinner."

He put his face into her hair. "Tell me your secret. I'll help you."

Still pressed into him, she said quietly, "Tommy, you're right that I have a secret. It's something from my past. I'm taking care of it but it's complicated and I can't share it with you."

He pulled back, searching her face. "Why?"

"Because it would put you in danger."

"I don't care."

"I need you to promise me you won't ask me about it again."

He peered at her. "I don't know."

"Just promise me."

"Fine. For now."

She heard footsteps on the gravel driveway. She pulled away from Tommy just as Ellen came around the corner of the house. But she forgot her embarrassment in the instant it took her to stifle a gasp. Ellen's braid had been replaced by an attractive pixie style cut. She had on new clothes too, a floral-print skirt and lilac-colored blouse.

Ellen clapped her hands when she saw Tommy. "I'll be, I didn't know this was a party."

"I kind of invited myself," said Tommy.

"It's just you two. And Alder. Not really a party," said Lee.

"Haven't seen any lights down here in two nights." Ellen looked from Lee to Tommy and back again. "You been busy?"

Lee felt her cheeks blaze with heat and saw Tommy stifle a smile. "Ellen, your hair looks nice," said Lee.

"The ladies down at the salon talked me into it." Ellen waved her hand in the air, as if it was the ordinary course of things. "I thought I might ask that nice Verle out on a date."

"A date?" said Lee.

Ellen chuckled. "What? The old biddy can't have some fun?"

"But, I mean…" Lee stumbled on the words. "How old is Verle anyway?"

Tommy laughed. "Old enough to go on a date."

Ellen picked lint off the front of her skirt. "How old is he, Tommy?"

"I think he's sixty-eight."

Ellen clapped her hands together, beaming. "Perfect. I always went for younger guys."

Tommy laughed again and then lowered his voice, as if Verle were in the next room. "Now, don't tell him I told you this but he has a little crush on you."

Ellen whipped her head around to stare at Tommy. "Are you sure?"

Lee sat in the rocking chair and put her head in her hands.

"As a matter of fact," Tommy glanced back at Lee, "I think he might be free tonight." He reached in his pocket and pulled out his cell phone. "Can we invite him?"

Lee held up her hand. "We don't have enough food." She gave Tommy a pointed look, which he ignored.

Ellen's face fell. "Well, that's just fine. We'll do it some other time."

Lee's heart softened and she waved her hand in the air. "Fine, invite him. I hope Annie can feed all of us."

Tommy went to where she sat in the chair and kneeled, putting his hands on her thighs. "Don't try to control it, just let it unfold."

She smiled, wanting to kiss him, but instead said with a tease and a mock pout in her voice, "You two have to do the dishes."

Tommy whooped, kissed her full on the mouth, and then pushed a couple of buttons on his cell phone. "I should've brought my guitar." He shuffled to the other end of the porch and murmured into the phone.

The pair of hummingbirds hovered near the hibiscus, invisible wings a loud buzz. "I should get a feeder," said Lee.

Ellen stared at Tommy but spoke to Lee. "What's that?"

Lee smiled to herself and sighed. "Never mind." She walked to the kitchen where Annie was cutting onions into large chunks on a thin wooden cutting board. "There are two extra guests coming. Is that okay?"

"There's plenty of food." On the counter were peeled and quartered Golden Delicious apples and small white potatoes washed but still in their skins.

Lee leaned on the counter and looked around the remodeled kitchen. Joshua, the handyman, was good, she had to admit. He'd started with the kitchen and had sanded and painted the cabinets eggshell white, the color Lee had in her condo kitchen. He'd then resurfaced the counters with white tiles that he found on sale at a large discount home repair store. He'd ripped the old linoleum floor out and installed the manufactured wood slabs that would also go in the rest of the house once he was through with the other repairs. The walls he painted a pale yellow and Ellen had made simple white linen curtains for the windows. Ellen lent her the money to replace the old appliances with a black General Electric gas stove and refrigerator. Joshua convinced her to install a dishwasher too, as it would add to the salability of the house. "You've got to have a dishwasher or the ladies won't want to buy," he had said, with a toss of his ponytail. Standing here now, even though she preferred stainless steel appliances, overall, she was pleased with the clean, crisp feel of the new kitchen.

But it wasn't clean tonight. Dirty pans covered the counters, flour powdered the floor, and grease spots speckled the wall by the stove.

Annie saw her looking around the kitchen. "Sorry for the mess." Her plump cheeks were flushed a deep pink and she sounded breathless. She ran her hand down the front of her stained and flour-coated apron. "I'm a sloppy cook. If I keep things in order the food isn't as good."

Lee fluttered her hand and smiled. "It's fine. I'm not here to interfere with an artist at work." Lee peered through the glass door of the oven and breathed in the smell of warm chocolate. "Do I smell chocolate?"

"It's a flourless chocolate hazelnut cake. It has another thirty minutes to bake." She looked at her watch. "It's served cool with a dollop of whipping cream sprinkled with hazelnuts." Annie was wrapping bacon around a long skinny piece of meat. "Pork tenderloins look like a big 'ol tongue, don't you think?" Annie chuckled. "Maybe that's just me." She stabbed toothpicks through the fatty bacon, securing it to the fleshy pink tenderloin.

The timer on the oven began to beep. "That's the crostinis," said Annie. She slipped her left hand into a mitt, yanked open the oven door, and pulled out a baking sheet with three lines of toasted golden pieces of thin bread. She dropped the baking sheet on the counter and a few crostinis slid off the pan onto the floor and broke into pieces.

"My main course tonight is pork tenderloins with apples, dates, and baby potatoes," said Annie. She took string from the pocket of her apron and tied four pieces around the tenderloin, yanked out the toothpicks and tossed them in the sink. Coarsely cut romaine and chunks of Parmesan were piled on a plate. Next to the lettuce was a bowl with a mixture of purple and green grapes. Annie pointed at the salad with the wooden spoon she held in her hand. Drops of the sauce propelled through the air, landing on the fronts of the cabinets. "Every cook should have a Caesar salad with their own secret tweak." She wiped a greasy hand on the front of her apron. "We'll sell a lot of Caesars." She giggled. "I mean, if you choose me." She chopped the grapes in halves, one by one, the juice making puddles on the surface of the cutting board. She pulled out a package of soft goat cheese from the refrigerator and mixed it with finely chopped fresh thyme and oregano. Using a butter knife, Annie spread the goat cheese on the bread and placed three grape halves on the top of each one.

Lee leaned on the sink, filling a glass with tap water and drinking it in two gulps. "This pregnancy makes me hot all the time." She heard Annie sniff and turned to see her wipe something from her cheek. "Annie, are you alright?"

Annie spread the cheese on the last crostini. "I broke up with my boyfriend, and the weird thing is I don't feel that bad, and that makes me feel bad, like why did I waste time with him if I don't even care when we break up? Does that make any sense?" Tears drifted down her flushed cheeks and she wiped them with the back of her hand. Her voice warbled and saliva caught between her tongue and her teeth. "Mostly, I just want this job more than anything in the world. I'm afraid to even think I might actually get the kind of life I've dreamt about, because things like this don't happen to people like me."

"Oh, Annie, what kind of person do you think you are?"

"A mess." She grabbed a paper towel and blew her nose. "I'm always so emotional. They used to mark me down for it in culinary school." She pulled a bowl of uncooked croutons out of the refrigerator, dumped them onto the empty baking sheet, and spread them over the surface of the pan with her bare hand.

A memory came to Lee of college. It was the last day of her junior year and Lee sat before the art professor assigned to judge her final project for the year. It was a series of ten paintings, the culmination of her year's work. She needed a passing grade in order to remain in the program for her senior year. Her professor was a crusty man in his sixties and had taught at the school for at least thirty years. He sat behind his cluttered desk in his small office in the basement of the art school and peered at her over his reading glasses. His office, stacked with art books and papers, smelled of dust and musty paper. She sat before him, quivering with fear, praying silently that he would pass her. He shook his head and stroked under his loose chin. "I'll pass you on for next year, but I'm disappointed in your work. It's good technically and you obviously work hard and you have talent. I can see all that, even though it's not reflected in the pile of crap you turned in this year. Let me tell you something, no one wants to see landscapes of some obscure little village in Oregon. It's been done and no one cares. The modern art world wants edge, excitement, a unique point of view." He took off his glasses and leaned back in his chair, resting his hands on the surface of the desk. His fingernails were long and there were dry irritated patches of skin around his knuckles. "You're the type of student I find hard to teach—detached, insecure, shying around here like a scared little mouse, painting in corners. Your paintings are overworked and empty of anything real. Go out and get laid for Christ's sake, instead of acting like a child. Find some goddamn passion to put in your work. Otherwise, there's not much point. You're just another silly bitch amongst hundreds of other silly bitches. Wouldn't you agree?"

Not only had she not agreed, she had no idea what he was talking about. That afternoon she'd flung all her oil paints off the balcony of her campus-housing apartment and watched as they tumbled and splattered on the concrete into a puddle of brown. The next day she'd gone to the academic office and changed her major to business.

She shook her head and refocused on Annie's face. "Women get accused of being too emotional in business all the time."

Annie peeked up at her. "You too?"

"God no, not me. I was always levelheaded, detached enough to make good decisions."

"What were you thinking about just now, then, that made you so sad?"

Lee looked at her, surprised. Had she been that obvious? "I was just thinking about something one of my professors said to me about my work in college. I used to study art. I wanted to be a painter. Have I told you that?"

"No. What happened?"

"I gave up too soon." She let criticism from an old, worn-out, bitter man determine her path. She gave away something she loved, her life work, because she believed what he said that day to be truth instead of one person's opinion. "I was young, without anyone to tell me, 'Stay in the game, fight harder, paint what you want no matter what anyone says.'"

"It's never too late, right?"

"I used to think it was, but since Dan, I don't know anything I used to think I knew. Lately, I keep thinking life is so unpredictable and no matter how hard you try to order it into something manageable, it gets ripped to shreds anyway, so you may as well do what you love while you can."

"But, it's not as easy as all that, is it? Look at me."

Lee smiled and tugged at the sides of Annie's apron, wanting to say she was perfect the way she was but something held her back. "I can't wait to taste this dinner."

Annie lurched forward and hugged her. Lee stood stiff for a moment but then put her arms around her in return. When she pulled away, Lee saw tears at the corners of Annie's eyes. "I've never been this close to my dream before," said Annie. "It kinda sucks."

They laughed and Lee walked to the door, peering into the yard. She turned back to see Annie twist the knob of the largest burner to medium, place a large pot on it, and douse it with several streams of olive oil. Lee cocked her head, staring into the yard again. Her eyes were heavy, like she could fall asleep at any moment. The meat crackled and the kitchen infused with the aroma of bacon.

Lee sat at the table and popped a piece of the Parmesan in her mouth. The texture was grainy, the flavor nutty and salty. "Verle and Tommy are joining us."

Annie turned the tenderloin with tongs, the cooked side crispy brown. She held the tongs in the air over the pot. "Tommy, from Los Fuegos?"

Lee felt her stomach flutter at the mention of his name. She kept her voice low. "Yeah, we've been kind of spending time together."

Annie turned from the stove. "Like dating?"

"I guess. Don't tell anyone. It's nothing serious."

"Holy crap." Annie put her hands on her hips and wagged her finger at Lee with a teasing smile. "Be careful of his heart. I hear he's the sensitive type."

Lee's eyes filled with tears and, before she knew it, she began to sob into her hands. Annie kneeled and put her arms around Lee. "What's wrong? What did I say?"

She wanted to tell her the whole truth, but what came out was just part of it, but a bigger part than she knew until it tumbled out of her mouth. "I slept with him. Two nights in a row and it was really wonderful and I feel like I'm cheating on Dan. I'm pregnant and I'm falling for someone new. What's wrong with me?"

One of Annie's corkscrew curls brushed Lee's cheek as she hugged her again. "Don't you think you deserve to be happy after everything you've been through?"

Lee wiped the tears from her cheeks. "I don't know."

Back on the porch, Lee watched Verle pull up in a beat-up truck with layers of dust covering other layers of dust. Stout, red-skinned, he reminded Lee of a photo of a Scottish sheepherder. He carried a bouquet of white flowers that looked like big cupcakes and reached into the back of his truck, pulling out two kitchen chairs. Tommy ran down the steps and took the chairs from him, murmuring something that made them both chuckle.

Tommy slapped Verle on the back and led him to one of the chairs. "Good thing you got here when you did. I wanted to eat your crostinis but Ellen saved them for you."

Ellen sat in the other chair, back straight, legs stiff, smoothing the front of skirt with her weathered hand. "They're cold now." She sniffed.

"An old widower like me ain't one to turn down food, cold or no," said Verle.

Ellen's eyes darted around, only stopping at Verle for a second. "Beggars can't be choosers."

Verle held the crostini close to his eyes. "That sure is a small piece of toast." He put the entire crostini in his mouth and chewed in a round motion, closing his eyes and making a little appreciative grunt. "My, now, that is good." He reached for another. "We always had goat cheese when I was a kid and my sister and I wished we had orange cow cheese like all the rich kids. If only my mother could see how it is now, goat cheese in all the fancy stores and all."

Alder darted by with a long stick in the air, screaming and running from a pretend foe.

Verle looked Ellen up and down, wiping his mouth with one of the paper napkins. "Something looks different about you."

Ellen's gaze was fixed on the yard, her hand playing with a tuft of hair. "Just a haircut."

"Looks real nice," said Verle.

Ellen smiled, waving her hand in the air and shrugging her shoulders as if the whole thing was an afterthought. "Figured after fifty years, it might be time to change it up a bit."

Verle picked up another crostini, nodding his head and grinning. "Good not to get in a rut, that's for sure."

Tommy caught Lee's eyes and she chuckled, feeling like a chaperone at a junior high dance.

It was dark now and the woods behind the fence were quiet. The candles threw shadows across the faces gathered around the table. Verle sat next to Ellen, Lee with Alder on her side, and Tommy opposite them. Annie brought the Caesar out in a large serving bowl and tossed the salad at the table. After dropping a generous portion of the dressed lettuce on each plate, she sprinkled slivers of Parmesan over the top. Using a pair of silver tongs, she placed a whole anchovy and seven croutons on each salad. They all stared at Annie. Lee felt transported by the artistry of Annie's graceful movements and the quiet beauty of the candlelit table, enclosed next to its dark backdrop.

Annie stepped back, glancing around the table. "Go ahead. Eat." She excused herself and headed back to the kitchen.

They all grabbed their forks and took a bite. "I haven't had anything this good since I went on my honeymoon," said Ellen. She took another bite and shook her head in appreciation. "And that was 1951." The dressing was traditional, full of garlic, Parmesan cheese, hints of lemon, and strong overtones of anchovies. But the croutons were the highlight. Still warm, they partially melted the slivers of hard salty cheese, and the crusted outer layers were crunchy and tasted of garlic, salt, and Parmesan. The insides were soft and exploded with the green earthy taste of olive oil.

For several minutes there was only the noise of silver hitting the ceramic dishes as morsel after morsel disappeared into their mouths. Except for Alder's plate—Alder said anchovies made him want to throw up—there was not a lettuce leaf left. Seeing that everyone was finished, Tommy jumped from his place.

Lee moved to help, but he touched his hand to her shoulder. "I'll be the server tonight." He gathered the plates and disappeared into the kitchen.

Alder whispered to Lee, "I think he's nice. Not at all like asshole."

"Stop saying that word." She looked at him and wrinkled her brow, trying to be stern. "I mean it."

"Sorry." He continued to whisper but it was loud enough Lee

knew both Ellen and Verle could hear him. "Are you in love with him?"

Lee blushed. "Never mind."

"I think you are."

Lee ignored the chuckles of Ellen and Verle and spoke through clenched teeth. "Just be quiet."

Alder threw up his hands. "Okay, okay."

Lee brought her napkin to her mouth to hide her smile and glanced across the table at Ellen, who gazed at Alder, eyes glistening with what might be tears. She's thinking of her son, Lee thought. Heart constricting, she ruffled Alder's hair. "Are you excited for your mom to be a real chef at a fancy restaurant?"

"Yeah, except for one thing." He looked at his plate. "What about me? She told me she'll be away more. Will I have to stay with you-know-who?"

Ellen shifted in her seat. "You can stay with me."

Lee looked at her, surprised. "You?"

Ellen's gaze focused on Alder. "You like puppies and gardens?"

"You have a puppy?"

"My boy used to have one a long time ago. Been thinking I might get one again. That interest you?"

"You bet!"

"You'll have to help me with the dog. I'm an old lady."

"Except for your wrinkles you don't seem old."

Verle chuckled and gazed at Ellen, with his face in the palm of his hand. "I agree."

Ellen smiled but Lee saw a glimmer of the sadness still in her eyes. "It's settled then. Your mom can help Lee and you'll help me."

He grinned. "Lee, does that mean Mom has the job?"

Lee shushed him with a finger to her lips. "Let's announce it at dessert."

Alder leapt from his chair, jumping up and down. "Yay." He ran into the kitchen, the screen door slamming behind him. "Mom, Mom, Lee says you have the job and Ellen's getting a dog."

Tommy and Annie brought the second course, penne with shrimp and morel mushrooms. "This is a simple white wine and cream sauce, flavored with hints of rosemary and garlic," said Annie. "The morel mushrooms are cooked with the white wine and cream so they soak up the flavor of the sauce." Alder was wriggling in his chair and swinging his feet until Annie gave him a look to be still. "The shrimp are simply sautéed in butter and garlic," she said, filling the empty wine glasses. "We're serving a sauvignon blanc with this course, from a winery outside of town, that pairs nicely with shrimp." She looked around the table at each face. "Thanks for allowing me to cook for you. It's great to be back in the kitchen."

Verle held up his glass to Annie. "This is a real treat for a lonely old man."

Tommy held up his glass. "Here's to the chef. Our compliments."

Alder toasted with his milk. "To my mom, the greatest cook in the whole world."

Everyone laughed as Annie slipped back to the kitchen.

Lee forked a shrimp, a piece of pasta, and a mushroom and brought it up to her mouth. The morel mushrooms seeped cream and white wine, the penne was al dente, the shrimp tender and buttery. As she took another bite she noticed Alder's eyes were drooping and then his head flopped onto her shoulder. She shifted and guided his head to her lap. She felt him drift to sleep, his head resting there next to her baby.

Annie brought the next course. "This is a pork tenderloin with apples, dates, and baby potatoes. The tenderloin is pan fried and then baked wrapped in bacon and spiced with cinnamon, cumin, and garlic. I have two cabs for you to try with it, one from a winery in Woodinville, Washington, the other from Walla Walla. Enjoy." Lee looked down at her plate. Three pieces of pork were arranged on the middle of the plate, surrounded with a mess of potatoes, slices of white onion, quartered apples, a thick whole date, and a small amount of sauce speckled with the spice. She took the first taste: a perfect blend of bacon, onions, cumin, and cinnamon mixed with the sweetness of the apples and dates.

Tommy caught her eye from across the table. "The girl can cook."

"I'll say." Verle took a swig of water and stuffed another big forkful of pork into his mouth.

Tommy sipped his wine, regarding Lee from across the candlelight. "You may just pull this thing off."

"Of course she will." Ellen wiped her mouth with the corner of her napkin. "She's done harder things than getting a little restaurant put together."

Tommy gave his attention to Ellen. "Like what, for example?"

"Raised herself for one. Took care of her mother for two. Got accepted to college at seventeen with an art scholarship for three. Earned an MBA from Wharton for four. Should I continue?"

Lee watched Tommy swirl his wine, the dark purple liquid like a small wave, the droplets catching the light as they crept down the inside of the glass. "Ellen's exaggerating a little," she said, moving a mushroom around her plate.

Ellen's napkin snapped as she waved it in the air. "I am most certainly not. I didn't know what a mess Eleanor was until I came over here one day after Lee left for college to see her drunk at eleven in the morning." She looked at Tommy. "Make no mistake, this is one tough, smart girl."

Tommy peered over his wine glass at Lee. "I can see that for myself."

Lee sipped primly from her water glass and pretended to dismiss their compliments. "You guys have had too much wine."

Ellen giggled. "Oh my, I do feel a little lightheaded."

Lee wiped the condensation off her water glass. "It won't matter one iota how clever or tough I am if this restaurant tanks."

Tommy raised his glass. "You know what they say in my business, it's always good to follow a bad act."

Ellen hiccupped and grinned. "Here's to second chances."

"To second chances," said Tommy as they all toasted.

"I'm naming the restaurant Riversong," said Lee.

Verle pulled on his ear. "River what now?"

His eyes on Lee, Tommy said softly, "Riversong, Verle. She's calling the restaurant Riversong."

Ellen raised her glass again. "Here's to you two kids. You're perfect together."

Tommy smirked at Lee and raised his eyebrows. "And why's that, Ellen?"

"You're the only two people in southern Oregon who don't own a gun."

They were all still laughing when Lee called Annie out to the table and gave her a glass of wine. Tommy stood and raised his glass. "Here's to the launch of a beautiful partnership. To Riversong." They all raised their glasses and toasted. "To Riversong," they all repeated.

CHAPTER EIGHTEEN

TOMMY ROWED LEE ACROSS THE RIVER in his rowboat. His muscular arms pulled the paddles in a steady rhythm. A picnic lunch and a beach umbrella were at their feet. The water appeared like the surface of a green glass table, broken only by the ripples made from the paddles. It was early June and the river was full and clear of nature's debris, no sticks, algae, or dead leaves like there would be in late summer. She wondered if she would still be here then.

As Tommy rowed, Lee felt like someone from another time, as if she should be dressed in a long lace gown and carrying a frilly umbrella. She loved it, this way he had of making her feel taken care of, like a treasure. He opened doors for her. He handed her a towel when she came out of the shower. His hand rested on the small of her back when they walked together. Just now he'd helped her into the boat, holding her hand and guiding her onto the bench. So much for feminism, she'd thought. It was nice, after the difficulty of Dan, to let go, to let Tommy take care of things, even if it was just the simple act of rowing her across the water.

At the deepest part of the river Lee looked down into the ever darkening shades of green. There was no discernable bottom. Lee shivered despite the warm sun. They neared a large gray rock scattered with moss and the mineral deposits left from evaporated rain. It jutted from the surface of the water like the head of a hippopotamus.

After they reached the sandy side of the river and departed the boat, Lee stood ankle deep, feeling the fine sand sifting between her toes, and watched with apprehension as Tommy waded up to his waist. He turned to her, his wet shorts clinging to his lean frame. "You ready?"

"Do I have a choice?"

"Not really." He motioned for her to come deeper into the water.

She moved towards him, gasping a little at how cold it felt on her hot skin, wading in past her knees and then her waist. When she reached him he held both her hands in his.

"You alright?" he said.

She answered yes, thinking it was now or never, and let him gently guide her onto her back, closing her eyes to block out the bright light of the sun, ready for his instruction. One hand was under her legs, the other under her back, so that she was almost nestled against his stomach. She held her body stiff, her neck slightly bent and tense, ready to put her feet on the ground if he let go. "Just allow yourself to relax and pretend like you're a board," he said. "I won't let go until you tell me you're ready."

Her eyes were screwed shut as she tried to imagine herself as a relaxed board. But the harder she worked on it the more tense she became. She opened her eyes. "I can't do it."

His brown eyes looked down at her. "You can. Think of a time when you were totally relaxed, totally happy. Picture yourself there again."

She closed her eyes. Several weeks ago that would have been difficult but now she thought of the night before. After dinner, she and Tommy had watched the stars from his patio, side by side on the chaise lounge. It had been clear and warm, the fir and pine trees next to his house rustling in the slight breeze. She had a soft blanket wrapped around her legs, the fresh dry air touching her bare arms and face. The stars scattered across the sky dazzled so that they seemed close, like a high ceiling instead of light years away. Tommy reached over and took her hand in his and they stayed like that, gazing upward, for several minutes. She'd let herself have the moment without guilt or worry, had allowed herself to feel safe.

Thinking of it now, she felt her muscles unclench and she relaxed. She began to feel the water as a surface, like a soft cot, there to support and restore her. She felt Tommy's arms relax a little too. "You ready for me to move away?" he said.

"I guess."

He backed away a few inches and then removed his arms from under her. She was floating. She opened her eyes, turning her head to look at him. "Hey, I'm doing it." No sooner were the words out of her mouth than she felt herself go under. She put her feet against the small stones and pebbles as she jerked out of the water. She coughed and sputtered, wiping her eyes with her hands.

Tommy grinned at her. "You did it."

"For about a second."

He instructed her to try again and this time to stay still until she felt him next to her again. She leaned back into the water but found her feet unwilling to leave the bottom. He scooped under her legs and held her until she indicated she was ready for him to let go. This time she floated for a long moment before he was next to her again. They practiced eight more times before he wrapped her legs around him and walked with her to the dry sand of the beach. They plopped down on beach towels next to one another, under his blue and white striped umbrella. "You did well," he said. "I told you it wasn't so hard."

She put on a straw beach hat and sunglasses, resting under the shade of the umbrella while he rummaged in the small ice chest. Handing her a bottle of water, he said, "Tomorrow I can show you how to blow bubbles." Then he began to play with the left thigh string of her one-piece bathing suit. His eyes half closed in that look she knew already from the week they spent together.

She scooted closer to him, putting her hand on his stomach. "So far swimming lessons are good," she said.

"Told you."

They couldn't keep their hands from one another. Every free moment they were together it was the pulling of clothes, grabbing and caressing of skin and hair. Sometimes they couldn't even get free of their clothes before they were intertwined, in every spot of Tommy's house, before breakfast, after lunch, before Tommy's gigs, in the middle of the night.

A week went by and then another. In between planning for the restaurant, she would think of him and hurry to finish the day's work to rush to his house. They developed a pattern where they worked during the days and met in the late afternoons at his house for her swimming lesson. After the lesson they would make dinner together and if he didn't have a gig to go to in the evenings, she stayed the night. After several weeks she brought a few clothing items over, going home every other day to check on the progress at her house. She knew she was getting involved too soon, and too deeply, but she couldn't make herself stop.

One afternoon on his couch he made her cry out twice before he let himself go. Afterwards, they lay together, half clothed, still flushed. He played with her hair. "Do you want to stay at your house sometime? We don't always have to be here."

"I don't know. Maybe." That afternoon she had stopped by to see the progress and was amazed to see Joshua up on a ladder painting the ceiling of the living room. Joshua had explained, gesturing with his wet paintbrush at the old floors, "Better to paint before I put the new floors down." She'd chosen a soft yellow called "Butter" for the living room and a beige named "Eggnog" for the foyer, stairwell, and upstairs hallway. "Better on your walls than in your fridge," she'd said to Joshua.

Now, she ran her finger along Tommy's lower lip, thinking how even with the cosmetic changes to the house, it was still stacked with memories better left covered. "Paint fumes are pretty strong. It's better to stay here."

"Whatever you say."

Weeks went by and Tommy taught her how to blow bubbles, rhythmic breathing, and a basic flutter kick and paddle stroke. On the afternoon of her twentieth week of pregnancy, she sat on a beach towel under the umbrella working on a list of items still left to do before the grand opening of Riversong.

To do:

Negotiate terms with local produce farmers

Develop a marketing plan

Meet with the local art group about the rotating shows

Hire staff

Just then she heard Tommy yell from the other side of the river and looked up to see him dive into the water and swim towards her. In less than a minute he stood at the edge of her blanket, shaking the water from his hair. He plopped beside her, looking like a child at the ice cream shop. "Did you see the doc?" he asked.

"I did."

"Well, is it a boy or a girl?"

She closed her notebook, stretching her legs out on the blanket. "I didn't find out."

His face changed in a way she couldn't decipher. "You didn't find out?"

"I couldn't decide if I wanted to or not. Then I was in the ultrasound and the doctor asked if I wanted to know and suddenly I didn't want to know." She laughed. "It was the strangest thing."

He looked away, made circles in the sand with a twig. "Everything okay, though?"

"Yeah. Everything's good."

Tommy broke the twig in two, threw one piece into the water.

"Measurements all on track? Weight gain good? Any signs of problems?"

"Nothing," she said. "We going to have a lesson?"

He looked at her, his face blank. "What's that?"

"A lesson. A swimming lesson?"

"Oh, yeah, sure." He got up and waded into the water.

She followed him, calling out. "Tommy, is something wrong?"

"Not a thing." His voice sounded tight, almost monotone.

"You have to work tonight?"

He shook his head, no. He turned away, picking up a rock from the river bottom and chucking it up the river.

She kept her voice light. "You never said whether you thought I should find out or not."

He shrugged, staring across the river. "You never asked."

She smiled, teasing. "That doesn't usually stop you from having an opinion."

His eyes were hooded. "I don't get to have an opinion. I'm not the father. Isn't that right?"

"Tommy, I'm sorry." She watched old grief play across his face. "I don't know what to say."

"I know."

He turned towards her then. "Lee, promise me that if you leave you'll let me know."

Suddenly she felt a sensation in her lower stomach like butterflies. She reached for him. "Tommy, I think I just felt the baby move for the first time."

He strode through the water, putting his hand on her stomach. "Really?"

She put her hand on top of his and whispered, "Yes, it's just like they say in the books. Like bubbles or butterflies."

They stood like that for a moment until Lee said, "I'm glad you were here for it."

His eyes glistened and then he hugged her, holding her tightly against his wet body. "Me too."

CHAPTER NINETEEN

LEE COLLAPSED on a blanket at Ellen's swimming hole, the river water beading on her sunscreened skin. She squeezed water from her hair, at her shoulders now, and perched her sunhat over her face, closing her eyes. She smiled, hearing Alder's body hitting the water as he jumped from a rock and then the splashing of his arms and legs swimming through the water. He called out to the yellow Labrador puppy playing at the shore. "Sunshine, come here, girl."

Ellen brought Alder and Sunshine to the river every afternoon while Lee and Annie worked. Watching Ellen and Alder interact over the last several months, Lee couldn't help but fill with sadness, thinking of the mother Ellen must have been and the unspeakable tragedy of her loss.

The midsummer air was hot and dry. The sun's rays felt as if they were healing some broken part of her as she lay there, thinking of nothing, swatting the air to thwart a buzzing dragonfly from resting on her hat. Down closer to the river were Ellen and Annie, their feet in the water, chatting amiably together. It was a rare day off for them all, after two months of intense focus on the building and planning of Riversong. The restaurant would open in five weeks. Four weeks had gone by since she first felt the flutter of her baby and in that time her stomach seemed to have doubled in size. Annie called it "the pop." It had popped alright, she thought. She wondered if it would ever pop back in?

She heard the crunch of rocks, lifted her hat, and saw four feet, two with white socks and tennis shoes, and two brown feet in Tevas. She removed her hat to see Verle walking toward the others and Tommy peering down at her. She knew at once he was agitated because he was rubbing the scar on his cheek.

He plopped next to her and caressed the side of her arm with his finger. "I hope you have sunscreen on."

"Twice now." She sat up. Her stomach practically reached her knees, she thought, wishing she'd worn a t-shirt instead of the maternity swimming suit that left nothing to the imagination. She shielded the sun with her hand. "Thought you had rehearsal?"

"Cancelled." Tommy took off his shirt and Lee resisted the urge to touch his lean, hairless stomach.

She sat up and reached for her sunglasses as he lay beside her, turning on his side and resting his head in the palm of his hand. She thought of his music, how sad some of the songs were and how his rich voice could make her want to weep.

"You remember the twitchy guy?" said Tommy. "Zac's buddy?"

Lee watched Alder and Sunshine try to capture a minnow from the school that swam together in the sandy shallow water along the river's edge. "How could I forget?"

"They found him and Deana dead in her trailer last night. Stabbed to death. Rumor is, tweekers gone crazy fighting over drugs." He sat up and moved closer to her, arms around his knees. She felt the heat radiating from his skin but her lips had gone numb.

"Do they think Zac was involved?" she said.

"No way to know for sure except to say he supplied the drugs at some point. I saw him stumble out of the Squeaky Wheel just now, barely recognized him. Skinny, like he's sampling the wares."

He spoke in almost a whisper. "I don't want you at the restaurant alone. If he's taking that crap, I don't trust him not to go crazy."

"Annie's there with me most of the time."

"I'm picking you guys up when you work late, and you're staying nights with me."

"Like I don't already?" For weeks now, she stayed with him almost every night in a false domesticity. They ate together, slept together, and stayed up late into the night talking. Last week she allowed him to take her to the monthly pregnancy checkup but made him wait in the lobby. Sometimes she felt that her old life was a dream and this new one with Tommy, her growing stomach and the building of Riversong, was the real one. Since the evening of Annie's dinner party she and Tommy formed an unplanned silent agreement to leave the subject of the future, in particular their future, alone. It was there anyway, under the surface of conversations and in the look of longing on Tommy's face when he didn't know she watched him and especially in the desperate way they made love like it could be their last time, each time.

"Zac shows up at the restaurant, I want you to call me immediately," said Tommy.

"He hasn't shown since the day he threatened me." She glanced around at the others. Verle sat next to Annie, a sandwich in his hand as Ellen dug in the ice chest.

"Maybe I should pay him a visit, make sure he knows to stay away."

"Are you out of your mind? Do you know how dangerous he is?"

"As a matter of fact, I do, and I'm not afraid of him. Should I tell you some of the details of my youth?" He sat up and rubbed his scar, with the same injured look he had when he talked about his brother.

"Regardless, Mike wants him at the restaurant." She picked up a smooth pebble from the sand next to the blanket and rubbed it with her thumb.

"Mike needs a reality check."

"Tommy, Mike's the owner. If he wants Zac there, I have to let him."

He sat up and kicked the sand with his foot. "I do not want him anywhere near you, do you understand?"

"How am I supposed to stop him?"

"Dammit, Lee, that's the point."

"You can't protect me from everything, even if you wanted to."

He went still and studied her. "What else do you need protection from?"

"It's just an expression." She leaned forward and rested her head on his shoulder, brushing sand off her legs. "Let's not fight when I feel like a cow."

He appeared to want to say something more, but instead ran a sandy hand through his hair, the gray bits sticking between his dark wavy strands. He rested his other hand on the roundness of her stomach. "It's starting to look like a big basketball. Come swim with me. The water will make you feel light."

He stood and pulled her next to him. She followed him into the water, the sand soft on the bottoms of her toes. They waded to their waists and when he drew her to him, she wrapped her arms around his neck. They floated together, drifting on the surface, the cool water lapping alongside them. "I love this river," she said to Tommy, putting her lips on his warm neck. "You know that?"

"I do." He kissed the side of her face and brought her closer to him.

With Tommy and the river water next to her skin, she surprised herself by thinking how good life would be if it were just the threat of Zac that worried her. As she rested her head on Tommy's shoulder and absorbed heat from his brown skin, it was the danger of DeAngelo that lurked alongside this tranquility, like an illness in remission, affecting everything with its subtle dread.

The next afternoon Tommy convinced her to take a much-needed nap at his house. She awakened to paint fumes and found Tommy in his spare bedroom painting a crib, headphones from his iPod in his ears, humming along with the music. She stood in the doorway, watching his strong hand brushing the white paint on the slats of unfinished wood. After a few moments, she turned from the doorway and walked to the bathroom. She turned on the water and sat on the shower floor, face in her hands, weeping without making a sound.

The next day, a Monday, in a moment of uncertainty about the restaurant and a pang of nostalgia for Linus, she bought a disposable phone and texted her friend. "I've been fine. Miss you. Call if safe." She received no response the rest of Monday and regretted sending it, wondering if it jeopardized her safety, if by some chance Von had intercepted it and traced it to her. All that night she lay awake next to Tommy, sweating and fretting that Von might show up at any moment. The next morning she sat across from Tommy at his breakfast table, picking at a cheese omelet. She felt him observing her in the way he did, intuiting something was amiss. "You tired this morning?"

"I didn't sleep well."

"Something bothering you?"

"No, just anxious about the restaurant."

He looked at her and she read on his face a mixture of disappointment and frustration. He put down his spoon and folded his napkin. "How long will this go on?"

"What do you mean?"

"This thing where you don't tell me the truth. How we avoid talking about the future, or the baby, or us?"

She rubbed her eyes and sighed. "Do we have to do this now?"

"If not now, when?"

She moved pieces of omelet around her plate and thought about DeAngelo and how she endangered Tommy with every moment she chose to stay with him. She was able to cajole herself into a false security when she was with him, like they were just an ordinary couple instead of the truth, which was too horrifying to face. "I'm working some things out. I need more time."

He picked up his butter knife and rubbed his finger along its shiny surface. "Do you want to be here, with me?"

She reached across the table and squeezed his forearm. "Isn't that obvious?"

On Tuesday, Linus appeared on her doorstep in the middle of the morning, wearing a tan linen suit with a light blue shirt, no tie, and a floppy straw hat. He draped across the opening of her front door. "Any rooms to rent?"

She threw her arms around him. "How did you find me without directions?"

"The address. GPS took me right here."

"That's bad."

"Only if he figures out where you are. Which he won't."

"Have you seen him?"

"Not for a while."

"How do you know he didn't follow you here?"

"Impossible. I've been in Chicago, visiting Will's mother."

"Chicago? Will's mother? What made you do that?"

"Just felt the urge to see her suddenly. When I left Seattle I got on a bus six blocks from my apartment that took me north to Greenlake, another bus west to Ballard, another bus back down-town, and finally an express bus that took me over the lake to Bellevue, where I walked five blocks to the mall, hung out in Nordstrom's for an hour, and finally hailed a cab to Boeing Field, where my rich friend Jake flew me to Medford on his private plane. No one followed me."

"Are you sure?"

"I promise, my little worry wart." He backed away and looked at her stomach. He paled. "Lee?"

Her eyes filled. "Yes."

He rested on the doorframe, appearing as if he might faint. "Did Dan know?"

"No. I found out after he died."

"How come you didn't tell me?"

"I didn't think I was going to go through with it."

He took a tissue from his pocket and wiped his forehead. "What changed your mind?"

She looked at the floor, blushing and feeling tears prick her eyes. "I had a spiritual moment after an incident with a bear."

He smiled wanly and took off his hat, fanning himself. "A bear? I'm going to need a drink."

"Come on in. I have some beer in the fridge. What got into you, coming all this way?"

"I haven't had a vacation in three years."

"Ever heard of Hawaii?"

"Hawaii doesn't have you in it."

Later that day Linus perched on a chair by the remodeled windows of Riversong and took off his reading glasses. "Opening a restaurant. Didn't see this coming."

"Yeah, well, desperate times, you know?"

"The aesthetic of the place is fabulous. I couldn't have done it better myself." He looked around the dining area. The floors were refinished and stained a rich dark brown. The walls were the color of the skin of green pears and the baseboards and bar matched the floors. Hanging fixtures dangled over each of the nineteen small tables and radiated soft yellow light. In addition to the tables, there were six booths with lush brown velvet fabric covering the bench seating. The tablecloths were a white polyester/linen blend that gave it an old fashioned crisp feel. On each table perched a glass flute waiting for the flowers of the season.

They heard the sweep of the kitchen doors and looked over to see Tommy, paper bag in his hand. He stopped when he saw the two of them sitting at the bar. Lee waved and motioned him over.

"Tommy, my friend Linus from Seattle showed up out of the blue." As she introduced them Tommy looked Linus up and down, his eyes in a squint as if he had an eyesight problem. Then he handed Lee the paper bag. "I can't stay but I brought you some lunch." He leaned over as if to kiss her, but she moved slightly and he stopped, looking at her with a mixture of confusion and anger. "Can I see you in your office for a moment?" he said.

She glanced at Linus, who appeared amused, and shrugged, scooting off her chair and following him into the back.

"Who the hell is he? Why is he here? Is this an old boyfriend or what?"

She laughed. "No, he's my best friend from Seattle. You know, my gay friend? I've mentioned him before."

That seemed to take the edge off Tommy's anger but still he glared at her. "Why didn't you tell me he was coming here?"

"Because I didn't know. He surprised me."

"Oh. Well, why is this the first we've seen him or heard from him if he's such a great friend?"

She opened her mouth to answer but then couldn't think of what to say. "I don't know."

"That's not good enough."

She sat on the edge of her desk, crossing her arms, struggling to think of a way to answer his question without lying. It would have to be a lie by omission, just like she did every day with him. "Linus was a big part of my old life with Dan and I just needed a little break from that world."

He let out a long sigh and slumped against the wall. "I'm sorry. I'm a jealous jackass."

She hugged him, wanting to tell him that none of this was what it seemed and that he was perfect in his passion for her, his need for her. He was good, she thought. She was a liar. "There's no reason to be jealous of Linus. You'll love him and he'll think you're hot."

He squeezed her. "He must have very discerning taste."

"That he does."

A few minutes later, seated back at the bar, Linus cocked his head and looked her up and down, waving his hands in the air. "You're stunning. Is it the pregnant glow or this new life?" He tapped his pen on the bar. "I've never seen you look better. I love your hair long like this, kind of free flowing and sexy."

"I'm a fat cow."

He continued to stare at her, lips pursed. "I think you're happy. You don't have that little pinched look around your mouth and that nervous little twitch you did with your foot."

"I'm pregnant and stuck in Lodi with a business that's going to flop."

"Now you're just being negative." He leaned back on the barstool. "Speaking of Lodi, how long have you been sleeping with that sexy Tommy?"

She flushed. "None of your business."

"I knew it. That's what's giving you the all over body glow."

"Maybe. But, I haven't told him all of it. Y'know, about the debt to DeAngelo and all."

"Why?"

"I don't want to put him in danger and there's nothing he could do to help me. He's the kind who would try." She went behind the bar, sprayed soda water into a wine glass, and wiped her forehead with the back of her sleeve.

Linus looked at her, serious. "You in love with this guy?"

She put up her hand. "I know, it's shameful. Dan's not even been gone six months."

"Lee, I've been thinking a lot about things and I wonder if you were happy before, with Dan?"

She felt tears spring to her eyes and grabbed a cocktail napkin, swiping at her eyes. She didn't say anything for a moment, thinking about what he'd asked. Tommy had asked her the same thing. Happiness, what did it mean exactly? "Linus, towards the end I used to daydream about leaving him and being free to start over. He was so dark, so driven towards this idea he had for success. There was no room for me. It took me a while of being here to realize he had come to feel like a burden, just as my mother had been. I was spinning on this wheel, thinking that once Dan reached the kind of success he wanted, he would be happy and I could be happy too. And not so lonely." She ran her hand over the bar. "But I can't help but think it's my fault for what happened because I wished for a different life instead of being grateful for the one I had."

"Does this Tommy make you happy?"

"Yeah. Even though he's not my type at all. He's a sentimental, liberal, Jesus-loving musician." Her voice broke. "And he's got this way of seeing right into me. He's nice to me and bought a crib at an unfinished wood furniture store for the baby and he's painting it white. We have incredible chemistry. He thinks we're soul mates." She took a shaky breath and wiped a tear from her cheek. "I'll just leave it at that."

Linus smiled, but his eyes were sad. "And, he doesn't know how much trouble you're in."

"Right."

He squeezed her hand. "We'll get this figured out so you can be with him. I'm here now."

She managed a shaky smile. "Great. Now I'll have both you and Tommy bossing me around."

"What more could you want?" Linus shuffled through her notes. "Anyway, I'm afraid I must agree with your assessment about Riversong." He lowered his voice. "The main issue is finding staff." He put his glasses back on and glanced at Annie's summer menu. "Your chef is quite capable and the young man, this Billy." He interrupted himself and whispered, "Well, he seems trainable." He flipped behind the menu and pulled out a spreadsheet, shaking his head, as if contemplating a problem of deep concern to humanity. "However, I'm worried about finding staff." He glanced askance towards the window. "In this town."

"The local druggies won't do?"

He rolled his eyes and pursed his lips. "Oh, no, no, no. That's just a shame." He looked up at the ceiling, sighed, and spread his hands on the surface of the table. "We must find the starving artists. Surely you have some of those here?"

"Why artists?"

"Smart and hungry." He scrawled something on a blank sheet of paper with his fountain pen and presented it to Lee.

Wanted. Artists of any kind to train for high-end server positions at new local restaurant, Riversong. No previous experience necessary but must be detail oriented, personable, and display exceptional customer service. Interest in fine wine and food a plus. Please contact the Manager at (541) 555-5970 for details and interviews.

"Don't put your name in the paper, just to be on the safe side." He took his glasses off, folded the handles, and put them in his shirt pocket. "Now, the other problem is publicity."

Lee heard Mike's booming voice calling her from the kitchen and a second later he came through the swinging doors. She felt Linus pop to attention. Mike stopped and took off his hat. "Who's this now?"

"My friend from Seattle. He came to help me with the opening."

"Wasn't aware you needed help." Mike shoved his hands in his pockets and squinted at Linus. She saw the two men take each other in and suddenly she was seeing them as they might see each other. Mike, with his cowboy hat, ruddy sunburned skin, and a ridiculous large belt buckle the shape of Oregon: rough, unsophisticated, the type that might hate a gay man. And, Linus, with his linen suit, soft hands, his graceful way of moving and almost upper crust way of speaking: a pansy, a phony, someone you called a queer to your poker buddies.

"Linus manages Figs Bistro in Seattle. He knows the restaurant business inside and out. Mike's the owner of Riversong."

"Lee's my partner here," said Mike. "No offense to you, but she's done this whole thing herself. Not sure why she'd bring you in now."

"I called him for advice. Figs is perfect. Because of Linus," Lee said.

"We do things different here than in Seattle. Lee knows that 'cause she's from here."

Linus sat back in his chair and crossed his legs. "No offense, but perhaps if you tried some of our big city techniques you might have some businesses that last more than a year."

Mike looked at her, betrayal in his eyes. "You tell him that?"

"What? No, he—"

Linus interrupted her, directing his gaze at Mike. "In my experience, the most important thing in the restaurant business is good publicity before an opening. I can make a few calls, see if we can get some press from some of the Northwest foodie magazines, maybe the Oregonian." Linus looked back and forth between them. "But we need a story to pitch."

Mike, his face red, crossed his arms over his chest. "That some kind of big city bullshit? We don't need a story, just old fashioned good business."

"I beg to differ. It's of the utmost importance we have a story that will prompt interest from the papers or foodie rags. Mostly for the tourist crowd. We want to create a buzz so people go out of their way to come here."

"I'm just a blue collar guy myself but look around. This is gonna be a special place and you—" He interrupted himself and looked at Lee. "Well, he hasn't even tasted Annie's grub yet."

Lee looked at Linus and begged him with her eyes. Play nice, please. Linus, perspiration on his forehead, gave her a hard look and looked at his feet. Then, he looked up, face composed, and flashed Mike a coy smile. "Now, don't you play that blue collar stuff with me. I can see you know more about business than Lee and I put together."

Mike smiled and uncrossed his arms. "Well, I'm old as dirt, been running the mill here for forty years."

"Well, what you say is exactly right. But, still, the public has to know about us."

Mike sat and angled his chair so his full attention was directed towards Linus. "What have you come up with so far?" He rested his hands on the table.

Linus stood and paced in front of the table, hands in the pockets of his pressed white linen pants. "I see two angles." Linus stopped in front of them and moved his hands in the air for emphasis. "One, talented young female chef dreamt of opening her own restaurant but is the mother of a young son and chose a small town for his benefit. We talk about her vision around local ingredients. We talk about the seasonally based menu, about the serendipitous event of meeting two business people, unnamed of course, who were willing to back her idea."

"But that's not what happened," said Mike. "Lee came up with this idea, not Annie."

Linus took off his glasses. "The papers love stories about the chefs. It's more compelling than the owners or managers."

Mike looked at him and shook his head. "If you're right about this story thing it should be about Lee. She's one of our own. Moved to the big city and became a bigwig, and came home after the death of her husband to start fresh with people who love her. Who understand her. If that isn't a story I don't know a pine tree from a cedar."

A picture of Von's tobacco-stained teeth sent a shiver down Lee's spine. She tried to keep her voice steady. "Mike, I can't be featured in any of the publicity."

"Why the hell not?"

"I have a good reason and I need to leave it at that. Can you trust me?"

Mike looked at her for a long moment. "Okay, darlin' whatever you say. I just wanted you to get the credit you deserve."

"How about the credit you deserve?" She looked at Linus. "Mike's trying to save the town single handedly. That's the real story."

Mike's face relaxed and he patted Lee's arm. "You're a good girl, but I'm not some Hollywood starlet looking to get in the paper." He shifted in his chair, one eyebrow lifted as his fingers tapped on the table. "Linus, what's the other angle?"

"This one's more of a stretch, but could be integrated with Annie's story. I'm seeing the headlines like, 'Best new restaurant you never heard of in the sweetest town in the West.'" He stared into space, visualizing. "Annie is just one of many young savvy talents moving in and transforming this town into a cultural oasis."

Mike leaned forward. "That sounds real good."

Lee rolled her eyes. "Our story has to be plausible."

Linus raised one eyebrow and pursed his lips. "Yes, it is a bit of spin. But, you've got the wineries here already." Linus shrugged. "Plus, if it's written about in that way, perhaps it might start to happen."

Mike jumped up from his chair and paced around the room. "Like it could attract other businesses like this one? High end? For tourists? That kind of thing?"

Linus plopped in a chair and wiped his brow with a cloth handkerchief from his pocket. "Precisely."

Mike slapped his leg. "That's just a doggone great idea." He glanced at his watch. "Shoot, I've got to go. It's payday and I like to pass out the checks myself."

"I do the same," said Linus.

"Shows respect."

"Exactly right," said Linus.

"Kids, I've got to go. I'm going to pay my respects to Deana. They're having a service at the Baptist Church. Her father used to work for me out at the mill long time ago. Such a waste, the way it ended for her."

"Do they have any suspects?" said Lee.

"Not a one. They're pretty sure it was a fight over drugs. Couple of people testified she had a party that night but everyone swears she and the other guy were alive when they left. These drug people, they're so far in the muck, we'll probably never know what happened." Mike gave Lee a slight smile. "But you don't need to worry about all that. You two are the wave of the future for this town. Darlin', good idea to bring this ol' boy down here. Real good idea."

Linus crossed his legs and gave a prim smile. "This little town isn't going to know what hit them."

Lee hid a smile behind her hand and pretended to write a note in her book.

Within two days, Lee had a dozen calls from interested candidates for the staff positions. Linus screened them first over the phone and selected five to come into the restaurant for interviews. The initial four yielded two solid hires. The first, Karen, was a woman in her mid-fifties, a local watercolorist and recent empty nester whose husband had been injured in the woods and couldn't work. They were out of money, she'd said, and hoped they didn't think she was too old to learn new things, because she'd raised four kids and nothing could be harder than that. The second was a former technical writer turned fiction writer working on his first novel. Frank was outgoing, articulate, and cultured. He'd moved from San Francisco six months earlier and loved River Valley because it was inexpensive and quiet, perfect for writing, but he was almost out of money. Linus thought he was trainable, especially after he confessed to love food and wine almost more than a good book.

The final interview was with a glass-blower in his mid-thirties named John. He had clear blue eyes, bleached blond hair, and wore a diamond stud earring in his left ear. Lee asked him to sit down at the table, noting his fuchsia silk shirt, and read through his application while she waited for Linus to begin asking questions. Several minutes slipped by in complete silence, with Linus staring at the candidate as if he'd forgotten where he was. Lee cleared her throat. "Linus is a consultant from Seattle helping me hire serving staff." She looked at him out of the corner of her eye. "He's going to ask you some standard questions."

Linus squirmed in his chair, crossed and uncrossed his legs, and knocked his stack of notes on the floor. "Yes, right." He leaned over to pick up the papers and banged his head on the edge of the table. "Ouch. Sorry. Let's see here." He massaged the side of his head and traced the candidate's name with his index finger. "John." He looked back at the candidate, smiled, and flushed. "How are you, John?"

"Fantastic."

"Good, good." Linus looked at the application. "So, you're an Aquarius?"

John brushed a lock of hair out of his eyes. "That's me. Independent. Kind of eccentric."

"Really? How interesting." Linus leaned forward. "I'm a Virgo."

"My former partner was a Virgo."

Lee pinched the area right between her eyes and took a deep breath. "Tell us, why are you interested in this job, John?"

He fluttered his fingers. "I loved your ad. I mean, who puts it out there like," he made a frame with his hands, "Wanted, artists. That was just so fabulous." He crossed his legs. "Plus, my glass doesn't sell enough to make a decent income."

Linus grinned and dipped his head to the right. "The ad was my idea."

Lee stared at him for a moment and then glanced down at the resume. "You have a theatre degree. How did you get into glass?"

"I spent ten years in Los Angeles. Had an agent, did stupid television commercials, the whole bit. I took a glass-blowing class for fun and fell in love with it. Just happened to see an ad for a glass studio for sale up here and bought the whole darn thing from this crazy hippy lady." He took a breath. "I love the drama of nature here. The mountains, the river, the vegetation are all mirrored in my glass." He smiled and played with his earring. "Of course, the problem is money."

Lee sipped from her glass of water. "So you must have worked in a restaurant before, being an actor?"

"It's been a long time but, yes." His eyes drifted around the room. "I didn't think I'd ever do it again but this place is so beautiful, I think I could bear it." He looked back at Lee. "The windows are faboo." He smiled and looked at Linus. "I had a theatre professor who used to say even a bad play could be hidden if the lighting was good."

Linus twittered and smoothed his hair. "When can you start?"

The entire staff, including Cindi, Annie, and Billy, sat scattered amongst the various tables, scribbling notes onto their pads. Linus stood at the flipchart, going over the sequence again. "Within one minute you must greet your table, welcome them, and take their drink orders." He scanned the faces. "Who can tell me what's next?"

Karen raised her left hand. "Bring their drinks within three minutes."

"Excellent. And what next?"

Karen started to answer but was interrupted by John. "Answer menu questions. Describe the Italian tradition of eating in three courses. Tell them the menu is prepared from fresh local ingredients."

Billy leaned forward. "Then take their orders."

This was the third and final day of restaurant boot camp and Linus had taught them everything from how to set the tables, timing of courses, wine 101, how to answer questions about the food, and the nuances of customer service. This afternoon he would complete the training by teaching them how to open a bottle of wine at the table and giving them their white aprons.

Lee left them with Linus and went outside. She squinted into the sun to watch the construction workers hang the royal blue awnings onto the top of the restaurant directly above the framed windows. The window frames and outside walls were all painted marinara sauce red except for a foot wide brown strip that ran along the bottom of the outside walls. The door was red too and had a large rectangular window, a shiny gold cylinder handle, and matching foot shield. On the sidewalk were planter boxes which would soon be filled with seasonal flowers chosen and planted by Ellen. Next to the flower boxes were two wooden benches, made by a local wood-worker, where patrons could wait for their tables, if by some miracle they were ever lucky enough to have more customers than tables.

She was about to go inside when Mike came around the corner of the building, wearing his cowboy hat and aviator style sunglasses. "Looking good," he called out. "Makes the rest of the town look like the ugly stepsister." It was true, on the left, with an alley separating them, was an empty two-story building with boarded up windows. On the other side, not attached to, but within feet of the restaurant, was a used clothing store.

She could see herself, misshapen, in his sunglasses. "Come by to see our progress?"

"No, I'm looking for Zac."

Lee's stomach clenched. She knew it was only a matter of time before Mike realized Zac hadn't shown since the day he threatened her. "I told him I didn't need him for the last several days before the opening."

"Lee, don't bullshit me."

"What do you mean?"

"What kind of food and beverage manager isn't here before the grand opening?"

Lee looked at the sidewalk. "I don't know what to say. I haven't seen him for a while."

"How long?"

"Since the day we announced the new plan."

"Gosh darnit, Lee, this wasn't part of the deal."

"I know, but he doesn't want to be here. What do you want me to do?"

"I'll take care of it."

She sighed and wondered if that meant Zac might appear this afternoon? She couldn't have him here, disruptive and hostile, when she had so many things left to do. "Mike, I don't want him here."

He stared at her. "You're telling me an extra body wouldn't help you open this place? He should be pulling down his share of the work." Mike's face was red and he growled, "He's on the damn payroll."

It was midnight, three days before the opening. The restaurant was dark except for the overhead lights above the bar, where Linus sat sipping a Syrah from Walla Walla. Lee, next to him, poured over the long list of things to do before the opening, feeling so fatigued that the edges of objects appeared gray and out of focus. "How are we ever going to be ready?"

"We will." He took another swallow of wine. "This is excellent. Did you know the climate and soil in Walla Walla is almost identical to the Rhone region in France where they make Syrah?"

"Do I care?"

"You should. You're a restaurateur now." He caught a drip of wine from the side of the glass and wiped it into a paper cocktail napkin. "Isn't the Northwest just a fabulous part of the country?"

"Your chipper mood's starting to bug me." Lee rubbed her eyes and yawned.

Linus laughed and then they were quiet except for the scratch of Lee's pen. After a few moments, Lee looked up and asked the question that was on her mind for over two weeks now. "How is it that you can be gone from Figs for three weeks?"

He tipped his glass, swallowed the remainder of his wine, and reached for the bottle. "I got fired."

"What?"

Just then the sound of pots banging on the tile floor erupted from the kitchen. Lee's insides turned to hot liquid, thinking of Von. She grabbed Linus's hand and tried to talk but no sound came out.

His eyes were fixated in space, listening, body upright, muscles tense, his voice a whisper. "I thought you locked the door?"

"I did."

Linus's eyes got big. He put his finger to his lips, picked up a wine opener from the table, pulling out the one-inch blade and holding it above his head. They tiptoed to the kitchen, catching the swinging door so it didn't make any noise. The door to Lee's office was open several inches. Linus grabbed one of Annie's chef knives, nudging Lee behind the cook's island. They knelt, peering through the opening in the office door.

It was Zac, with a freezer bag full of money grasped in his hand.

The desk was askew, pulled out about a half of a foot from the wall and she knew by his unsteady and exaggerated movements he was drunk. He dropped the bag several times and had to steady himself on the desk to keep from falling. He fumbled with the zipper of the bag for several more seconds before stuffing it into what appeared to be the space between the wall and the desk. He stumbled to his feet and pushed the desk back in place with both hands. Linus grabbed Lee and they ran on their toes through the swinging doors to the front of the restaurant. They perched on the barstools, tense, listening for Zac's next move. They heard the clattering of what Lee supposed was Zac colliding with the busboy cart, and then the back door opened and slammed shut. The engine of his vintage Firebird roared and they turned to the window in time to see him zooming down the alley and onto the street, wheels squealing. They jumped from their stools and headed for the office. Linus yanked back the desk, revealing an opening in the wall the size of an apple box.

It was stuffed with Ziploc bags full of money.

They sat on the floor in the office, staring at the pile of cash at their feet. After counting it twice, they determined it was 778,000 dollars. Neither spoke for several minutes until Linus flopped against the wall, gazing at the ceiling with a dumbfounded expression. "I didn't realize there were no banks here."

Lee stared at the pile of money. "This is enough to pay DeAngelo."

He jerked to his feet. "We've got to get this back in the hole."

Lee began handing him the bags. "No wonder he threatened me."

"How dangerous is he?" asked Linus, stuffing another into the hole.

"He threatened to hurt me if I got in his way."

"Would he know it was you if it disappeared?"

"I think so. He and I are the only ones who have keys to this office." She handed him another bag. "Why is he keeping it here?"

"I don't profess to understand the criminal mind but having watched a lot of police shows, I say he figures you would never assume he would keep it right under your nose." He gave her another baggie to fill. "Or, maybe he's really stupid."

A horrible thought came to Lee. "What if the drugs are here too?"

"No way, he hasn't been here enough. Should we go to the police?"

She put her head in her hands. "I don't know, I'm so tired. I need time to think."

"Let's sleep on it," he said.

She raised her head, watching his long fingers zip another baggie. "How did you get fired?"

"Von started showing up every night at Figs. He'd sit at the bar for hours. A couple of times he got rough with me at the end of the night."

Horrified, her body went hot and then cold. "To get you to tell them where I was?"

"Right."

"Linus, how rough?"

He fluttered his hands. "Beat me to a pulp a couple of times. The first time he broke my arm." He pulled the sleeve of his shirt past his elbow. "Broke it right here. I had a cast for eight weeks. The second time he beat me so badly I had to spend a week in the hospital." He looked at her, his face crumpling. "Now, don't cry, love. It's okay." He bent his arm several times. "See, it's fine."

"How did you get him to stop?"

"When I was in the hospital they gave me a cop outside the hospital door. Unfortunately, the owners of Figs thought the whole situation unseemly—bad for business and all that, so they fired me while I was in the hospital. After I was well enough to be released I hired one of those rent-a-cop types to help me pack up and escape to Chicago."

"When did this happen?"

"Couple of months ago."

"Why Chicago?"

"I wanted to see Will's mom. I figured they couldn't find me there, since I have no family there or anything."

"Why didn't you tell me this before?"

"I didn't want you to fret. What could you do at this point? I'm fine now."

"I don't know what to say." She began to cry. "I'm sorry Dan and I have managed to ruin your life too."

He shrugged and took her hand. "Change is good. I've been in a rut and would never have left Figs if I wasn't forced. I was bored and lonely. There are other jobs, other towns." He looked at her fingers. "Good God, you need a manicure. Your hands look terrible."

CHAPTER TWENTY

FINALLY THE DAY OF THE OPENING ARRIVED. Before they opened the doors for the first dinner, Lee, Linus, and the entire staff sat at a rectangular table eating their before-shift meal of pasta with red sauce that tasted of garlic, fresh tomatoes, basil, onion, and another ingredient Lee couldn't discern.

Twirling spaghetti around his fork, Linus said from the head of the table, "Opening night. It's like Christmas." He gazed at the staff. "Are you all as excited as I am?" His fork hung in mid-air, the strands of spaghetti coiled in perfect symmetry.

No one said a word.

"Excuse me, is anyone out there?" said Linus.

Billy and Annie sat together on one end of the table picking at their food. Cindi, at the other end, studied the wine list between bites of pasta, her forehead glistening with a mixture of orange-tinted make-up and sweat. The servers sat together, memorizing the Specials list.

Linus snapped his fingers, waving his other hand in the air above his plate. "In a mere ninety minutes, history will be made. Gourmet food will have invaded this hungry town and by hungry, I mean starving for something decent to eat." He motioned to the three high-school kids, hired for washing dishes and bussing tables, as they shoveled pasta into their mouths. "Just look at these three, for example." Lee couldn't help but notice the wiry one's acne was the same hue as the pasta sauce. Linus pointed his fork at the boys. "Have you gentlemen eaten in the last several years?"

The tall one with sloped shoulders grinned and murmured into his bowl. "Lee had us here at seven this morning and wouldn't let us take a break to eat." He blushed and peeked up at Lee, only to blush a deeper pink and stare into his pasta bowl before shoveling another sloppy bite into his mouth.

There were twitters from various corners of the table. "Please," said Lee, rolling her eyes in jest, "I let you have a little break for bread and water around noon."

The one in the middle, the handsome, letterman-wearing one, raised his eyebrows at Lee. "Oh yes, master, give us some more."

The other boys laughed. "Finish your dinner," Lee said. She noticed Annie was rocking in her chair with one arm pushed into her stomach. "What's the matter with our chef?"

"I think I'm going to be sick I'm so nervous."

Linus laughed and sat back in his chair. "You artists are all the same. Describe the specials to the servers and you'll be fine."

Annie grabbed a note card from her apron pocket. "We've got two main dishes for specials. The first is cabernet-braised pork short ribs served with gorgonzola polenta and mixed-herb gremolata. The ribs were seasoned and chilled overnight and then braised in the oven for several hours, spiced with fresh rosemary and thyme, and the sauce, obviously, is made from cabernet wine and butter. The second is grilled New York steak with San Marzano sauce. This was chosen because of our seasonally based menu, since tomatoes are ripe." She cleared her throat and an abrupt self-conscious laugh escaped. She clamped her mouth shut for a moment and stared at the table. "Sorry, I'm freaking out a little. So, yeah, the sauce is made from a plum-type tomato and fresh basil. We're serving it with a side of goat cheese ravioli in a simple brown butter sauce. It complements the complexity and acidity of the tomato sauce in contrast to the richness of the steak."

Linus leaned back in his chair and crossed his legs. "Who wants to recommend a wine for the ribs? Karen?"

"Let's see. I'm not much of a drinker myself…"

Linus shook his head. "No, no, darling, you're not a mother of four housewife when you're wearing the white apron. You're a sophisticated wine and food connoisseur, whose obligation is to help the less privileged lead a more fabulous existence."

Karen grinned. "Right, sorry, I forgot what you said about that." She closed her eyes for a moment.

Linus raised both hands in the air. "Before you answer, what are we, gang?"

The servers said in unison, "We're educators."

He nodded his head and turned his gaze to Karen. "And, the winner for wine selection is?"

Karen grimaced. "A merlot?"

Linus pursed his lips. "Have I taught you nothing? Merlot for short ribs, no, no, no. It needs something bold to hold up against the meat and the only choice is a cabernet, or for the adventurous, a Syrah. As we talked about during training, suggest two different bottles, one on the less expensive side and one on the medium scale, unless you think they're rich. And, do we remember how to discern if one's patron is loaded?"

John raised his foot above the table and everyone called out, "Look at their shoes."

Linus smiled and put his hand on his chest in mock reverence. "I've taught you so well."

Lee stood, looking at her watch. "Alright, finish your dinners. We open in exactly seventy-seven minutes. Don't forget to check your teeth for bits of basil." She picked up her empty plate to head for the kitchen, but Linus caught her eye and, stepping next to her, whispered, "You're hopeless."

She shrugged and mouthed, "What?"

Linus put a hand in the air. "Before you all run off, I have a few words on behalf of our management staff." He indicated to Annie and Lee with his water glass before pausing and looking around the table. "We realize most of you are either artists or this job is your secondary, how shall we say, less favored work, perhaps on your way to somewhere else. I've been in this business a long time and know this is the curse of restaurant staff." He smiled and looked around the table at each face. "We thank you and celebrate you for your hard work these last few weeks, especially given that it's not your dream job. And, on the cusp of my departure, I give you two last challenges for tonight and all the nights you work here. The first is to find joy in the doing of something with excellence, whatever your task. Know there is meaning in that pursuit of perfection, whether it's pouring a glass of water without splashing, or gracefully taking back a steak to the chef even though it's cooked to their specifications, or making a martini with the perfect amount of vermouth, or my personal favorite, opening wine tableside without the tacky pop of the cork." He smiled at the servers. "The second is to notice the artistry in the ordinary, perhaps an image to paint later, a conversation overheard to use for fiction." He gazed at John for a moment. "Choose something every night that inspires you, so that your time here is not just about money. Know this, my dears, beauty, inspiration, can be found in the most astonishing places." He raised his water glass. "I toast you. As for your nerves, in the words of a good whore, fake it till you make it." Everyone laughed and raised their glasses with cheers all around.

Lee raised her water glass, tears prickling the insides of her eyelids. She inhaled and steadied her voice. "Cheers."

Annie wiped tears from her cheeks and stood. "This is a dream come true for me. Cooking is what I love and, well, thanks for all being here and Lee, thanks for believing in me." Her face crumpled and she collapsed into her chair. "I'm just so happy."

After everyone departed for their last-minute duties, Lee went to her office and closed the door. It was organized now into a tidy space, the desk bare but for her laptop and several bins for paper items. The files were tucked in their drawers, alphabetized and sorted between vendors, personnel files, and various other subjects. She sank into her office chair and closed her eyes for a moment. She thought about the money behind the desk.

There was a knock on the office door and Linus stuck his head through the opening. "Hiding out?"

"What? No, just gathering my thoughts."

He closed the door. "Guess where I slept last night?"

"Please say you haven't slept with one of the staff."

He grinned and tugged on his ear. "John's not my staff." He flicked a piece of lint from his trousers and fussed with the starched crease.

"You sure that's a good idea?"

"He's a good person, Lee. I really like him."

"Just don't leave him with a broken heart."

"Speaking of that, I have some news. I've decided to lease Mike's building next door and turn it into a bed and breakfast. I leave tomorrow to fetch my things from Grace's house in Chicago."

"Funny."

"No joke. Mike's agreed to co-sign for a bank loan."

Lee stared at him, speechless.

"Will's been dead for ten years. Do you realize that?" His eyes drifted to the ceiling. "I was spared the virus and I thank God for that every day but I think there was a part of me that felt like I shouldn't live if Will didn't get to. Something about the last couple of months made me realize I haven't really been living. Even Will's mother has moved on. Did I tell you she finally remarried after being divorced for twenty years? Her new husband has two grown daughters and they call her their second mom. One of them has this toddler who follows Grace around like a puppy, crawling on her lap every chance he gets. Do you remember how she seemed like she'd crawl into the grave with Will at the service? Yet she lived to love again."

Lee nodded, remembering too, how Linus had practically carried her back to her seat. "I remember."

"I look at you, how you've blossomed into the person you're supposed to be here, how you're flushed with love. I want that too."

Lee rubbed the goose bumps on her forearms. "But I may not be here. What if I have to run?"

He thumped his torso on the door and his voice was louder than normal. "Why don't you just tell Tommy the truth and give him a chance to help you?"

"Tommy doesn't have that kind of money." She gazed at the desk. "If he knows, he'll try to do something and it's too dangerous. I cannot bear the thought of him getting hurt or worse, killed." She nodded towards him. "Do I have to remind you what happened to you?"

He looked at her, hands on his hips for a moment. "No, you don't." His eyes glittered as he adjusted his tie. "Goddamn bastard."

"Dan or DeAngelo?"

"Both."

"I want more than anything to be free."

His face softened. "Free to stay here. Free to stay with Tommy."

She said in a soft voice, looking at her hands, "Yes, more than anything to stay with Tommy. And I don't want you to stay without me." She put her head in her hands. "I'm a terrible person."

"I said it before and I'll say it again." He knelt, putting his hands on either side of her face. "We'll get this guy paid off one way or the other. I have some things to take care of in Chicago but when I return we'll sit down with Tommy and figure out a plan." He opened the door an inch before turning back to her. "Lee, being truthful with the people who love you is the only way to be truly free."

There was a soft knock and Mike's voice came through the

opening of the door. "You guys in there? I have great news. A reporter's coming from the Seattle Times."

Lee froze, chest tight. Linus stuck his head around the door, his face impassive, his voice even. "No pictures of Lee, right?"

"Just Annie and the restaurant," said Mike.

Lee let out a breath. "Good."

Thirty minutes later, Lee grabbed the Grand Opening sign and swung open the front door. She placed the sign on the sidewalk and looked up and down the street. It was a Friday in early August, the air hot and dry, the traffic through town steady, with as many out-of-state license plates as local. She blinked, thinking the buildings seemed less turquoise than they used to be. Must be the way the sun glows this time of year, she thought. Linus was right that the town was charming, in its own humble way. A little facelift in the way of new paint on the businesses could do wonders. She would convince Mike to organize the effort, or maybe Ray. He needed a project, and the town might flourish with a little love and care from such a kindhearted man leading the effort. Like her house, she mused, and herself for that matter, thinking of the way Tommy had held her for an extra moment that morning before she left his house for the restaurant. His arms around her made her feel cherished and filled her with warmth that lasted all through this busy day. She looked across the street at Ray's office, knitting her brow—when had he changed his store-front paint to the attractive muted brown?

She stood for a moment, admiring the front of the restaurant and the portable We're Open sign. John had given it to her for a grand opening gift, and, she suspected, to impress Linus. It was an A-frame wooden sign, made of cedar, decorated with fragments of his failed glasswork. "Riversong" was written out in cobalt blue, and around the edges were bits of yellow and green. In the last several weeks there were articles about Riversong in the Medford, Eugene, and Portland newspapers, plus a blurb in the latest Alaska

Airlines flight quarterly magazine along with a small mention in the Northwest version of Sunset magazine. She gazed at the sign and said a silent prayer, "Please let them stop. Please, someone come."

Lee grabbed a small bag of trash from behind the hostess podium and walked to the kitchen. Rock music blared from someone's iPod. The garlic and butter aroma from Annie's croutons filled the air.

The chef herself was at the stove stirring something in a large frying pan that let off the aroma of blackberries. Billy stood at the prep island, using a knife to julienne zucchini. He chopped with rapid succession, fingers wrapped around the zucchini and the knife moving a hair away from his fingernails, just as she'd seen Annie do. "Billy, the way you're using that knife, you look like a real chef," said Lee.

He looked up, adjusting his chef hat and grinning. "Annie taught me. I've been practicing with a bunch of potatoes every night before I go to bed."

"Billy, I'm impressed."

"I'm kinda impressed with myself."

Lee walked down the back steps to dump the trash in the bins. There were two skinny young men standing behind it, smoking cigarettes with one hand while their remaining limbs twitched and jerked. Lee opened the bin and threw the trash in, holding her breath against the stench of rotting food and cigarette smoke. She turned to walk back inside, looking at the ground to avoid eye contact.

"What's up your ass, lady?" They both laughed.

She walked towards the back door, feeling their eyes on the back of her head.

One of them called out to her, "Where's Zac?"

She turned back to them. "He won't be here anymore, so whatever you need, ask around town, because he's no longer associated with this restaurant."

One of them threw his cigarette on the concrete, stomping it with his ratty tennis shoe. "We need to find him." He pulled on his ear and then bit the nail of his thumb.

"Sorry, can't help you." She started up the stairs.

"Tell him Arlie's looking for him if you see him."

She slipped in the door, slamming it shut and pulling the lock. She told herself as she walked to the front and opened the reservation book, just focus on tonight. There were eight names listed, all for parties of two to eight. Mike, Ray, Ellen, and Linus were listed but besides them, she didn't recognize any of the names.

She heard someone come through the kitchen doors and turned to see Tommy, dressed in long pants and a dress shirt, carrying a wrapped present. "The place looks fantastic," he said, putting his arms around her from behind. "I brought you something." His hair was damp on her cheek as he leaned down to kiss her neck.

"Oh, you didn't need to do that."

"You're shaking." He let her go and came around the front of the small hostess station.

"Just had a run-in with some guys out back," she said.

"I'll get rid of them."

"They may be gone by now." She gestured towards the stage at the other end of the restaurant. "You and the band ready for tonight?"

"Can't wait." He lowered his voice to a whisper. "I'd give you a proper good luck kiss but I wouldn't want the staff to talk."

She smiled. "Do you have a reservation, sir?"

He reached over the podium and found Ellen's name on the list. "That's Ellen and Verle and me. They took pity and invited me to go with them."

"You're crashing their date?"

"My girl's busy tonight." He grinned. "Open your present."

She untied the bow and opened the box. Nestled on soft cotton was a silver chain with a row of small crystal stars. "It's beautiful. Thank you."

He moved behind her and placed the necklace around her neck, his fingers brushing her skin as he fastened the lock. "Perfect.

Muy bonita." He reached over and kissed her cheek. "Don't worry, they'll come. I'll go scan the back, make sure it's clear."

He walked toward the kitchen and she turned to see a young woman, in black pants and a clingy knit blouse, come in the front door. "I'm looking for the owner. I'm here from the Seattle Times." The woman's collarbones and hipbones jutted against the clingy fabric of her clothes.

Lee stuck out her hand. "I'm the manager, Lee Tucker. The owner, Mike Huller, will be here in a moment."

"Yeah, he's the one knows my boss. He made me come down here as a favor to him. My name's Sylvia. Sylvia Nox."

"Welcome to Riversong. May I seat you in the dining room?"

"Wherever." Sylvia studied her. "You look familiar. Have we met before?"

"I don't think so." Lee looked at the floor and ushered her to a table by the front window. "You been doing this long?"

"No, I'm new to the paper. The food guy moved up to features, so they gave me the restaurant beat." She had a petite face and short, spiky, bleached-blond hair, arranged in angry peaks on the top of her round head. "To be honest with you, I don't know a thing about food. I don't really eat." She sighed and touched a plastered bit of hair that hung over her forehead. "I keep thinking, shit, I have a degree in journalism and I'm stuck writing about a restaurant in Podunk Oregon. No offense. I'm looking for a big story, one to show them what I can do." She looked around at the empty room. "Guess I won't find it tonight. My boyfriend and I both got hired out of journalism school but he gets assigned to the business section and I'm stuck writing about food. Sexism is alive and well, let me tell you." She brushed sweat from the sides of her nose with her fingertips and wiped them on the top of the crisp white table cloth. "Christ, it's hot down here and what's up with all the fat people at the rest stops? The paper's so cheap I couldn't take a flight and had to drive. I drink diet cokes by the gallon." She reached into her bag and plunked a pack of Marlboro Lights on the tabletop. "Can you still smoke down here in the wild west?

In Seattle you practically get arrested for buying a pack of cigarettes."

Lee cleared her throat, placing her finger on the twitch next to her right eye. "No, this is a nonsmoking restaurant. You can smoke outside if you want."

Sylvia took a cigarette out of the pack and stuck it in her mouth. "I'll ask you a few questions and then take a little smoke break."

"You should probably just talk to our owner. Our chef is busy getting ready for dinner hour. I'm just the staff, really."

"Whatever. Let's just make it quick. I've got to drive home tonight."

"Will you be having dinner then? We'd love to have the opportunity to show off our menu."

She waved her cigarette in the air. "Sure thing. Whatever you want to send out, is fine. Except, did I mention I'm a vegetarian?"

"Will you excuse me a moment?"

Lee found Mike in the kitchen, sampling the specials. "Reporter's here. You ready to talk to her?"

He clapped his hands together. "Yeah, get Linus too. I want to make sure we tell the story the right way."

She tasted blood and realized her teeth were clenching the insides of her cheeks. "Just leave me out of it."

He took her hands and nudged her into the office. "Lee, you don't have to tell me again to keep you out of the paper. You gotta learn to trust a little. I'm not gonna let anything happen to you." He patted her on the top of the head. "I'm growing real fond of you and I don't want you running off like a scared little bunny rabbit."

She relaxed her shoulders and sighed. "Alright." She pointed towards the dining room. "Just get out there and talk to the skinny reporter, or I could commit a murder before we sell our first steak."

Tommy, alone on stage while his band took a break, was perched on a stool, singing an old folk song into the microphone. Lee nibbled on an appetizer at one of the tables, swollen feet on a chair hidden beneath the tablecloth, and listened to the music, feeling relieved. Then she walked to the bar and ordered a soda water from Cindi, replaying the night in her mind. The minute the first customer had entered, Lee didn't have time to fret over anything but keeping up with the flow. By 7:00 every seat was filled, along with people waiting in the bar for a table to open. The local women were all turned out in full garb and make-up, the men in nice shirts. Several of the women thanked Lee for opening someplace nice they could make their husbands take them. Everyone raved about the food. At one point a couple called for the chef to come out to their table and when Annie entered the dining room, Ellen and Tommy stood and clapped and the entire restaurant followed. Annie, red-faced, tears in her eyes, took a small bow and returned to the kitchen.

Lee glanced at her watch. It was a few minutes after midnight, and the dining room had closed an hour ago. But the bar was packed with people ordering drinks and appetizers. Linus perched on a barstool, chatting with Cindi while she made drinks. Mike remained at a table in the dining room with a group of men, beaming at Lee from time to time. Lee assumed they talked business by the way they leaned their heads together and scribbled notes onto the paper bar napkins. She heard Cindi say to Linus, "Those guys with Mike, they ordered a 150-dollar bottle of wine. Think of the tip." Think of the margin, Lee thought.

Annie came out of the kitchen and plopped down next to Linus at the bar. Out of the corner of her eye, Lee saw the men with Mike get up from the table and circle in the doorway. She heaved out of her chair and moved towards them, smoothing her dress over her extended stomach. The three men, dressed in Tommy Bahama shirts and trousers and smelling of expensive aftershave, nodded and smiled at Lee.

Mike stepped back, allowing her into the circle. "Lee, these are the gentlemen I told you about. They're developers from Seattle and we've been talking about how to turn this town into a tourist destination."

The oldest of the group, a handsome, polished man in his fifties, slapped Mike on the back. "Now, we're fly fishermen more than developers. But, we're interested in this little town. Have been for a while and I think Mike's finally got us convinced." He smiled at Lee. "This place has certainly helped sway our opinion. And, the bed and breakfast going in next door. Just great."

They said their goodbyes and the door was no sooner closed than Mike squeezed her in a bear hug. "I've been working on those suits for three years to partner with me to build a hunting and fishing lodge on the river. I own some choice property out there along River Road and it's perfect for a fishing lodge. They agreed to do it tonight." He led her to a table, calling Annie to join them. "Now you sit back down and take a load off." He pulled out a chair for Annie, slapping the table. "Girls, just super job tonight. Super. Annie, I would never have thought of lamb shanks with that blackberry sauce on top of it."

Annie laughed. "You talking about my blackberry reduction?"

"Sure, sauce, reduction, whatever you want to call it, but heck, it might've been the best thing I ever tasted." He reached into his jacket pocket and pulled out a checkbook. "I'm giving you both a little opening night bonus." He scribbled on two checks, tore them out of the register and placed them on the table in front of them.

They were made out for 5,000 dollars each. Lee was unable to speak, but Annie held her check in both hands and shook her head back and forth. "Five G's." She leapt from the table and hugged and kissed Mike.

He blushed, brushing her aside. "You two deserve it, working in here these last months with hardly a paycheck." He looked at Lee. "This was a gosh darn miracle."

Annie's eyes glistened. "This is the most money I've ever had at one time."

Mike looked between them. "I want to make sure you two stick around. There's more of that in your futures if we keep turning them out like tonight."

After he left, Lee glanced around the restaurant and felt her heart swell with pride and, dare she say it, happiness. She thought about Linus's proclamation earlier that he was opening a bed and breakfast while throwing his heart into a love affair. She thought about Mike's steadfast resolve to change the town and of Tommy and her staff and her friends. It all felt like her real life now and she didn't know how she could walk away if, when, Von found her.

She thought of Zac's money behind the desk and wondered for the hundredth time if she should steal it to pay off DeAngelo. She knew it was too dangerous. She, Mike, and Zac were the only three with a key to the office. He'd figure it was her as soon as he discovered the money was gone. It was trading one danger for the other, except Zac knew exactly where she was. As long as Von didn't find her, she could keep saving until she had enough money to buy her freedom. She turned and watched Tommy's strong hands tuning his guitar, a gnawing emptiness in the pit of her stomach.

CHAPTER TWENTY-ONE

LEE OPENED HER EYES to sunlight peeping through the blackout shades in Tommy's bedroom. It was Monday morning and Riversong was three weeks old. She stretched and thought it felt like three years instead of three weeks. She rested her hand on her stomach, which moved with the rhythm of the baby's habitual morning hiccups. There was a note on the bedside table from Tommy saying he went for a run and would be back by 8:30. It was 8:40. She turned and rested her head in the indent of his pillow and breathed in the scent of his hair and the salty smell of his skin that lingered on the soft cotton.

Twenty minutes went by, and another twenty. She paced the floor, trying to ignore the butterflies in her stomach, sweating, fighting the nausea. She showered, trying to scrub away the panic that invaded her, but crazy thoughts ran like a wildfire and she was helpless to stop them. She sat on the floor of the shower, gripping her knees, water hammering the top of her head. She imagined him dead on the side of the road from a hit and run. Maybe it was a heart attack or a rattlesnake hidden in the tall grasses that lashed out to bite his ankle. Either way he writhed in pain, dying in the hot sun. Perhaps he decided she was too much work and had pushed his truck without starting it to the highway so as not to wake her and snuck out of town. Maybe he ran into one of the women from the bar and decided to follow them home.

Or did Zac come after him?

Or Von.

Or maybe he shot himself.

At ten after ten, sitting in his large armchair in the corner of the bedroom, she heard his keys drop on the front table. He called out, "Baby, I'm back. You up?" He came into the bedroom, sweaty and more alive than ever. He tore off his shirt. "I smell awful but it's the most fantastic day. There's some crispness in the air and it felt so good I decided to run all the way to the farmer's market to buy blackberries. I had a plan to get Ellen to make me a pie but when I got there I realized I had no way of getting them back. I mean, can you imagine me running back with a flat of blackberries in my arms?" He paused, considering her while slipping off his sneakers by pushing the toe of his shoe into the heel of one, then the other. "Why is your hair wet? You shower already?"

She stared at the floor in front of the chair, resting her arms on top of her pregnant belly. "I was about to go home." The panic lingered and she felt as though she might suffocate.

"What? I thought we're spending the day together?"

She shrugged. "I have a meeting at the restaurant."

He kneeled next to the chair and covered one of her bare knees with his hand. "This because I'm later than I said in the note?" He scooted in front of her and leaned closer to her face. Although she didn't meet his gaze, she felt him analyzing her and his voice was tender. "I worried you. I'm sorry. I didn't realize how long I was gone. I'm back now and it's okay, right?"

"I thought you were dead."

"Sweetheart, I'm so sorry. I didn't think about how much it would scare you if I was late. And I should have."

She jumped up from the chair and grabbed her clothes. "I've got to get to my meeting."

He sat on the floor and watched her getting dressed. "I know there's no meeting. Can't we talk about this?"

She held up a hand. "What's there to talk about?"

"Lee, I will always come back. No matter what. You need to understand that."

She sobbed, making angry swipes at her cheeks with the back of her hand. "You don't know that. You don't know all the things that can happen that could wreck your life."

He looked at her, his face helpless. He opened his mouth but seemed to think better of it and shut it without another word. Although her insides roared with the desire to stay, she left the room and headed for the door.

At her car, he put his hand on the handle to stop her. "Just stay, let me fix you breakfast." There was fear in his eyes, his need for her palpable, but instead of softening her, it made her angrier still.

"It's way past breakfast," said Lee.

"Will I see you later?"

"You're playing tonight, right?"

"Of course."

"Then I'll see you later."

She drove away, angry that he stood in his yard, watching her car move down the dirt road, a cloud of dust billowing behind like a giant apparition. She could feel his eyes bore into the back of her car and imagined she felt the pull of him saying, come back, come back.

Later that same night, she allowed him to take her to his home after the restaurant closed, feeling grateful he seemed the same as always. Her panic having subsided, they continued as if nothing had happened. But Lee was filled with dread, a foreboding that she could not shake.

The next morning, she awakened when the front door slammed. She heard Tommy throw his keys on the table next to the door where he always tossed them. It was thirty minutes after eight. She turned over, facing away from the door and closing her eyes to feign sleep. The bedroom door creaked and she heard his muffled footsteps move across the wood floors and a small thud on the bureau like he dropped something. Seconds later, she heard the bathroom door swing open and thump on the wall and then the gush and patter of the shower. She turned over and looked into the bathroom. The outline of his body showed through the opaque glass of the shower stall, his hands in his hair, his torso leaning backwards into the water stream. Steam wavered in the open door-way, illuminated by the streaming sunlight from the large bedroom window. After a few minutes he turned off the water and his brown hand reached for the towel that hung on the rack next to the shower. She closed her eyes until she smelled his clean skin as he walked by the bed. She stirred to let him know she was awake and opened one eye. He had the towel wrapped around his waist, hair sticking out in every direction, a day's growth of stubble on his face.

He sat on the side of the bed and touched her hair. "Did I wake you?"

She stared at the wall behind his torso, trying not to purr like a cat with his touch upon her hair. "I heard you in the shower."

He traced the skin under her eyes with his thumb. "You get enough rest?"

She touched a vein in his forearm. He looked into her eyes and murmured, "Don't do that, unless you want me back in bed."

She shifted her gaze from his eyes and watched the muscle on the side of his neck twitch. "You have someplace to be?" She pulled closer to him, kissed him on the mouth, slipped her hand under his towel and touched the sinewy muscle of his leg.

"I haven't shaved."

"I don't care."

He threw back the covers and got into bed. He looked into her eyes, touching her face with his long fingers. "I won't be late again. I feel terrible I scared you yesterday."

"It doesn't matter." She escaped his scorching gaze and looked at the ceiling, the room suddenly airless until he shifted to kiss and lick her neck.

He ran his hands down her body, his touch familiar now but still possessing the power to move her. His fingers moved between her legs, where they tapped and flicked in the same way he plucked the notes from his guitar. No longer shy, she caressed him with freedom, enjoying the feel of his muscular frame in her hands.

He nudged her on her side, his mouth on her shoulder, hands on her hips, round belly protected from his weight as he positioned behind her and their legs entangled like two pairs of scissors. Her mind emptied and she was simmering liquid, unsure of where her flesh began or ended.

His callused fingertips gripped her skin and she quivered, excitement building as he thrust harder into her and she touched his face with the back of her hand. His mouth was next to her ear, his voice hoarse, and his breathing fast. "Te amo," he said.

She gritted her teeth and shut her eyes to shut out the light coming through the windows. "Don't say it."

His voice was low in his throat and his words cracked. "I love you. Why can't I say it?"

She bit the inside of her bottom lip. "Just don't."

His fingers clutched the insides of her thigh, his wet mouth hot against her shoulder. His energy was frenetic, intense, no longer playful or teasing, his words breathless. "I can't help myself."

She willed her body to separate from him but the climax was upon her and like something slippery and unconnected, invaded her and she shuddered and cried out, half wail, half scream. Still inside her, he cried out too, a low abrupt gasp, and buried his face in her neck. After several seconds, he pulled away from her onto his back. She stayed on her side, drew her legs up and lay in the fetal position, the sweat from him still wet on her skin, the dampness between her legs warm and ripe. He was stiff beside her and she felt him shiver and cover himself with the blanket. She stared at the sunlight drifting through the spaces in the slats of the shades.

The bed moved and she heard his feet on the floor, the closet door creak open and shut. She turned to see him pull boxer shorts over his lanky legs. Her eyes drank him in until he faced her and she pretended to look at the ceiling.

His voice sounded tired and sad. "You want breakfast?"

"I should shower first."

"Eggs or oatmeal?"

"Oatmeal."

Tommy's oatmeal sat in his bowl, untouched. He appeared to be reading the paper but he hadn't turned a page in fifteen minutes. She dropped her spoon into her empty bowl and it clattered in the thick, silent room. "I'm the one that should be angry."

He turned a page of the paper with a deliberate movement, his mouth a thin line.

She shook the newspaper. "I don't think a person should be hijacked right before an orgasm. It's hardly fair."

In two paces he was at the kitchen sink. "You're making a joke." His shoulders sagged and he hung his head over the sink. He pushed on the side of the counter with his hands, as if it took all his strength to hold himself up, his voice resigned. "I can't do this anymore."

Frigid fear crept up her spine but she used a scathing tone as if his statement was juvenile and needy. "Do what?"

He turned to her and his eyes were glassy with unshed tears. "I can't be in limbo with you anymore."

"I don't even know what that means."

"What are you hiding?" She saw he noticed her flinch and his face softened. "What are you so afraid of? We need to talk about the future. The baby's going to be here before you know it and I want to be a part of it."

She glanced down at the spoon and saw her face reflected in its shallow curved cup, deformed and ridiculous. "I'm not ready."

"You say that, yet you're here every night." He picked up the newspaper and threw it across the room. "Stop lying to me. Tell me what you're so afraid of."

She stood, pushing the chair into the table. In one heated shrieking breath she screamed at him, "You're right. I have a secret and it's something that you could lose your life over if I get you involved." She stopped and took a deep breath, willing herself to gain control. "I'm trying to protect you."

He was next to her in one stride and grabbed the tops of her arms in his large hands. "What is it? Tell me the truth, so help me, Lee."

She bit the words. "You cannot help me, even with all that love for God and your mother and this house that pulls in sunshine."

"I will do whatever it takes to help you. Do you get that? Anything."

She stared at his Adam's apple and spoke through tight lips. "Life is not a sentimental three-chord song." She started to shake from her insides. Her teeth chattered and she clamped her mouth shut, pulling away from him.

He inched towards her and put his hands on both of her shoulders. His eyes were dim and red rimmed. "You're running from something or someone. Who is it?"

Her lips trembled and there was a lump in her throat so big she couldn't swallow. "Tommy, I love you. There, I said it. I love you but this is something you need to leave alone."

He jerked away from her and paced, pressing his eyes with the tips of his fingers. He stopped at the sink, crossed his arms and looked at the ceiling. "See, the thing is—I know you love me. I know you. You think keeping this secret is to somehow spare me from whatever it is. But I can't be with you if you will not tell me the absolute truth about your life."

"Why are you pushing this? Why can't it just stay the way it is?"

"Because I need to know if you're going to be here in a month, or a year, or ten. Because I don't want to fall in love with the baby too, only to have you leave me."

She didn't know what to say, except that he was right. The truth was she wasn't free, couldn't be free until she paid DeAngelo.

"This thing that happened between us this morning in bed…" His voice broke and he looked at the ceiling. He drew in a deep breath, the vein on his forehead popping. "I'm in too deep. I can't go on this way, not knowing where we stand, feeling like you've got one foot out the door all the time, reserving the right to leave."

She reached for him, took his hands. "I don't want to leave you."

His eyes filled and he put his hands on her stomach. "Lee, I'm begging you, tell me what it is so I can help you."

She stared at him, helpless to think of what to say. "No good will come from you knowing the truth. It will put you in danger and I can't risk it. Can't you just trust me?"

He turned from her, sinking into a chair and burying his face in his hands. "You need to go now."

"Tommy, I—"

His hands still covered his face. "Come back when or if you decide to tell me the truth."

Her legs shook as she walked to his bedroom to gather her things. She reached for her bag and there on the bureau was a small jewelry box. Unable to stop herself, she opened it. Sitting inside was a diamond engagement ring. She snapped it shut and left it on the bureau. She ran to her car and drove half blind down his dirt driveway. She didn't allow herself to cry until she pulled onto the highway.

CHAPTER TWENTY-TWO

AT HOME, Lee stumbled to her bedroom. Joshua had left the upstairs windows open but the paint fumes permeated the thick August air. Lee shivered as if her blood, bones, every organ were slush. She phoned Annie's voicemail and left a message that she was ill and to have John act as host for the next several nights. She pulled on long sweatpants and a sweater and fell into bed, pulling the covers over her head.

She dreamt of her mother, her slender hands moving in a white bowl sprinkled with cobalt blue flowers. Eleanor took a warm cloth from the bowl and laid it gently on Lee's forehead. Her mother's skin was unwrinkled, dewy with youth, her eyes clear, her brown hair in a shiny sheet on her shoulders. Lee's star necklace, Tommy's gift, nestled in the hollow of her mother's neck. She put the cloth back in the bowl and her green eyes, so like Lee's own, were sorrowful. "There's so much you don't know."

Lee awakened with a start, the feel of her mother on her skin. The windows were wide open and the night's breeze smelled of dust, dry grasses, and the sweet rose of late fading summer. A memory of another dry August night, long forgotten, surfaced.

The August Lee was thirteen was hot, the temperature running up to 108 in the late afternoon for five days in a row. Day after hot day Lee sat on the front porch sketching and making lists, longing for the feel of the water on her scorched skin. With each day of intense heat Eleanor seemed to disappear further inside herself. On the 16th of August Lee awakened around midnight, heart pounding, alarmed from either a dream or sound. The air had cooled slightly but her skin harbored the day's heat. She threw her feet onto the hardwood floor, the fine hairs on her scrawny arms sticking up under her worn cotton nightgown. She tiptoed to her mother's room and peeped through the crack in the door. The bed was empty. She sprinted down the stairs and searched the living room and kitchen. She was not in the house. Lee went to the screen door. Her mother was sprawled across the thirsty grass. The screen door creaked as she opened it and her mother called out, "Come see the stars. They're falling." She sounded as if she had a mouthful of cotton balls. Fully clothed in a flowered cotton dress with puffy sleeves and a full skirt that seemed a size too large and that Lee had never seen before, she held a half empty bottle of vodka next to her slack and puffy face. Lee looked up at the sky and indeed a meteor shower was in full expression across the Milky Way. Stars dripped across the black sky, brilliant as they took their final journey and disappeared as if they were an imaginative fancy, or nothing more than a memory.

Lee crept to her and rested her fingertips on the pale flaccid skin of her mother's forearm. "Mommy, it's late. Come inside."

"They were supposed to come home on the sixteenth of August. Everyone's gone. I'm all alone."

"Mommy, I'm here."

"You don't count."

Stunned, Lee raised her head and stared at her, disoriented for a moment. Then she was above the scene. She saw her mother's emaciated body and unfocused eyes that moved around the night sky as if on fire. Her cheeks were stained with tears and dust, her hair tangled and scattered on the parched grass. A girl, her skinny white arms wrapped around stick legs, a pinched nervous face, leaned over the woman. And she knew her mother was right, she didn't count. She might not even exist, she thought.

Now, she went back to sleep, knowing it was the only relief she would find.

"Lee, wake up." She opened her eyes to Ellen shaking her. "You sick? I've been calling you for two days."

Lee rolled over and pulled the cover over her head. "I'm just tired."

Ellen yanked the covers from the bed. "Have you eaten?"

"I don't know."

Ellen opened the shades and threw back the covers. "Take a shower. Come down for lunch."

Lee flopped onto her other side, squinting at the bright light bolting through the window. "I don't want to."

Ellen stood over her, hands on her hips. "I don't want to have to drag you by the hair, but I will."

Ellen stood at the stove, frying a frozen turkey burger on the skillet. There were slices of wheat bread on the plate next to the stove, covered with mustard and mayonnaise. Ellen looked up when she came into the kitchen. "Sit. Eat." She dropped the burger onto the bread and set the plate in front of Lee. "Annie says you haven't been to work in two days."

Lee took a small bite of the burger. It tasted like dust in her mouth. She choked down another bite and pushed the plate to the middle of the table. She rubbed her eyes and felt pain in every part of her body.

Ellen washed the pan in the sink and dried it with the cotton towel hanging on the stove handle. She crossed her arms over her cotton dress. "Rumor has it Tommy's sick too." She raised her eyebrows and gave her a quizzical look.

Lee felt tears start in her throat and turned to grab a napkin from the holder. There was a weathered envelope on top of the stack of napkins. There was a sticky note from Joshua that said, "Found this behind the dresser in one of the bedrooms. See you next week." The postage date stamp said August 14, 1974. It was addressed to Eleanor Johnson. "What is it?" said Ellen.

"Some old letter addressed to my mother. Joshua found it."

Ellen peered over her shoulder and Lee felt her stiffen. "That's from Christopher. My son."

Lee looked at the address in the corner and saw the name Christopher White and Ellen's address scrawled in black pen. "It's to my mother?" She glanced up at Ellen and noticed her suntanned face was white.

Ellen put a trembling hand on her shoulder and spoke in a strangled voice. "Open it."

Lee lifted a weathered school-lined paper from the envelope and tried to hand it to Ellen. Ellen stared at the wall above the kitchen table, gripping the back of the chair so that her knuckles were white. "You read it to me."

Lee took a deep breath and read, "August 14, 1974. Ellie, I've thought of nothing else since you told me about the baby and I hate that I've been at the fair knowing you are home alone, scared and unsure of the future. I can't get the look of your frightened eyes out of my mind or the way you waved at me as I drove away with my mother, so small and fragile. I don't want you to worry anymore, because I have a plan. When I get back on Saturday, we'll sit down and tell our parents about the baby and that I'll forget Princeton and go to the University of Oregon with you. I called this afternoon and they'll enroll me for the fall. We can live in campus family housing. I'll work and go to school and all our dreams will still come true, just not exactly as we planned. But, I love you and you love me and we will love this baby. I know you're worried about my mother and your father, but their love won't disappear just because we've made a mistake. I'm going to sleep now and dream of sunning on our favorite rock before we plunge headfirst into the deep, deep water of the river. All my love. Chris."

Lee stared at the letter. "What does this mean?"

Ellen's face had the shell-shocked look of a warrior after a battle. "It means Chris was your father."

"That's impossible. That would make us related."

Ellen nodded yes and reached for the letter but then pulled back her hand and smoothed the front of her dress. "I had no idea." She pulled out a chair and looked as if she might sit but jerked up and stood next to the counter instead. "I wanted to die myself when I got the news. For years and years every night before I went to sleep I prayed I wouldn't wake up in the morning. If I'd known about you..." She trailed off and stared into space as if the past were there on a screen.

Lee picked up the letter. His cursive looked like her own, especially the way he looped the p's and b's. "How can this be?"

Ellen spoke as if she hadn't heard her. "I told Christopher he wasn't allowed to date, so they must have hid their relationship from us. I wanted him to concentrate on his studies. He wanted to go to Princeton more than anything in the world and I knew the only way we could pay for it was for him to get a scholarship. He did, y'know. He got that scholarship."

"But why didn't she tell you?"

Ellen sank into a chair and absently rubbed one knobby hand with the other. "I think she tried, once. Your mother went away to college the fall after they were all killed. When she came back in the spring, you were with her. She came to see me one day. You were several months old. I wouldn't look at you or hold you. It's no excuse, but I couldn't without breaking down about my own baby and maybe it was that bitterness that drove me to it, I don't know, but I told her she should've put you up for adoption, that she had no skills and no business trying to raise a baby when she was a helpless child herself. I gave her a lecture about morals and I don't know what else." She paused and took a long shaky breath. "It's my own fault she didn't tell me."

Lee was too shocked to speak.

"Next thing I knew she was living here and instead of trying to help her, I judged her every time I drove by and saw the yard going to weeds and the paint on the house peeling."

Lee cradled her stomach and stared at the letter. "What was he like?"

She looked at Lee with new eyes. "He was kind of like you. Whip smart. Kindhearted but reserved at the same time. The way you figure and plan things, that was him too." A trace of a smile crossed Ellen's face. "He used to rescue all these animals he found in the woods, lizards with no tails, birds with hurt wings—always bringing them in my clean house." Her eyes snapped and she chuckled. "Those hurt animals were kind of like your crew at Riversong, now that I think of it. He was ten when his dad died in the woods and overnight he had to grow up and take on things a boy shouldn't have. Just like you did." She studied Lee's face. "These months since you've been home, I've dreamt of him almost every night." She smoothed Lee's hair, her eyes sad, even as her mouth moved to a half smile. "I should've known."

"Did it never occur to you?"

Ellen shook her head no, gazing out the window. "You get these ideas about the people you love, these stories you tell yourself. I couldn't imagine my little boy grown enough to make a baby. I still saw them as the children they once were, swimming and splashing at the river's edge."

Lee's words were choked as she tried to fight the lump in her throat. "I had these elaborate fantasies as a kid about my father, that he would come rescue me from her, from all this. But he never came and I hated her for that." She shook her head and wiped the tears from her face.

"If I'd known, I would've looked after you."

Lee wiped her face with a napkin, bitterness rising from her gut. "If I'm like him, why didn't my mother love me?"

Ellen pulled Lee to her spare chest. "Your mother felt alone in this world and it made her crazy."

"Just like me."

"No, you're strong and steady. And, you have me. And your gang at Riversong. And, Tommy."

The next morning, Lee hiked to Ellen's swimming hole, carrying a small shovel. The early morning dew glistened on the flowers that poked through the wild grasses above the river. A decayed wooden swing swayed from a large oak, as if a child, moments before, had rocked and gazed at the blue sky while he swept his toes above the tickle of the grasses' dry blades. Lee peered down the steep rocky trail to the patch of sand but her stomach made her too unsteady to risk taking the trail. She perched on the grass under the oak tree instead, breathing in the sunny rock smell of the river and watching the still luscious late summer leaves that rustled in the branches.

Clumps of buttercups tickled her bare legs. She picked one and stroked the petals underneath her chin and tried to remember the childhood game—if you see yellow reflected on your skin are you made of butter or are you a princess? She closed her eyes and rested her head against the trunk of the oak tree, smelling moss and wet bark. Something scurried and she jerked her eyes open. A lizard ran up the trunk and some other hidden creature scampered through the grass. Overhead a hawk circled. She shivered and changed the focus of her eyes to the tree branch above her head. She thought of her father, who and what he was, and how much she wished to have known him.

She pulled out the picture of the baby's ultrasound and placed it in a small silk bag that had once held her engagement ring from Dan. She dug a foot deep hole, placed the silk bag in it and covered it with dirt. She closed her eyes and remembered Dan running across the soccer field and waving to her in the stands—how vital and happy he'd seemed in that moment. She picked a red wild-flower and placed it on top of the mound of dirt and closed her eyes, envisioning Dan's face. She let herself be overwhelmed with the thought of him so that she felt him there. She told him she was sorry she was unable to reach out to him and to love him as he should have been loved. In that moment, next to his makeshift memorial, she filled with forgiveness. She sensed that wherever he was, Dan was at peace and wished her happiness. She forgave herself too, for her inability to save him, and for moving on, for moving into the love Tommy offered her. The baby shifted inside her womb and she felt Dan beside her, blessing their child. She felt how sorry he was to miss the child's life on the earth. He asked that she make sure the child knew about him and how much he would have loved her. And Lee said, silently, I will, I will.

She opened her eyes and gazed at the blue sky, and a peace, an acceptance of what is, settled between her shoulder blades.

CHAPTER TWENTY-THREE

THAT AFTERNOON, she turned her phone over and over in her hands, saying a silent chant, Tommy call me, Tommy call me. It rang and she yanked open the cover but it was Mike, not Tommy. "Lee, my buddy at the Times just called. Said there's a big spread on Riversong. I haven't seen it yet but I'll call you later to compare notes." She walked to the end of the driveway to pick up her edition from the newspaper box. Four weeks had passed since the reporter came to the opening and with everything that had happened since, she'd forgotten about the hope for an article altogether.

Back in her kitchen, she shifted in her chair, wincing because the baby was heavy now, just weeks from her due date, and opened the paper to the food section. Her stomach dropped. The headline read, "Disgraced Seattle Entrepreneur Reinvented as Food Maven." There were two bylines under the headline, Sylvia Nox and Alex Wright. Instantly Lee knew Sylvia's boyfriend was the business section writer that cornered her at the press meeting the day Dan died. Sylvia had said, "He gets assigned to the business section to follow all the high tech companies." Next to the article was a large photo taken at a fundraiser she and Dan attended two years previously. In the picture, Dan, dressed in a tuxedo, had his arm around Lee in front of the Seattle Art Museum. The Seattle Times must have had it in their files and pulled it for the article. The reporters had done their homework and rehashed it all, detailing Dan's suicide and the crumbling of Existence Games, Inc. The only item the reporters didn't detail, because they didn't know, was the debt to DeAngelo, who would now know where she was.

Lee ran upstairs and pulled a suitcase from the shelf in the closet, stuffing it full of clothes and toiletries. She called Ellen's house but there was no answer. She left a message on her voice-mail, saying she had to leave unexpectedly and would call her when she was safe, but not to expect to hear from her for some time. She hung up the phone, opened the door a crack and surveyed the yard, saw nothing and ran to her car.

On the highway she headed south, with no plan other than escape. She drove through town, not looking at Riversong, afraid she'd break down if she glanced at the familiar blue awning. Her mind was a tumble of half thoughts and images: Von's gun, the menu at Riversong, Alder's head in her lap, Tommy's voice, and the baby. She glanced in the rearview mirror and saw a car approaching from the distance. Her heart leapt to her throat and she pushed harder on the gas pedal. The car was right behind her and it was a man in the driver's seat, his hand gesturing and waving. She couldn't think, couldn't see. She pushed the gas pedal to the floor and the car lurched forward. She saw the odometer read 70, then 80 and she was a mile out of town. All of a sudden, the road curved and she steered to correct but it was too late. Her car spun out of control, across the opposite lane, and began to roll. In midair she heard herself scream and thought of the baby. She felt the car land upright and heard a thundering crash and shattering glass. The seat belt held her tight but her head wobbled and her teeth rattled. She clutched her stomach. Then it was quiet but for the sputtering and spitting of steam and fluid from the car's engine. Outside of the car, the air above the dry earth wavered with the late summer heat. She looked across the road. The other car was stopped. A man got out and ran across the highway towards her. Run, she told herself, run. She opened the door, hundred-degree heat blasting her like an oven door. She stumbled in the gravel on the side of the road, sweat dripping in her eyes. She fell, her mind acknowledging pain in a distant way as small sharp stones embedded into the skin of her knees. Hair plastered to her scalp, she scrambled up and started to run again. Then the man was upon her. He tackled her from behind and they both fell, his body cushioning Lee from the hard ground. She heard a voice that seemed familiar and still she couldn't think. The man shook her. "Lee, it's me. What's the matter with you?"

She wiped the sweat from her eyes and Mike's face floated before her like a mirage. "Mike?"

He carried her across the hot pavement to his car and placed her into the passenger seat. He got in the driver's side and started the engine. The air conditioning blew on her face and she tried to breathe but her chest was tight like she might suffocate. Mike tapped the temperature gauge and muttered a curse under his breath. "It's 103 degrees out there and dammit, you're about to have a baby. Do you have any sense?" He looked at her and shook his head. "What the hell is wrong with you?"

"I thought you were someone else."

"Is someone after you?"

"Do you have a gun in here?"

"Under the seat."

She twisted, eyes darting in every direction. "I have to get out of here. Now."

Mike took her shoulders. "Look at me. Calm down and tell me what's going on. I'll help you."

She sighed and her chest rose and fell as she breathed in the car's cool air. "I came here to hide. Dan took a loan for our company from a guy with ties in every direction to illegal activities. I owe him three quarters of a million dollars and now he'll know where I am. The newspaper article named my location." She looked at Mike's lined, handsome face and his eyes that mirrored the hazy, late summer sky outside the car's window. "I'm dead if he finds me and it's only a matter of hours."

Mike stared at her. "Holy Christ. You came here to hide. Tommy was right." He shook his head. "Tommy called yesterday to tell me what happened between you. He also told me what Zac's been up to. Said it was time I knew the truth."

"He told you?"

He gazed at his dry, chapped hands. "I'm an idiot but I had no idea. After I talked to Tommy I went out to Zac's place and there were these rough-looking guys." His voice choked and he gazed out the window. "These rough men hanging out in his living room, guns on the coffee table." He paused and rubbed his eyes. There was stubble on his usual clean-shaven face, and bags of skin pooled under his eyes. "I confronted him and he went insane. Started babbling about leaving town and the beach or some other nonsense I didn't understand. Then he sped off in the car."

She glanced at the windshield, and the squashed bugs on the glass appeared in the pattern of a quarter moon. She blinked her eyes and pushed her fingers into her forehead. "This is about a lot of money."

"Something I can't figure is where all the money's gone. Zac sure never acts like he has any extra."

"He's been hiding it behind the desk at Riversong. It's over 770,000 dollars."

He took in a deep breath and splayed his hands over the steering wheel. "I see." He paused and looked at her. "Why didn't you take it? Pay this guy off?"

"Mike, I'm sorry to say this, but it's because I'm as afraid of Zac as I am of this DeAngelo." She watched a jackrabbit hop to the middle of the road and look around, sniffing the air, and suddenly a log truck was upon him. Lee shut her eyes, hearing the truck whiz by. When she opened them the rabbit was on the other side of the highway, hopping away, almost blending into the beige colored, sun scorched brush and grasses. "Mike, I have to get out of here."

He shook his head, no, and took her soft hands in his big rough ones. "Listen to me, young lady. We're gonna sit right here and work this through until we come up with the answer to your problem. You cannot run away. That's not how we do things here. You understand?"

"I can't stay here. I bet he's in town right now."

He went on as if he didn't hear her. "Why did you keep this a secret from me? I could've helped you."

"It's my problem."

"Now see, that's where you're wrong. Part of being a friend is asking for help from the people who care about you."

"Why would you help me?"

"That's a complicated answer, but let me try to get it through your thick head. The first thing is, I knew your grandparents. My daddy called them friends and that meant they were friends to me, too. And that means you're my friend. You're one of our kids and it's our job to take care of you. That's how I do things, how we did things around here, until the drugs started taking over." He seemed like he wanted to say more but stared at the steering wheel instead.

"Mike, these guys, they're serious. They will kill me if I don't get out of here and I don't want any of you in danger."

"Listen, I've made no secret that I'm on a mission to save this town. I see it real simple, like God wants it, and part of that plan includes you."

"But it's not safe for you to even be here with me."

He held up a hand, shaking his head. "Just let me tell you something now. One night last year I had a dream I was swimming in the river on my property with my eyes open. A trout swam in front of my face, opened his mouth, and said the word 'flies.' Damnest thing, a talking fish. Anyway, the next night I dreamt I walked the length of Main Street with three people. I couldn't see their faces but as we walked, the street transformed into real fancy shops, restaurants, a bookstore, a bed and break-fast, that kind of thing. At the end of the street was a fly fishing store."

"Flies."

"That's right. Flies. I believe the three people with me were you, Tommy, and Linus. This is your destiny."

"My destiny?"

"If you need that money, you should take it because we need you here."

"It's impossible. He'll know it's me. You saw for yourself the thugs he hangs out with."

"I'll tell him I took it."

Lee's eyes filled with tears. "I can't let you do it."

Mike tapped her on the forehead. "Young lady, you've got to learn how to accept help when it's offered." He shifted in his seat. "It makes me sick, thinking what he's been doing. I don't know what I did wrong."

"That's what I always thought about my mother. If I could just be good, please her, maybe she wouldn't need to drink. But it never worked." She looked at him for a long moment, thinking of Zac's face the day she confronted him, an idea clicking in her mind. "The money gets me out of my mess, but what about Zac? I think he wants to get out but these thugs he's involved with have scared him. He needs a fresh start somewhere and he needs to get sober. But neither one of us wants him to go to jail. Right?"

"If you're talking rehab, he'll never go."

"Rehab's better than jail."

They locked eyes and Mike nodded. "Tell me your idea."

"It'll require a little help from our friends."

After agreeing to the plan, Mike pulled onto the highway and raced towards town. "We should have everybody meet at my house so I can lay out my plan," Lee said. "I just hope no one in town tells him where I live."

Mike reached in his pocket for his cell phone. "I'll call Ray and tell him to spread the word not to talk to any strangers about you."

"Tell him Von has a limp and always wears hats."

Mike called Ray and gave him the cautionary instruction. After he hung up, he glanced at her. "Tommy figured you were hiding from something. Why didn't you tell him the truth?"

"Because I didn't want him to die trying to save me."

"That's your problem, right there. You don't know anything about love. That boy couldn't be more in love with you if he tried and that makes it his job to die trying to take care of you. This is the burden of love."

"It's a lot to ask."

"You bet your ass it is."

She stared out the window as they crossed the bridge over the river, thinking about the risk she would ask her friends and Tommy to make. Would it be too much, she wondered?

She dialed Ellen and Tommy from her cell phone but there was no answer at either house. "Mike, I can't get Tommy or Ellen."

Mike took his eyes from the road and she saw fear in his face. "It's gonna be fine. Call the others."

She reached Annie, Cindi, and Billy one after the other, asking them to meet at her house with their guns and not to speak to any strangers. To her surprise, they all agreed without question.

Mike's car sped past the gas station. They were almost to River-song when she saw him, lurking under the blue awnings. "That's him." She pulled on Mike's shirt. "That's him, right there."

"You were right, he didn't waste any time getting down here." He handed her his sunglasses. "Put these on and get down."

Lee slid as far down in the seat as she could, her stomach higher than her head and her neck scrunched. "Do you think he saw me?"

Mike looked in his rearview mirror. "No, he's trying to see inside Riversong. He's got his grimy hands on our clean windows." He pushed the gas pedal harder and the car lurched forward. "You stuck down there?"

"I'm alright. Just get me home."

Mike's car tumbled down her dirt driveway. Neither of them spoke, the danger of their situation like another passenger. She thought to ask, "Why were you following me?"

"Divine intervention."

"You know that kind of stuff just makes you sound crazy?"

For the first time that day she heard his belly-laugh. "I was on my way to the mill and saw you driving so fast I thought you were having the baby. So I followed you."

They pulled up to the house. Tommy's truck was parked in the driveway. Her stomach lurched at the sight of him pacing the front porch. Ellen sat in the rocking chair, phone in her hand. They parked, dust so thick in the air she couldn't see for a moment. As it cleared, she saw Ellen run down the steps towards the car, grabbing her in a tight hug. Then she held her away with stiff arms. "I've called everyone from here to Kingdom Come. What happened to you? Are you hurt? You're bleeding. Get in this house right this instant."

Lee rested her head on Ellen's shoulder. "Thank God you're both alright. I'll explain everything." She headed towards Tommy, who stayed where he was on the porch.

His eyes, bloodshot, were cold. "What happened?"

"Had a little accident."

"Are you alright?"

"My car's a mess, but I'm fine."

His face betrayed no emotion. "I'm glad you're safe. Ellen was worried sick." He started down the porch steps. "I've got to go." As he moved past her she grabbed his arm and he stopped.

"Please, don't go. Give me a chance to explain."

He stepped past her like he was going to his truck but stopped, shook his head, and murmured to himself, "I should just walk away." But he started back up the steps, following Ellen into the house.

She turned back to Mike. "Can you keep watch out here while I talk to them?"

Mike reached under the seat of his car and pulled out a handgun. "I'll be on the porch."

She told them all of it, sparing no details and ending by saying, "The good news is I've come up with a plan."

Tommy said nothing for a long moment. "This was your secret."

Ellen's mouth was open and she shook her head back and forth in disbelief. "Why did you keep this to yourself?"

Tommy jerked from the couch and went to stand by the window. "Because she didn't trust us."

"No, that's not it," said Lee. "I didn't want to put either of you in danger. This guy hurt Linus so badly he was in the hospital for a week. I was terrified that one of you would get hurt too. This is not about me trusting either of you. This is about me protecting you."

Ellen stood, took Lee's hands. "This must've been a big weight on you."

"Ellen, I want you to go home and lock your door, keep your gun close," said Lee. "I don't want you in jeopardy."

Ellen brushed her hands aside. "Push aside the old lady, is that the idea? I don't think so. I'll get my gun and meet you back here. Whatever the plan is, I'm included. Got it?"

Lee thought of protesting but knew it was no use. "Go. Keep your eyes open when you come back. Make sure we're alone before you come into the yard."

"Tommy, don't leave her side," said Ellen.

Tommy stared at Lee, eyes unblinking, like he didn't know her. "I won't."

Ellen glanced between them like she was going to say something further but seemed to think better of it and left out the front door.

They were alone. Her blouse was damp from sweat, despite the cool temperature of her living room.

"Where were you going?" he said.

"I don't know. Just south. I panicked." She took a large breath and steadied herself on the back of a chair. "I know I don't deserve your help."

He paced by the window before he turned to her, his voice loud. "Lee, that has nothing to do with it. When you love someone and are intimate like we have been you tell them the damn truth. You trust them to help you out of messes. That's what people do."

"I'm sorry. I didn't want you to get hurt."

"I did get hurt. By you, not some criminal, Lee. By you." He looked like he wanted to go to her but instead lifted the shade an inch and peered into the yard. He said, quietly, "I begged you to tell me the truth."

"I'm sorry," she whispered again.

"You're asking me for help?"

She took a deep breath. "Yes. I'm asking you for help. I don't think I can do it without you."

"Lee, you remember that song we heard the night we came back from the coast? Boulder to Birmingham?"

Lee's eyes filled with tears and she moved towards him. "Tommy, I'm—"

He held up a hand. "Don't."

She nodded and stayed, vulnerable, in the middle of the room.

He looked at the floor, his voice tight. "What do you want me to do?"

She wiped her eyes and tried to control the shaking in her voice. "I called the Riversong gang. They'll be here in a few minutes. If you'll stay on watch, I'll take a shower before they get here."

He turned, pulled the curtain back and peered into the yard, his back like a wall.

Thirty minutes later, Tommy, Ellen, Billy, Cindi, Mike, and Annie were all gathered in Lee's living room, sitting in the vinyl chairs from the kitchen, except for Tommy, who stood at the window with his back to the group, and Mike, who was propped in a corner, his face rigid from worry. Lee stood before them and told them all the details about Dan's bad business deal, the debt it caused and the subsequent threat it caused to her safety. "After I buried my husband, this house and property was all I had left. I came here to repair it and sell it to pay the debt. And then an amazing thing happened. I found all of you. You took me in, rescued me—whatever you want to call it. I know Tommy and Mike would call it divine intervention and I'm starting to believe they're right. I fell in love with this town, with our restaurant, and most of all with you—my friends. Yet always in the back of my mind I thought, when will DeAngelo's people find me? When will I have to say goodbye? So I've held myself back a little, always with the idea that I might have to leave at a moment's notice." Tommy turned from the window and looked at her, swiping his hand under his nose. "This morning when I saw the article I knew without a doubt that my worst fears had come true. I knew they would find me within a matter of hours." Her words strangled but she continued, determined to tell them everything. "All I could think to do was run—to save myself and my baby." She smiled, her voice shaking, as she told them about driving out of town, crashing and being rescued by Mike. "Mike convinced me that all of you are both the reason to stay and the way to freedom." She told them of the money she and Linus found hidden in her office that night months ago. "It's drug money, tainted with the residue of destroyed lives. That I understand. But it's the only answer to my problem."

Cindi shook her head back and forth, lips pursed. "Lee, Zac will never give you that money." She darted a look at Mike. "No offense, Mike, but Zac and these people he's involved with—they're as dangerous as this DeAngelo character. Lee, trust me, you can't take that money."

"No offense taken. I know you're right." Mike came forward, hands in his pockets. "I didn't know the truth about Zac until Tommy had the guts to tell me last night. I've been kidding myself that he's alright. I know you've all seen it for yourselves and have probably asked yourself what was wrong with me, giving him the restaurant to run in the first place." He shrugged his shoulders. "He's my kid, and I was trying to do the right thing. I'm not saying Zac deserves any of your help, but maybe I do. And maybe Lee does."

Annie sat forward on the couch. "What can we do?"

Lee, hand on her stomach, directed her gaze at Tommy. "I thought of a way to get Zac to give us the money willingly. But it requires help from all of you and a little bluffing." Feeling like she needed a flipchart, Lee told them her idea in detail, including what parts they would all play. Cindi stared at her, mouth open. Annie looked like she might cry. Billy's cheeks were flushed and he rocked back and forth on the edge of his chair. Ellen glanced from face to face. Tommy looked at the floor. No one spoke for what felt like minutes, and Lee, cringing inside, thought it was too much to ask; she shouldn't have burdened them. After a moment Billy stood. "Lee, we don't want this man to hurt you."

Annie put her arms around Lee. "We would do anything for you. We love you."

"But, this could be dangerous, and you have Alder," said Lee.

"We'll be fine," said Annie. "And, I, for one, would love to see Zac get the help he needs, even if what he's been doing was wrong. I was given a second chance at the life I dreamt of when Lee found me and I believe everyone deserves the same. Mike and Lee, you've both given everyone in this room a gift with your vision and intelligence and we're not going to walk away when you need us. That's not what friends do."

Cindi leapt to her feet. "Oh, hell yeah. Anyway, this is a good plan."

"We can pull this off, no problem." Ellen got to her feet, gun in hand. "Let's do it."

"Oh, hell yeah," said Cindi.

After they left, Ellen watched the driveway while Lee called Linus. He answered on the first ring. "I've been trying to get you all day," he said. "I saw the article."

"I have a plan. Can you get down here by tonight?"

"I'm already at the airport."

She hung up and called Zac's cell phone. His voice was hoarse, like she'd awakened him from a hangover. "What do you want?"

"Somebody left something for you in a big envelope. Thought you might want to come by and pick it up."

"What time?"

"Two o'clock?"

"Fine."

She saved the hardest call for last. She dialed Von's phone number listed on the worn business card from all the months in her wallet. She almost hung up when she heard his chilling voice, but took a deep breath instead and caressed the bump on her stomach she believed to be the baby's knee. "Von, this is Lee Tucker, I mean, Lee Johnson."

"You have our money?"

"I do. Meet me at eleven p.m. at Riversong."

"Don't mess with me this time. Understand?"

"Yes. See you at eleven." She hung up, sinking into the couch, arms around her stomach.

CHAPTER TWENTY-FOUR

TWO MINUTES AFTER ELEVEN, the restaurant was almost empty. Tommy played without his band. The servers and busboys had all left for home. The remaining dinner guests, a young couple, were finishing the last bites of their desserts. Lee exchanged glances with Tommy and watched Cindi wipe the bar with a white bar towel. She turned back to her podium and played with her star necklace at her throat. She heard feet shuffle on the sidewalk outside and looked up to see Von limping by the window. He tipped his hat when he saw her and, despite the plan, she froze until she saw him reappear inside the doorway. He slipped inside and hovered beside the ficus tree, blending into the shadow except for his eyes that glittered between the leaves. The young couple stopped at Lee's podium, grabbing a business card. They said something to her that she couldn't hear for the pounding in her head and then stopped at the door when they saw Von, hesitating as if they sensed something amiss. The young man glanced at Lee with a questioning look and she mustered a reassuring smile. "Thanks for coming in. We'll see you next time." The couple smiled, grabbed each other's hands, and walked through the door.

Von turned to Lee, his mouth turned up at the corners in a smile that didn't reach his eyes. "I'm in a hurry, so let's get this done." She smelled cigarettes and the pungent spice of his cologne. His white-coated tongue flicked over his chapped lower lip as he reached inside his jacket, the glint of his gun reflecting in the light of her podium lamp.

Legs numb and shaky, she stepped from behind the podium, placing her hand on her stomach for courage. "Can you wait for me in the bar?"

He glanced at her midsection. She thought she detected shock and perhaps even shame cross his face but he followed her in silence past the empty tables to the bar. "Have a seat here and I'll be with you in a minute," she said.

Annie sat at the table next to the stage taking sips of white wine, her foot twitching under the table. Ellen was at the bar with her hands around a Bud Light draft. Billy pretended to read a newspaper at the table closest to the kitchen. Von chose a barstool in the middle of the row and Lee whispered to him, "Please don't make a scene in front of my customers. Just have a drink and I'll be right back."

He looked around the restaurant, avoiding her eyes. "Make it quick."

She heard Cindi ask what she could get him as Lee walked to the front door and locked it. As she walked back to the bar she gave Ellen a nod. Tommy put down his guitar and jumped from the stage, and in tandem they all surrounded Von, except for Billy, who ran to stand at the front door. Ellen and Tommy pointed guns into his back while Cindi pulled her pistol from under the bar and pointed it at his head. He reached to his belt but Tommy poked him hard with the butt of his gun. "Don't even think about it. Give me the gun, real slow."

Von pulled the gun out of its holder and handed it to Tommy. Von looked over at Lee. "You don't know what you're dealing with here."

276

Cindi wagged her gun at him. "I don't think you know who you're dealing with."

Linus came in from the kitchen. Von stared at him. "You."

Linus touched his forehead with his fingers and tossed his head. "Just little ol' me, only this time we have the guns."

Von squirmed on his stool. "I told my boss I should've hurt you worse than I did."

Tommy went to Annie, handing her Von's gun. Then he put his face next to Von's and said through clenched teeth, "We're going to get this settled."

"What is this, the hick brigade?" said Von, his eyes on Cindi.

Tommy yanked him off the barstool and threw him against the counter. "Listen, you piece of shit, I would love to beat you beyond recognition." The scar on his cheek twitched. His free hand tightened around Von's neck. "Do you have any idea what you've done to this woman's life?" Tommy raised his gun in the air like he was going to bring it down on Von's head.

Annie's eyes darted from Von's face to the gun in Tommy's hand. Sweat dripped down the sides of her face and she looked at Lee and mouthed, "Do something."

"Tommy, stop. We don't want to kill him here," said Lee.

Linus put one hand on his heart while waving the other in front of his face as though he might faint. "Too much blood."

The anger seemed to run out of Tommy as he let go of Von's neck, shoving him back onto the barstool and sticking his gun into his ribs again.

Ellen poked him with her shotgun. "We're gonna shoot you and feed your body to a bear."

Von's eyes darted to Lee. "You think this is over if you kill me? I don't work alone."

Lee went around the bar and stood next to Cindi. Her knees knocked together as she held onto the bar, thankful she didn't have to hold a gun. "Do you have another solution besides my friends killing you and feeding you to a bear named Clive?"

"It doesn't matter. If I come back empty-handed, after letting you escape, I'm finished. These people I work for, they're not part of the humanitarian movement. So I may as well let you idiots do it." She saw the fear in his eyes.

Lee nodded to Linus and Annie. "Go get him."

Annie and Linus walked to the kitchen. No one spoke while they waited for them to come back. Lee trembled and couldn't bring herself to look at Von, instead focusing on the popping vein in Tommy's neck. In less than a minute, Annie and Linus came through the kitchen door with Zac. His hands were tied behind his back and his mouth was gagged. His eyes darted around the room in an expression between confusion and rage. Ellen aimed her shotgun at Zac and pointed at the barstool next to Von. "Put him next to the scumbag." Linus lifted him up to the barstool.

Zac's eyes were wild, trying to talk through the gag. Lee directed her gaze on him. "We're sorry to have to bring you into this mess but I'm afraid you're the only solution to a very serious problem. You see, I owe this man money, thanks to a debt left to me by my late husband, and he's threatened to kill me if I don't give him 750,000 dollars." She shrugged her shoulders. "Do you know anyone who has that kind of money?"

Linus fluttered his hands in the air. "Say, lying around?"

Zac looked at Linus and back to Lee. He shook his head no.

Tommy kept his gun's aim on Von. "See, we know different. We know there's a whole lot of money from your little business. Blood money you've made hooking innocent kids on meth. So we decided you either give us that money or we kill you and blame it on this asshole here." He poked Von again.

Ellen rested her gun on the back of Zac's scrawny arm. "Of course, if you cooperate, we'll just forget this ever happened and keep your drug dealing ways from the police."

Cindi shook her head. "Unless you start up again, and then we're singing like canaries."

Linus leaned over and took off Zac's gag. "Now, why don't you tell us your decision?"

"You're all crazy." Bits of saliva flew out of Zac's mouth.

Ellen motioned at him with the barrel of the shotgun. "You're a very rude young man."

Tommy's face was flushed. "You know, I'd love an excuse to shoot this guy. Let's just do it and get our other friend back on the road before midnight."

Cindi cocked her gun. "I want to do it."

Zac spit at Cindi. "That thing isn't even loaded."

"Should we test it?" said Cindi.

Tommy prodded Von with his gun. "Why don't you tell us what you do when people don't cooperate?"

"We get people to do what we want, let's just say that," said Von.

"Like what, cutting off fingers, stuff like that?" said Cindi, leaning on the bar as if the idea intrigued her.

"I haven't personally done that one, but yeah, like that." He smirked and stared at Cindi. "We don't have a handbook, so to speak, we just use our instincts."

Cindi nodded and squinted, pursing her lips in agreement. "That makes sense."

"Annie, go get your meat cleaver." Tommy looked over at Zac. "I've seen Annie with a knife and she's good."

Annie ran back to the kitchen and came back with the meat cleaver, the lights from the bar glinting from its shiny surface as she raised it in the air. She said to Cindi, "This'll be fun. A little revenge for all the men who've treated us bad."

Cindi twirled her arm in the air like she was roping a cow with a lasso and whooped. "Say it again, sister."

Zac's eyes blazed and he lifted his chin. "You guys are so full of shit. No one's gonna cut off my fingers."

"Who wants to hold his hand up on the bar?" Annie raised the meat cleaver in the air.

Linus smoothed his hand along the surface of the bar. "Don't do it here and ruin the wood. Let's take him to the kitchen."

Tommy shifted his stance, keeping the gun on Von but looking at Zac. "Listen, these guys are having fun at your expense. Truth is we're not going to hurt you. None of us have it in us. However, Lee needs this money, so we're going to give Von back his gun and let you two work it out between you."

Von raised an eyebrow and surveyed Zac. "You gonna keep him tied up?"

Linus put his hand on his hip, with a mock innocence in his tone. "Don't you think that's best?"

Von grunted yes and nodded at Zac. "What's it gonna be, then?"

Zac's eyes widened and for the first time he looked frightened instead of just angry. He turned toward Von and spoke like they were old friends. "Listen, you and me, we could work something out. Between us, y'know?"

Von looked at him, his face stony. "You wouldn't last a day in the company I keep." He turned to Tommy. "Can I get my gun now?"

Tommy moved like he was going to give him the gun but before he reached him, Zac jerked in his seat. "No, no, I'll give you the money but you'll have to let me go so I can pull it together."

Linus tilted his head, tapped the back of Von's stool, and pursed his lips in a smirk. "I don't mean to be bossy but I wouldn't let him go before I got the money."

Von glared at Linus for a moment and then turned to Tommy. "You gonna give me my gun now so this idiot can get me the money?"

"We have an even better solution." Lee reached under the counter and placed a small suitcase in front of Von. "Zac, you needn't worry about getting the money together. We took the liberty of taking care of that for you." Lee opened the suitcase, which held stacks of money.

Zac stared at the bills. "What the hell?"

Lee pushed it closer to Von. "This is all of it, in hundred-dollar bills, but we'll wait if you want to count it."

He nodded, picked up several stacks and flipped the bills, his eyes snapping with what appeared to be silent counting. After a few minutes, he seemed satisfied and closed the lid of the suitcase and shut the clasps. "You people are crazy in this part of the country." He nodded towards Cindi. "Let me know if you're ever looking for work."

"I run the bar here and someday we'll be known as the best restaurant in Oregon, so no thank you." She fluffed her hair-sprayed coif, flushing a little as if she were flattered.

Tommy kept his gun aimed at Von. "Now that you've worked it out with Zac here, we'd like to keep your gun, make sure you leave without any trouble."

"Consider it a gift." He got off his barstool, gave a slight nod of his head, and limped to the front door. Billy unlocked it and Von disappeared into the darkness.

Annie went behind the bar and put her arms around Lee. "You're free." Lee slumped into her, fatigue and relief washing over her in equal measure. Annie helped her to one of the tables and had her sit, smoothing her hair. "It's okay now. Ellen, she's really pale." She pulled a chair next to Lee. "Put your feet up here."

Ellen pointed her gun at Zac. "You want him over at the table now?"

Tommy walked to the table. "Go get Mike and then wait for us in the back, in case we need you."

The others left as Tommy pulled Zac off the barstool and over to the table. Lee wanted to tell Zac that everything was going to be fine, that he just needed to get himself cleaned up and then he could go to the beach. She might say, you don't need a million dollars, you could live there anyway, start to make a life for yourself slowly, get a job and an apartment. She wanted to tell him that her mother's life could have been different if she'd faced her pain instead of trying to kill it with vodka. She wanted to tell him that rehabilitation would help him, and that he could rest there and heal from the years of drowning all that rage and sorrow with booze, drugs, and women. But Zac wouldn't meet her eyes, kept his gaze on his hands, slumped forward, so she stayed silent too.

She peeked at Tommy across the table. He looked tired, deep circles under his brown eyes. She put her hand on his arm and he looked at her. She mouthed the words, "Thank you," and he nodded but then looked towards the door. Her heart filled with remorse and she wondered if she could win him back after all she'd put him through. After a moment, Mike came in from the back and joined them at the table.

Mike nodded at Zac. "Son." Zac didn't respond, except for a twitch and shift in his left leg.

Tommy leaned back in his chair and crossed his legs. "We've got video of you dealing drugs in the parking lot, copies of your client book, and pictures of the sacks of money. More than enough evidence to get you thrown in jail for a long time." Lee went to the bar and pulled out the copies she made months before of the contents of his Fairy Book, photos of the money, and fake tapes, and placed them on the table in front of Zac and sat again.

Zac looked at them, sullen for a moment and then his face turned purple like it did the day Lee confronted him, all those months before. His body shook and his eyes darted back and forth. "What do you want?"

Mike pulled his chair closer to the table and looked as if he might reach for Zac's hand but instead crossed his arms across his chest. "We don't want you to go to jail. We think you need some time to dry out and there's a place down in California that will take you. It's a full ninety-day drug and alcohol treatment program. Get you cleaned up and help you deal with stuff. They even have the family participate. I talked to your mom and she's willing to come out for it. And me, too, of course."

Zac looked up then, his eyes wide and his voice haggard and dry. "You talked to Mom about this?"

"Yes, and she was concerned about you. Wanted to help," said Mike.

"I'm sure. 'Cause she's been so involved the last twenty years.

You can't make me go to rehab. I just drink a little too much. I'm not like those people."

Mike glanced at Lee, looking uncomfortable. She caught Tommy's eye and motioned towards the kitchen. He nodded and they headed for the back. As the doors closed she heard Mike say, "Rehab or jail. Your choice."

CHAPTER TWENTY-FIVE

THE REST WERE HUDDLED around the chef's island in the kitchen. They all looked up when Lee and Tommy came through the door. "Are they still out there?" said Annie.

"We wanted to give them some privacy," said Lee. She plopped into the chair by the walk-in freezer just as she felt a little pop and then a gush of fluid between her legs. And then there was a pool of water underneath her chair. She stared at it for a moment, unable to make out what happened and then it occurred to her. "I think my water just broke."

The women circled and Annie took control. "Tommy, get your truck and pull around front. Ellen, call the doctor and have her meet us at the clinic."

Lee shook her head, dazed. "But the baby's not due for three more weeks."

Annie gripped Lee's hand. "Don't worry, after what we just pulled off, having a baby's going to be a piece of cake."

Tommy, his face wan, appeared at her side and guided her towards the door. A pain like severe cramps started in her groin and she felt her belly tighten. She gasped and leaned against him until it passed. She grabbed his arm and whispered, "Please stay with me."

"I will."

The doctor, hair disheveled, was between Lee's legs. "Just one more push and we've got a baby."

Lee flopped back onto the hospital bed, looking first at Tommy and then Ellen. She'd pushed for two hours and she was beyond fatigue, almost delirious. "I can't do it. I'm too tired."

Tommy's voice was in her ear. "Just one more push and you get to see the baby."

She looked in his eyes and anchored to that pool of brown. "It hurts."

He wiped the sweat from her face with a soft cloth. "You're tough, you can do this."

The doctor's voice sounded far away. "Alright, it's time, just one more push, Lee. Tommy, get behind her on the bed and prop her up."

She leaned into Tommy's torso and tried to breathe through the burning pain and the intense pressure of the baby's head pushing through the small opening of her body. She concentrated on Tommy's voice in her ear, took a deep breath, and pushed with her remaining strength. There was burning pain like she might rip in half and then she knew the baby's head was out. Then there was a gush of fluid and the sensation of the rest of the baby slipping into the world. Then crying that sounded like the exaggerated mew of a frightened kitten. The doctor held it in the air and Lee saw flailing limbs and a slightly bloody head thrown back. "It's a girl and she's got red hair," said the doctor. A nurse wiped the baby with a cloth and placed the naked bundle in Lee's arms. The baby's stunned eyes, only minutes ago in the protected warmth of a womb, locked to her mother's face. Lee scanned her features, for clues about who she was, who she looked like, if Dan were etched anywhere. But she was so small that Lee couldn't see anything recognizable.

The nurse said, "Hold her close to your skin. That way she knows you're her mommy." Lee did as instructed, holding the baby to her chest and kissing her damp forehead. She held one of the petite wrinkled hands in her own, gazing at the miniature fingernails and then back to the round newborn eyes, which hadn't moved from Lee's face. Lee shushed the baby, her baby, rocking her and kissing the top of her head. "Don't cry now, we're all so happy to see you."

Lee looked up at Tommy. His eyes brimmed with tears and he murmured something in Spanish as he touched the top of the baby's head. Ellen, on the other side of the bed, sniffed and patted Lee's shoulder, "You did good, girl, really good."

The nurse took the baby from her and put her on a scale that looked like a bigger version of the one Billy used at the restaurant. "Six pounds, nine ounces. Now all she needs is a name."

It was morning when she awakened to the antiseptic smell of the clinic's recovery room. She lay back onto the pillows, wincing from the pain in her groin. Tommy was asleep on the cushioned bench next to her bed. Ellen rocked and cooed to the baby, who was wrapped in a pink blanket and cap. Lee watched them for a moment, swallowing the lump in her throat. Ellen looked up and came to the side of Lee's bed. "How're you feeling?"

"A little sore, but better."

"You ready to feed her?"

"You think she's hungry again?"

"She's rooting around for something over here and I had to tell her that ship's long since sailed." Smiling, Ellen placed the warm bundle in her arms. Lee stroked the small features before opening her hospital gown, guiding the mouth that looked like a rose petal onto her breast. The baby clamped on and sucked, her cheeks moving in nature's patterned rhythm of suck, suck, breath. Ellen clucked and patted Lee's shoulder. "I knew you'd be a natural. Your father was giant, almost ten pounds. Did I ever tell you that? He had a cone head the whole first month, but this one's so petite her head just came out perfectly round. To me she looks just like your Grandmother Rose."

"I didn't think you'd be the gushing type."

"Well, shoot, she's perfect."

"Ellen, I'm terrified I'm going to screw this up. You've got to help me."

"This mean you're staying?"

She reached for Ellen's knobby hand. "I can't leave your pies."

Ellen's eyes misted and she pulled the baby's cap further down her petite forehead. "We've got a lot of pies to make up for."

"Ellen, I've been thinking about something. I want to call Dan's parents and tell them about the baby."

Ellen nodded, pursing her lips. "I think that's the right thing to do."

"She's going to want to know them. And it might give them a little peace."

"Having lost my own son, I can tell you that it will. You want your phone?"

She looked at Tommy's sleeping form and shook her head, no. She'd call them later, after some things were settled.

Tommy stirred and sat up with a start. "Was I asleep?" His eyes darted from the baby to Lee. "You alright?"

"Just tired."

He jumped from the bench and hovered next to the women. "Is the baby alright? I heard the doc say babies that are born a few weeks early sometimes get jaundice and have to sleep under special lights. Did they check for that yet? What about you? Are you still in pain?" He looked at Ellen. "Has the doc checked on Lee? Should I go get her? Maybe we should give her one of those pain pills the nurses left. Where's the ice pack?"

Ellen laughed. "Relax, Papa Bear, they're both fit as fiddles." She motioned to Lee to give her the baby. "It's been thirty-five years since I held a new life and I'm going to get my fill. I'll take her for a little walk around the clinic. Show her off to the nurses." Ellen left, never taking her eyes from the baby. After the door swooshed shut, it was silent except for the ticking of a clock and Ellen's footsteps making their way down the tiled hall. Tommy sank onto the bench, rubbing his eyes and scratching the stubble on his face.

"Thanks for staying," she said.

"Lee, I wouldn't leave, after all we've been through." Everything about him sagged, the lines in his face seemed deeper and his voice was hollow and sad. "She's beautiful."

"Did Ellen tell you what Joshua found?"

"Yeah, she showed me the letter when we were looking for you." He smiled and raised his eyebrows. "Can't believe I didn't see it before."

"Knowing I was wanted, that he wouldn't have walked away, well, it's made things easier to accept. And, knowing about Ellen is better than those fantasies I used to come up with as a kid."

He flinched and turned towards the window. "I'm glad."

"Tommy, you're better than any fantasy I could come up with, too. I know I've hurt you and I'm truly sorry. I don't want this to be ruined."

He turned to her, sat on the side of the hospital bed, sighing and running his hands through his hair. "All these months, keeping this secret."

"What would you have done if you'd known?"

"Sold everything I owned to pay him off and if that wasn't enough, gone after him myself."

"See, I knew that, and I couldn't let anything happen to you because of me."

He puffed his cheeks and threw up his hands. "You've got to be the most exasperating woman that ever lived. That's not the way this works. Love isn't like your lists. When you love someone there's nothing you won't do for them, and sometimes that means it's a colossal mess. I've felt from the first moment I saw you that we're connected in some kind of mysterious, otherworld way. You fought it instead of giving into it and I couldn't understand why, until I figured out your secret was bigger than my love for you. You allowed it to be bigger than my love for you. But it was an excuse because deep down you didn't believe you're worthy of my love. And that's where you're wrong, because you don't get to decide. Because the way I see you, the way I feel about you—I get to decide that."

"I know."

He stared at the floor, his voice soft. "I've been miserable without you." He rubbed his eyes and then looked at the ceiling. "I've been going insane. I can't sleep. I can't eat."

"I was too."

He looked at her. "It can't be like before. No more secrets."

She reached for his hand. "It won't be. I have nothing left to hide."

He turned his face towards her and his eyes were wet. "I want you to marry me and I want to adopt the baby. I want to be a family."

"I want that too."

He brushed her hair away from her face. "You sure? I know you never wanted to live here and I'll move if you want. I'll go anywhere you want."

"When I was a child I felt the landscape here run through me like it was part of my blood or bones, like it fed me somehow during those times my mother broke my heart. When I went to art school, I used to paint it from memory, the bend of the river, the arc of the mountains as the sun set behind them, the hue and sway of the dry summer grasses. When I left here I thought my love for these simple treasures would sustain me but as the years passed I lost that feeling. The emptiness, the difficulty of surviving in this world all alone, it took over. I tried to fill that hole with security, money, order, and with the heat of the anger towards my mother.

But I see now that this place and our friends, the work of River-song, these feed me, these fill me. And, you. Especially you."

Smiling, he took her hands. "I'll spend a lifetime making sure that remains true. You have my word on that."

"Me too," she whispered. "Always."

EPILOGUE

THE MORNING OF THE BAPTISM CEREMONY, Lee heard Ellie-Rose howling from the nursery. Knowing that particular cry meant the baby was hungry, she smiled to herself, thinking how desperate she sounded, as if the tiny person thought she might never be fed again. Lee padded down the hall and picked her daughter up out of the crib, nursing her in the glider rocking chair Linus had given her. Ellie-Rose ate ferociously while Lee listened to the wind rustling through the firs and the river's melody mingling with the notes of the winter sparrow. She caressed her daughter's delicate ear and smoothed the strawberry blond hair over the soft spot in the middle of her head.

After Ellie-Rose had her fill, Lee set the wriggling, grinning baby on the floor of the bedroom while she dressed. They'd decided the only solution that seemed right was for her to move into Tommy's house and for Annie and Alder to move into her house. Here there were no memories to haunt her sleep. And Annie and Alder loved the transformed home, with Ellen close by to help.

She heard the front door slam and Tommy's keys drop on the table. He was in the doorway then, sweaty, smelling of lime and the outdoors, watching her for a moment, carefully, like he did. "You look beautiful," he said to Lee as he kissed the baby on both cheeks. "How's Daddy's girl? Have you been good while I was gone?"

He sang in the shower. She held the baby in her lap, closing her eyes, listening to the sweet notes of his voice while breathing in the perfect smell of her daughter's head. She had no idea she would love a daughter this much. No one had told her it would be this way. She thought of Clive and her cubs then, and sent silent gratitude.

She sat in the front row of the church, cradling warm Ellie-Rose against her chest. It was a non-denominational Christian church built in the simple style of the Shakers, all clean lines and natural wood. The midmorning light of early December flooded in from the skylights and it smelled of vanilla and lilies that Ellen had grown in her greenhouse for this occasion. Tommy sat next to her, absently playing with his wedding ring and talking in a low voice to the pastor about the details of Ellie-Rose's baptism.

Dan's parents, Ralph and Betty, sat in the row across from them. For this, their third visit since her birth, they stayed at Linus's newly opened bed and breakfast, The Second Chance Inn. This morning, Ralph, back straight, eyes darting around the church as if looking for something to orchestrate, caught Lee's eye and nodded. Dressed in a dark pink suit, her feet held daintily together, Betty gripped a digital camera. Dan's sister was there too, without the husband and children, a hint of the former peace she had before Dan's death there on her face. Last night they'd all eaten at Riversong, passing Ellie-Rose from one to the other, kissing her and making funny faces to get her to laugh. After the dessert, a chocolate soufflé, Betty gave Lee a present to open. It was Dan's christening gown. Betty's eyes filled as she said, "I thought it might be nice for tomorrow, but only if you want."

Lee hugged her. "It would be lovely," she said.

Billy, sitting behind Dan's family, fiddled with his tie and looked uncomfortable in a suit a size too big for him. Cindi sat next to him, chomping gum and swinging her crossed leg back and forth. Mike came in with Ray. Lee smiled at them as Mike reached over to pat Tommy's shoulder. "Quite a day. Quite a day."

Ray nodded in agreement. "Glad to be here."

Lee rested her head on Tommy's shoulder. He kissed her cheek. She heard someone's coat scrape the back of the bench and turned to see Annie and Alder take the seats behind them. Ellen and Verle walked in next, holding hands like teenagers. Ellen sat next to Alder and whispered something in his ear that made him giggle, while Verle loosened his tie that looked circa 1973. Linus and John came in next, dress shoes clicking on the wood floor of the church and sitting on the other side of Annie. Linus leaned over the bench, resting his hand on her shoulder. "You three need anything?"

Tommy glanced at Lee and down at the baby. "No, we're all set."

The pastor smiled at them as he came up the aisle and took his place at the podium. Ellie-Rose stirred in her sleep, let out a short squeak, opened her sapphire-colored eyes and stared at Lee for a moment before closing them once again and falling asleep, her mouth slack and her little hands splayed on top of the pink blanket.

The pastor asked Tommy and Lee and the godparents, Annie and Linus, to bring the child up to the front. They all rose and joined the pastor. He sprinkled Ellie-Rose with holy water, blessed her, and said a few words.

Lee looked down at the bundle in her arms. Ellie-Rose gave a toothless smile and something in the quality of it reminded her of Dan. She thanked him, wherever he was, for giving her the precious gift of this daughter.

As they were walking out of the church, Lee saw Zac standing at the bottom of the church steps. He approached them, saying,

"Hope you don't mind if I was here. Just wanted to say hello, see the baby."

Tommy shook his hand. "Good to see you, man. We hear you're doing great."

His face was trim, the bloated look gone and his eyes clear. "Came back to get some stuff, see my dad. Don't know if he told you but I have a little apartment in San Diego, about six blocks from Mission Beach. Got a job at a little surf shop down there. Going to meetings, the whole bit."

Lee put her hand on his arm. "A surf shop sounds great."

"Wanted to say thanks, too, for y'know, pushing me to clean up my act."

"We're just glad things are going so well," said Tommy.

Mike came up behind them, kissing the baby, slapping Tommy on the back, hugging Lee. Then he put his arm around Zac. "You ready, son?"

"Yep. Hey, I'll see you guys around."

At Riversong, in the exact moment "The Hick Brigade" raised their glasses to toast their sweet Ellie-Rose with a pinot noir from the Willamette Valley, the sun appeared through the front windows, sparkling in the icicles that hung from the blue awning. Basking in the warmth of that rare December sun, they laughed and talked while dining on Annie's croissant bread pudding that was warm comfort in their mouths and stomachs. They reminisced about the opening of Riversong and the progress they hoped to make that coming summer in the transformation of their community. All the while, Ellie-Rose babbled from her bouncy seat next to the window, her hands playing in the streaks of sun.

ABOUT THE AUTHOR

Tess Thompson writes small-town romances and historical fiction. Her female protagonists are strong women who face challenges with courage and dignity. Her heroes are loyal, smart and funny, even if a bit misguided at times. While her stories are character driven, she weaves suspenseful plots that keep readers turning pages long into the night.

Her desire is to inspire readers on their journey toward their best life, just as her characters are on the way to theirs. In her fiction, she celebrates friendships, community, motherhood, family, and how love can change the world. If you like happy endings that leave you with the glow of possibility, her books are for you.

Like her characters in the River Valley Collection, Tess Thompson hails from a small town in southern Oregon, and will always feel like a small town girl, despite the fact she's lived in Seattle for over twenty-five years. She loves music and dancing, books and bubble baths, cooking and wine, movies and snuggling. She cries at sappy commercials and thinks kissing in the rain should be done when-ever possible. Although she tries to act like a lady, there may or may not have been a few times in the last several years when she's gotten slightly carried away watching the Seattle Seahawks play, but that could also just be a nasty rumor.

Her historical fiction novel, *Duet for Three Hands* won the first runner-up in the 2016 RONE awards. *Miller's Secret*, her second historical, was released in 2017, as were the fourth and fifth River Valley Series books: *Riversnow* and *Riverstorm*. The sixth River Valley book will (hopefully) release in the latter part of 2018.

Traded: Brody and Kara, the first in her new contemporary, small town romance series, Cliffside Bay, released on February 15th, 2018. The second in the series, *Deleted: Jackson and Maggie* releases May 7th. The subsequent three Cliffside Bay books will release every couple months in 2018.

She currently lives in a suburb of Seattle, Washington with her recent groom, the hero of her own love story, and their Brady Bunch clan of two sons, two daughters and five cats, all of whom keep her too busy, often confused, but always amazed. Yes, that's four kids, three of whom are teenagers, and five cats. Pray for her.

Tess loves to hear from you. You can visit her website http://tesswrites.weebly.com/ or find her on social media.